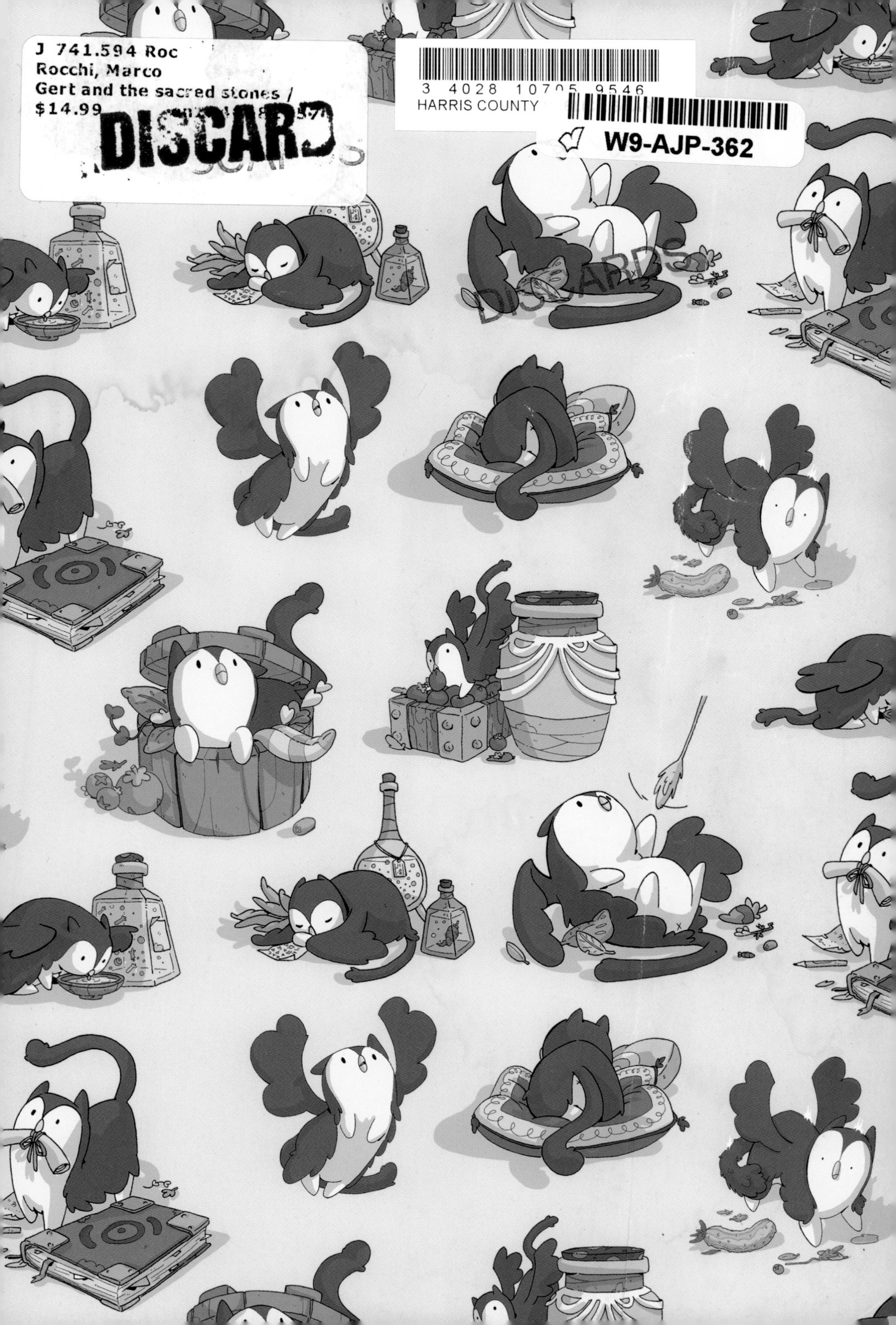

GERT™

AND THE SACRED STONES

STORY AND ART BY
MARCO ROCCHI AND FRANCESCA CARITÀ

DARK HORSE BOOKS

PRESIDENT AND PUBLISHER   MIKE RICHARDSON
EDITOR   KATII O'BRIEN
ASSISTANT EDITOR   JENNY BLENK
DESIGNERS   JEN EDWARDS AND KATHLEEN BARNETT
DIGITAL ART TECHNICIAN   SAMANTHA HUMMER
TRANSLATED BY   JAMIE RICHARDS
LETTERING BY   JOAMETTE GIL

Library of Congress Cataloging-in-Publication Data

Names: Rocchi, Marco (Comics creator), author, artist. | Carità,
    Francesca, author, artist. | Richards, Jamie, translator.
Title: Gert and the sacred stones / story and art by Marco Rocchi and
    Francesca Carità ; translated by Jamie Richards.
Other titles: Gherd, la ragazza della nebbia
Description: First edition. | Milwaukie, OR : Dark Horse Books, 2020. |
    Audience: Ages 12+ | Summary: Young orphan Gert sets out to protect her
    village from ferocious, fantastical animals by sneaking into the warrior
    initiation test, beginning an adventure which will teach her to rethink
    the glorification of war, and prove that she can be the unlikely hero to
    reimagine her people's future.
Identifiers: LCCN 2020010169 (print) | LCCN 2020010170 (ebook) | ISBN
    9781506719634 (paperback) | ISBN 9781506719641 (ebook)
Subjects: LCSH: Graphic novels. | CYAC: Graphic novels. | Fantasy. |
    Self-actualization (Psychology)--Fiction.
Classification: LCC PZ7.7.R635 Ge 2020 (print) | LCC PZ7.7.R635 (ebook) |
    DDC 741.5/973--dc23
LC record available at https://lccn.loc.gov/2020010169
LC ebook record available at https://lccn.loc.gov/2020010170

DarkHorse.com
Facebook.com/DarkHorseComics
Twitter.com/DarkHorseComics

Originally published in Italy by Tunué (www.tunue.com)

Published by Dark Horse Books
A division of Dark Horse Comics LLC
10956 SE Main Street
Milwaukie, OR 97222
Advertising Sales   (503) 905-2315
Comic Shop Locator Service   comicshoplocator.com

First edition: March 2021
E-Book ISBN: 978-1-50671-964-1
Trade Paperback ISBN: 978-1-50671-963-4

1 3 5 7 9 10 8 6 4 2
Printed in China

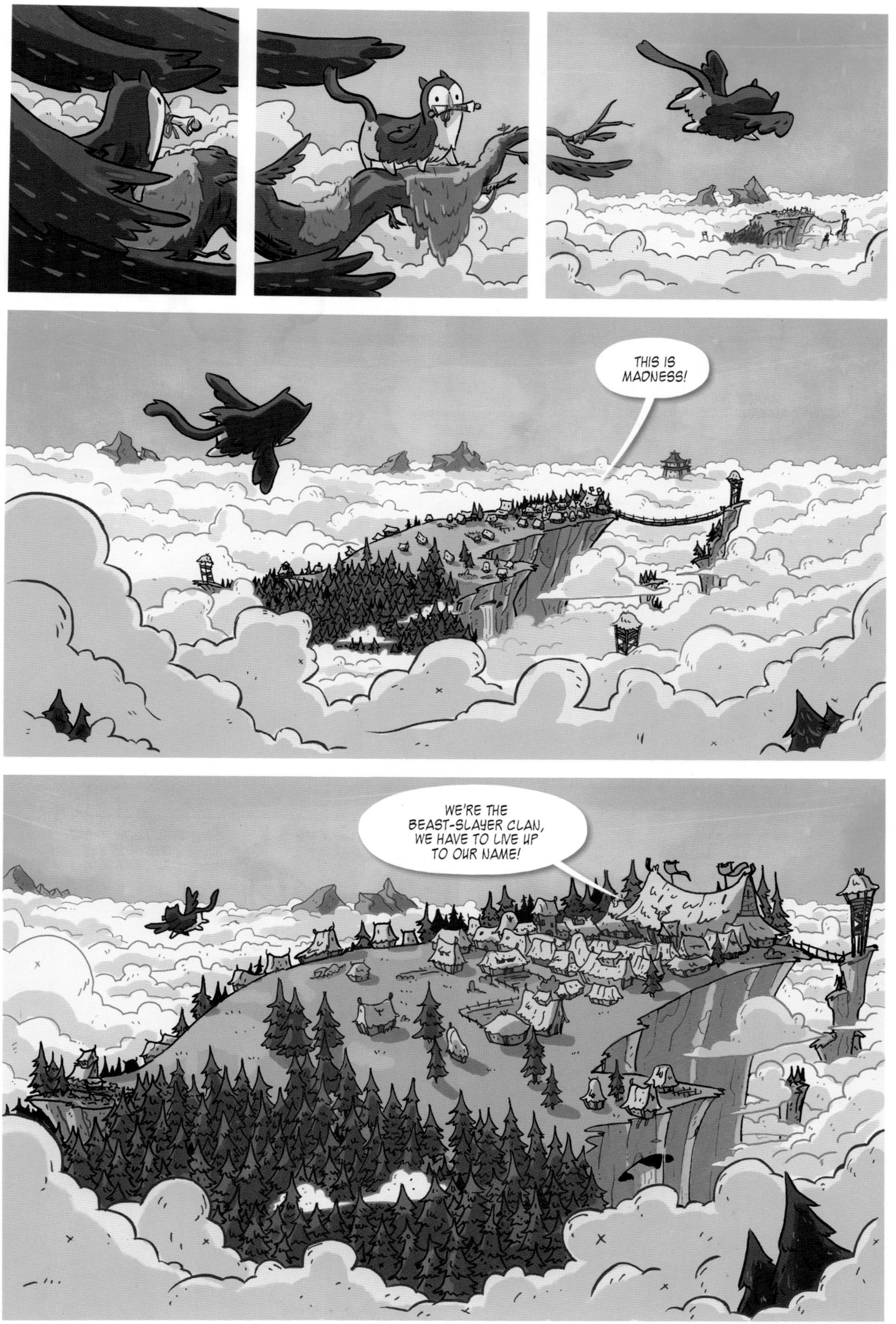
THIS IS MADNESS!
WE'RE THE BEAST-SLAYER CLAN, WE HAVE TO LIVE UP TO OUR NAME!

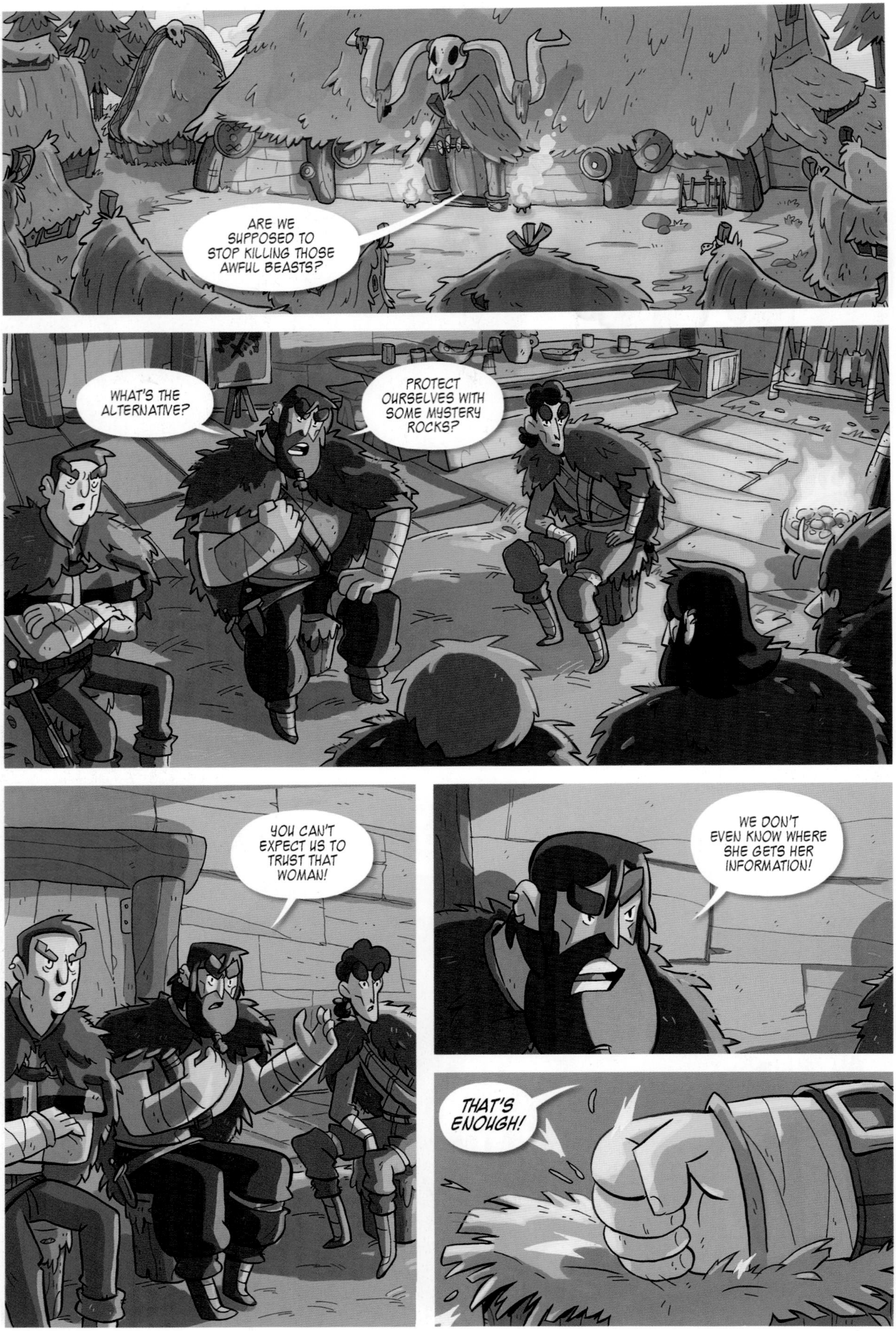
ARE WE SUPPOSED TO STOP KILLING THOSE AWFUL BEASTS?
WHAT'S THE ALTERNATIVE?
PROTECT OURSELVES WITH SOME MYSTERY ROCKS?
YOU CAN'T EXPECT US TO TRUST THAT WOMAN!
WE DON'T EVEN KNOW WHERE SHE GETS HER INFORMATION!
THAT'S ENOUGH!

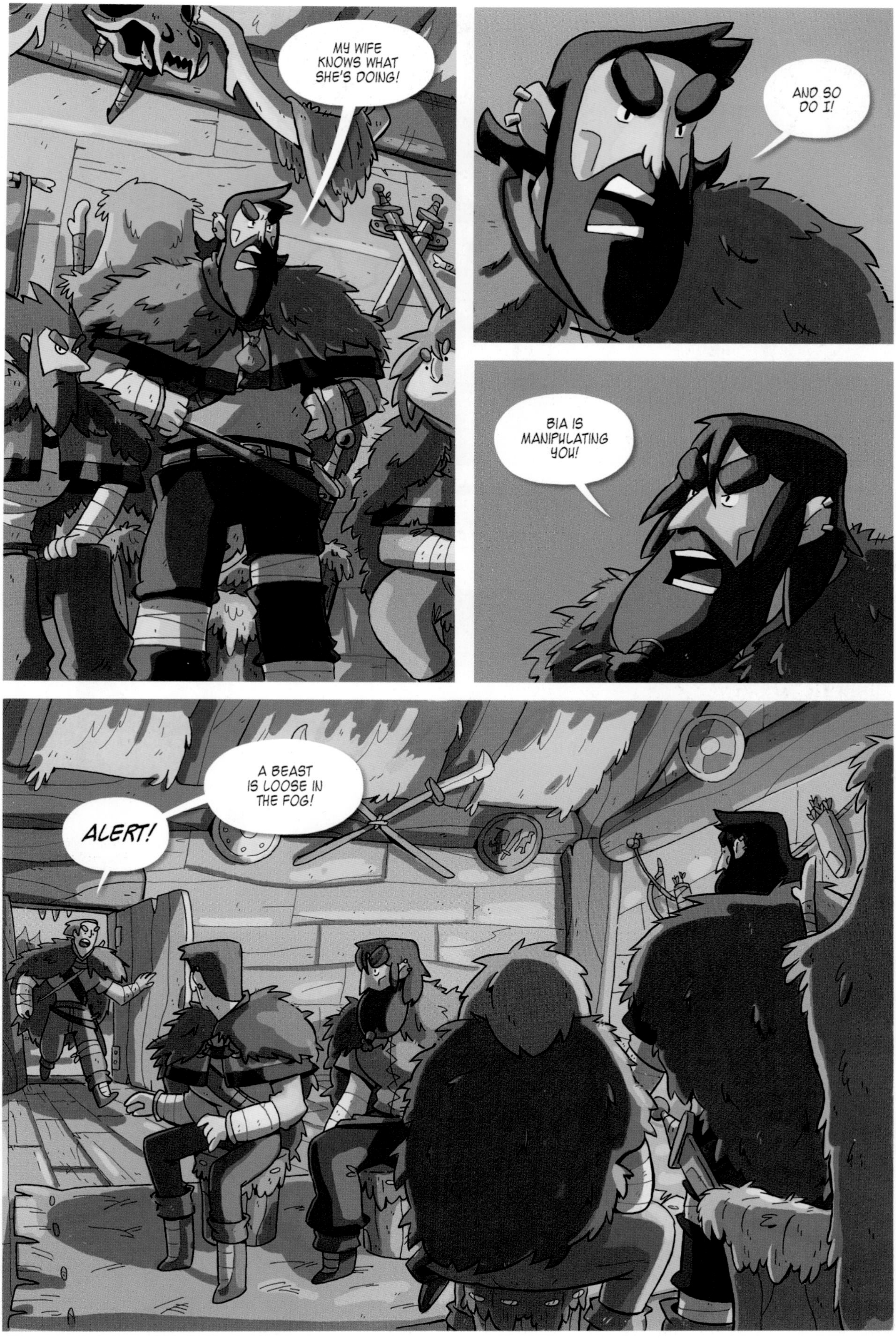
MY WIFE KNOWS WHAT SHE'S DOING!
AND SO DO I!
BIA IS MANIPULATING YOU!
ALERT!
A BEAST IS LOOSE IN THE FOG!

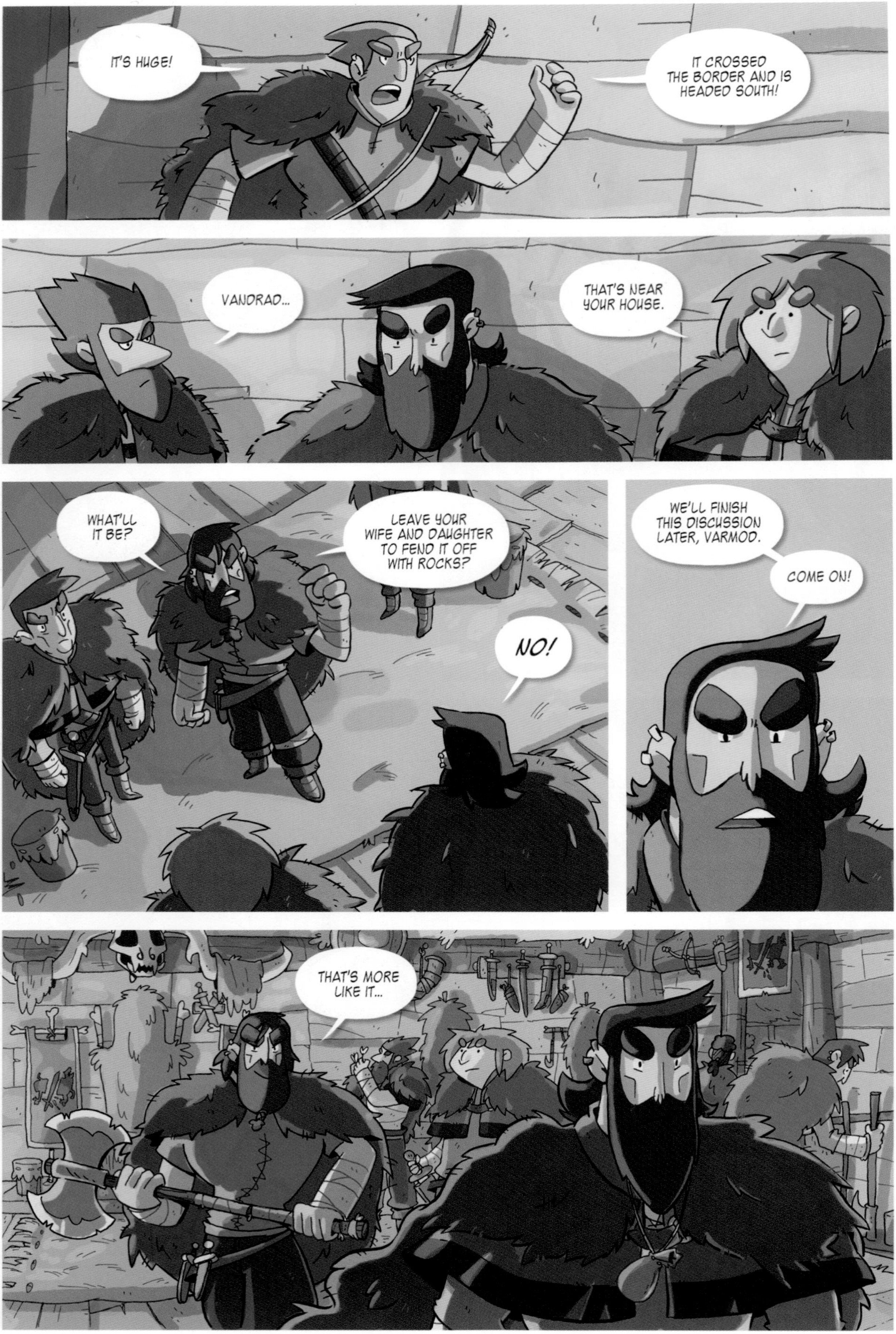
IT'S HUGE!
IT CROSSED THE BORDER AND IS HEADED SOUTH!
VANDRAD...
THAT'S NEAR YOUR HOUSE.
WHAT'LL IT BE?
LEAVE YOUR WIFE AND DAUGHTER TO FEND IT OFF WITH ROCKS?
NO!
WE'LL FINISH THIS DISCUSSION LATER, VARMOD.
COME ON!
THAT'S MORE LIKE IT...

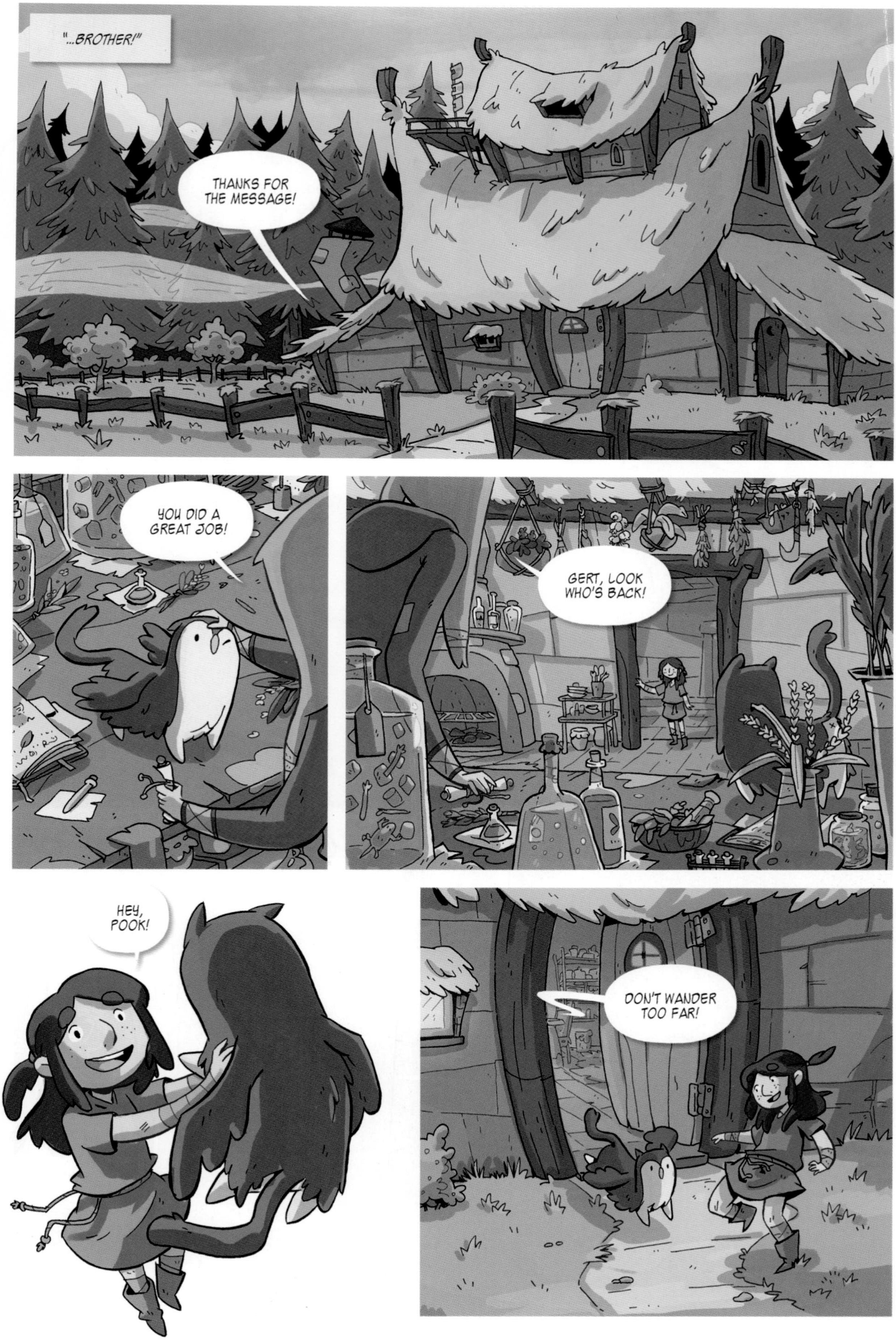
"...BROTHER!"
THANKS FOR THE MESSAGE!
YOU DID A GREAT JOB!
GERT, LOOK WHO'S BACK!
HEY, POOK!
DON'T WANDER TOO FAR!

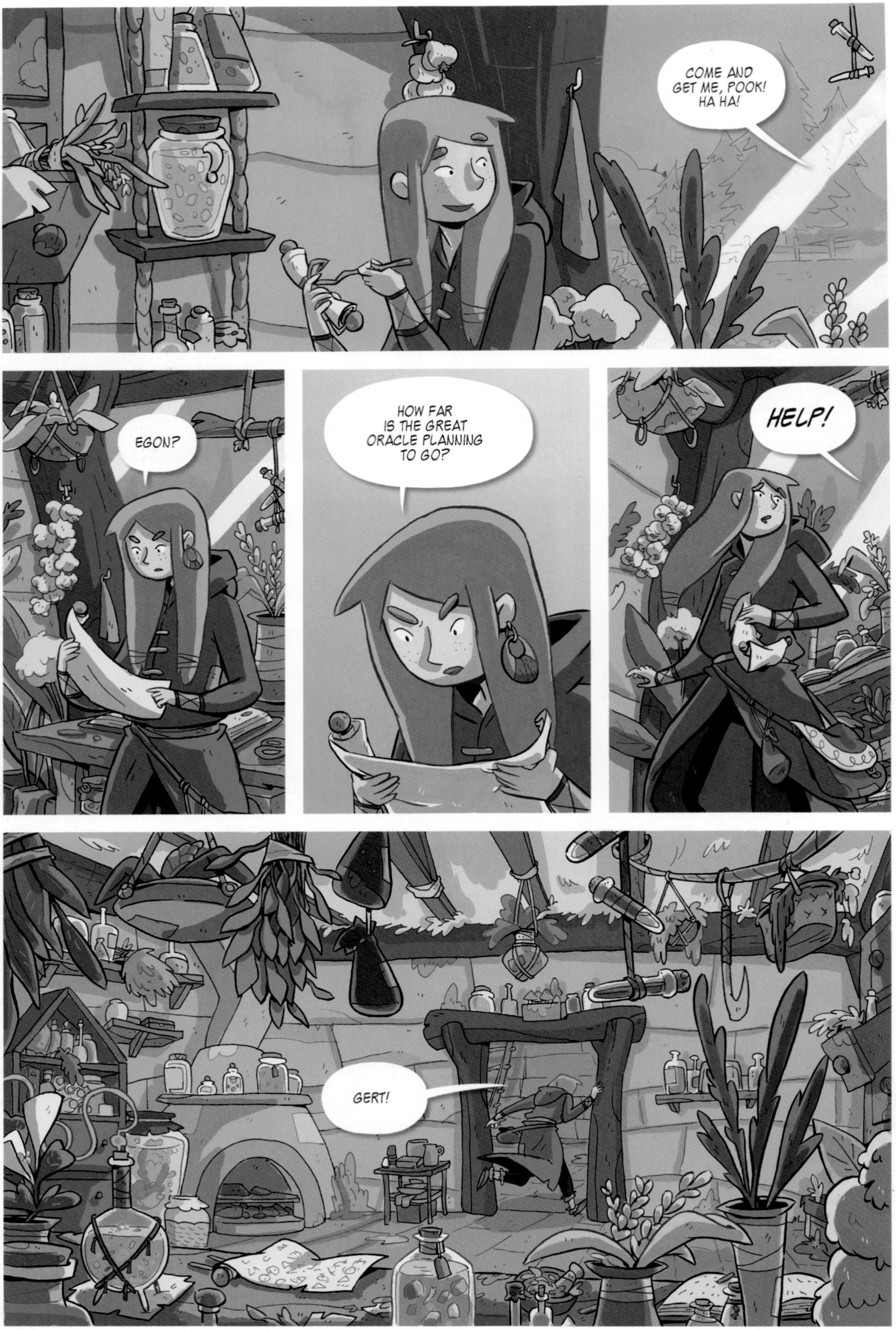
COME AND GET ME, POOK! HA HA!
EGON?
HOW FAR IS THE GREAT ORACLE PLANNING TO GO?
HELP!
GERT!

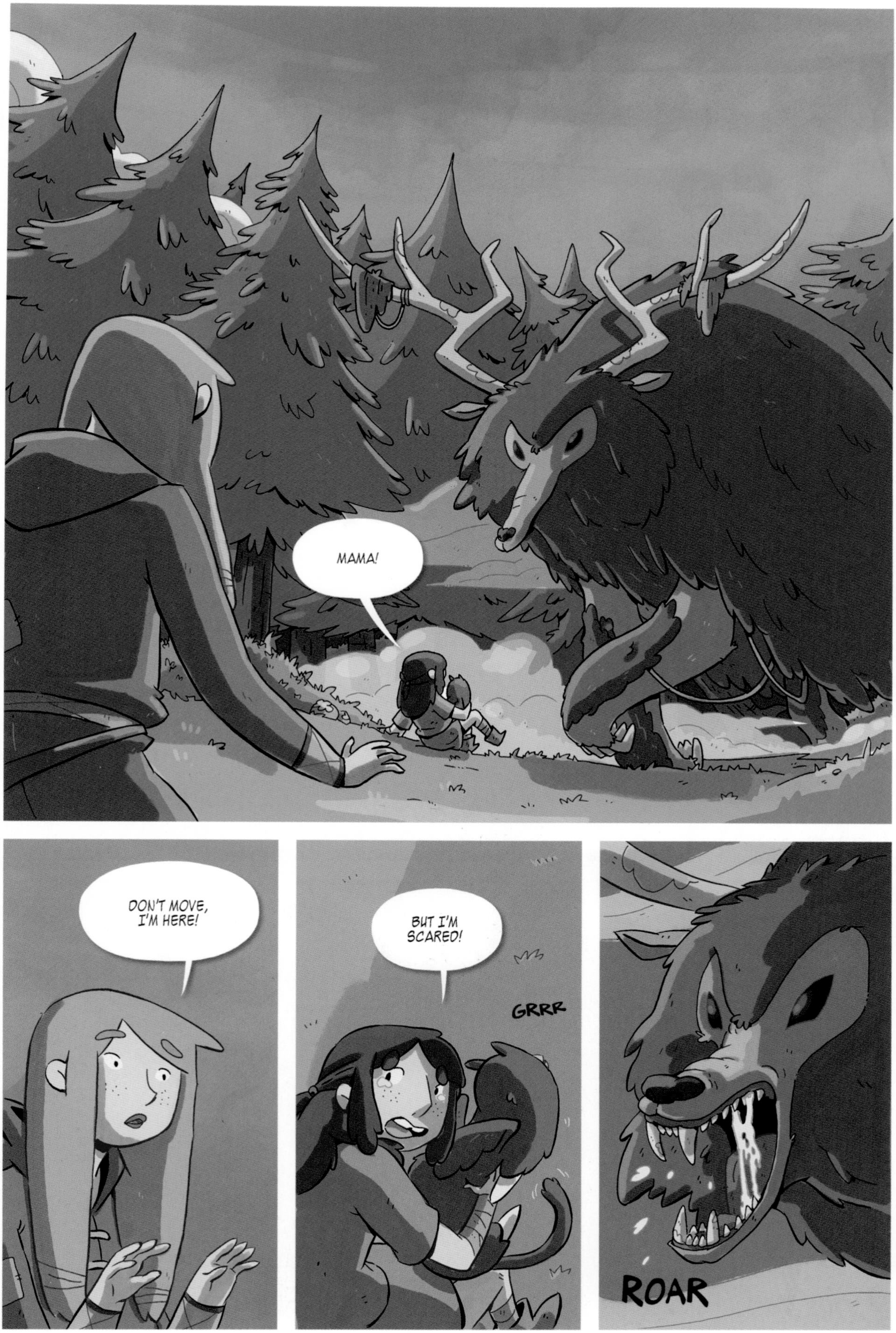
MAMA!
DON'T MOVE, I'M HERE!
BUT I'M SCARED!
GRRR
ROAR

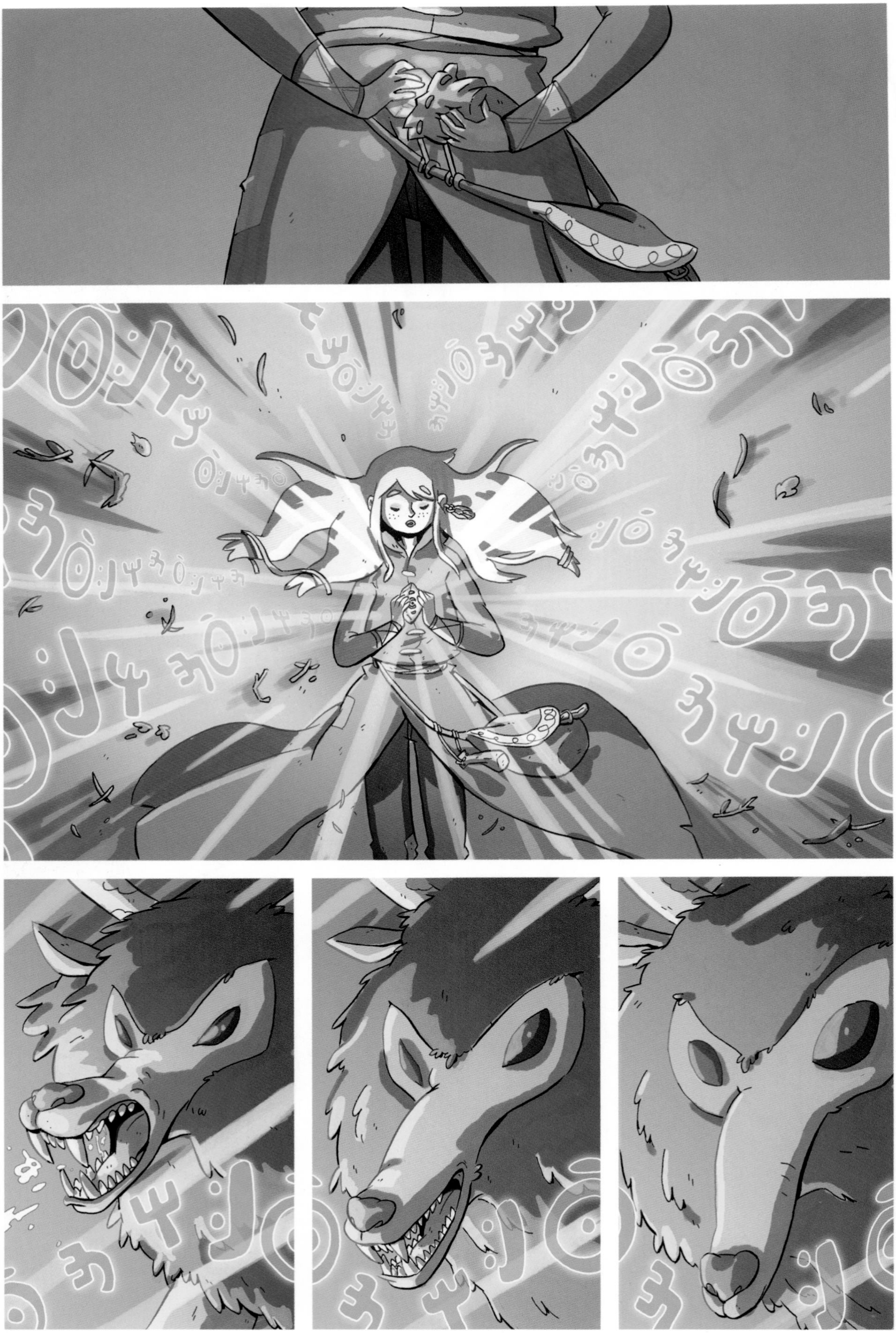

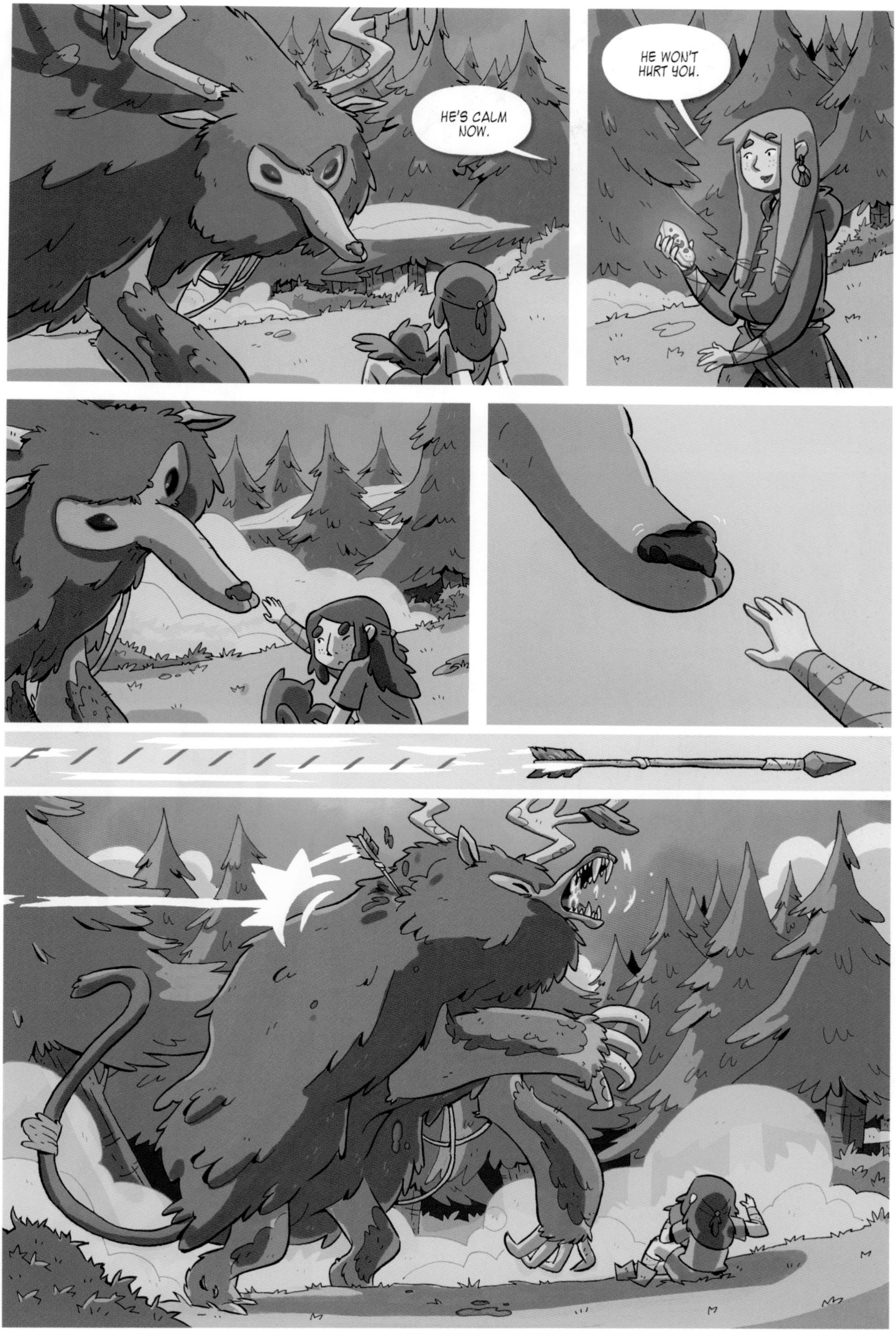
HE'S CALM NOW.
HE WON'T HURT YOU.
FIIIIIIIII

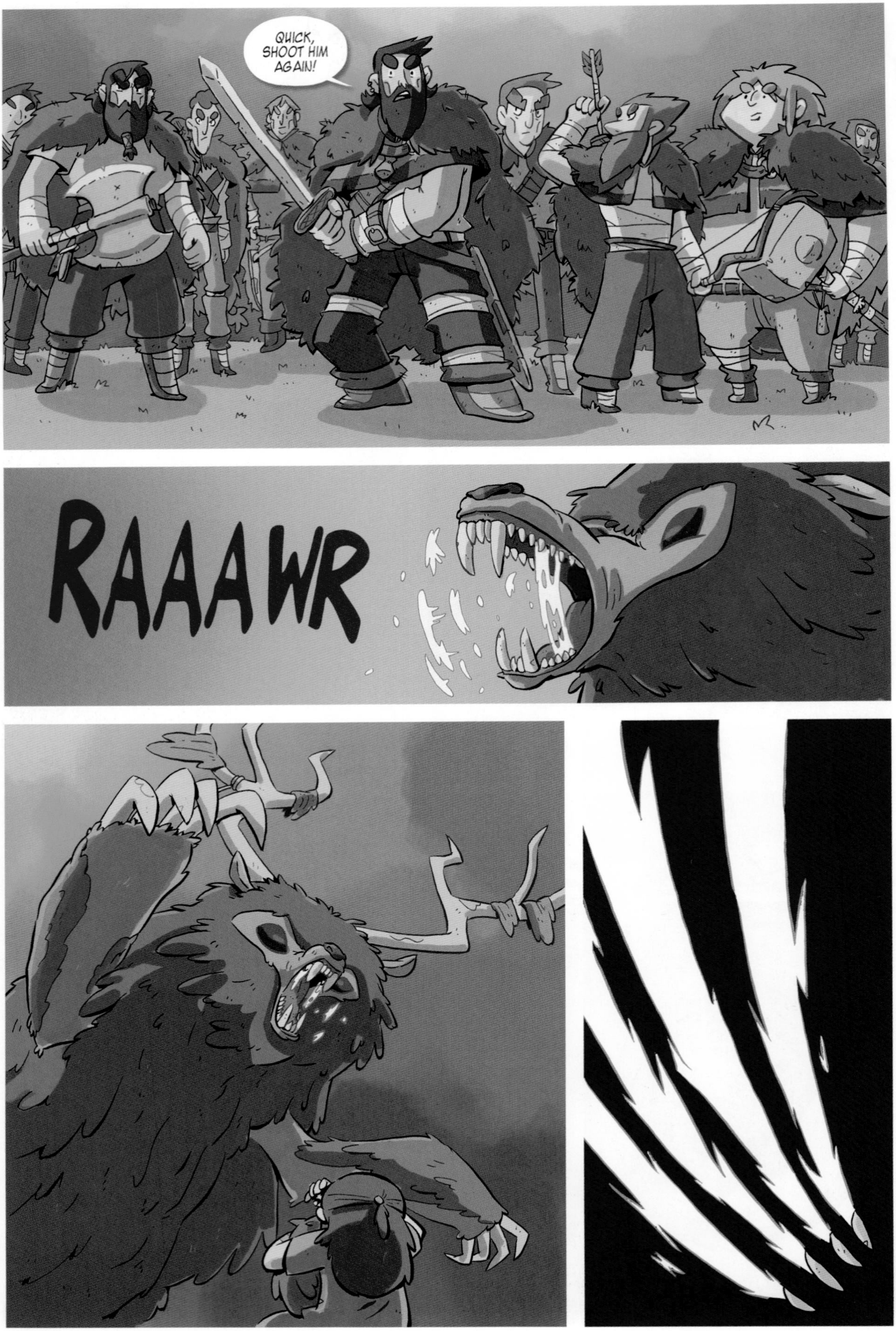
QUICK, SHOOT HIM AGAIN!
RAAAWR

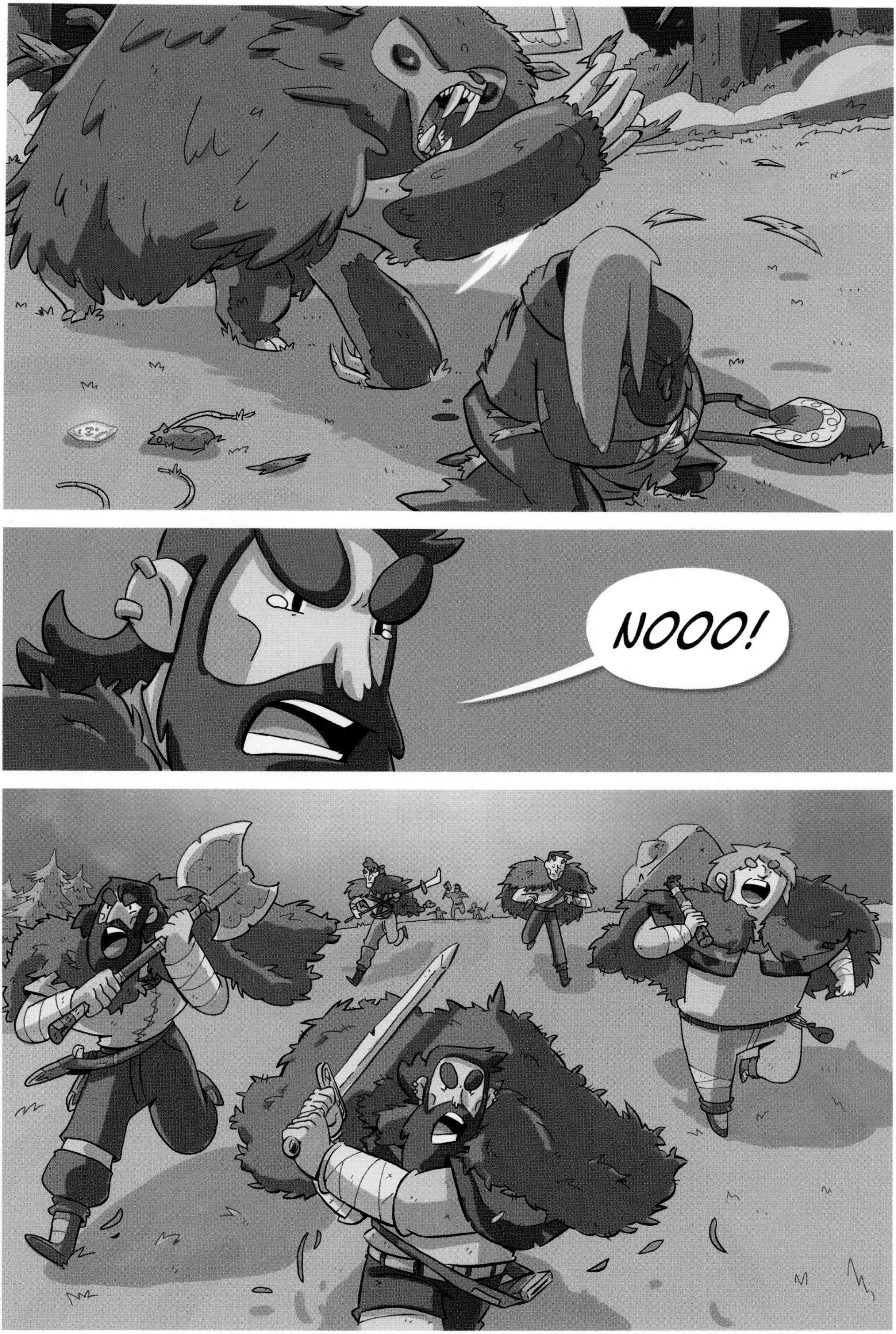
NOOO!

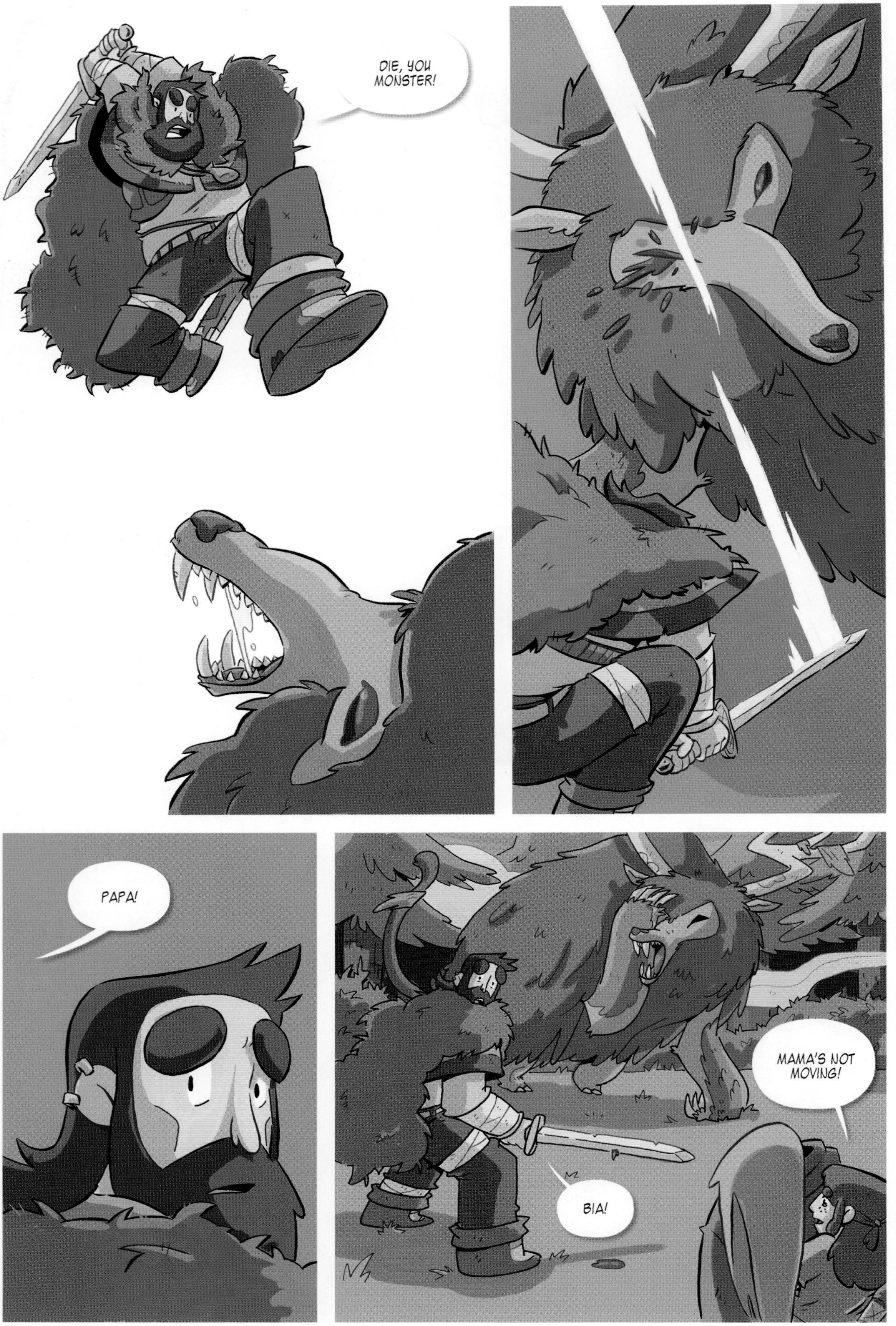
DIE, YOU MONSTER!
PAPA!
MAMA'S NOT MOVING!
BIA!

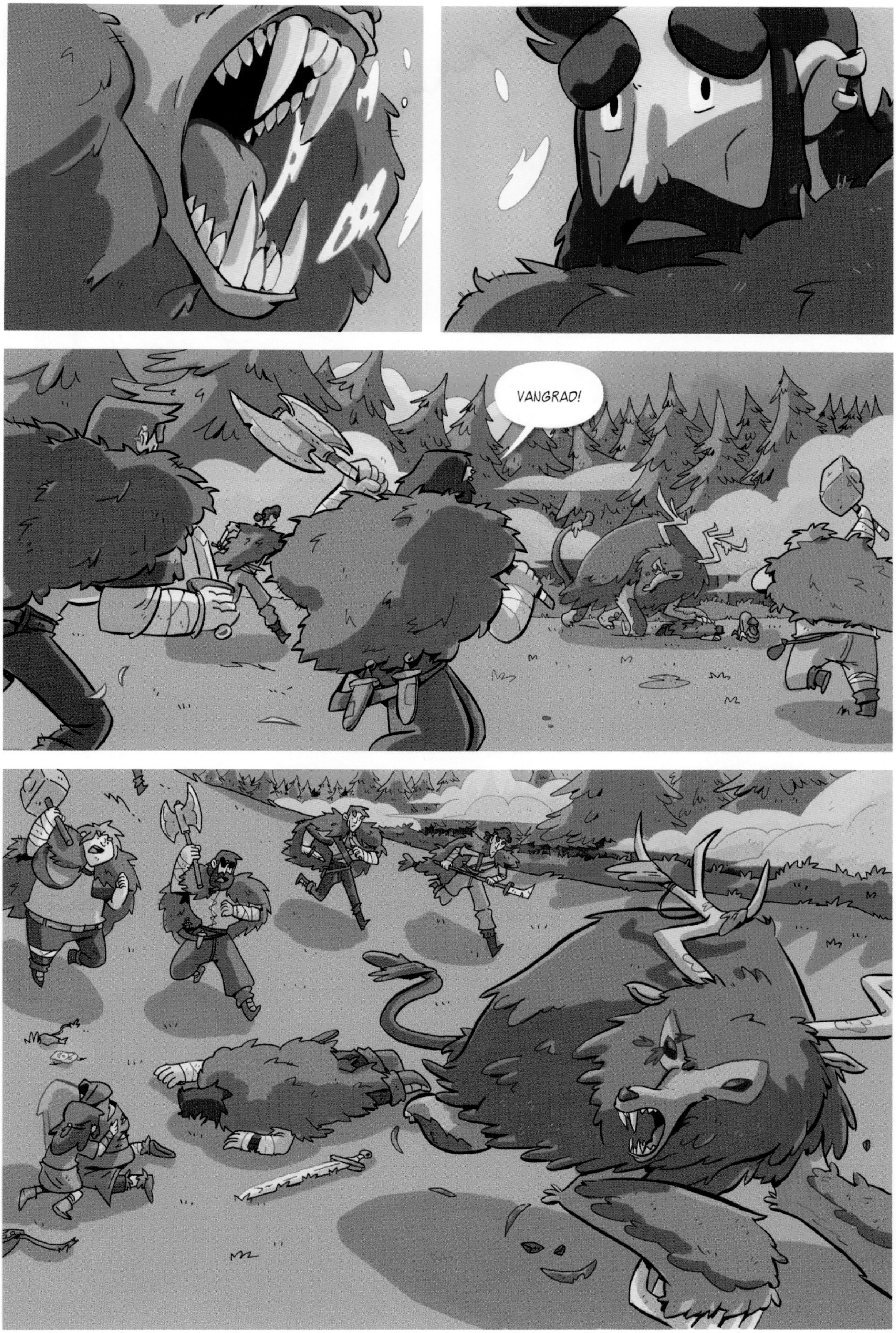
VANGRAD!

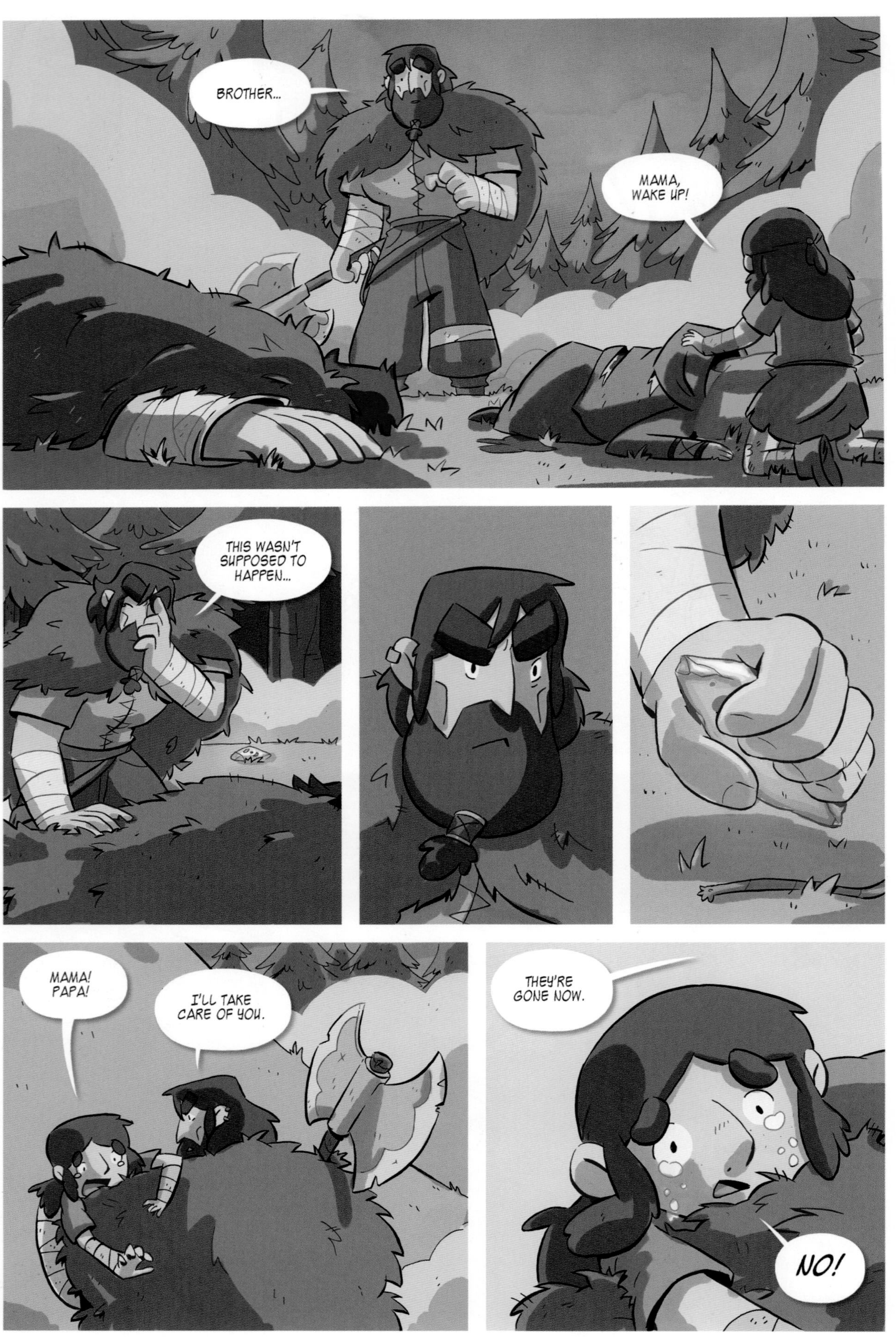
BROTHER...
MAMA, WAKE UP!
THIS WASN'T SUPPOSED TO HAPPEN...
MAMA! PAPA!
I'LL TAKE CARE OF YOU.
THEY'RE GONE NOW.
NO!

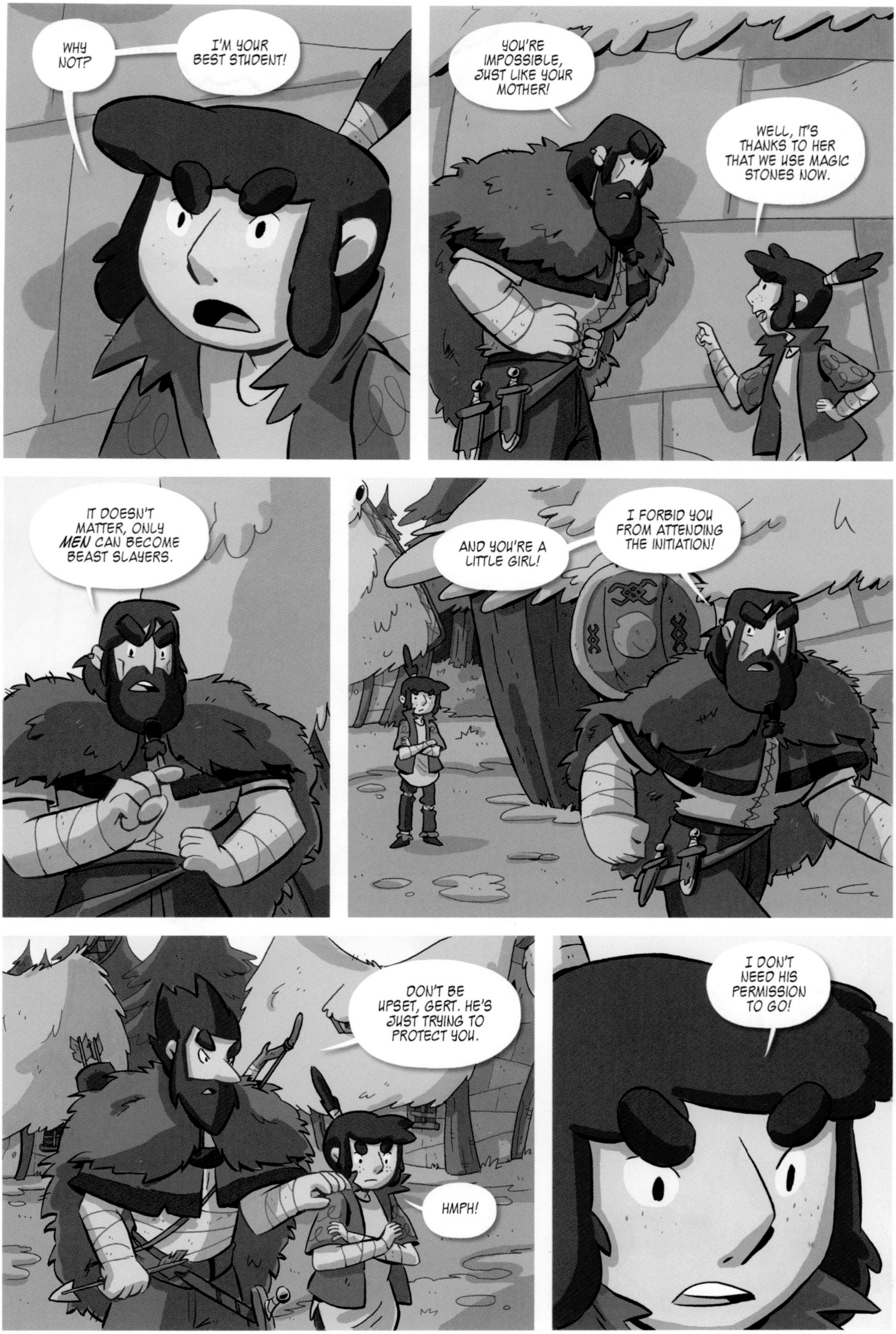
WHY NOT?
I'M YOUR BEST STUDENT!
YOU'RE IMPOSSIBLE, JUST LIKE YOUR MOTHER!
WELL, IT'S THANKS TO HER THAT WE USE MAGIC STONES NOW.
IT DOESN'T MATTER, ONLY MEN CAN BECOME BEAST SLAYERS.
AND YOU'RE A LITTLE GIRL!
I FORBID YOU FROM ATTENDING THE INITIATION!
DON'T BE UPSET, GERT. HE'S JUST TRYING TO PROTECT YOU.
HMPH!
I DON'T NEED HIS PERMISSION TO GO!

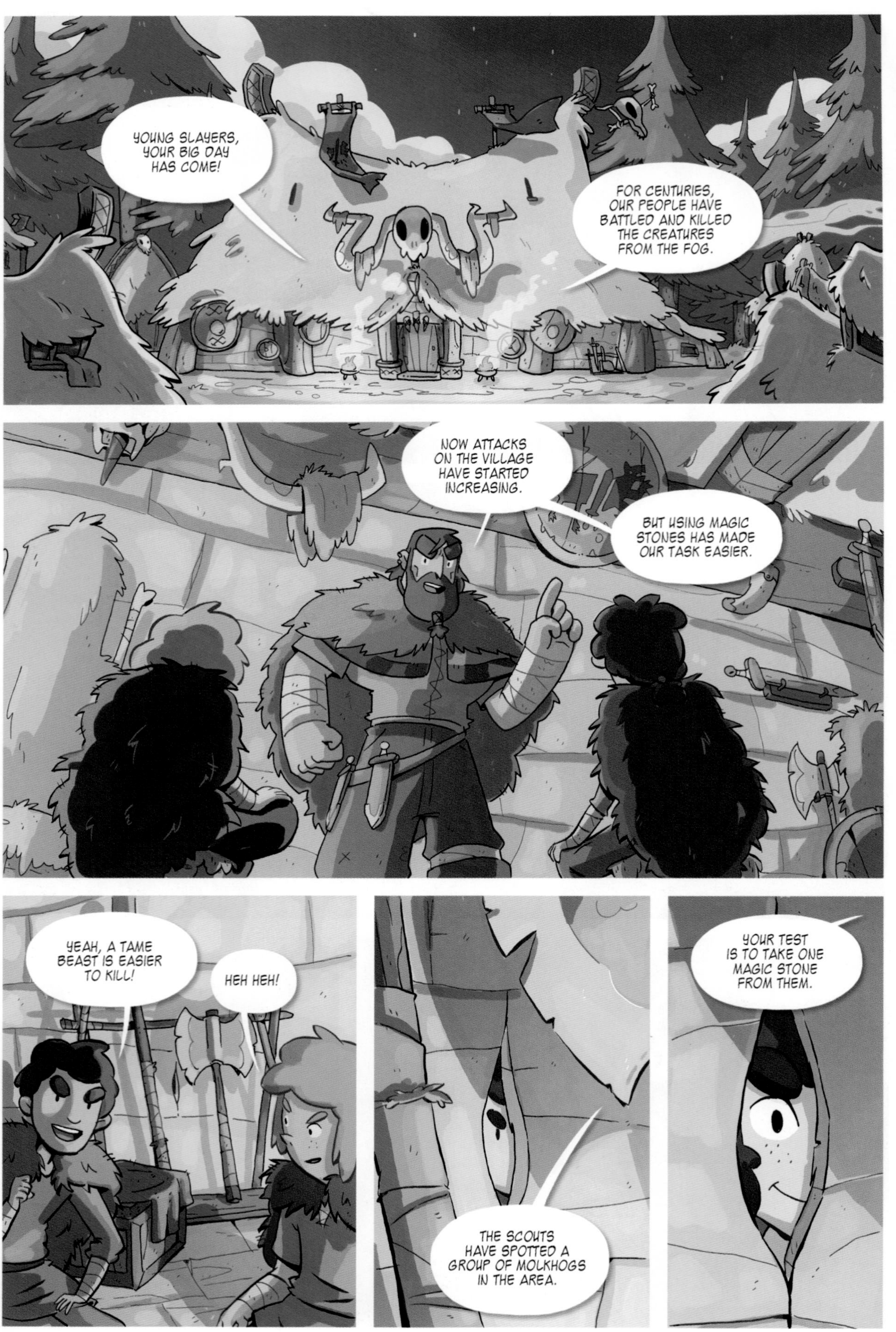
YOUNG SLAYERS, YOUR BIG DAY HAS COME!
FOR CENTURIES, OUR PEOPLE HAVE BATTLED AND KILLED THE CREATURES FROM THE FOG.
NOW ATTACKS ON THE VILLAGE HAVE STARTED INCREASING.
BUT USING MAGIC STONES HAS MADE OUR TASK EASIER.
YEAH, A TAME BEAST IS EASIER TO KILL!
HEH HEH!
THE SCOUTS HAVE SPOTTED A GROUP OF MOLKHOGS IN THE AREA.
YOUR TEST IS TO TAKE ONE MAGIC STONE FROM THEM.

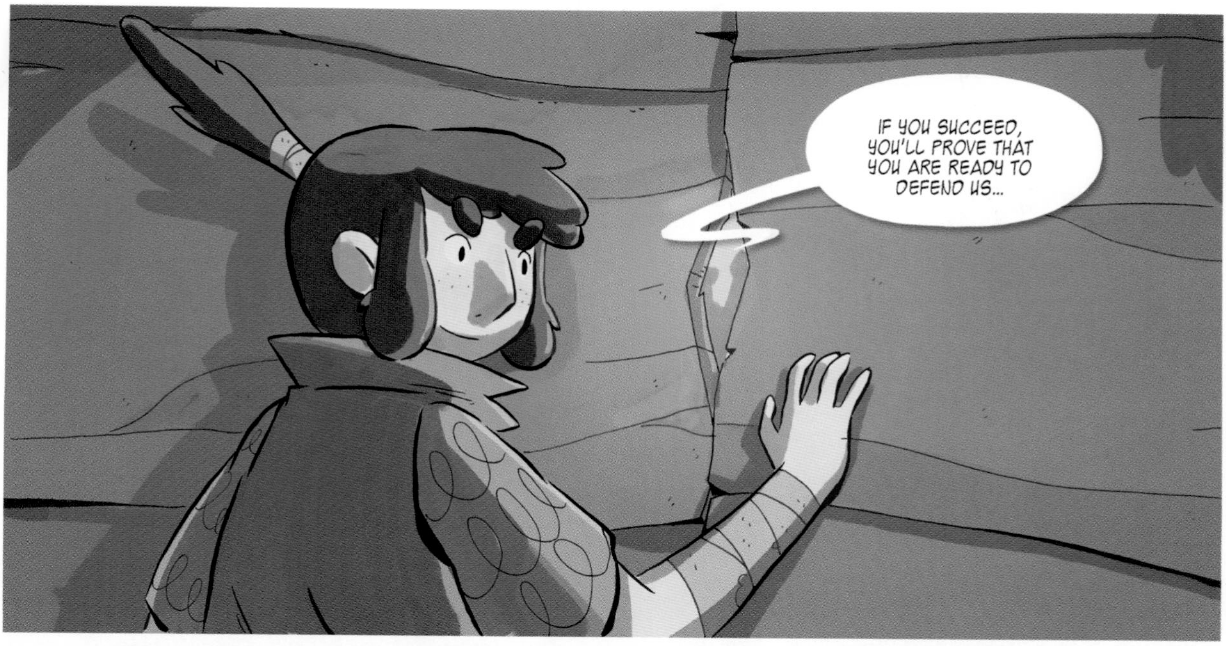
IF YOU SUCCEED, YOU'LL PROVE THAT YOU ARE READY TO DEFEND US...

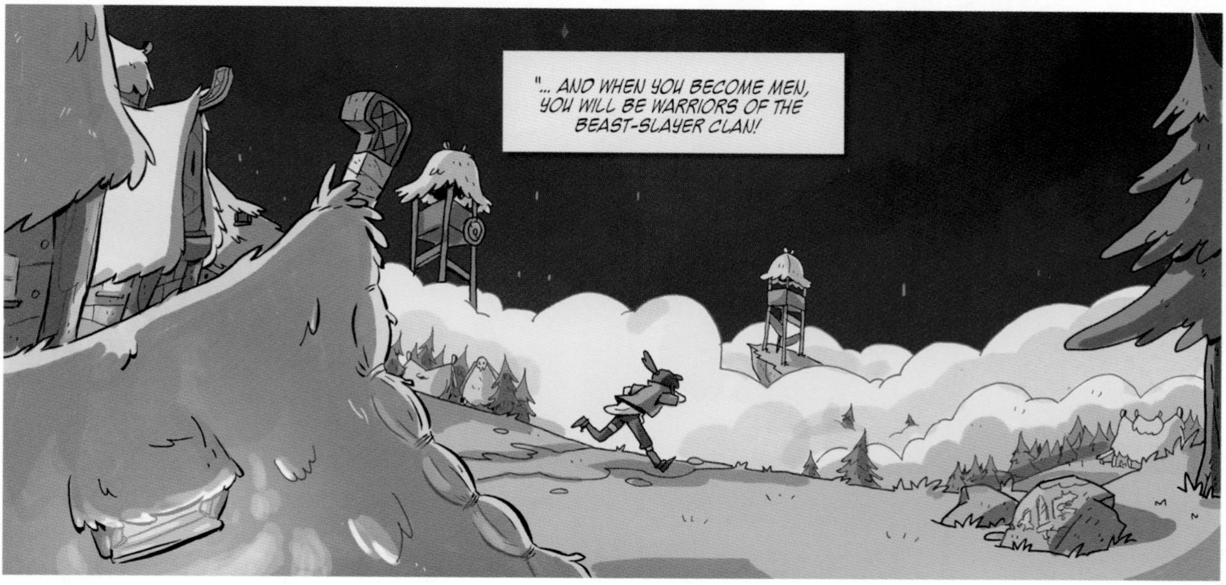
"... AND WHEN YOU BECOME MEN, YOU WILL BE WARRIORS OF THE BEAST-SLAYER CLAN!

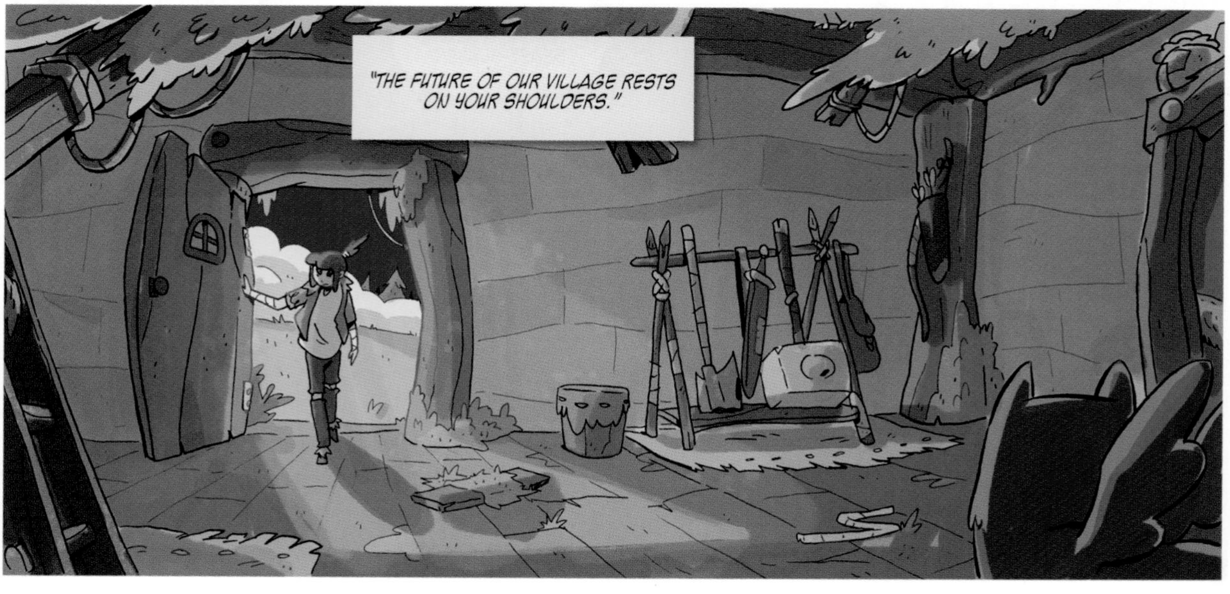
"THE FUTURE OF OUR VILLAGE RESTS ON YOUR SHOULDERS."

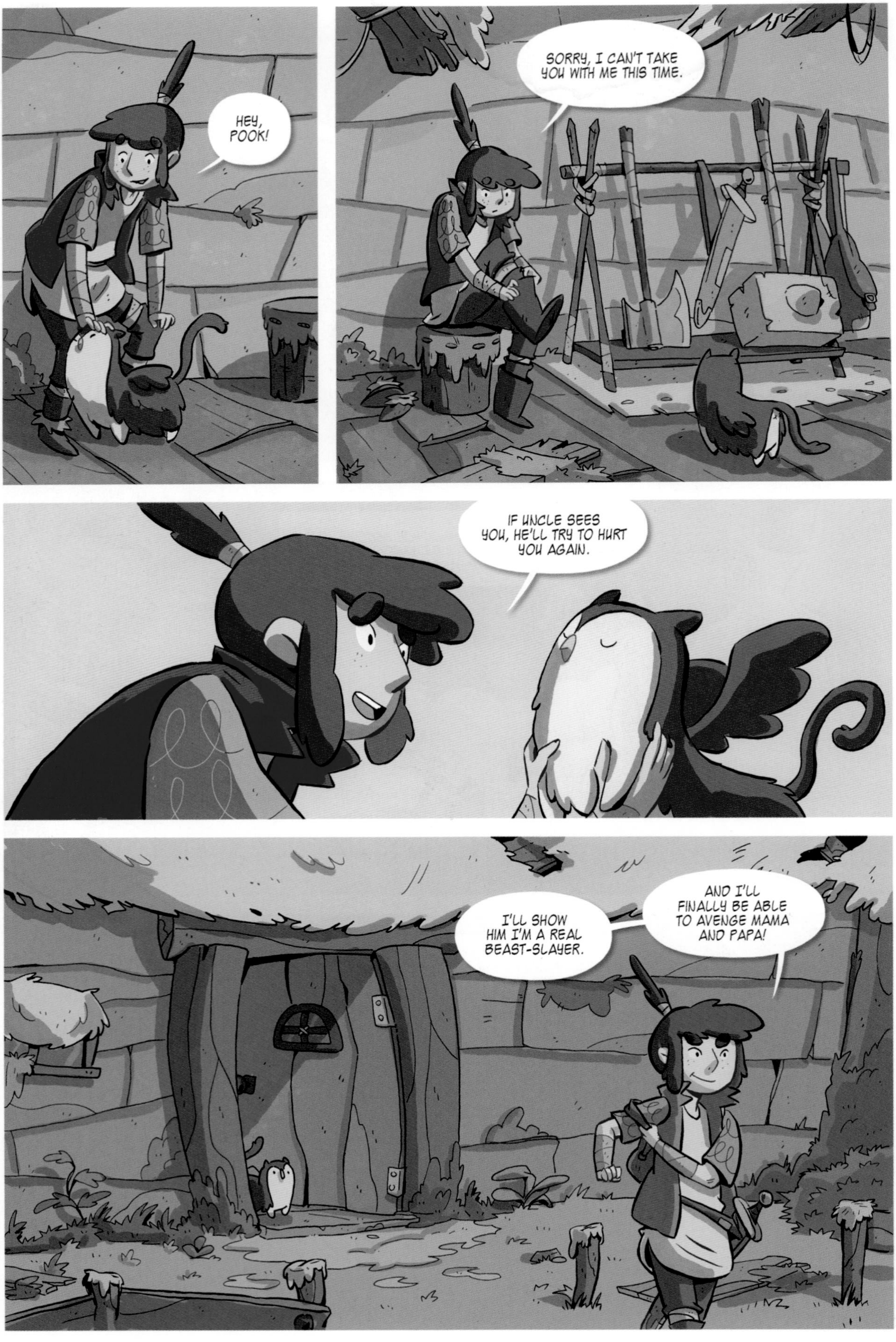
HEY, POOK!
SORRY, I CAN'T TAKE YOU WITH ME THIS TIME.
IF UNCLE SEES YOU, HE'LL TRY TO HURT YOU AGAIN.
I'LL SHOW HIM I'M A REAL BEAST-SLAYER.
AND I'LL FINALLY BE ABLE TO AVENGE MAMA AND PAPA!

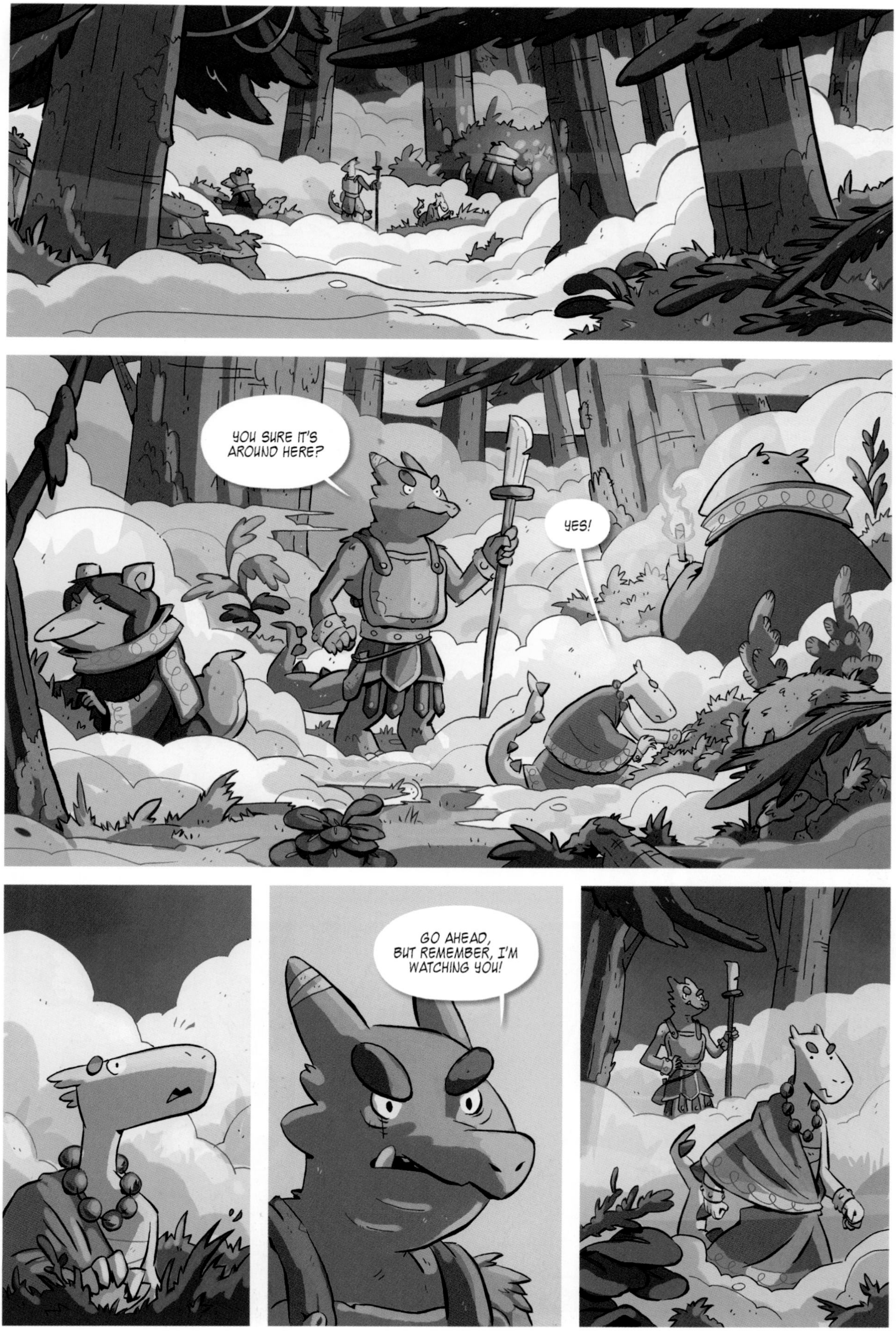

YOU SURE IT'S AROUND HERE?
YES!
GO AHEAD, BUT REMEMBER, I'M WATCHING YOU!

I KNEW I FELT IT HERE!

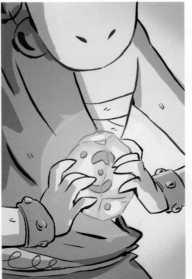

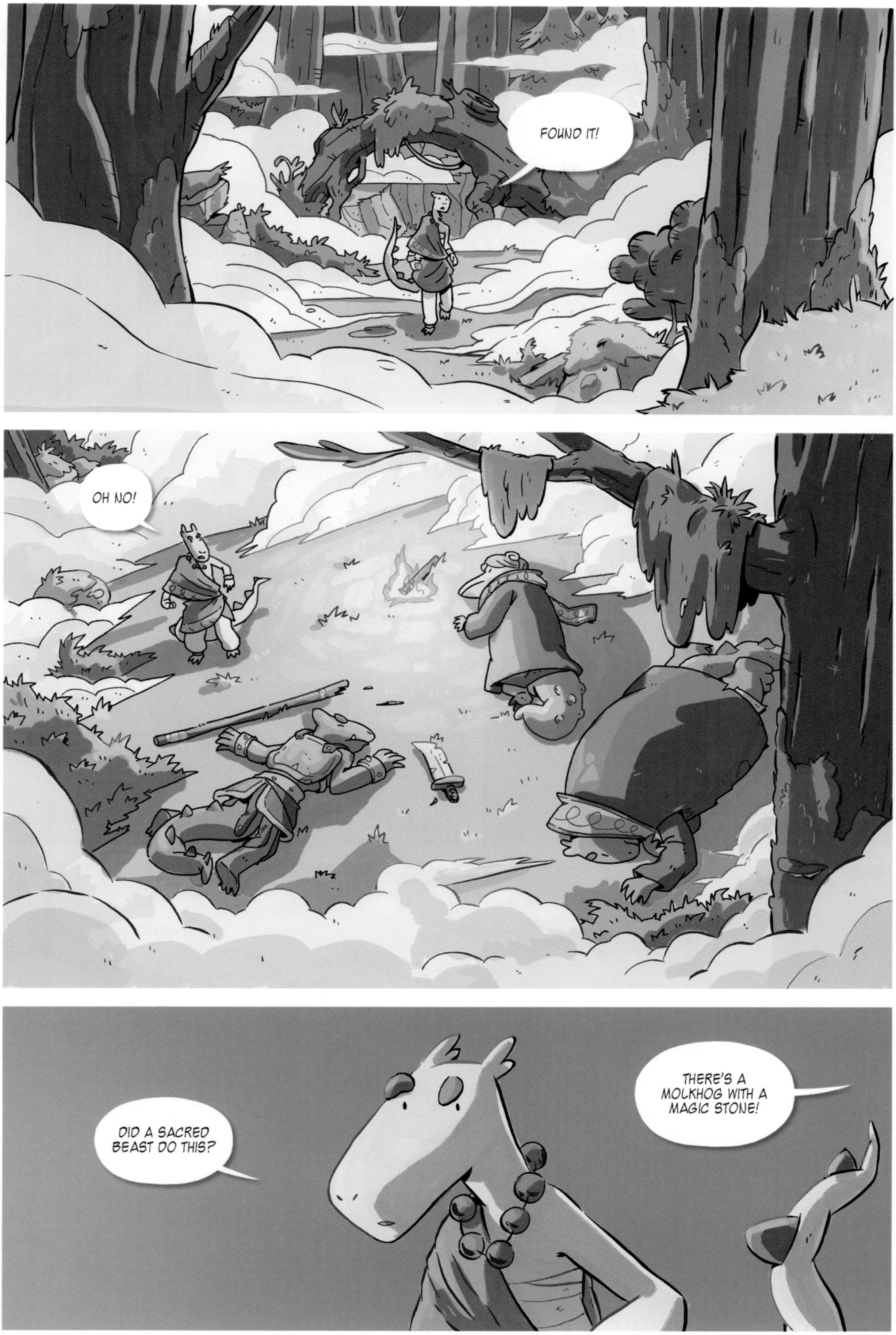
FOUND IT!
OH NO!
DID A SACRED BEAST DO THIS?
THERE'S A MOLKHOG WITH A MAGIC STONE!

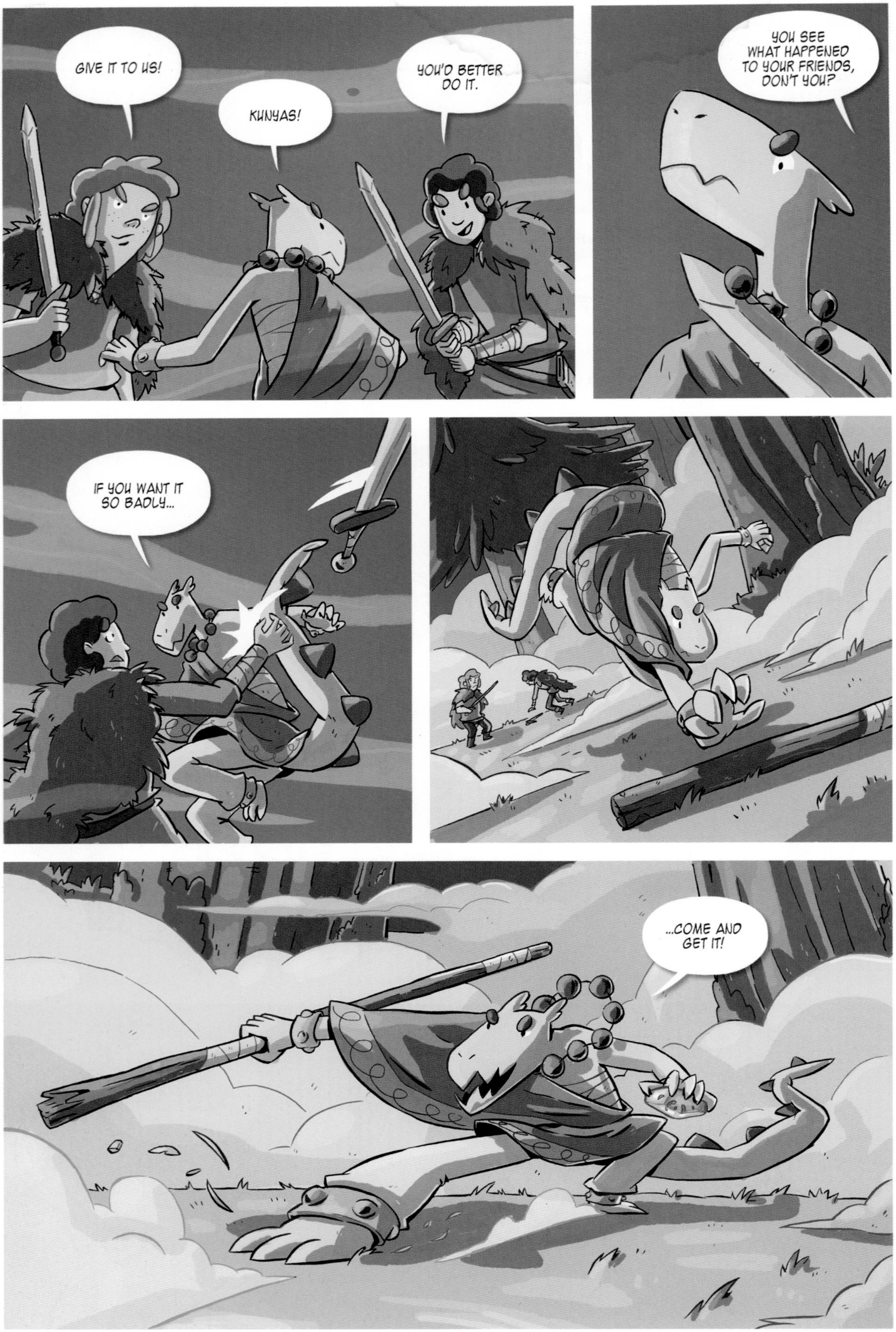
GIVE IT TO US!
KUNYAS!
YOU'D BETTER DO IT.
YOU SEE WHAT HAPPENED TO YOUR FRIENDS, DON'T YOU?
IF YOU WANT IT SO BADLY...
...COME AND GET IT!

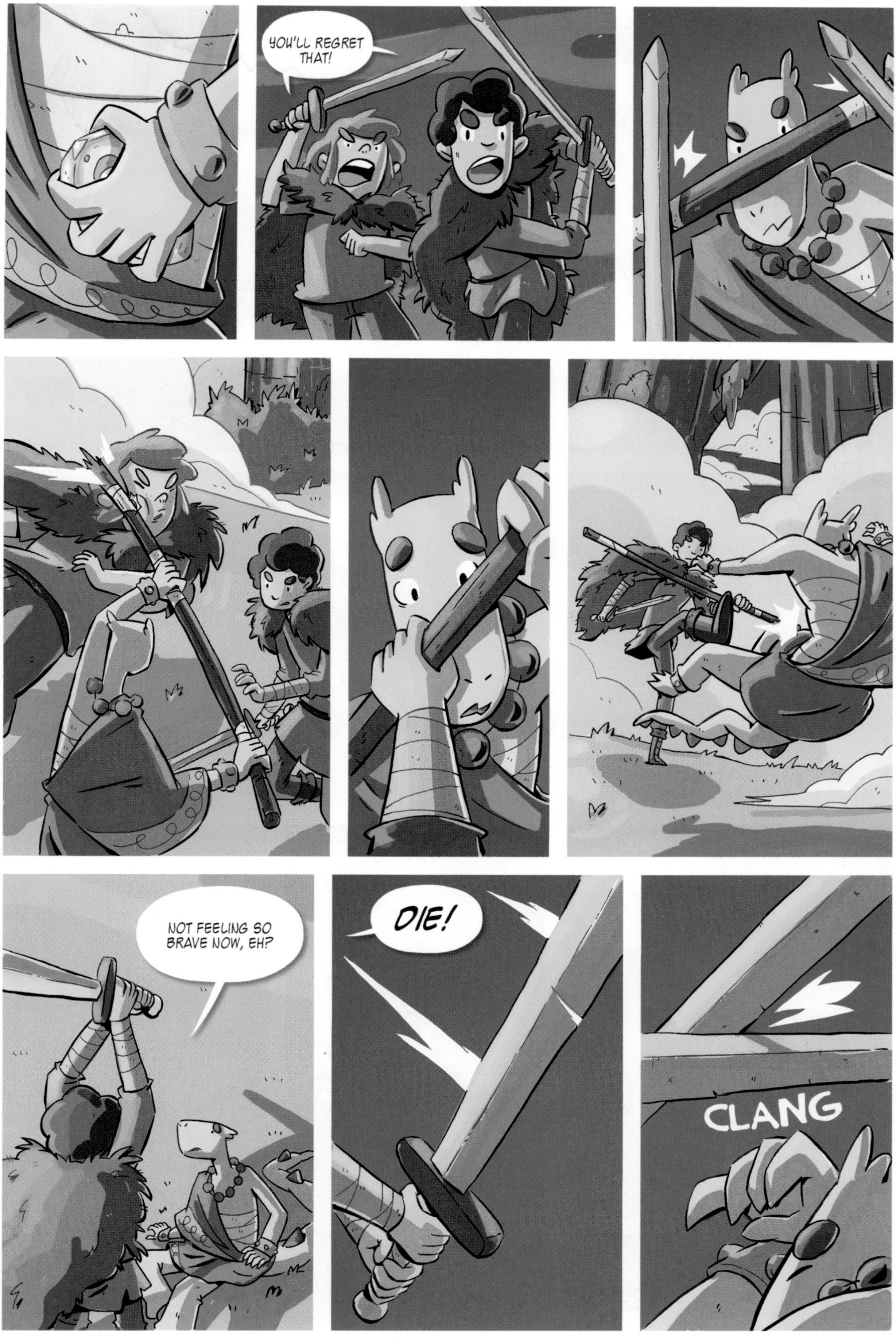
YOU'LL REGRET THAT!
NOT FEELING SO BRAVE NOW, EH?
DIE!
CLANG

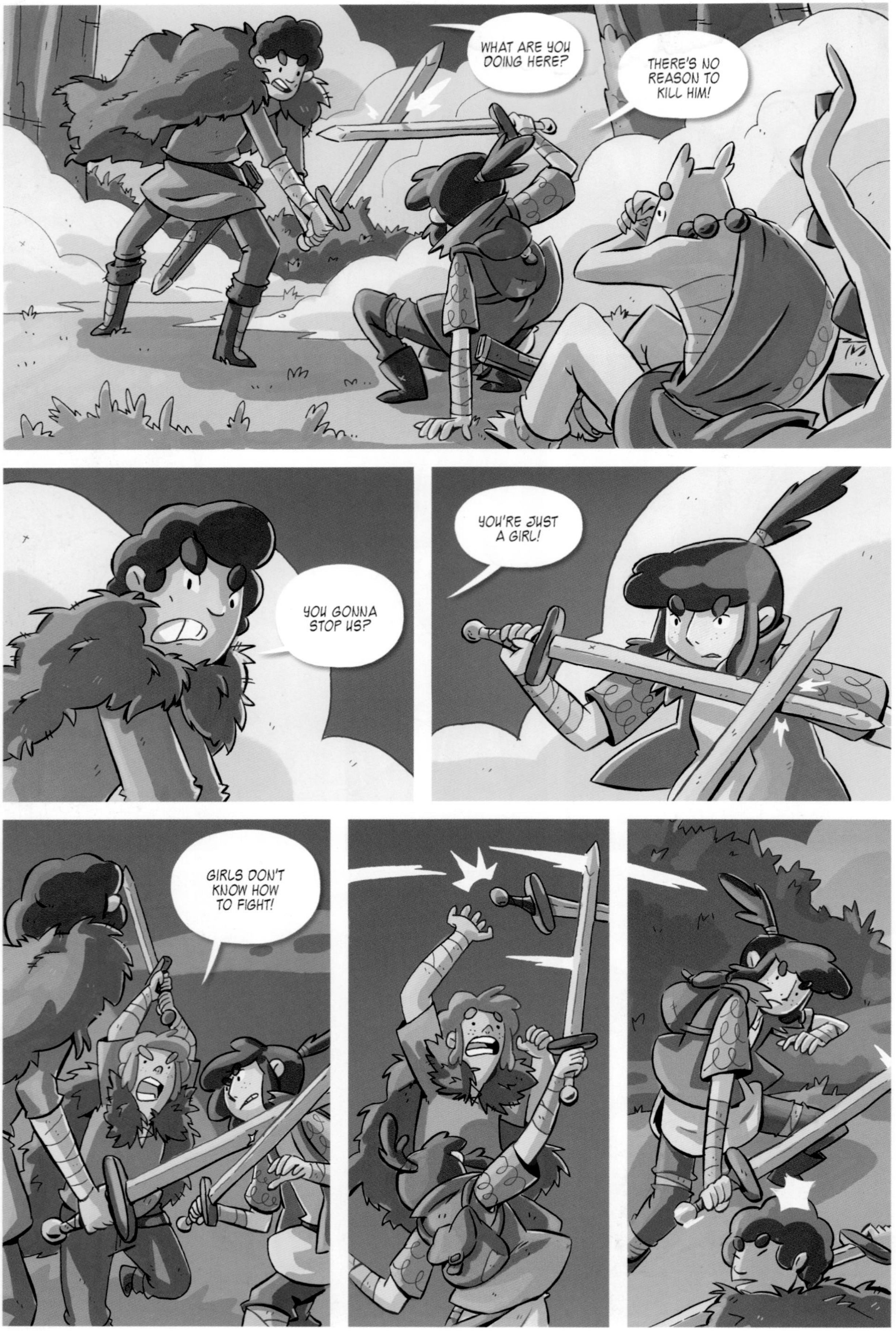
WHAT ARE YOU DOING HERE?
THERE'S NO REASON TO KILL HIM!
YOU GONNA STOP US?
YOU'RE JUST A GIRL!
GIRLS DON'T KNOW HOW TO FIGHT!

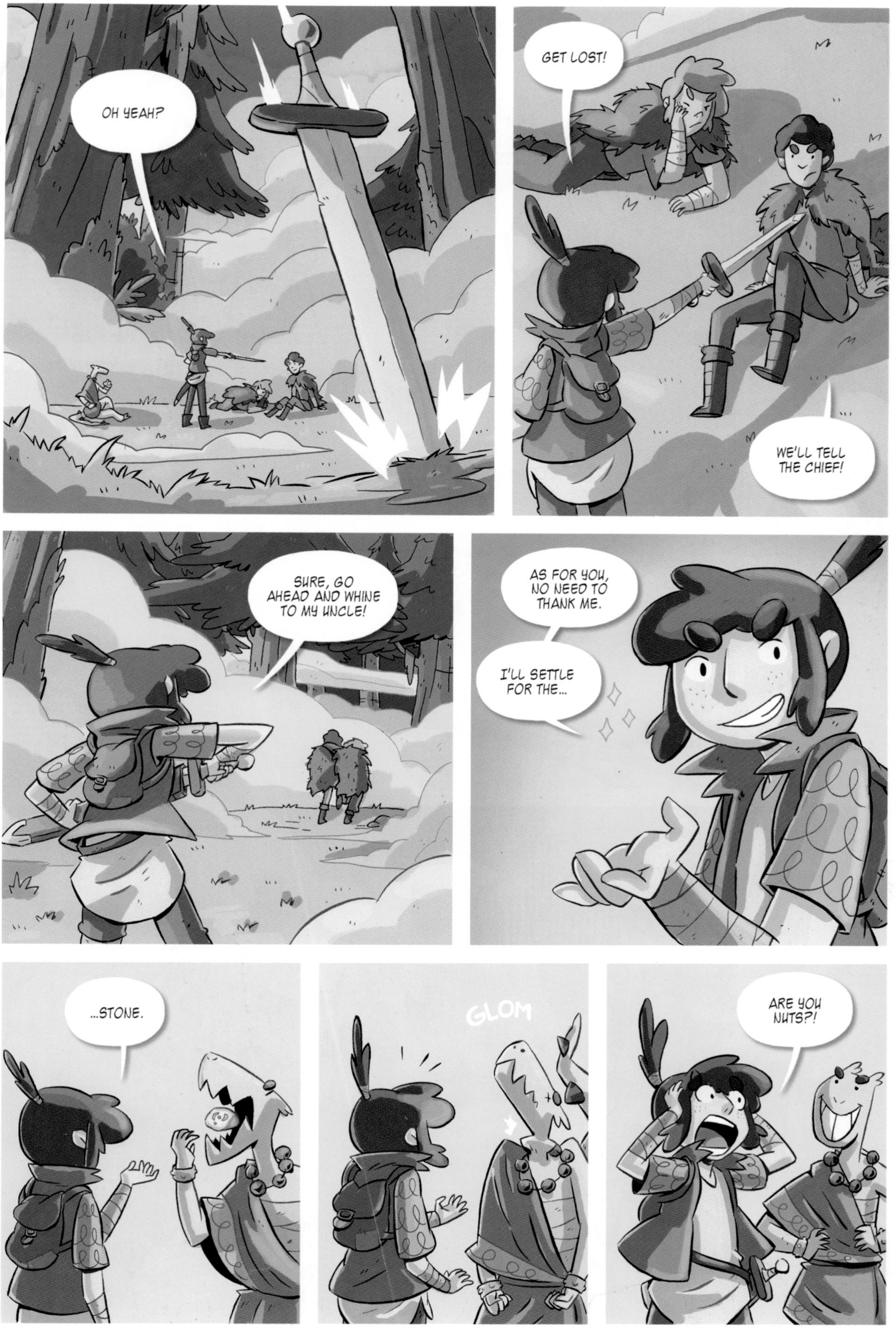
OH YEAH?
GET LOST!
WE'LL TELL THE CHIEF!
SURE, GO AHEAD AND WHINE TO MY UNCLE!
AS FOR YOU, NO NEED TO THANK ME.
I'LL SETTLE FOR THE...
...STONE.
GLOM
ARE YOU NUTS?!

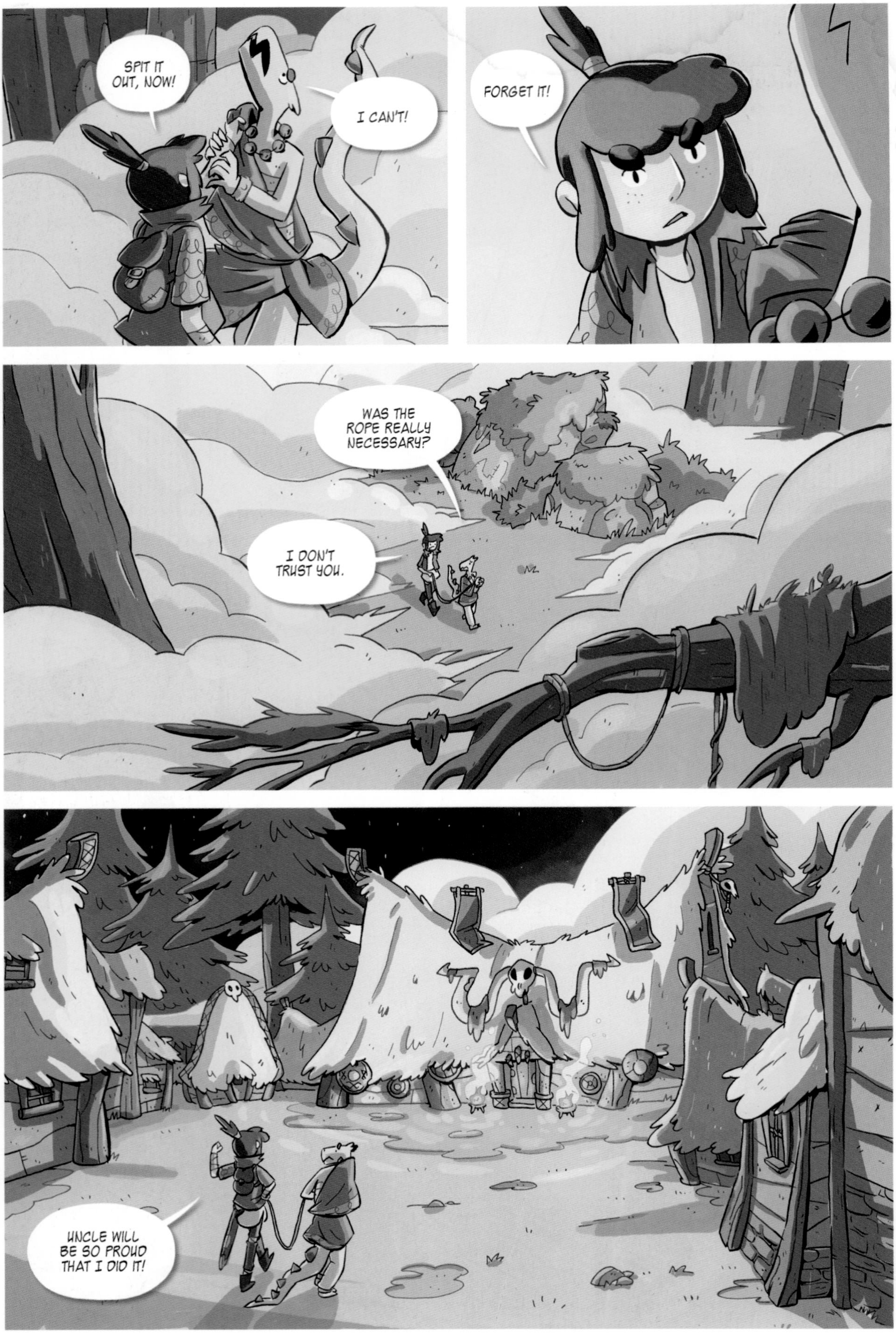
SPIT IT OUT, NOW!
I CAN'T!
FORGET IT!
WAS THE ROPE REALLY NECESSARY?
I DON'T TRUST YOU.
UNCLE WILL BE SO PROUD THAT I DID IT!

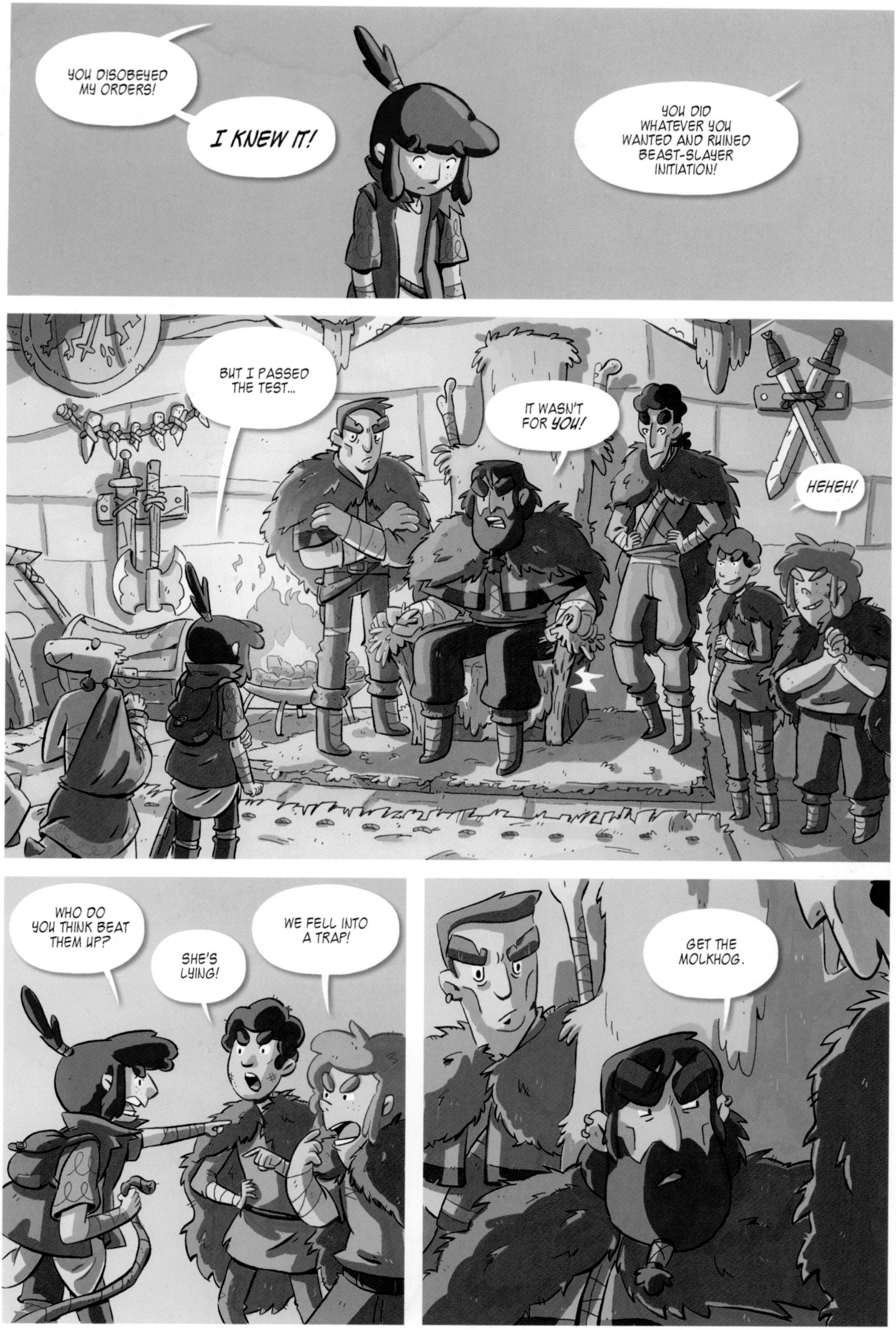
YOU DISOBEYED MY ORDERS!
I KNEW IT!
YOU DID WHATEVER YOU WANTED AND RUINED BEAST-SLAYER INITIATION!
BUT I PASSED THE TEST...
IT WASN'T FOR *YOU!*
HEHEH!
WHO DO YOU THINK BEAT THEM UP?
SHE'S LYING!
WE FELL INTO A TRAP!
GET THE MOLKHOG.

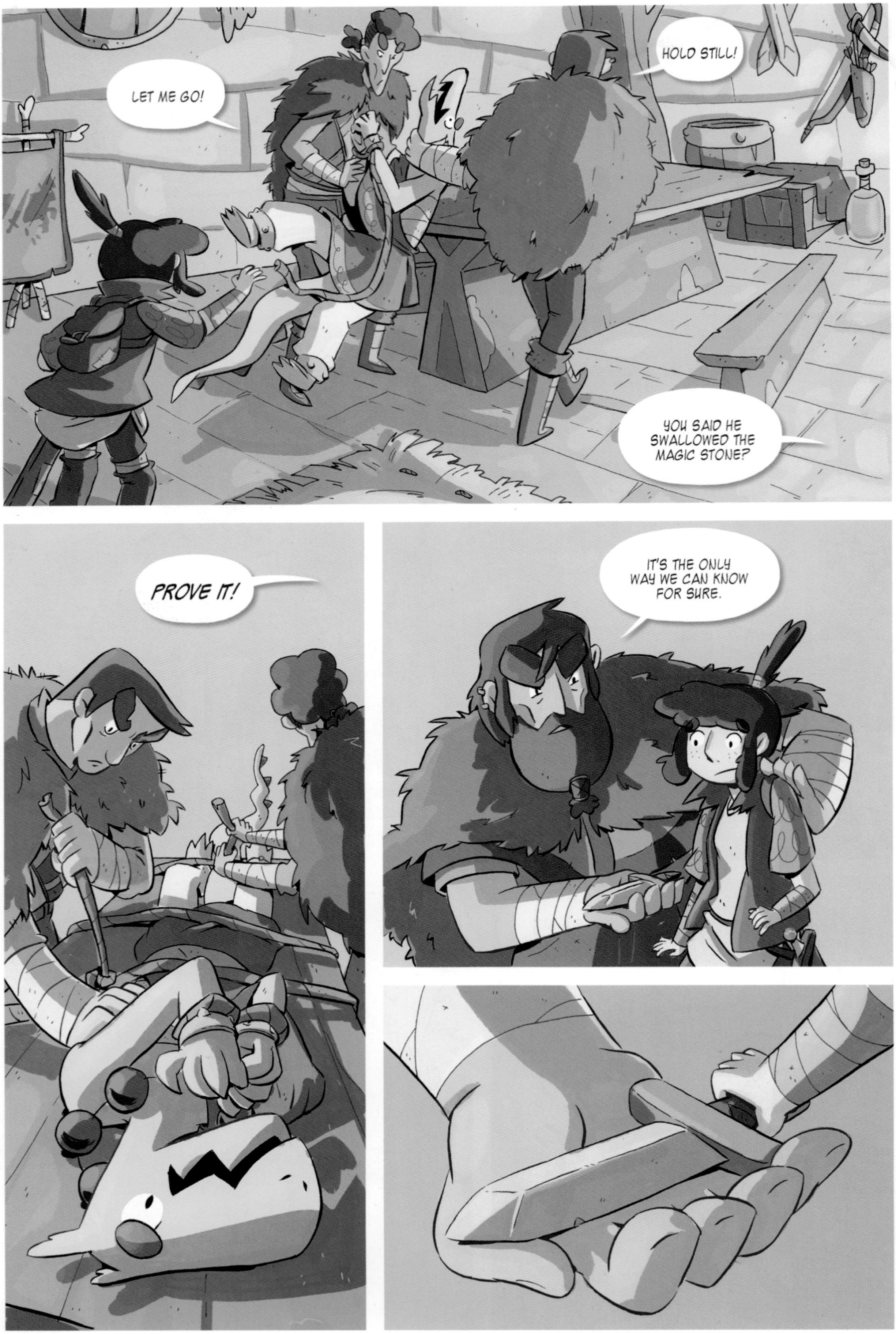
LET ME GO!
HOLD STILL!
YOU SAID HE SWALLOWED THE MAGIC STONE?
PROVE IT!
IT'S THE ONLY WAY WE CAN KNOW FOR SURE.

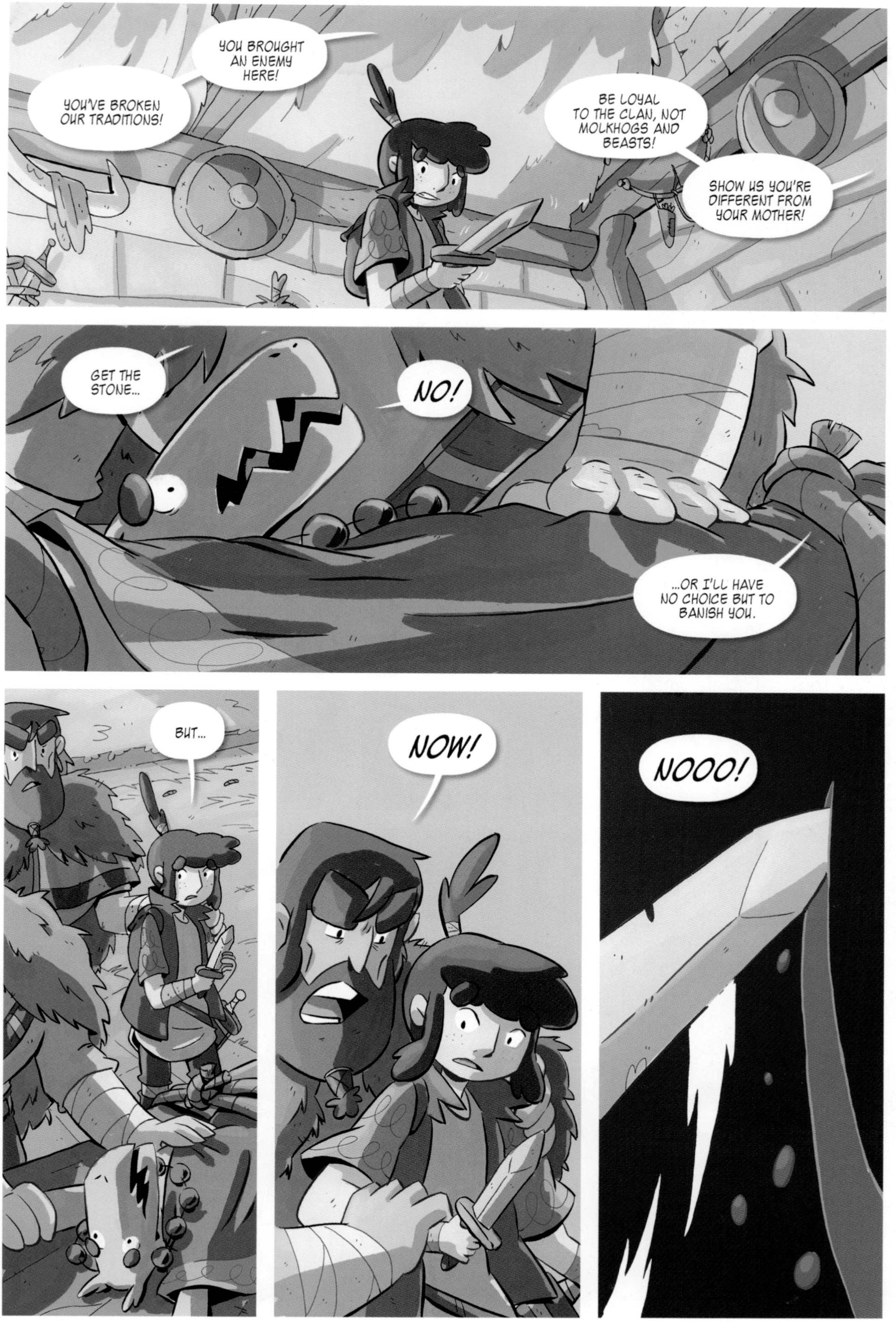
YOU'VE BROKEN OUR TRADITIONS!
YOU BROUGHT AN ENEMY HERE!
BE LOYAL TO THE CLAN, NOT MOLKHOGS AND BEASTS!
SHOW US YOU'RE DIFFERENT FROM YOUR MOTHER!
GET THE STONE...
NO!
...OR I'LL HAVE NO CHOICE BUT TO BANISH YOU.
BUT...
NOW!
NOOO!

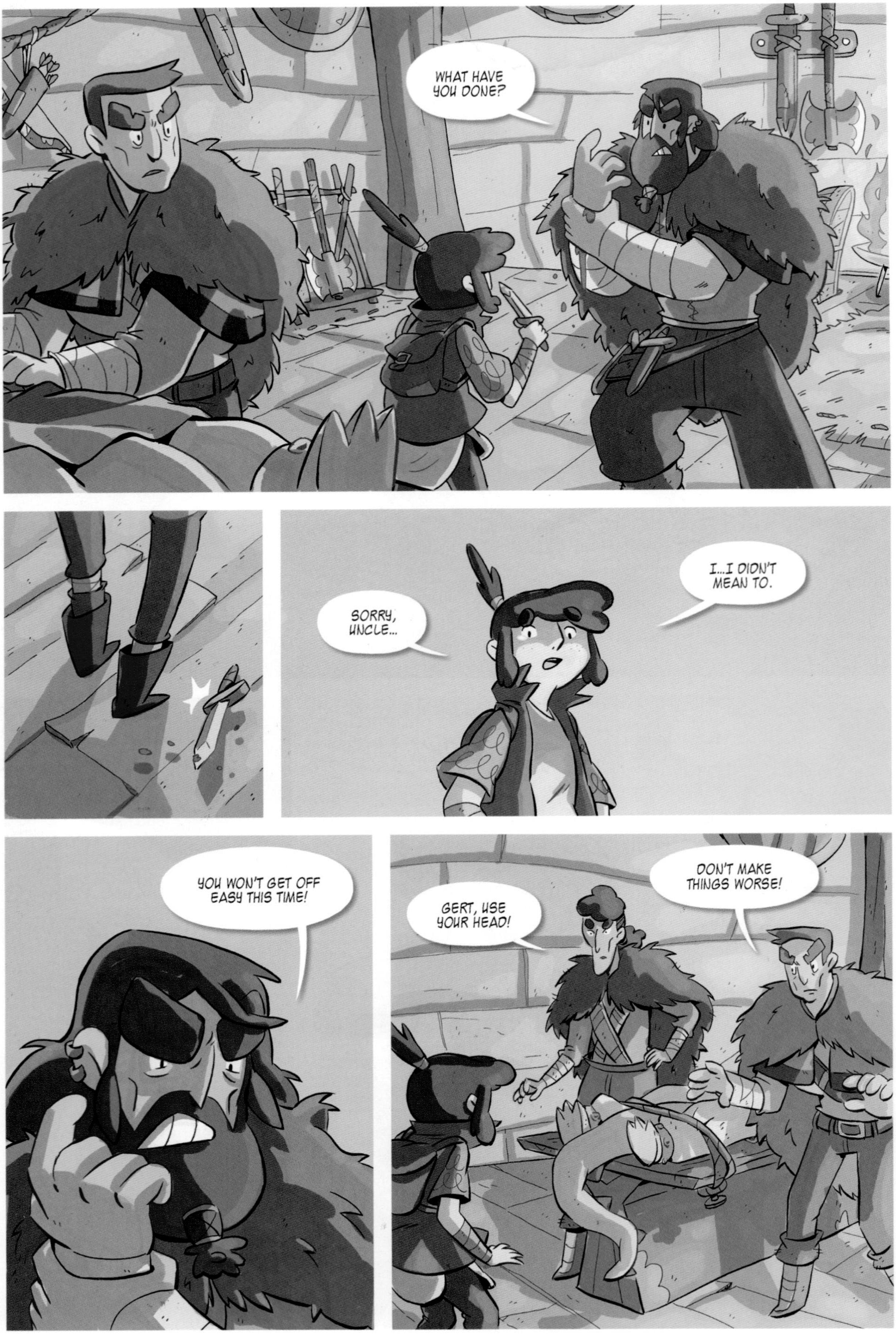
WHAT HAVE YOU DONE?
SORRY, UNCLE...
I...I DIDN'T MEAN TO.
YOU WON'T GET OFF EASY THIS TIME!
GERT, USE YOUR HEAD!
DON'T MAKE THINGS WORSE!

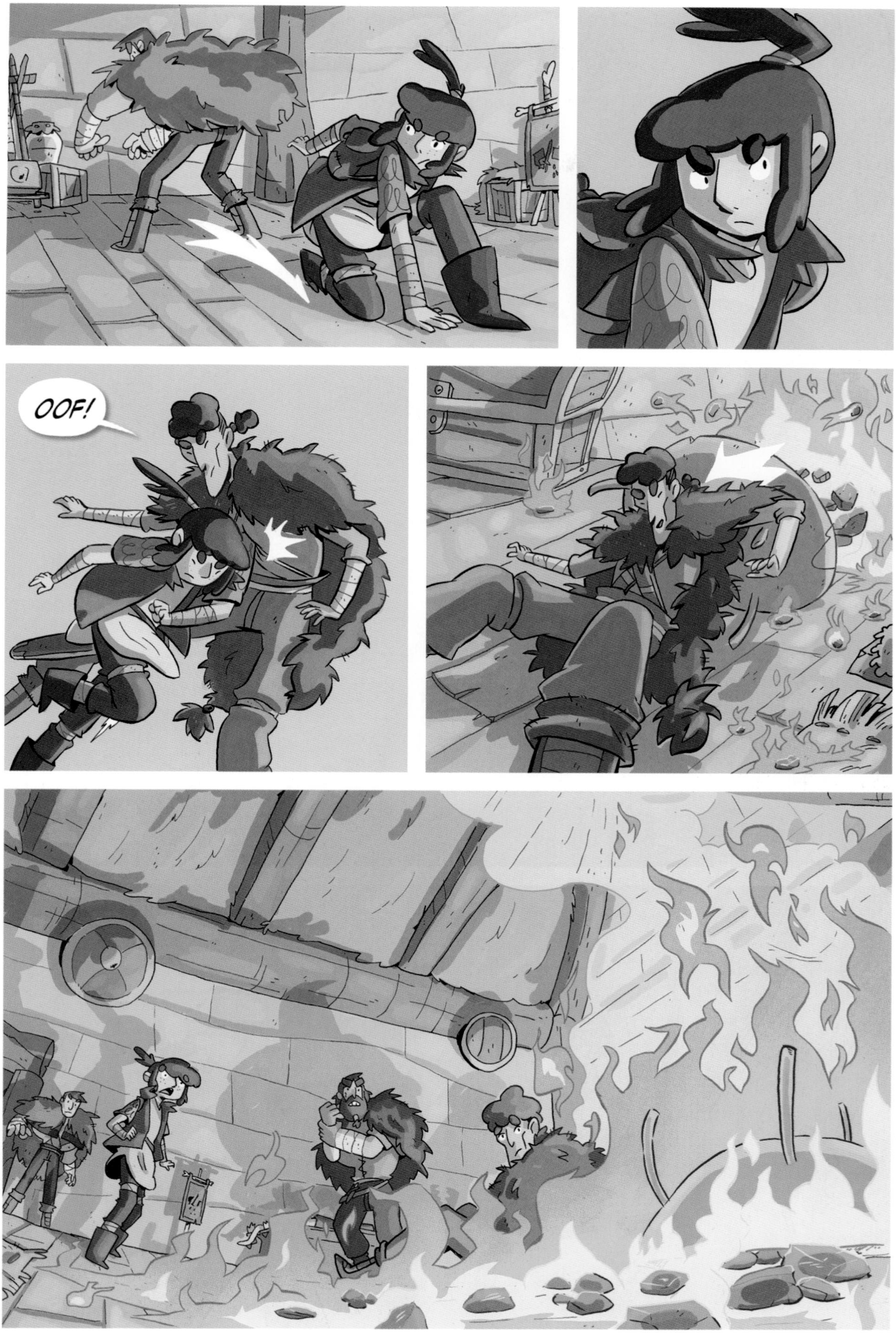
OOF!

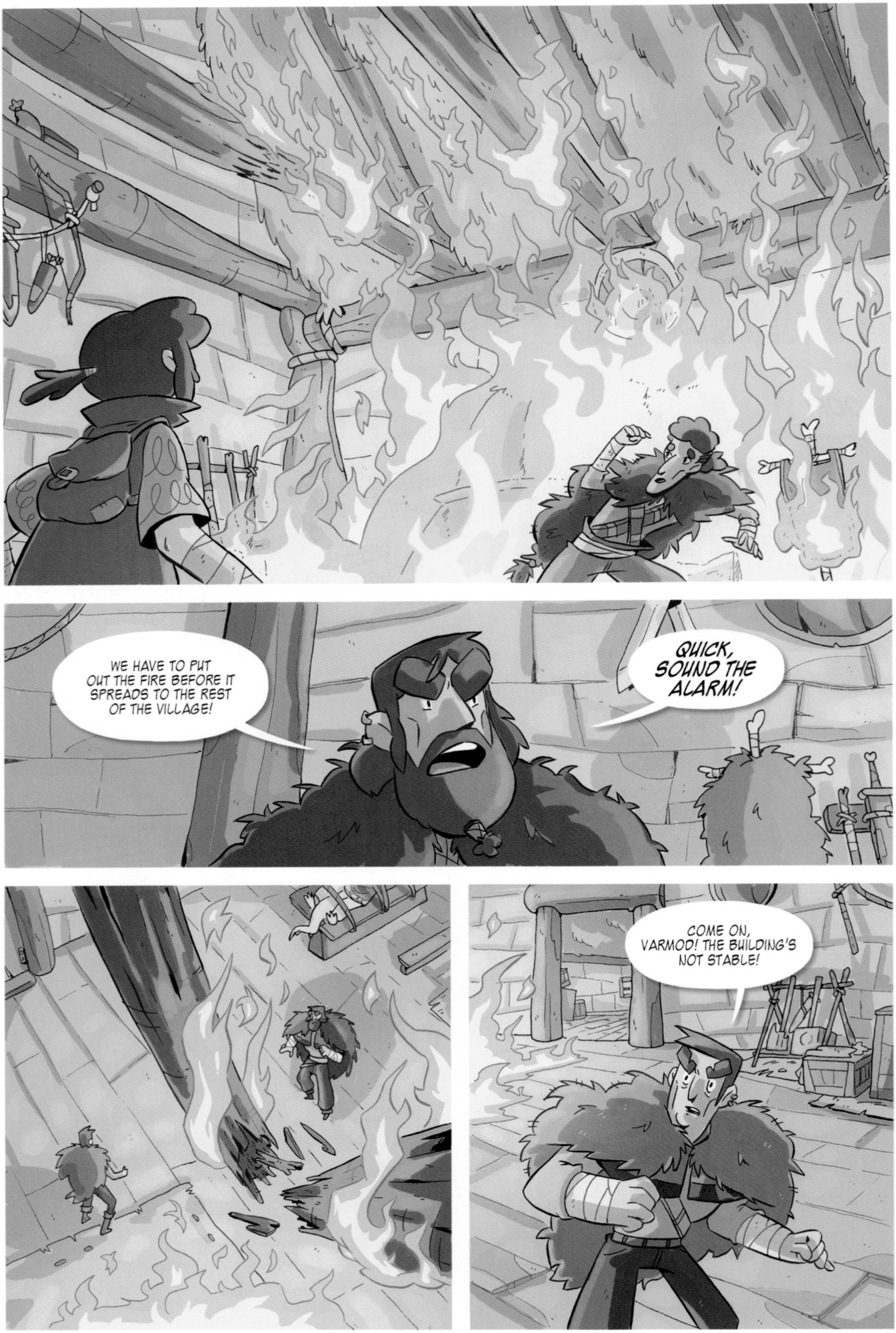
WE HAVE TO PUT OUT THE FIRE BEFORE IT SPREADS TO THE REST OF THE VILLAGE!
QUICK, SOUND THE ALARM!
COME ON, VARMOD! THE BUILDING'S NOT STABLE!

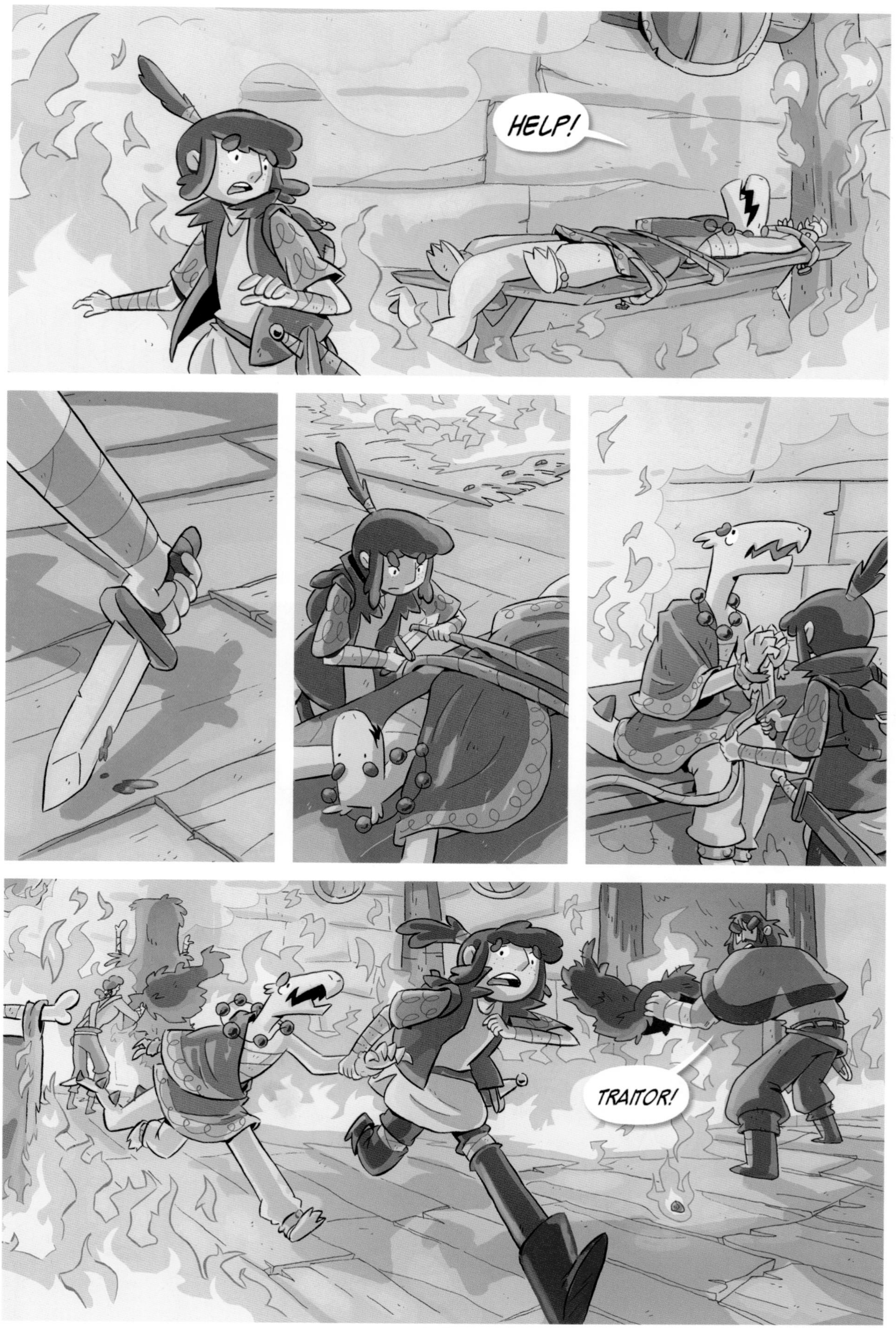
HELP!
TRAITOR!

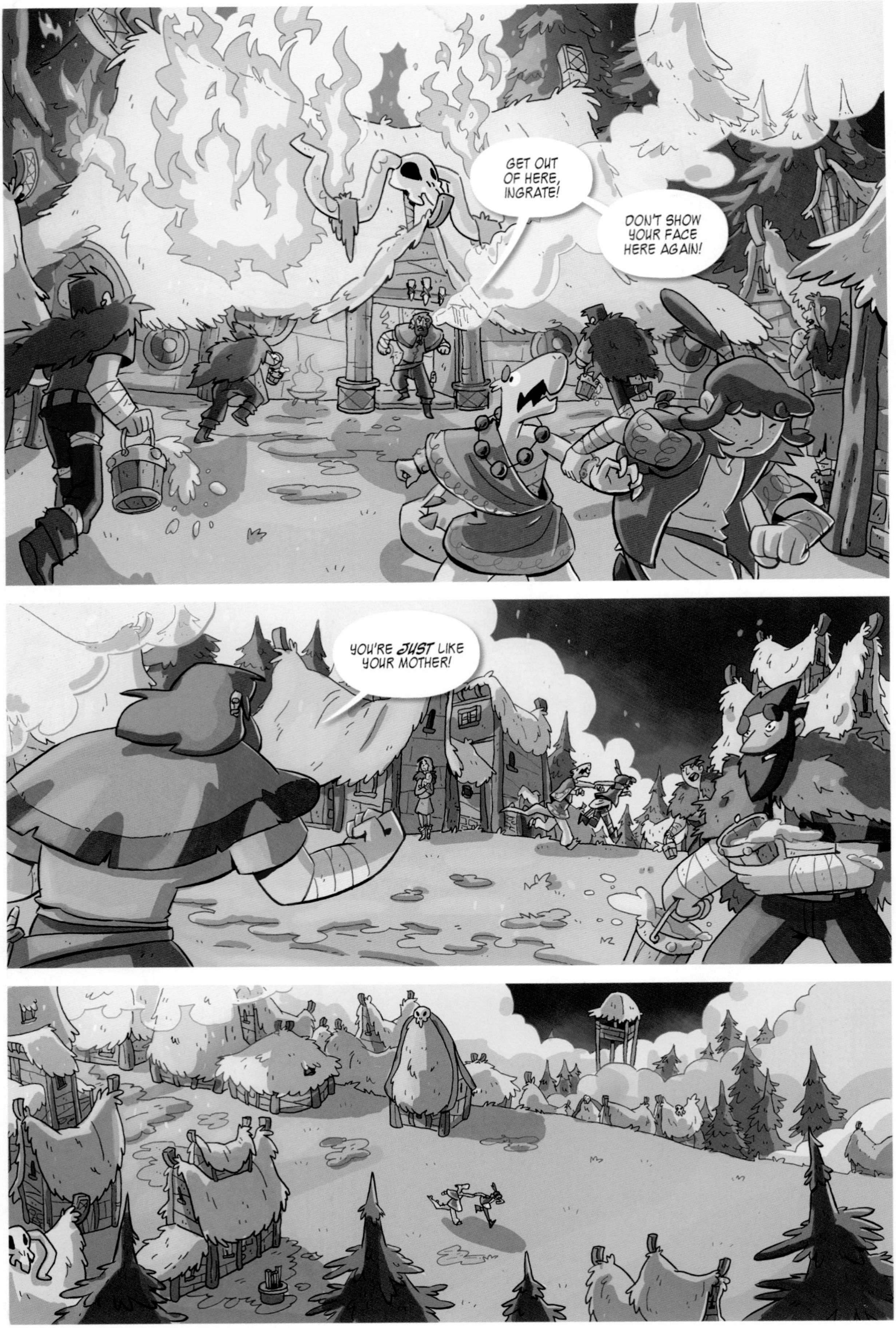
GET OUT OF HERE, INGRATE!
DON'T SHOW YOUR FACE HERE AGAIN!
YOU'RE *JUST* LIKE YOUR MOTHER!

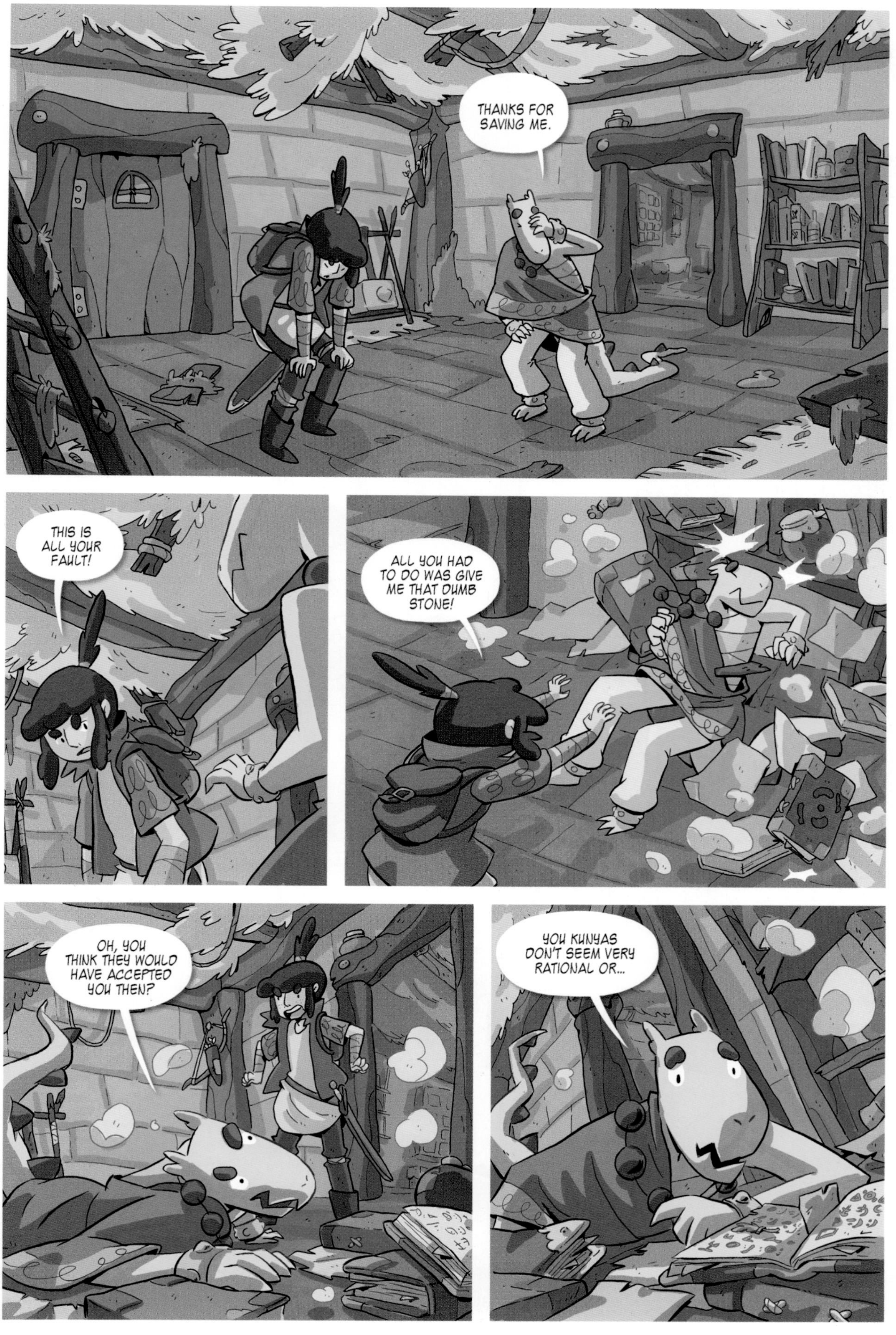
THANKS FOR SAVING ME.
THIS IS ALL YOUR FAULT!
ALL YOU HAD TO DO WAS GIVE ME THAT DUMB STONE!
OH, YOU THINK THEY WOULD HAVE ACCEPTED YOU THEN?
YOU KUNYAS DON'T SEEM VERY RATIONAL OR...

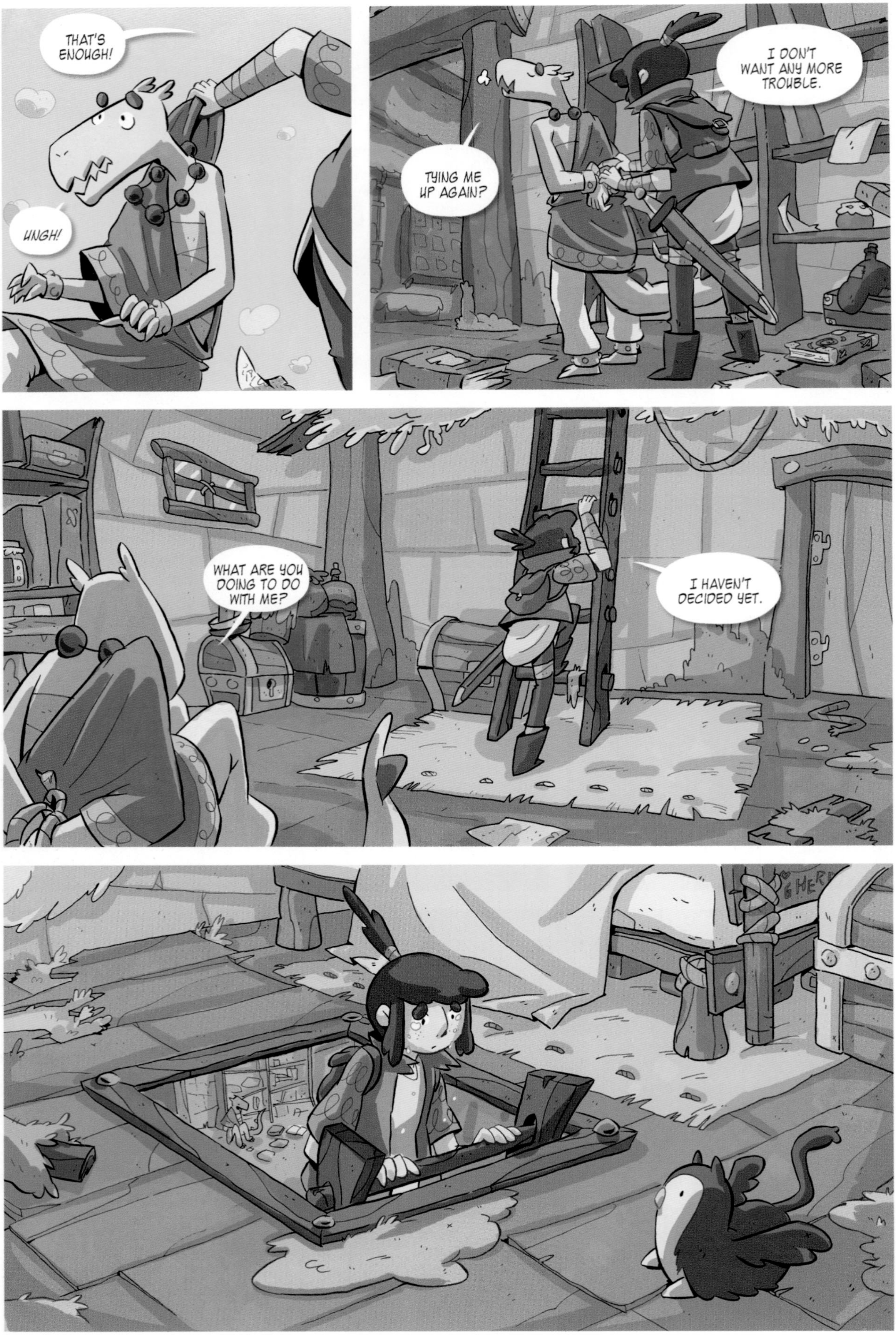
THAT'S ENOUGH!
UNGH!
TYING ME UP AGAIN?
I DON'T WANT ANY MORE TROUBLE.
WHAT ARE YOU DOING TO DO WITH ME?
I HAVEN'T DECIDED YET.

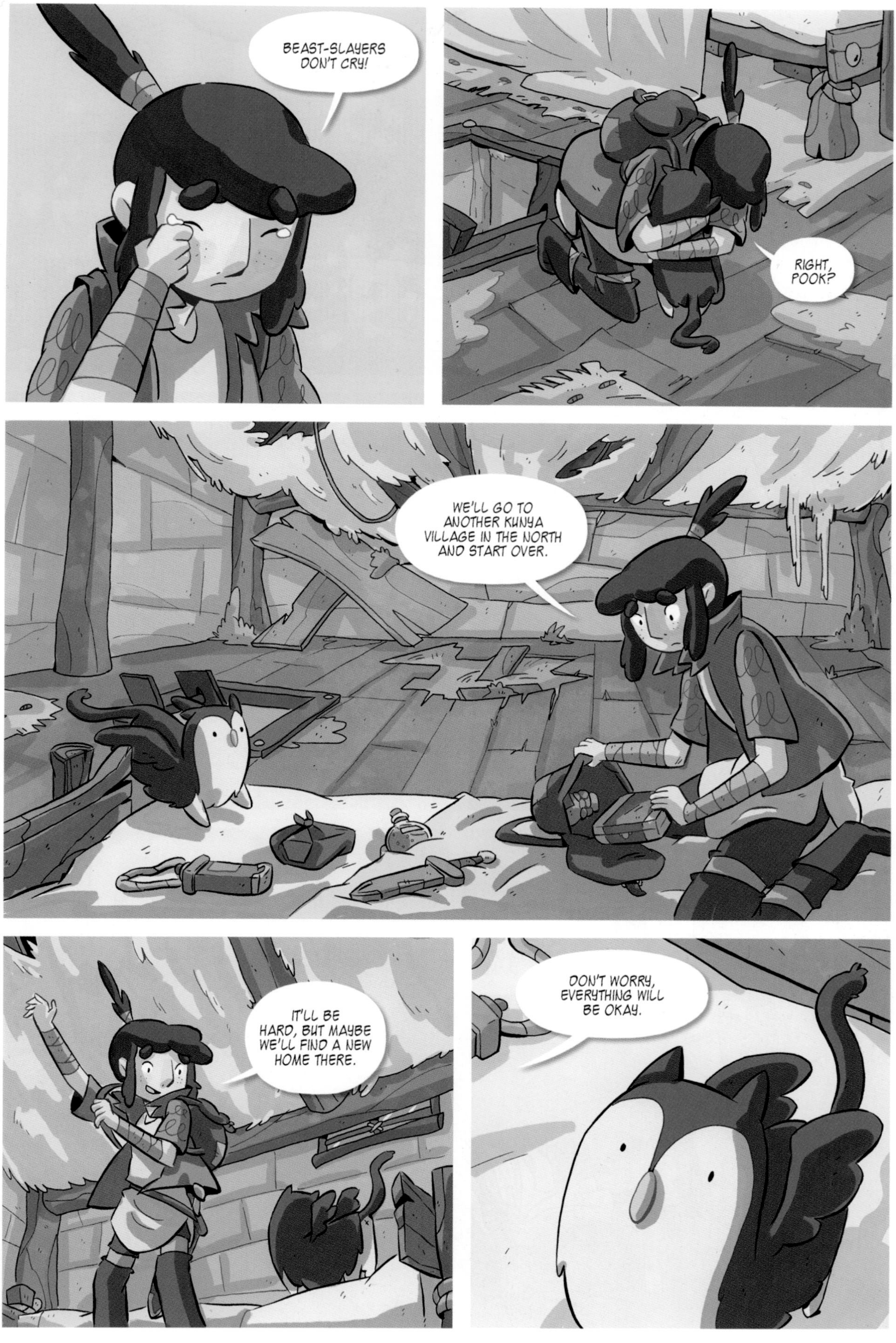
BEAST-SLAYERS DON'T CRY!
RIGHT, POOK?
WE'LL GO TO ANOTHER KUNYA VILLAGE IN THE NORTH AND START OVER.
IT'LL BE HARD, BUT MAYBE WE'LL FIND A NEW HOME THERE.
DON'T WORRY, EVERYTHING WILL BE OKAY.

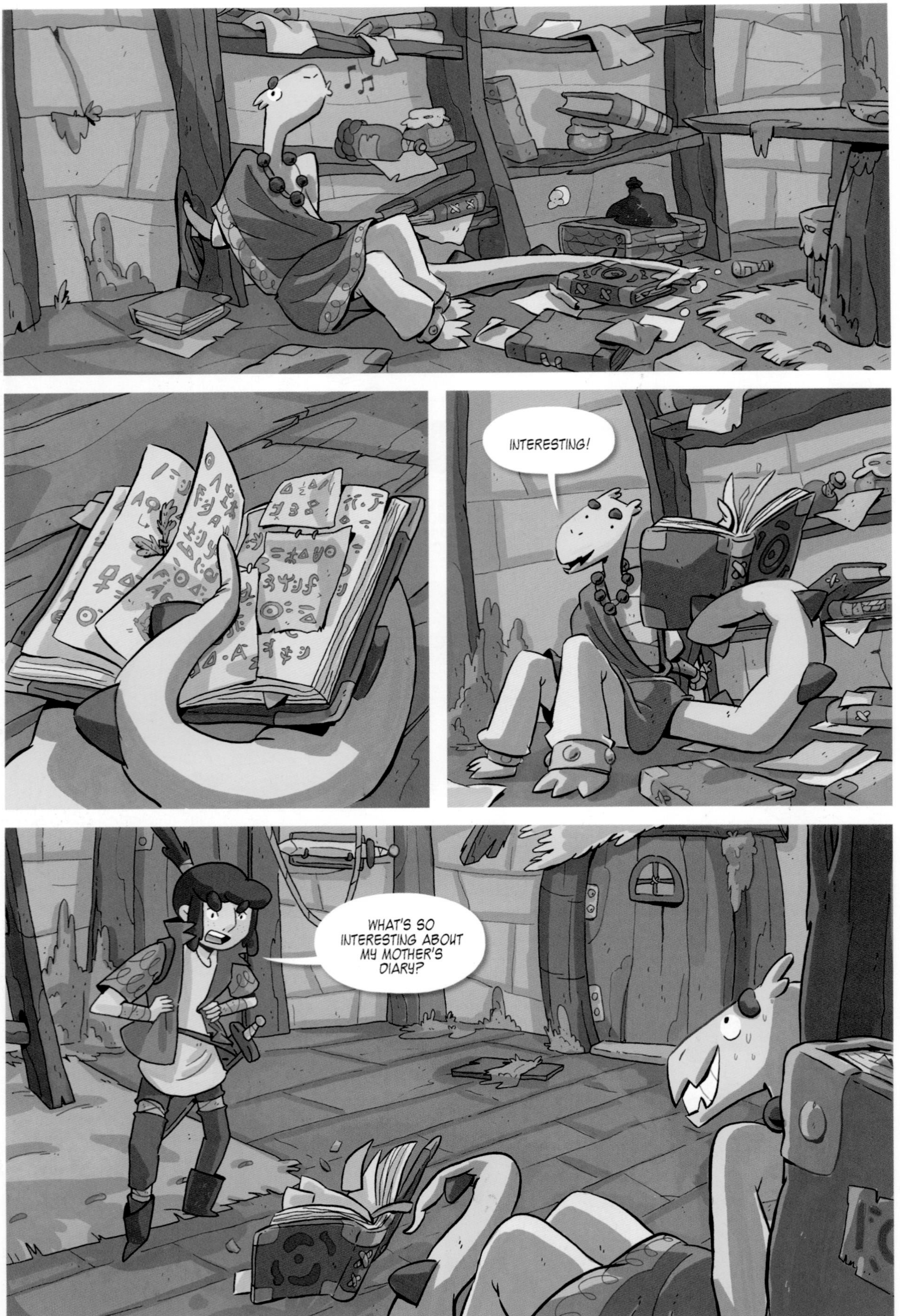
INTERESTING!
WHAT'S SO INTERESTING ABOUT MY MOTHER'S DIARY?

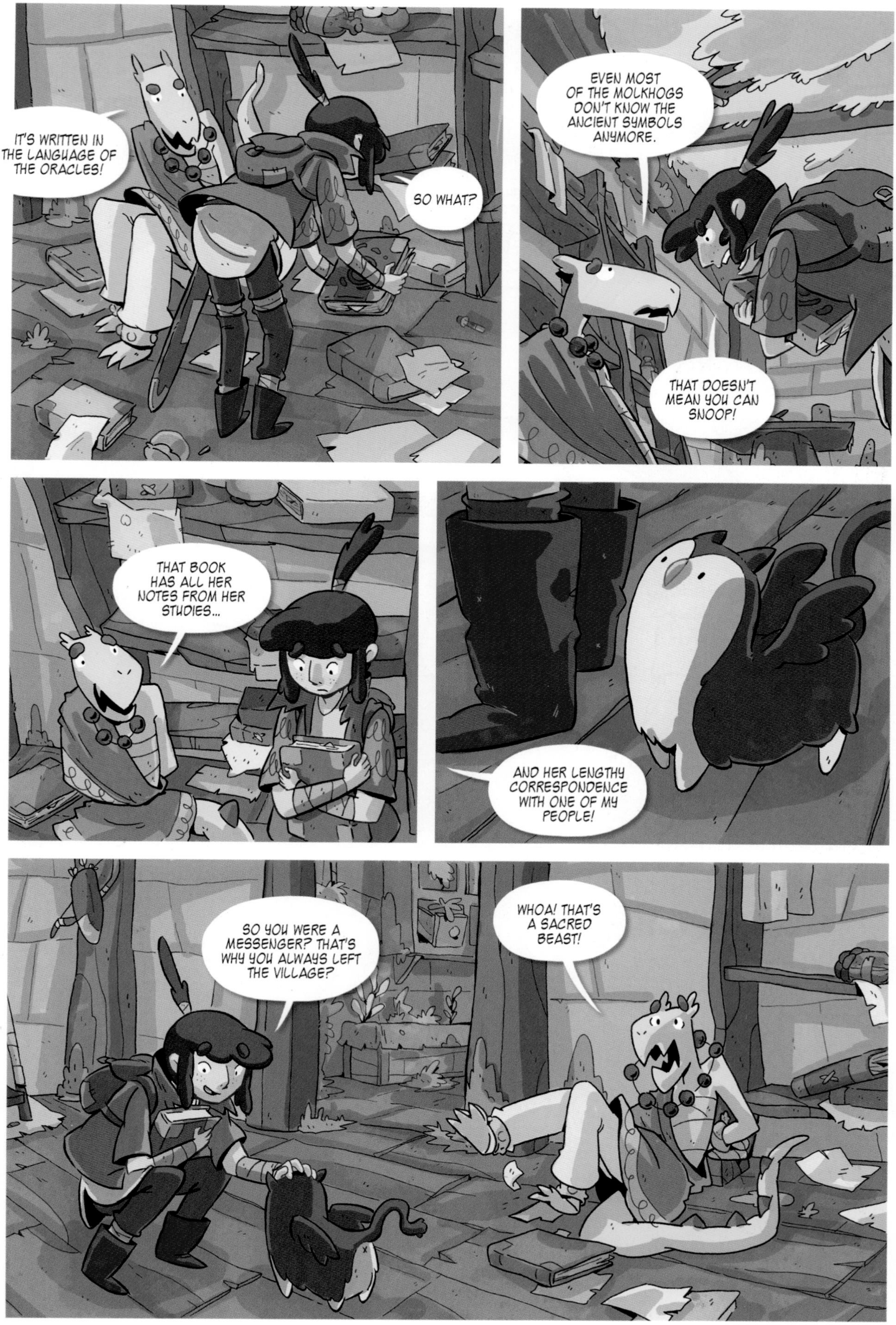
IT'S WRITTEN IN THE LANGUAGE OF THE ORACLES!
SO WHAT?
EVEN MOST OF THE MOLKHOGS DON'T KNOW THE ANCIENT SYMBOLS ANYMORE.
THAT DOESN'T MEAN YOU CAN SNOOP!
THAT BOOK HAS ALL HER NOTES FROM HER STUDIES...
AND HER LENGTHY CORRESPONDENCE WITH ONE OF MY PEOPLE!
SO YOU WERE A MESSENGER? THAT'S WHY YOU ALWAYS LEFT THE VILLAGE?
WHOA! THAT'S A SACRED BEAST!

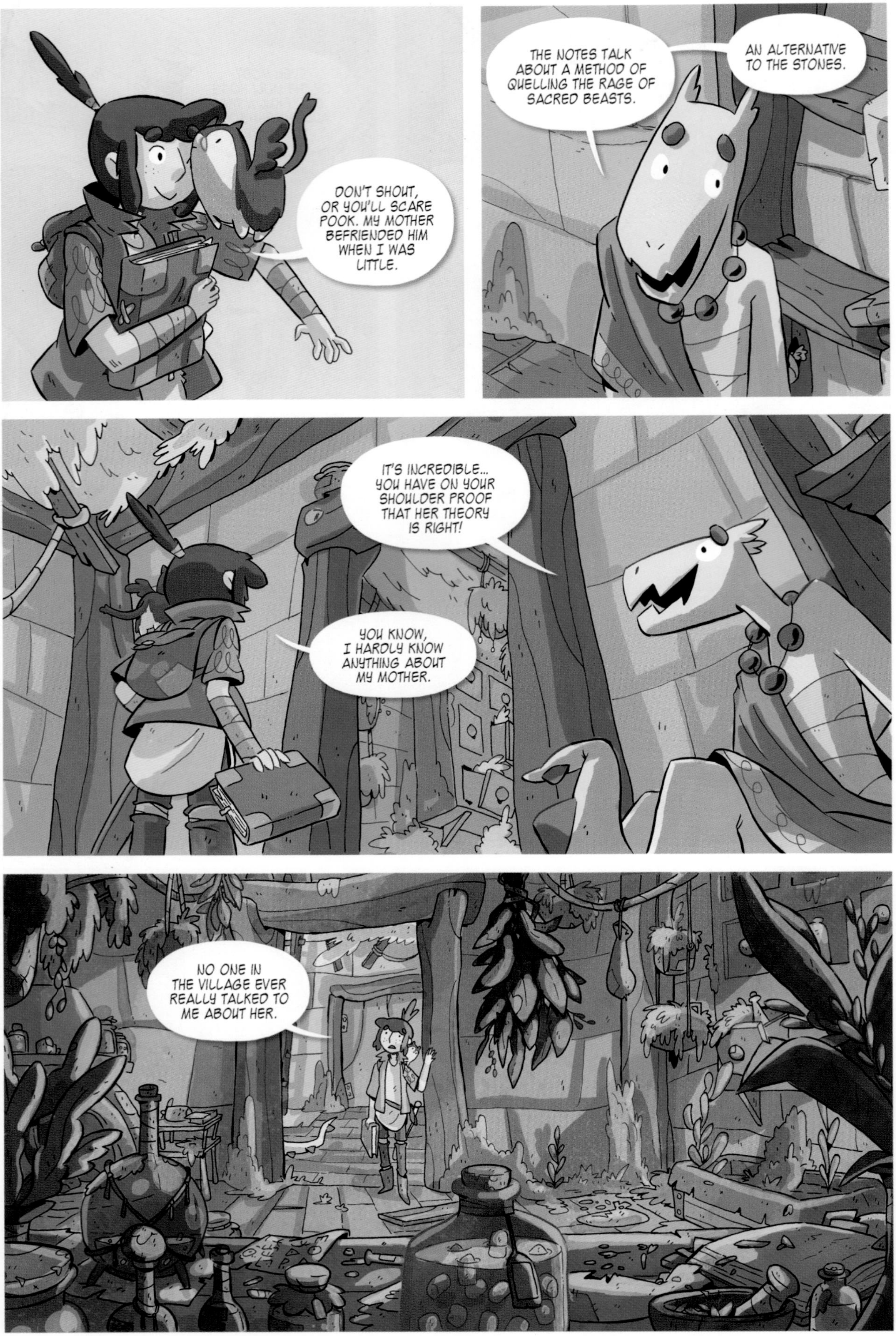
DON'T SHOUT, OR YOU'LL SCARE POOK. MY MOTHER BEFRIENDED HIM WHEN I WAS LITTLE.
THE NOTES TALK ABOUT A METHOD OF QUELLING THE RAGE OF SACRED BEASTS.
AN ALTERNATIVE TO THE STONES.
IT'S INCREDIBLE... YOU HAVE ON YOUR SHOULDER PROOF THAT HER THEORY IS RIGHT!
YOU KNOW, I HARDLY KNOW ANYTHING ABOUT MY MOTHER.
NO ONE IN THE VILLAGE EVER REALLY TALKED TO ME ABOUT HER.

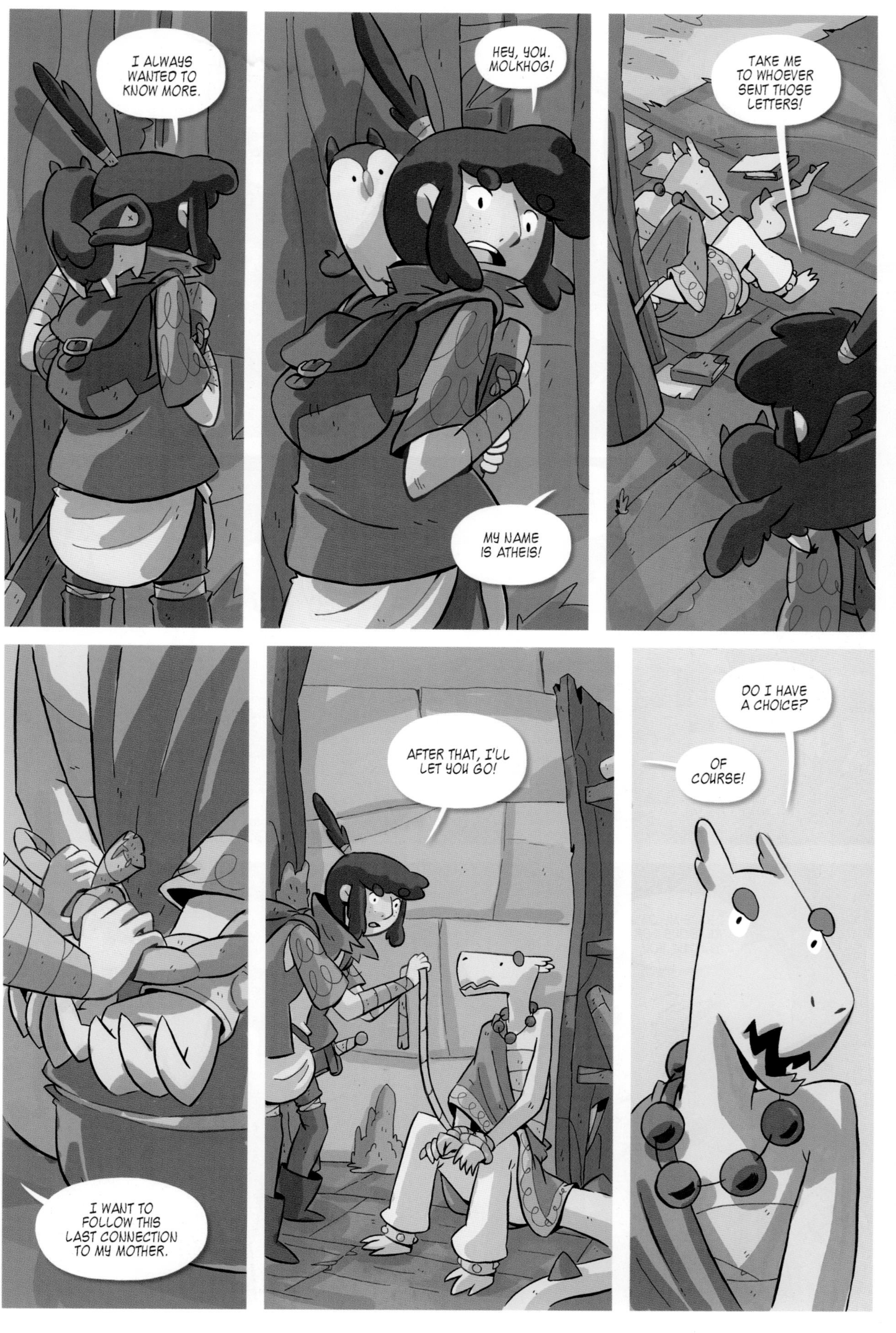
I ALWAYS WANTED TO KNOW MORE.
HEY, YOU. MOLKHOG!
MY NAME IS ATHEIS!
TAKE ME TO WHOEVER SENT THOSE LETTERS!
I WANT TO FOLLOW THIS LAST CONNECTION TO MY MOTHER.
AFTER THAT, I'LL LET YOU GO!
DO I HAVE A CHOICE?
OF COURSE!

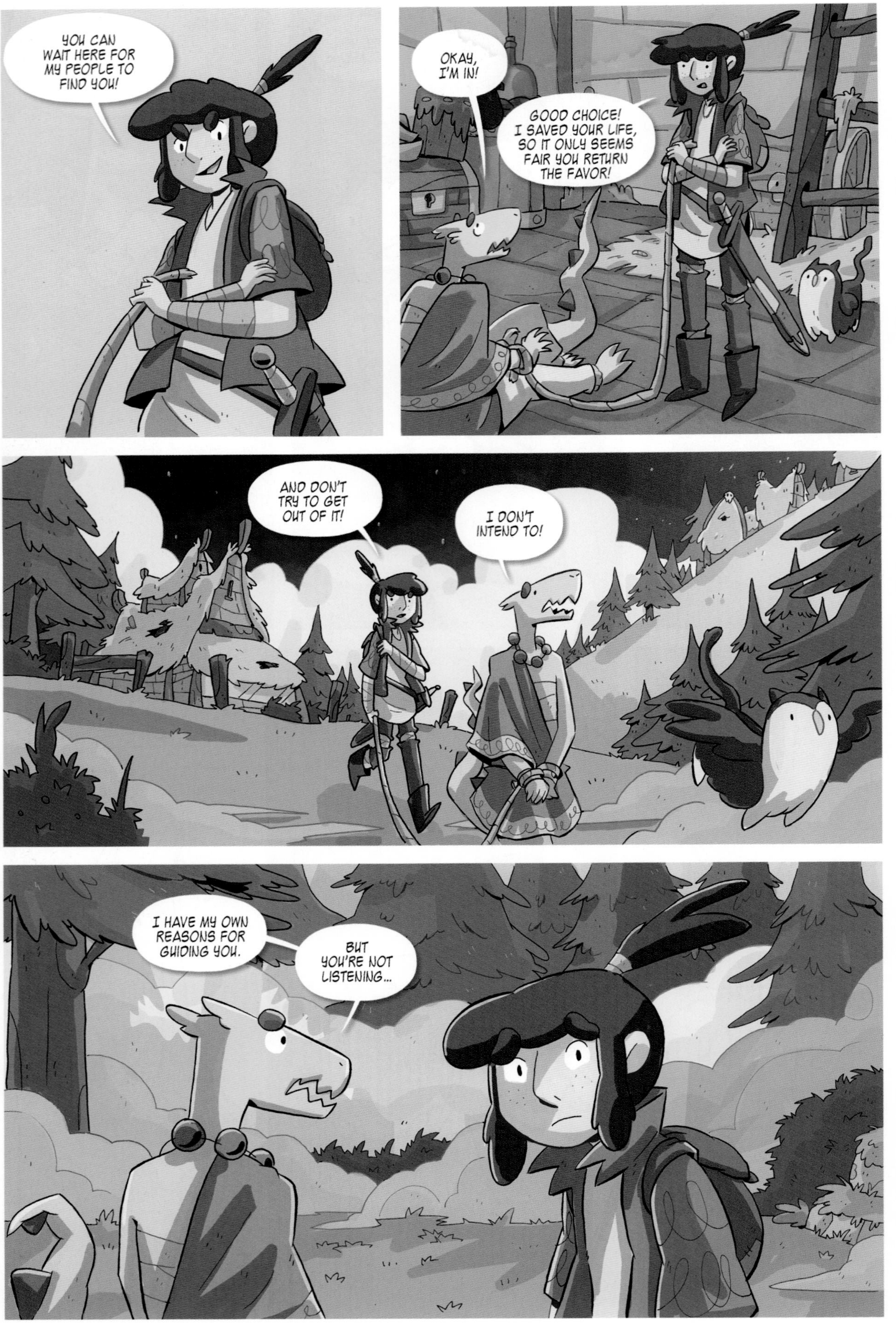

YOU CAN WAIT HERE FOR MY PEOPLE TO FIND YOU!
OKAY, I'M IN!
GOOD CHOICE! I SAVED YOUR LIFE, SO IT ONLY SEEMS FAIR YOU RETURN THE FAVOR!
AND DON'T TRY TO GET OUT OF IT!
I DON'T INTEND TO!
I HAVE MY OWN REASONS FOR GUIDING YOU.
BUT YOU'RE NOT LISTENING...

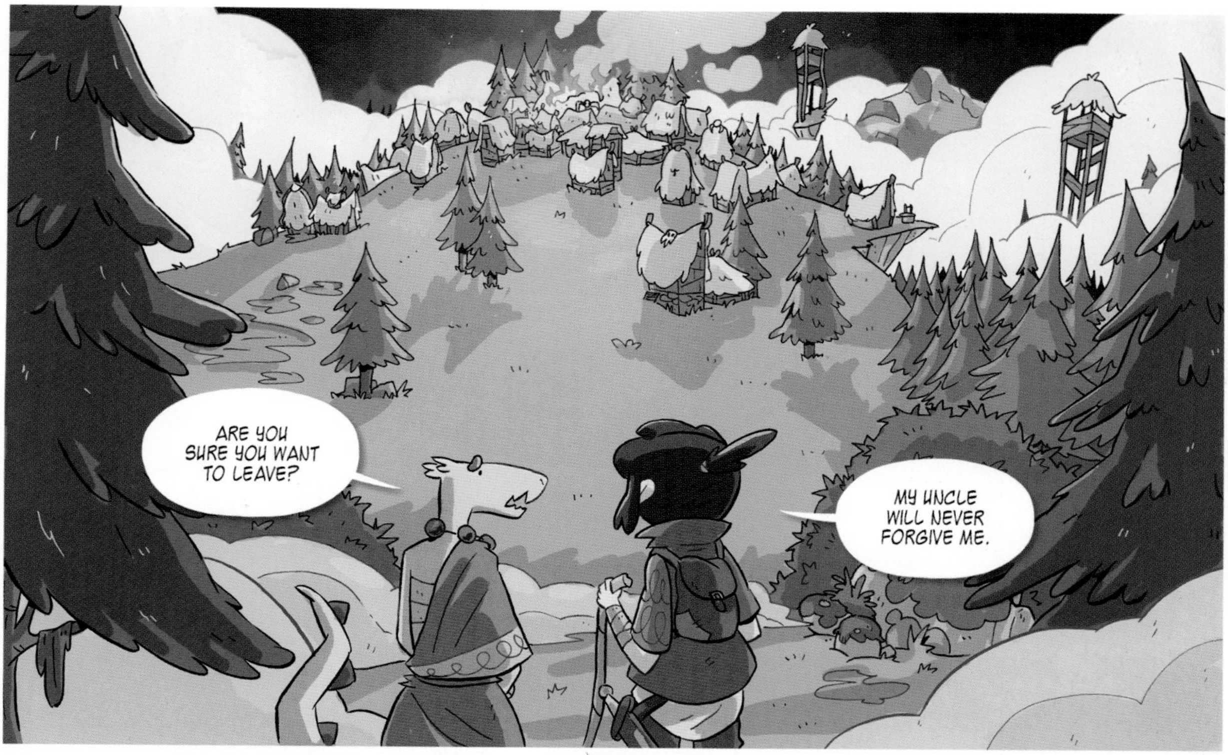
ARE YOU SURE YOU WANT TO LEAVE?
MY UNCLE WILL NEVER FORGIVE ME.

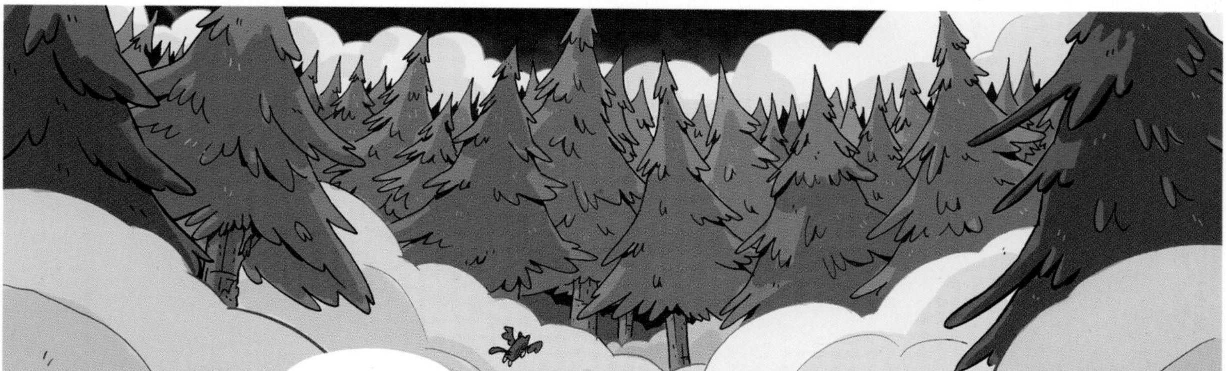
THERE'S NO PLACE FOR ME HERE NOW.

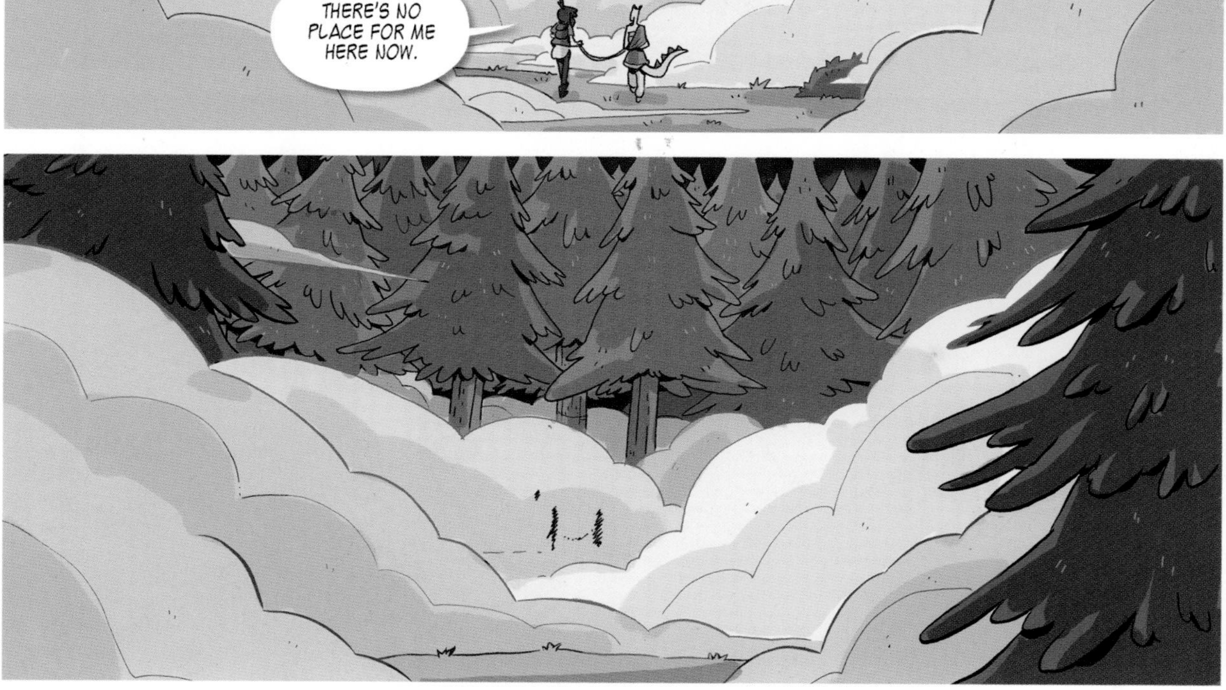

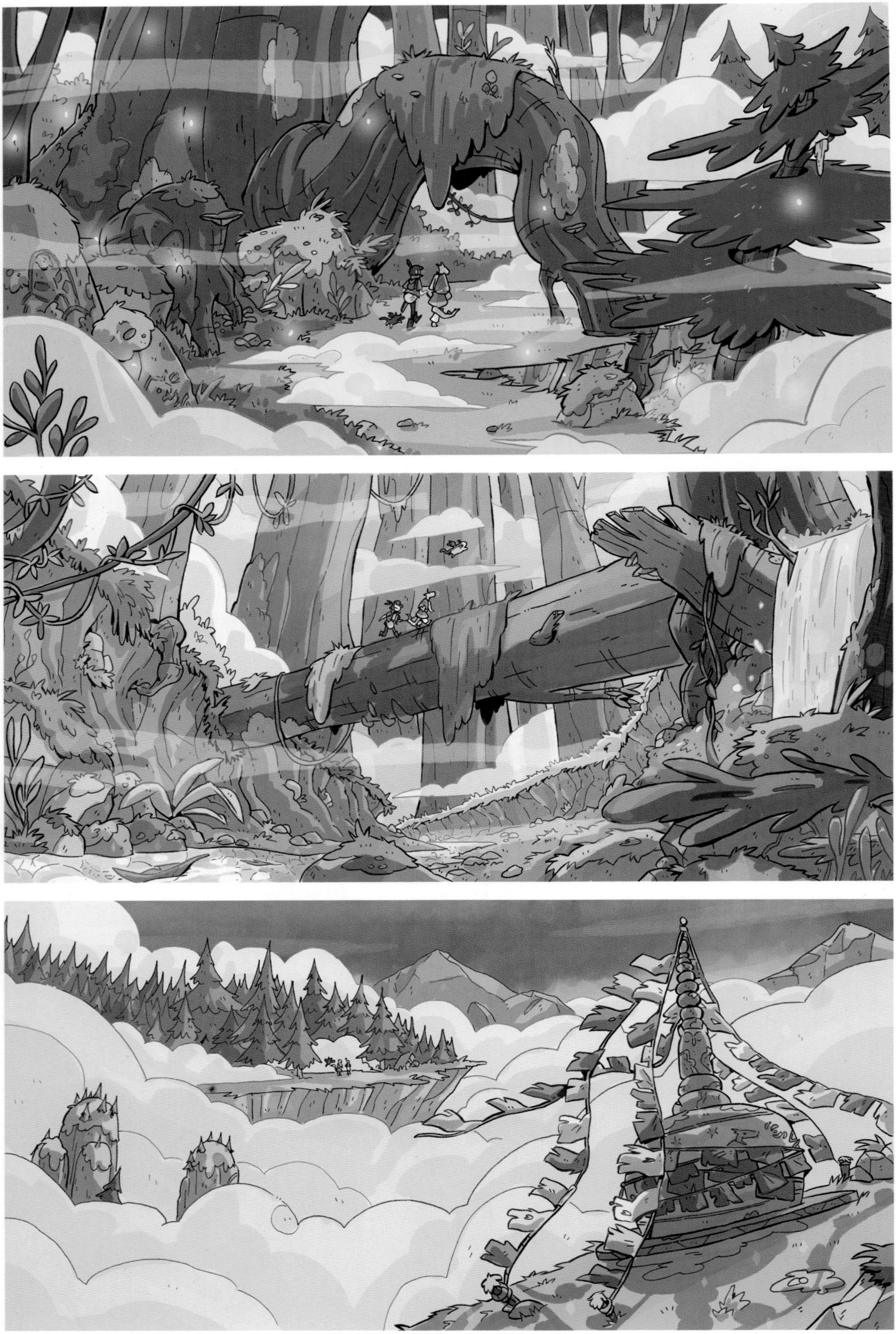

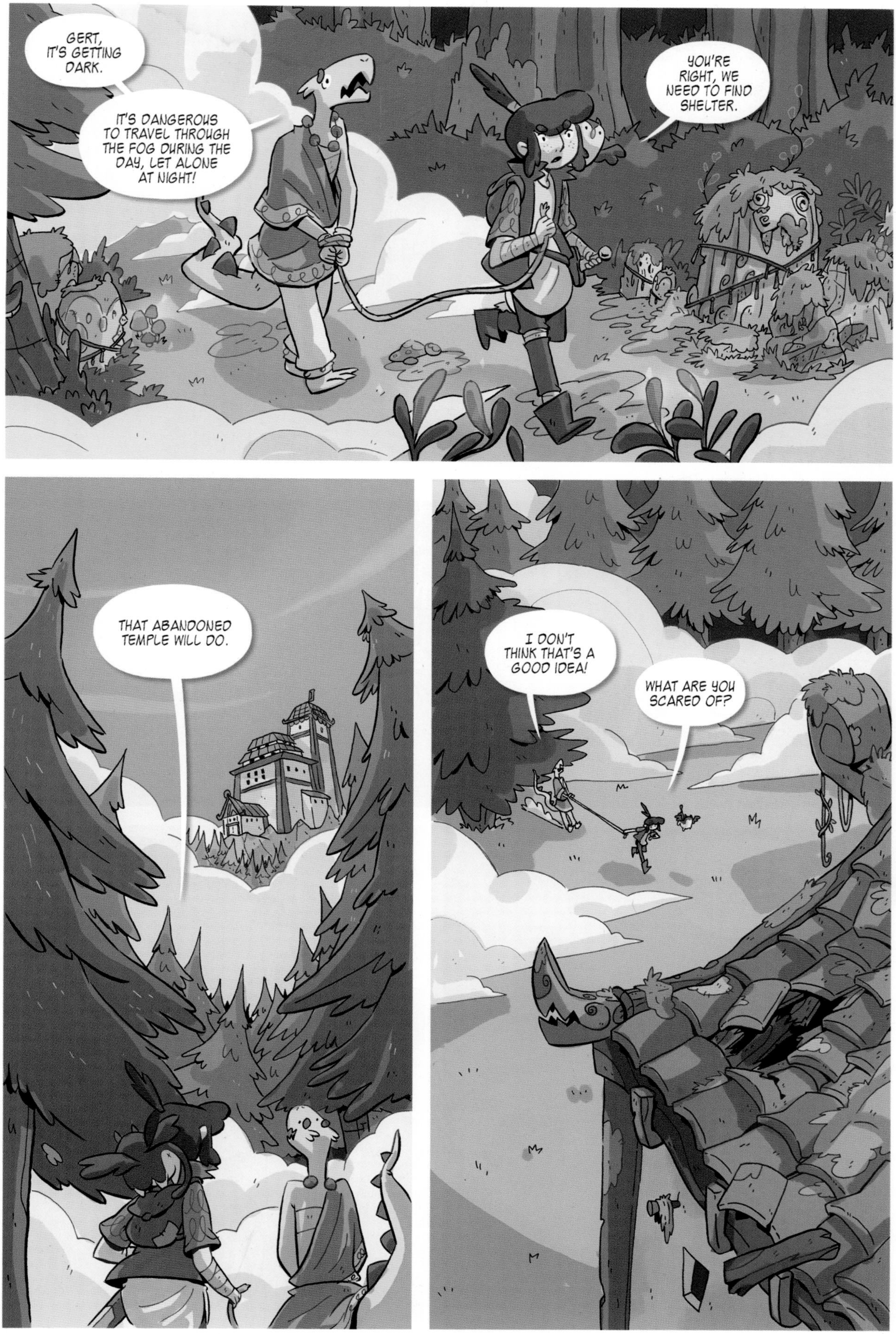

GERT, IT'S GETTING DARK.
IT'S DANGEROUS TO TRAVEL THROUGH THE FOG DURING THE DAY, LET ALONE AT NIGHT!
YOU'RE RIGHT, WE NEED TO FIND SHELTER.
THAT ABANDONED TEMPLE WILL DO.
I DON'T THINK THAT'S A GOOD IDEA!
WHAT ARE YOU SCARED OF?

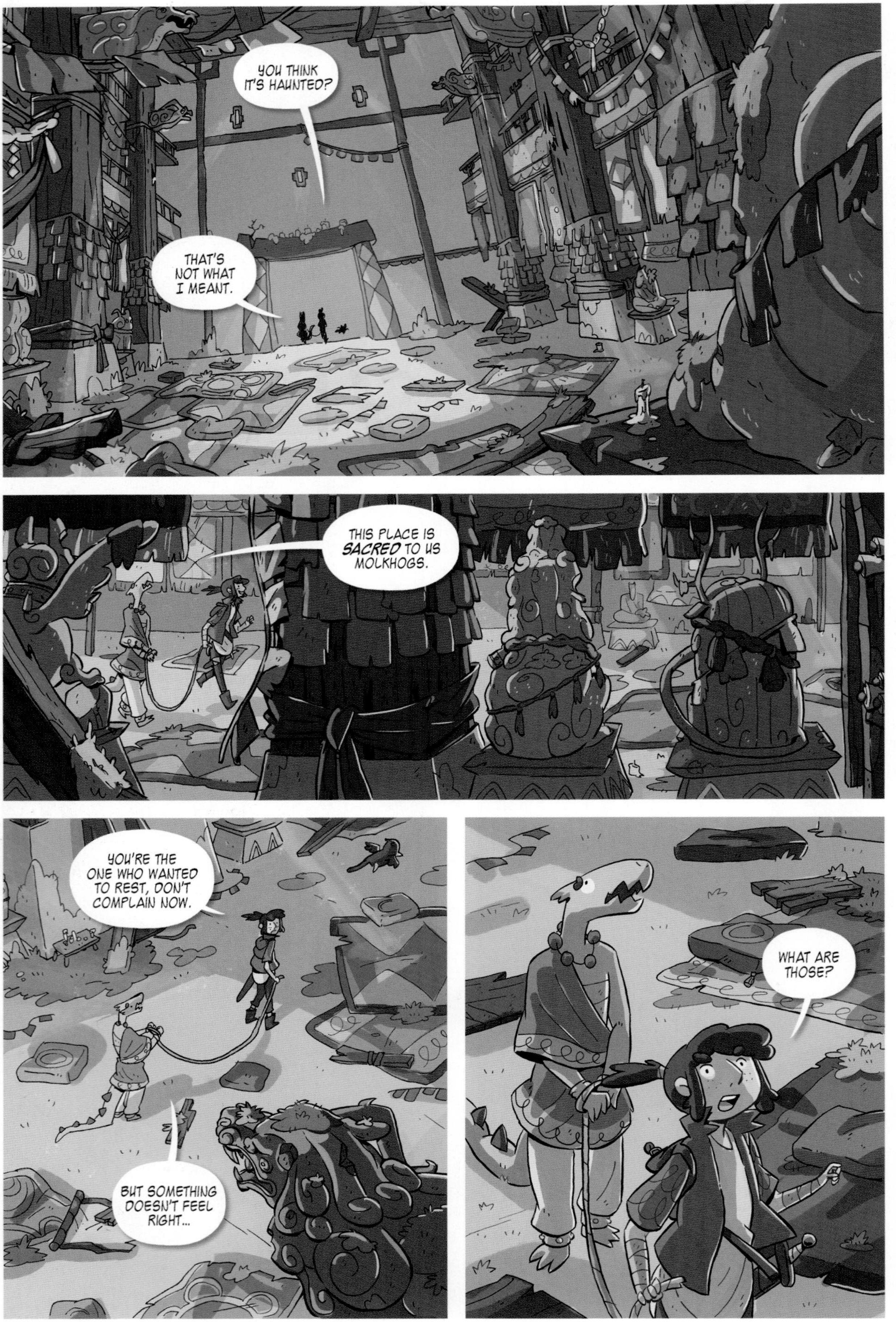
YOU THINK IT'S HAUNTED?
THAT'S NOT WHAT I MEANT.
THIS PLACE IS **SACRED** TO US MOLKHOGS.
YOU'RE THE ONE WHO WANTED TO REST, DON'T COMPLAIN NOW.
BUT SOMETHING DOESN'T FEEL RIGHT...
WHAT ARE THOSE?

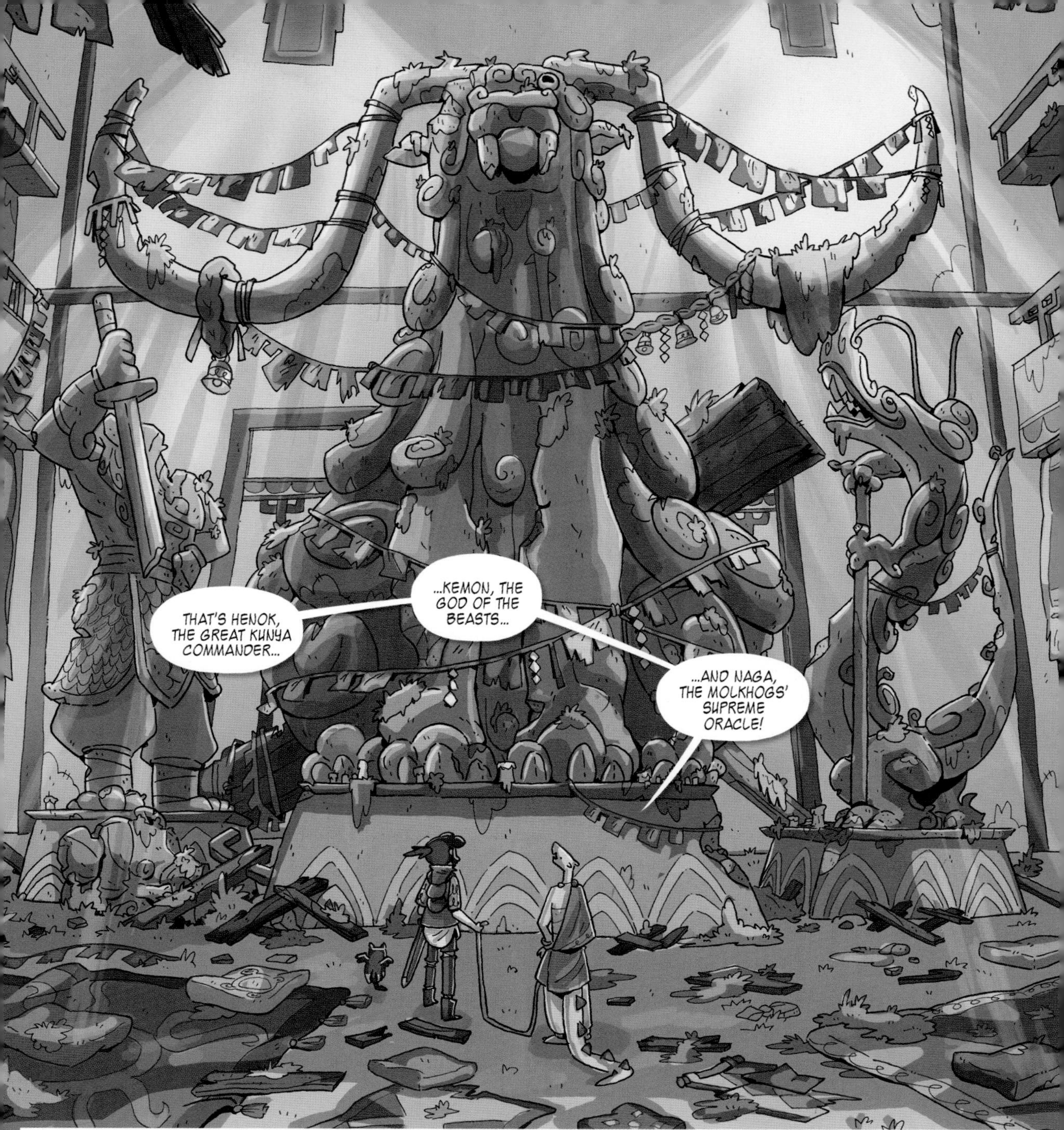
THAT'S HENOK, THE GREAT KUNYA COMMANDER...
...KEMON, THE GOD OF THE BEASTS...
...AND NAGA, THE MOLKHOGS' SUPREME ORACLE!

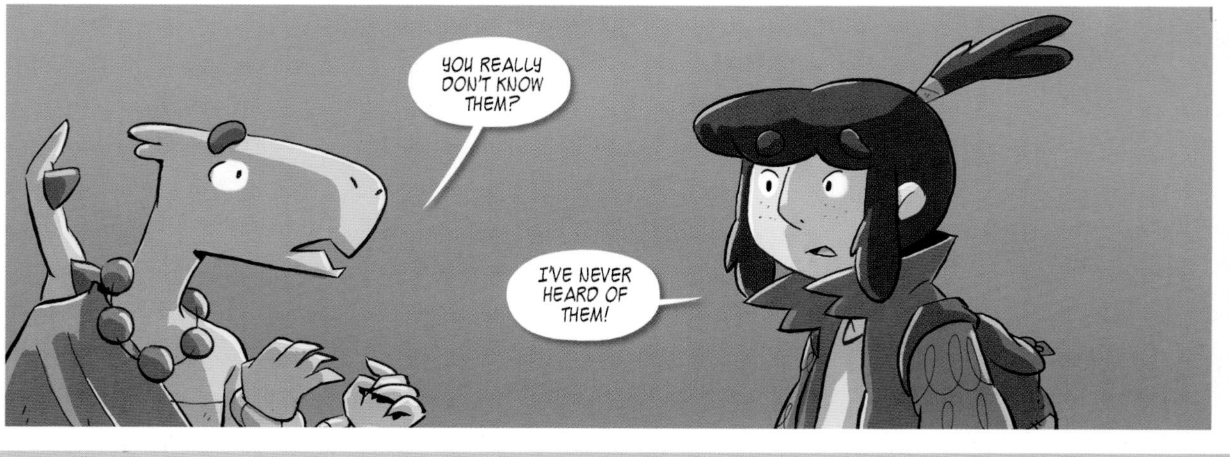
YOU REALLY DON'T KNOW THEM?
I'VE NEVER HEARD OF THEM!

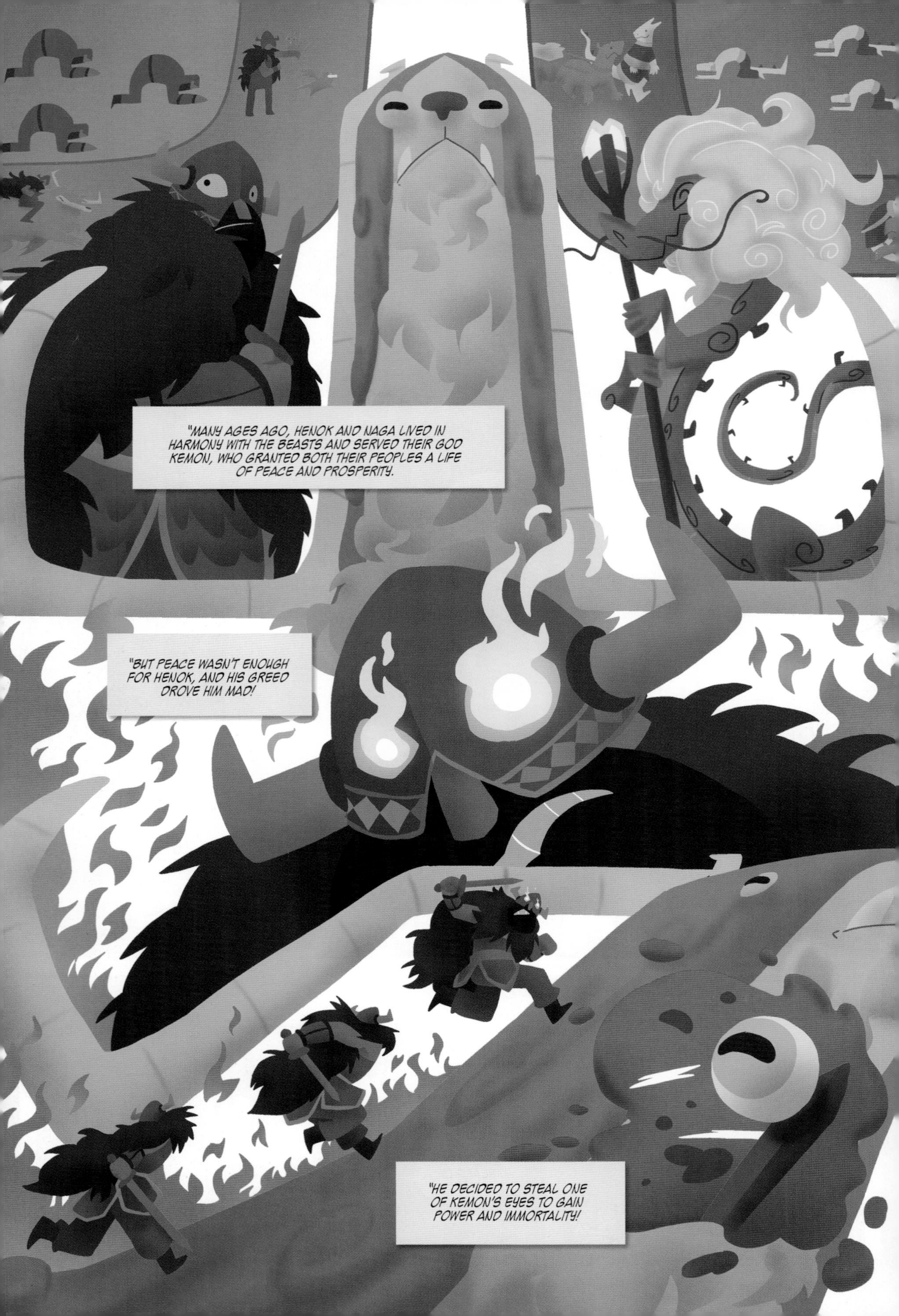
"MANY AGES AGO, HENOK AND NAGA LIVED IN HARMONY WITH THE BEASTS AND SERVED THEIR GOD KEMON, WHO GRANTED BOTH THEIR PEOPLES A LIFE OF PEACE AND PROSPERITY.
"BUT PEACE WASN'T ENOUGH FOR HENOK, AND HIS GREED DROVE HIM MAD!
"HE DECIDED TO STEAL ONE OF KEMON'S EYES TO GAIN POWER AND IMMORTALITY!

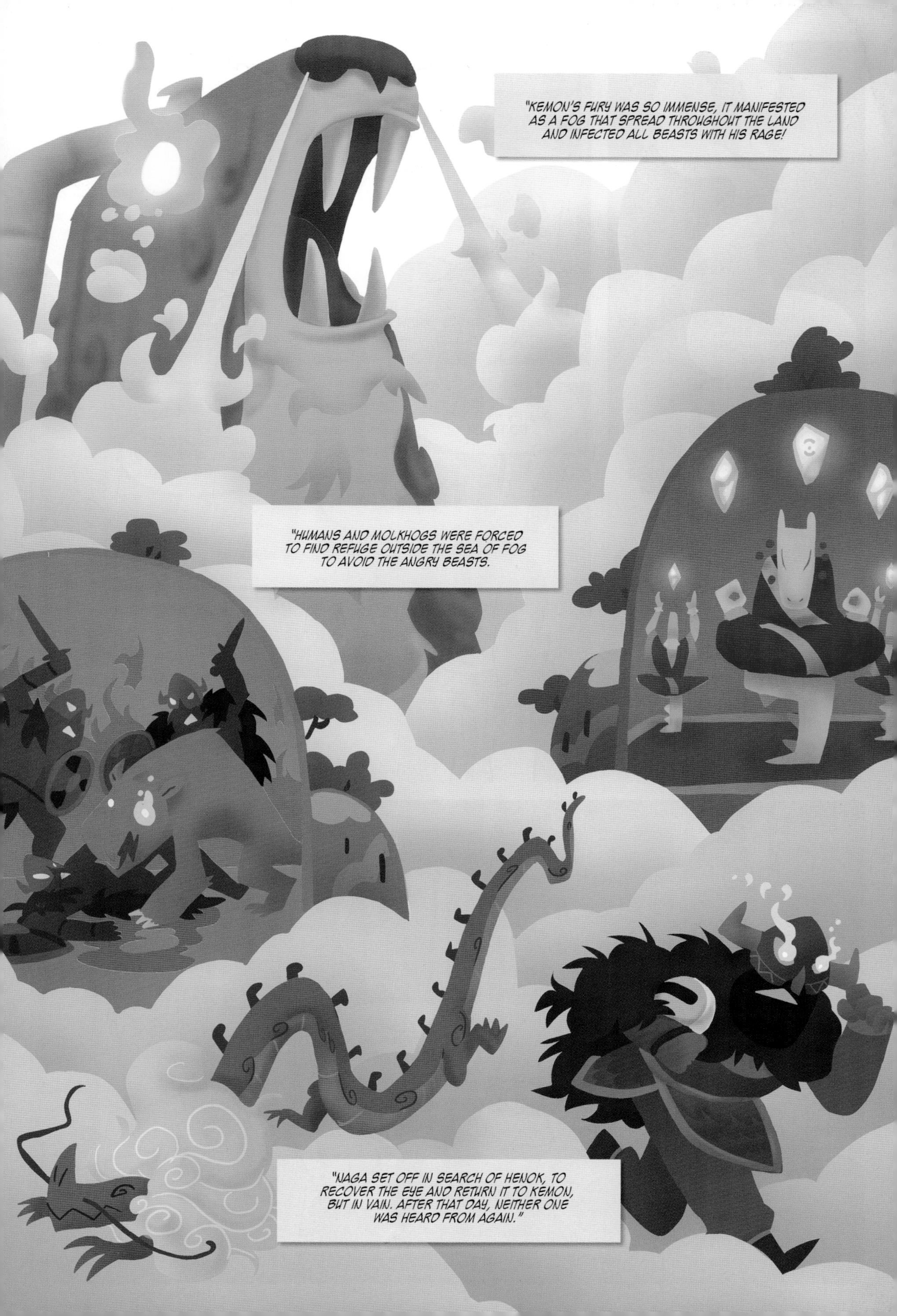
"KEMON'S FURY WAS SO IMMENSE, IT MANIFESTED AS A FOG THAT SPREAD THROUGHOUT THE LAND AND INFECTED ALL BEASTS WITH HIS RAGE!
"HUMANS AND MOLKHOGS WERE FORCED TO FIND REFUGE OUTSIDE THE SEA OF FOG TO AVOID THE ANGRY BEASTS.
"NAGA SET OFF IN SEARCH OF HENOK, TO RECOVER THE EYE AND RETURN IT TO KEMON, BUT IN VAIN. AFTER THAT DAY, NEITHER ONE WAS HEARD FROM AGAIN."

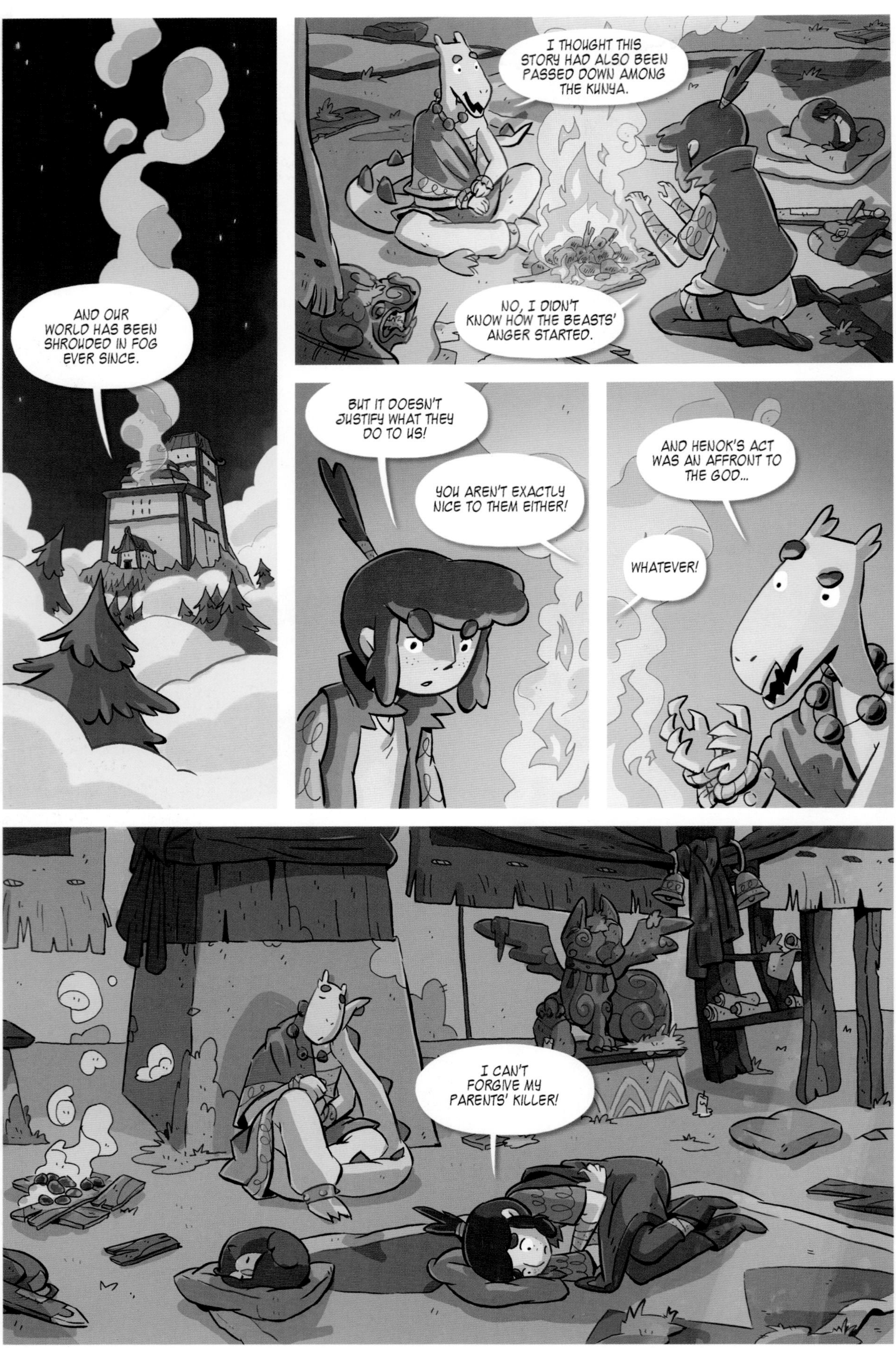
AND OUR WORLD HAS BEEN SHROUDED IN FOG EVER SINCE.
I THOUGHT THIS STORY HAD ALSO BEEN PASSED DOWN AMONG THE KUNYA.
NO, I DIDN'T KNOW HOW THE BEASTS' ANGER STARTED.
BUT IT DOESN'T JUSTIFY WHAT THEY DO TO US!
YOU AREN'T EXACTLY NICE TO THEM EITHER!
AND HENOK'S ACT WAS AN AFFRONT TO THE GOD...
WHATEVER!
I CAN'T FORGIVE MY PARENTS' KILLER!

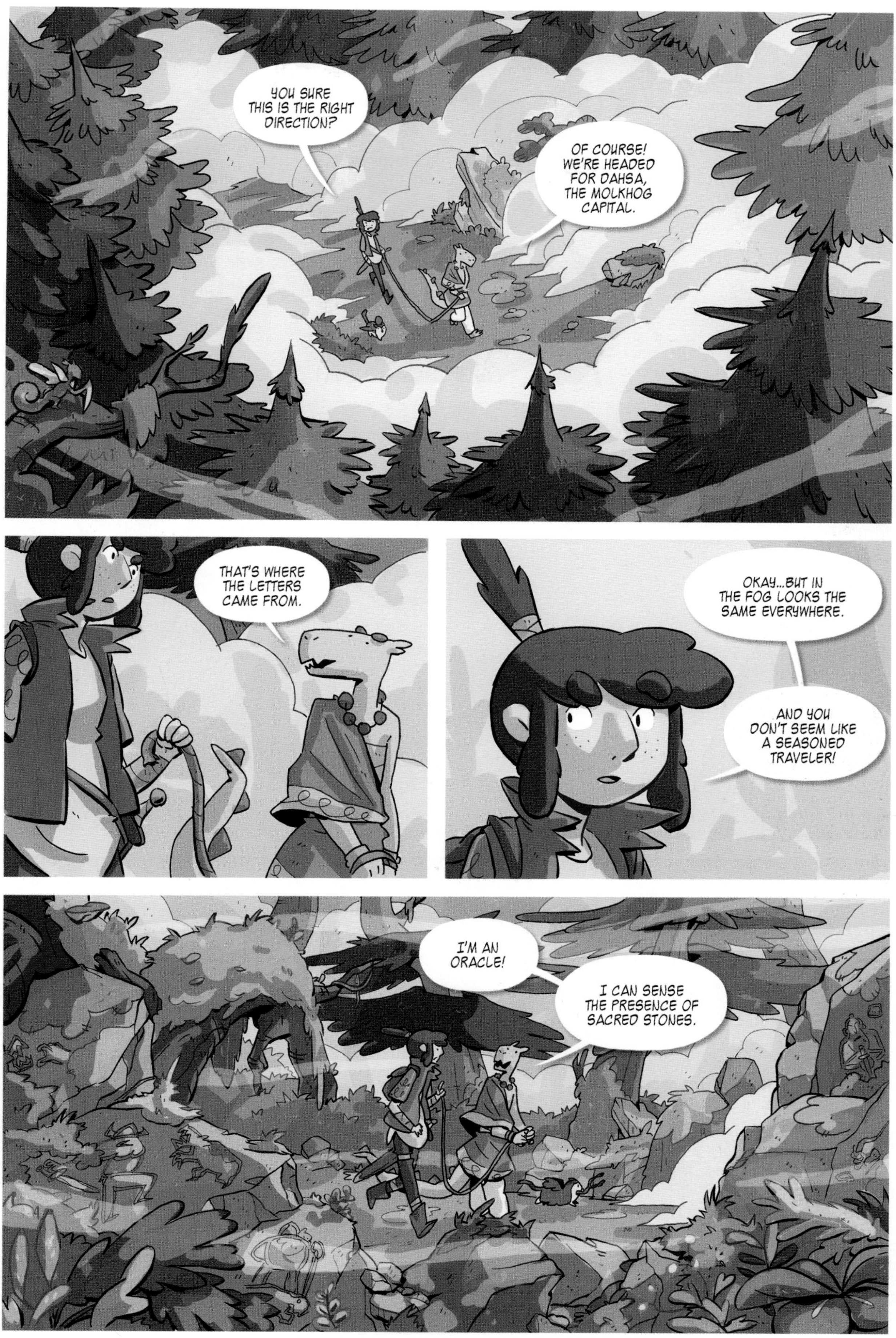
YOU SURE THIS IS THE RIGHT DIRECTION?
OF COURSE! WE'RE HEADED FOR DAHSA, THE MOLKHOG CAPITAL.
THAT'S WHERE THE LETTERS CAME FROM.
OKAY...BUT IN THE FOG LOOKS THE SAME EVERYWHERE.
AND YOU DON'T SEEM LIKE A SEASONED TRAVELER!
I'M AN ORACLE!
I CAN SENSE THE PRESENCE OF SACRED STONES.

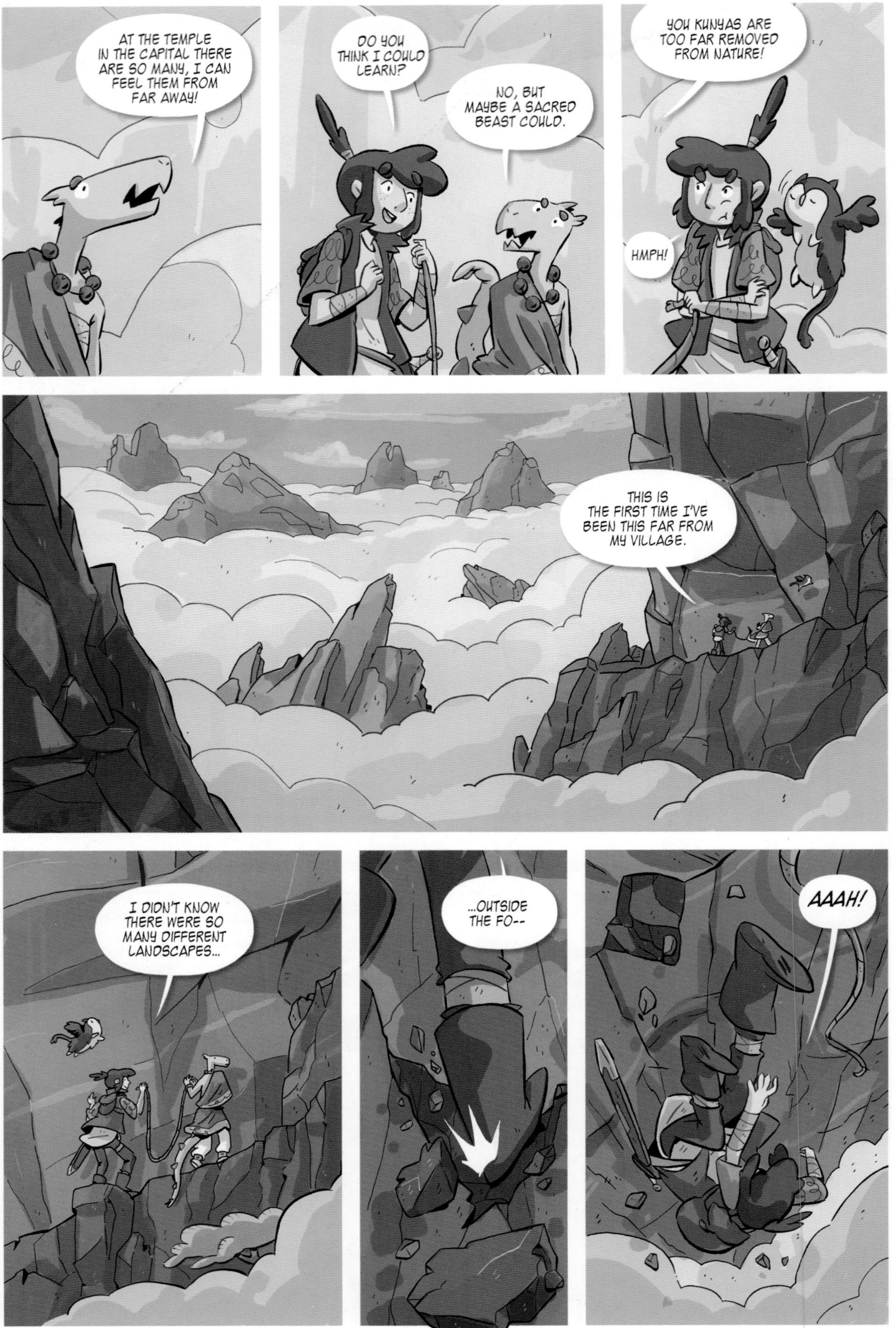
AT THE TEMPLE IN THE CAPITAL THERE ARE SO MANY, I CAN FEEL THEM FROM FAR AWAY!
DO YOU THINK I COULD LEARN?
NO, BUT MAYBE A SACRED BEAST COULD.
YOU KUNYAS ARE TOO FAR REMOVED FROM NATURE!
HMPH!
THIS IS THE FIRST TIME I'VE BEEN THIS FAR FROM MY VILLAGE.
I DIDN'T KNOW THERE WERE SO MANY DIFFERENT LANDSCAPES...
...OUTSIDE THE FO--
AAAH!

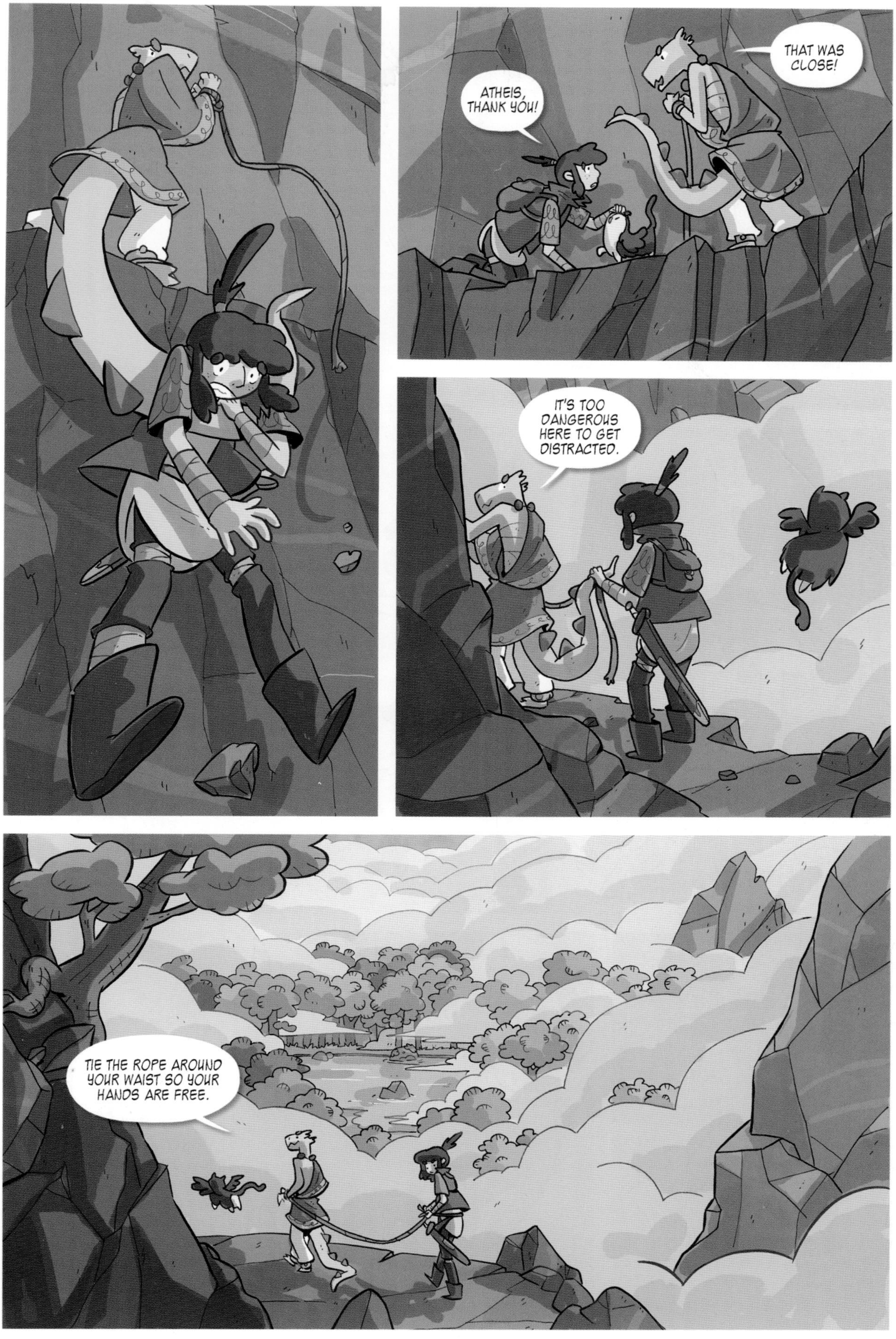

ATHEIS, THANK YOU!
THAT WAS CLOSE!
IT'S TOO DANGEROUS HERE TO GET DISTRACTED.
TIE THE ROPE AROUND YOUR WAIST SO YOUR HANDS ARE FREE.

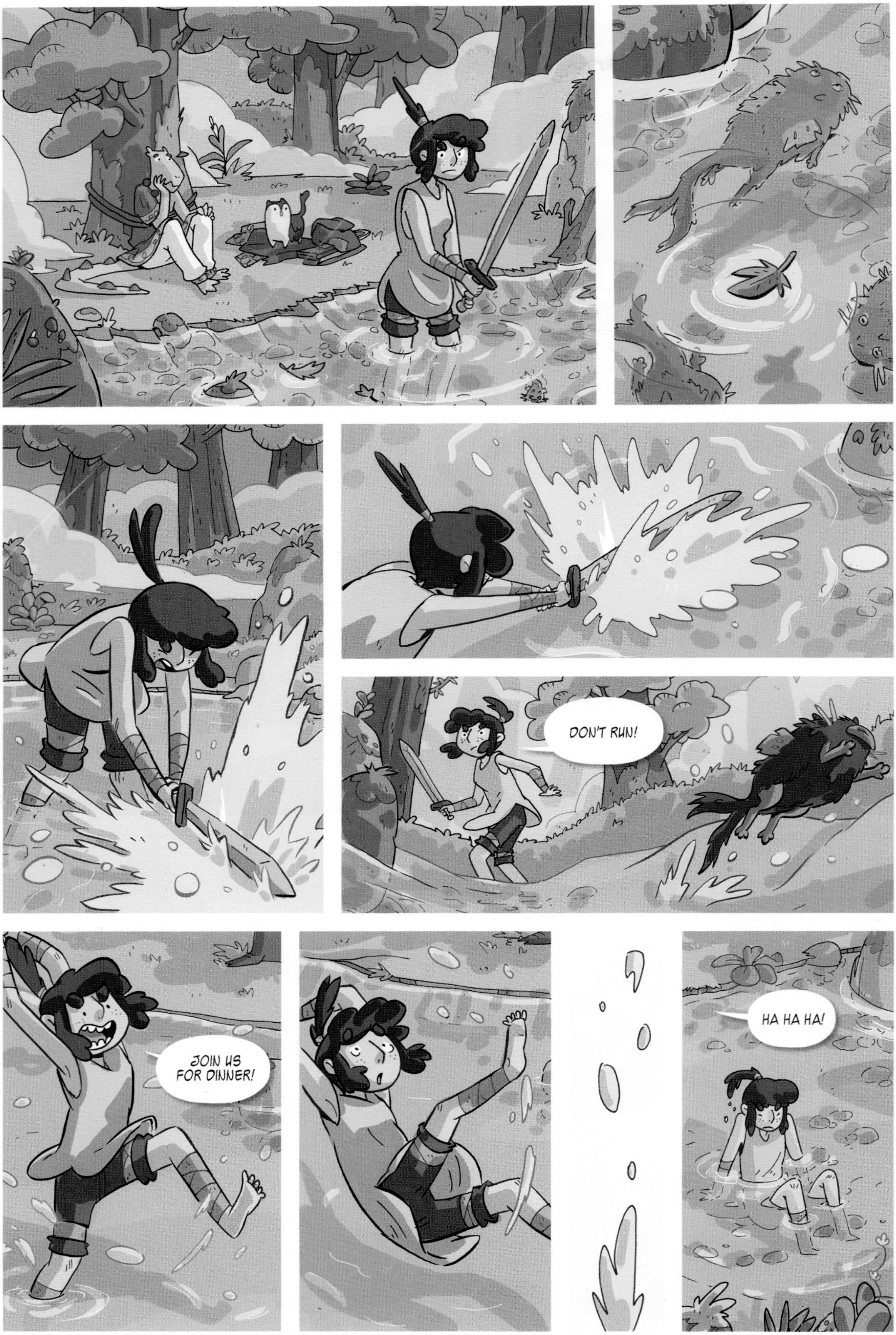
DON'T RUN!
JOIN US FOR DINNER!
HA HA HA!

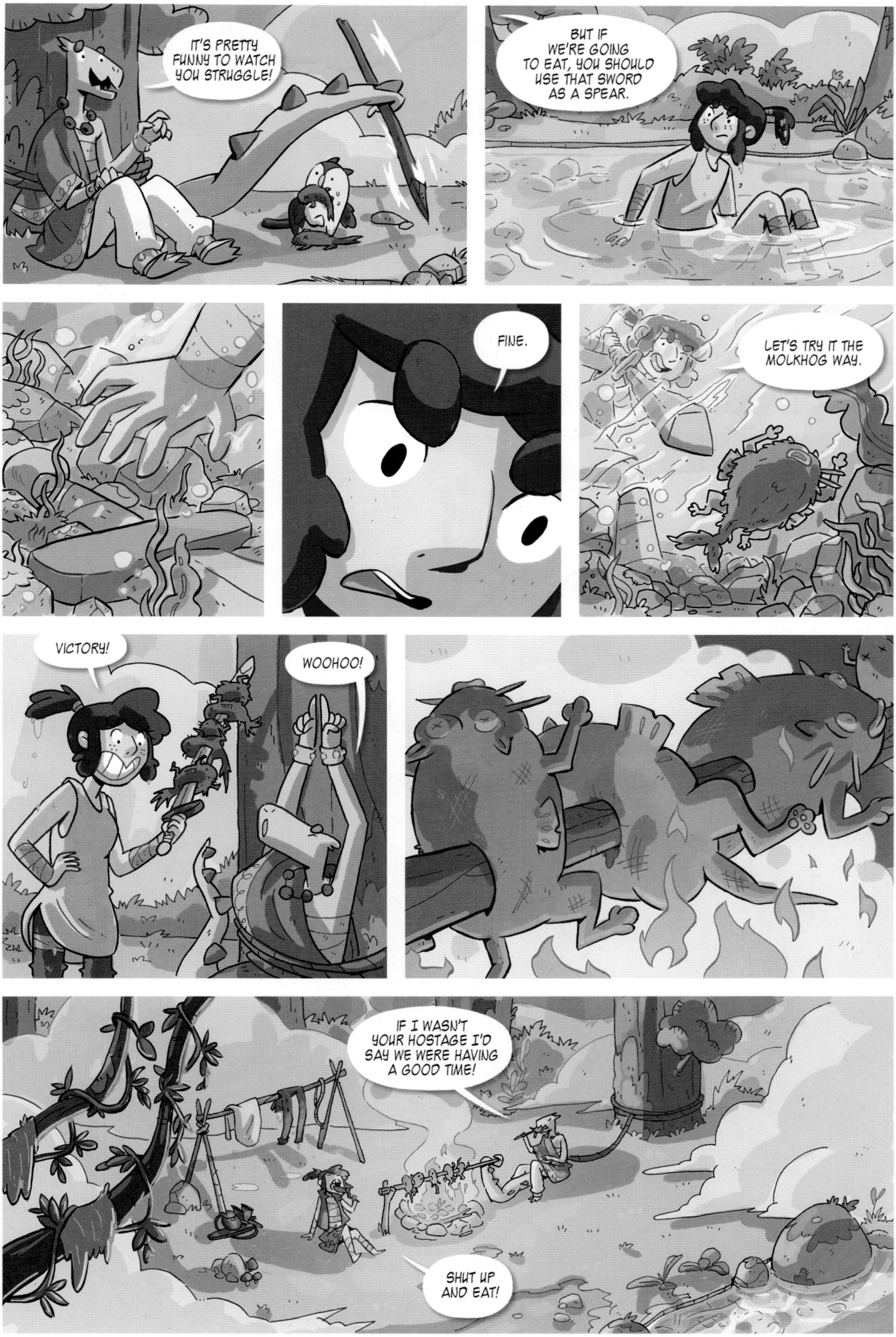
IT'S PRETTY FUNNY TO WATCH YOU STRUGGLE!
BUT IF WE'RE GOING TO EAT, YOU SHOULD USE THAT SWORD AS A SPEAR.
FINE.
LET'S TRY IT THE MOLKHOG WAY.
VICTORY!
WOOHOO!
IF I WASN'T YOUR HOSTAGE I'D SAY WE WERE HAVING A GOOD TIME!
SHUT UP AND EAT!

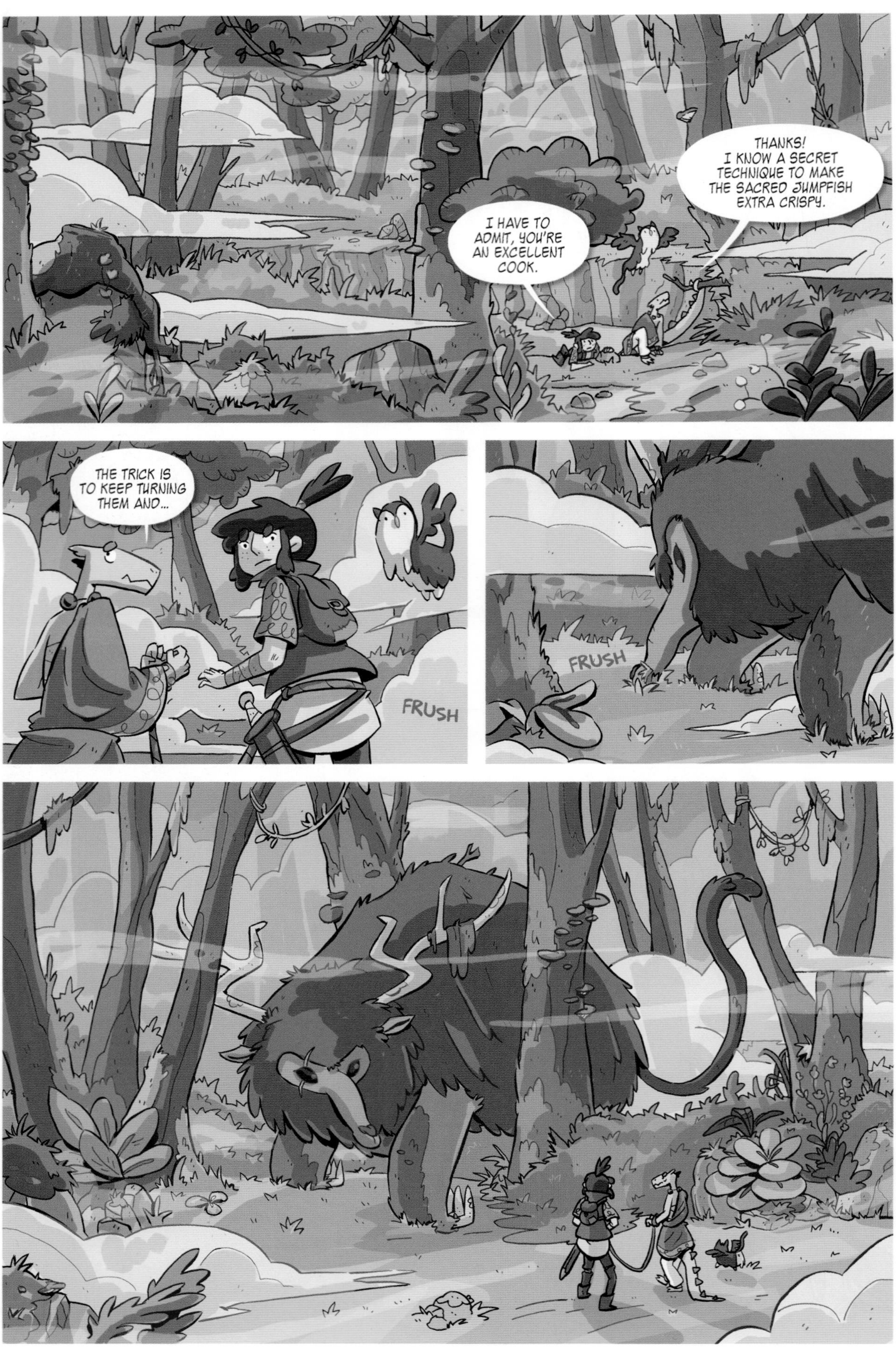
I HAVE TO ADMIT, YOU'RE AN EXCELLENT COOK.
THANKS! I KNOW A SECRET TECHNIQUE TO MAKE THE SACRED JUMPFISH EXTRA CRISPY.
THE TRICK IS TO KEEP TURNING THEM AND...
FRUSH
FRUSH

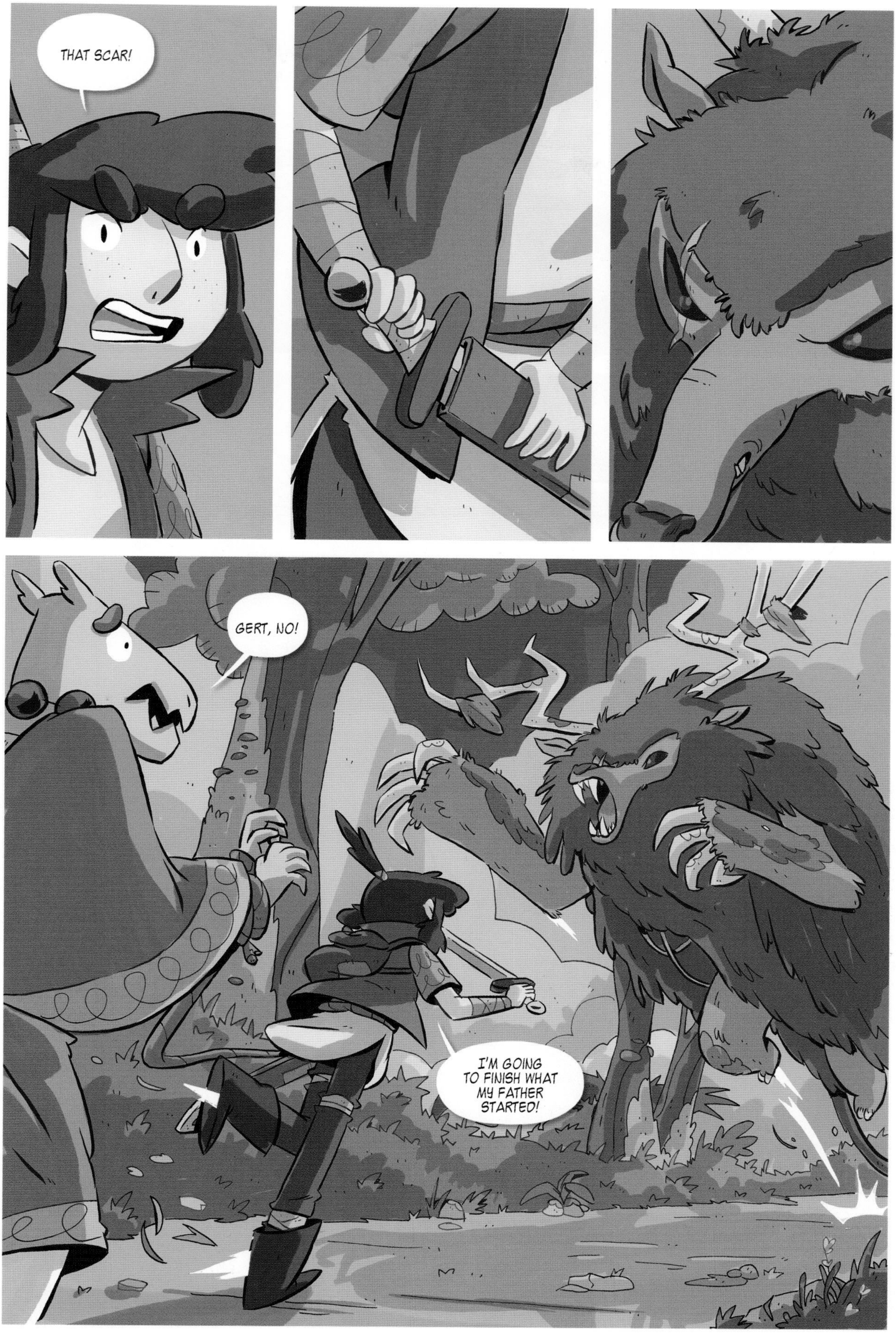
THAT SCAR!
GERT, NO!
I'M GOING TO FINISH WHAT MY FATHER STARTED!

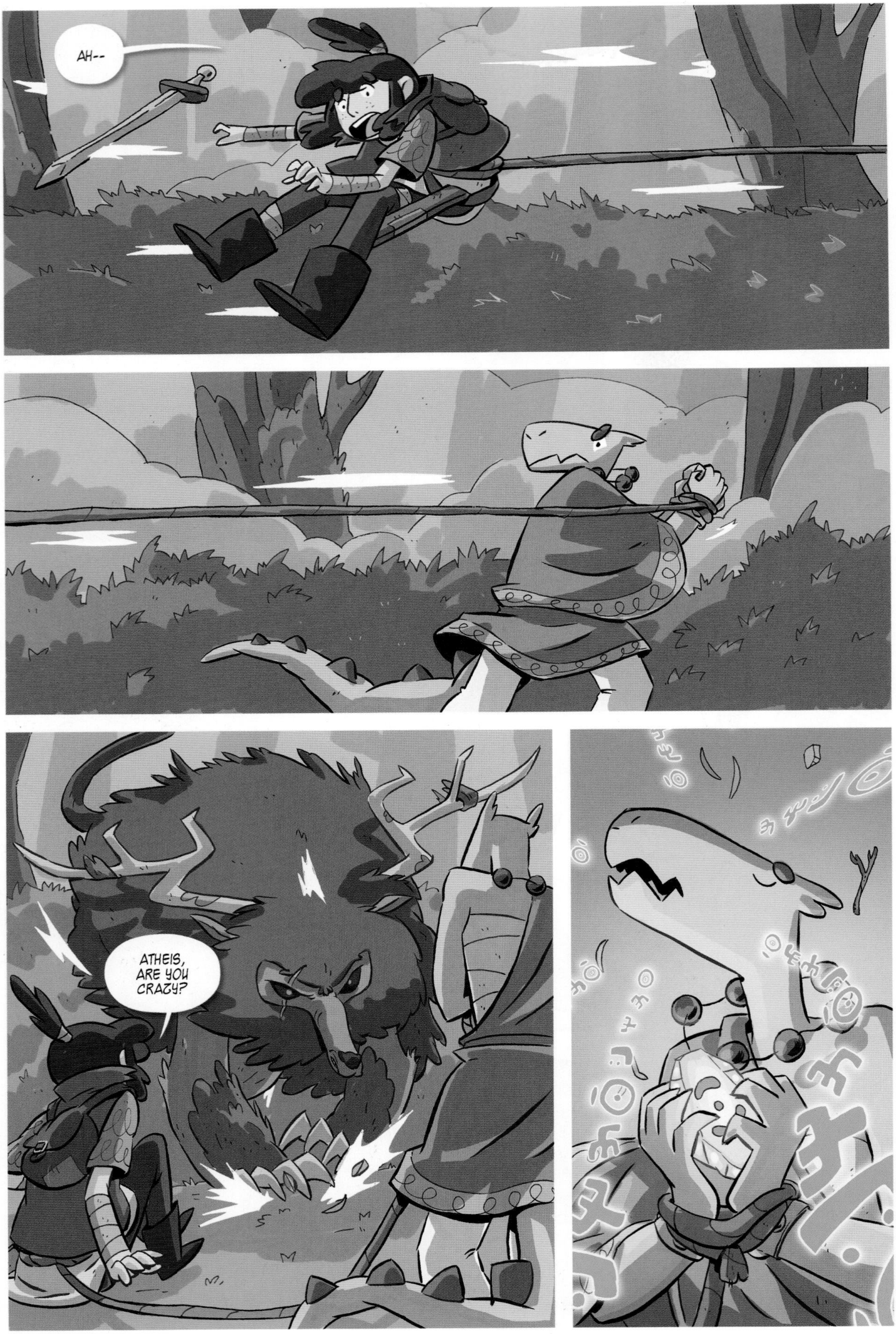
AH--
ATHEIS, ARE YOU CRAZY?

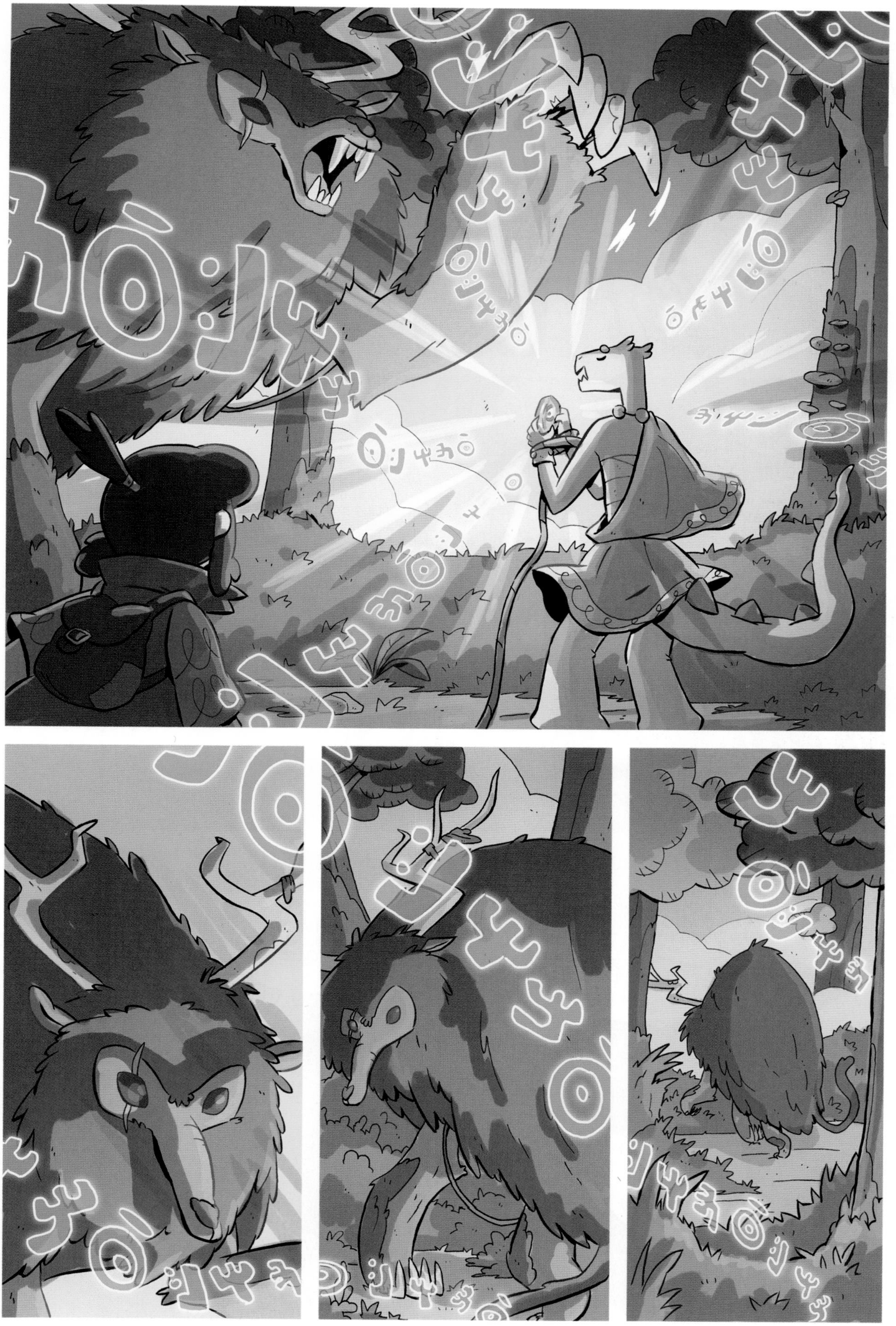

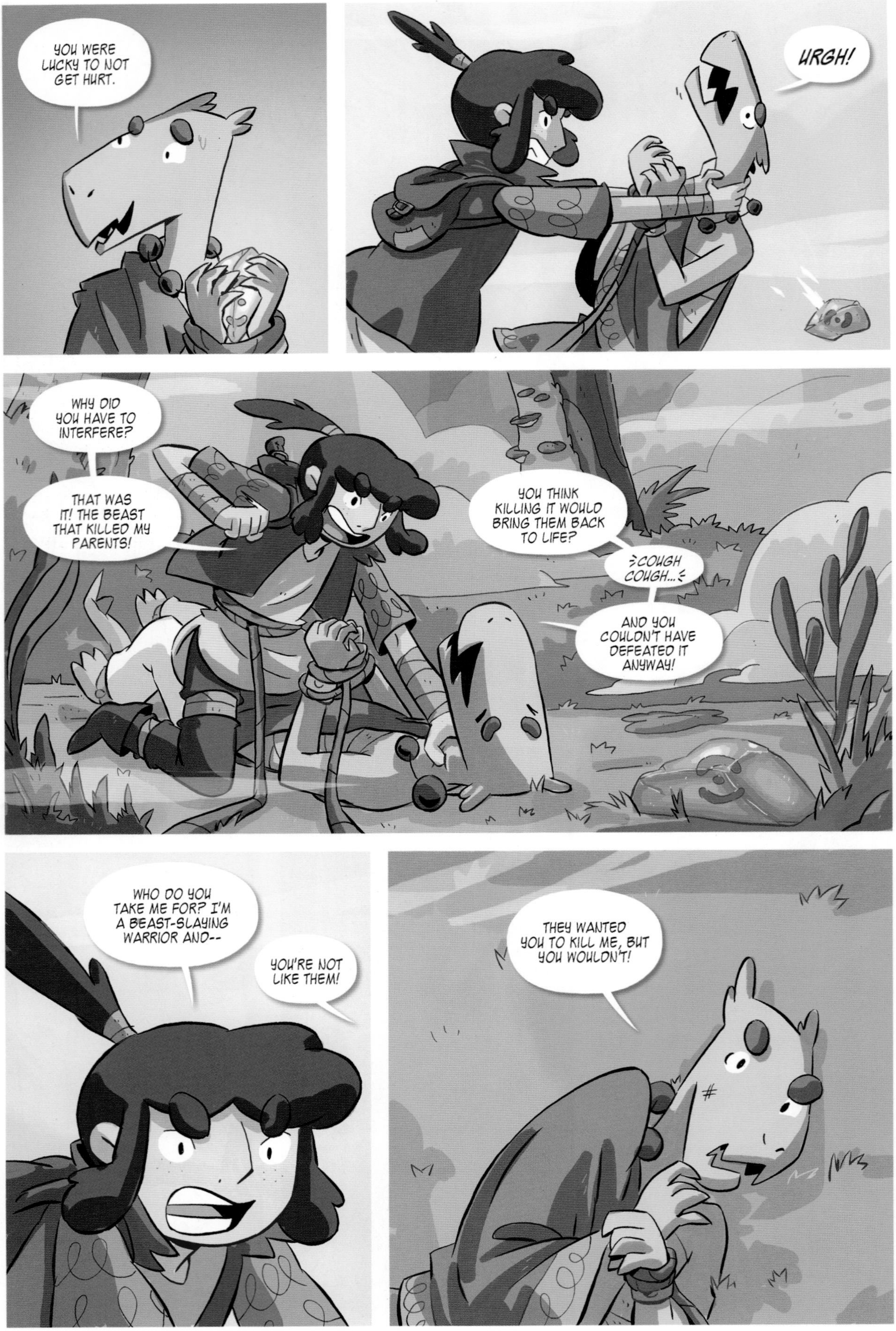

YOU WERE LUCKY TO NOT GET HURT.
URGH!
WHY DID YOU HAVE TO INTERFERE?
THAT WAS IT! THE BEAST THAT KILLED MY PARENTS!
YOU THINK KILLING IT WOULD BRING THEM BACK TO LIFE?
COUGH COUGH...
AND YOU COULDN'T HAVE DEFEATED IT ANYWAY!
WHO DO YOU TAKE ME FOR? I'M A BEAST-SLAYING WARRIOR AND--
YOU'RE NOT LIKE THEM!
THEY WANTED YOU TO KILL ME, BUT YOU WOULDN'T!

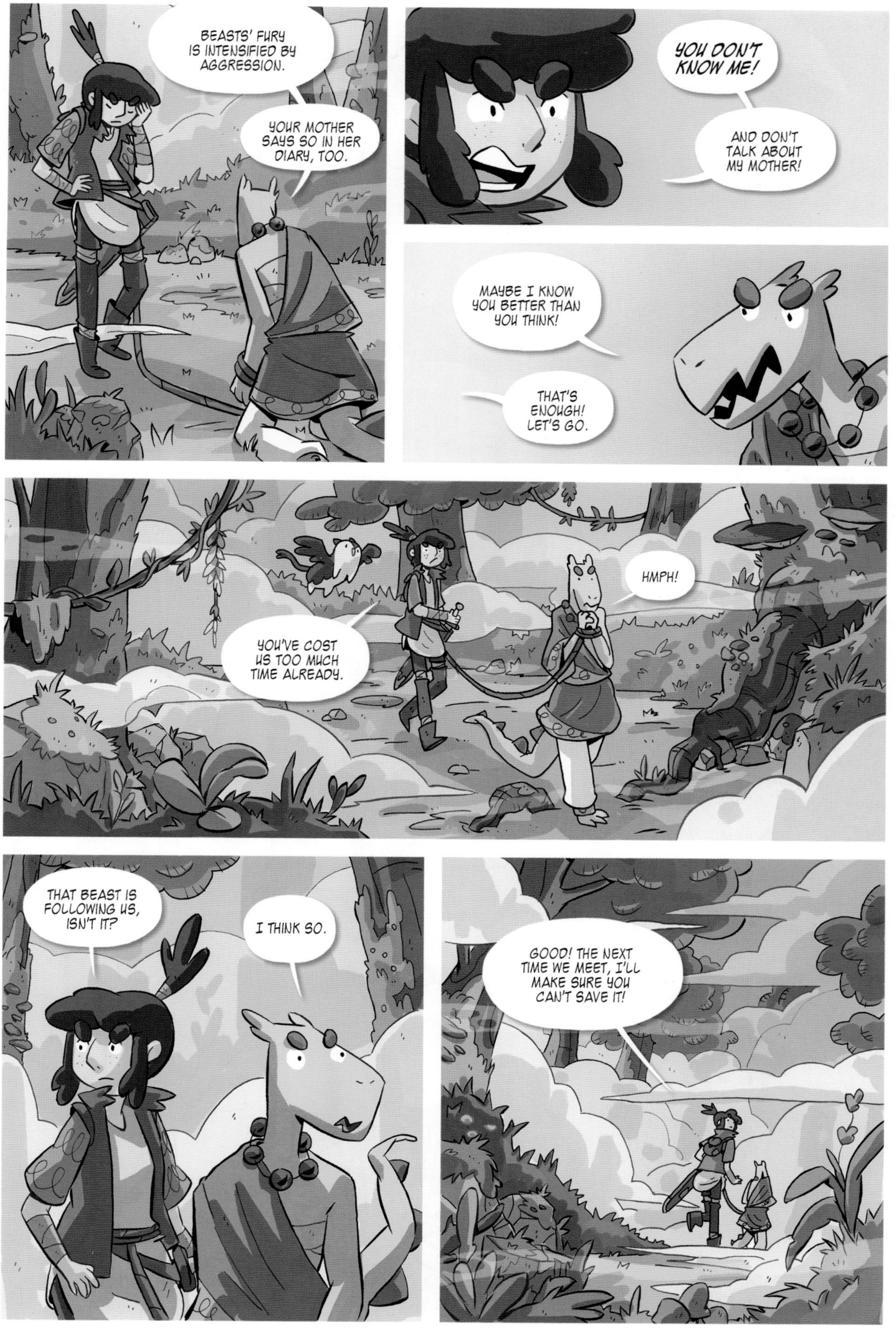
BEASTS' FURY IS INTENSIFIED BY AGGRESSION.
YOUR MOTHER SAYS SO IN HER DIARY, TOO.
YOU DON'T KNOW ME!
AND DON'T TALK ABOUT MY MOTHER!
MAYBE I KNOW YOU BETTER THAN YOU THINK!
THAT'S ENOUGH! LET'S GO.
YOU'VE COST US TOO MUCH TIME ALREADY.
HMPH!
THAT BEAST IS FOLLOWING US, ISN'T IT?
I THINK SO.
GOOD! THE NEXT TIME WE MEET, I'LL MAKE SURE YOU CAN'T SAVE IT!

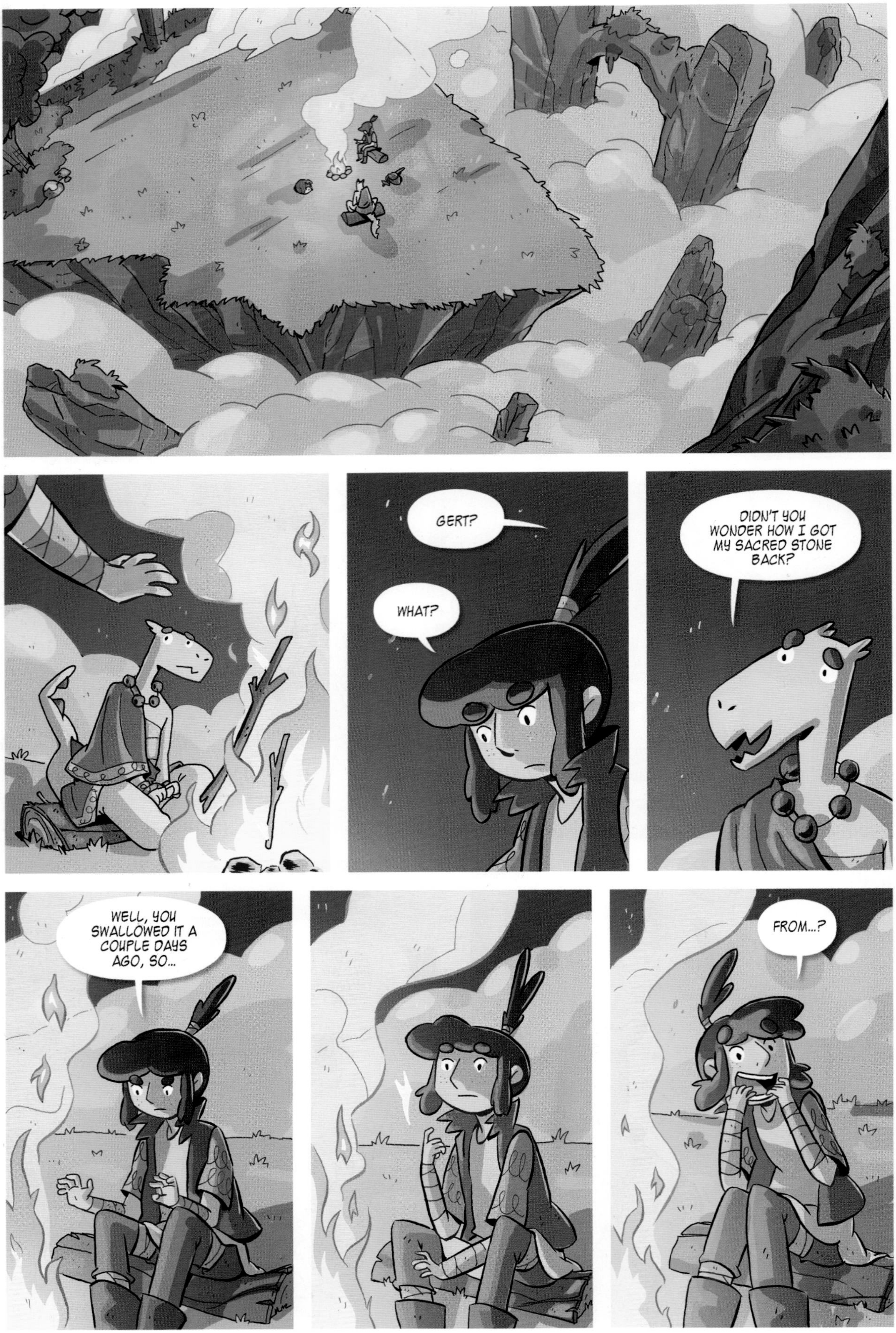
GERT?
WHAT?
DIDN'T YOU WONDER HOW I GOT MY SACRED STONE BACK?
WELL, YOU SWALLOWED IT A COUPLE DAYS AGO, SO...
FROM...?

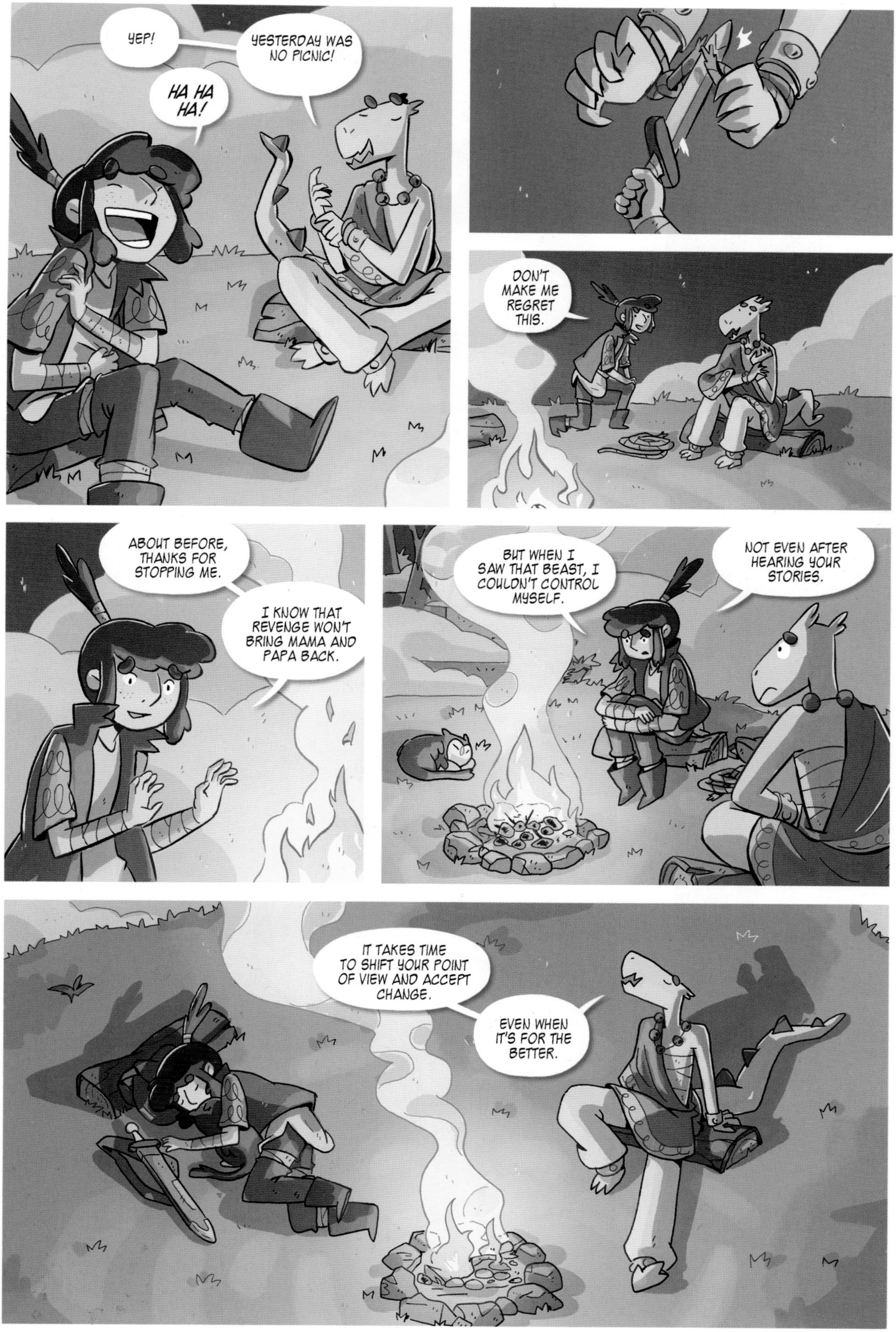
YEP!
YESTERDAY WAS NO PICNIC!
HA HA HA!
DON'T MAKE ME REGRET THIS.
ABOUT BEFORE, THANKS FOR STOPPING ME.
I KNOW THAT REVENGE WON'T BRING MAMA AND PAPA BACK.
BUT WHEN I SAW THAT BEAST, I COULDN'T CONTROL MYSELF.
NOT EVEN AFTER HEARING YOUR STORIES.
IT TAKES TIME TO SHIFT YOUR POINT OF VIEW AND ACCEPT CHANGE.
EVEN WHEN IT'S FOR THE BETTER.

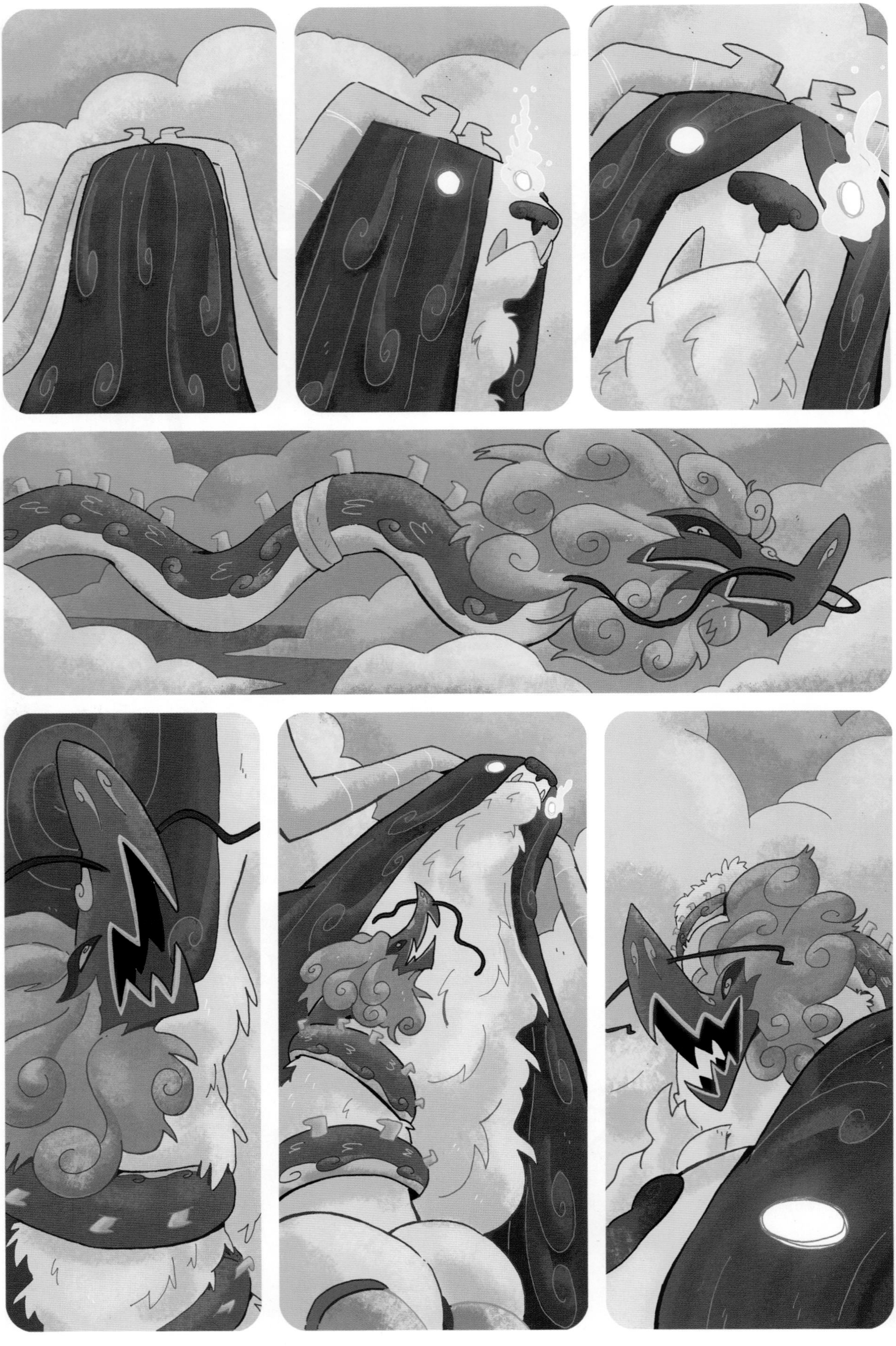

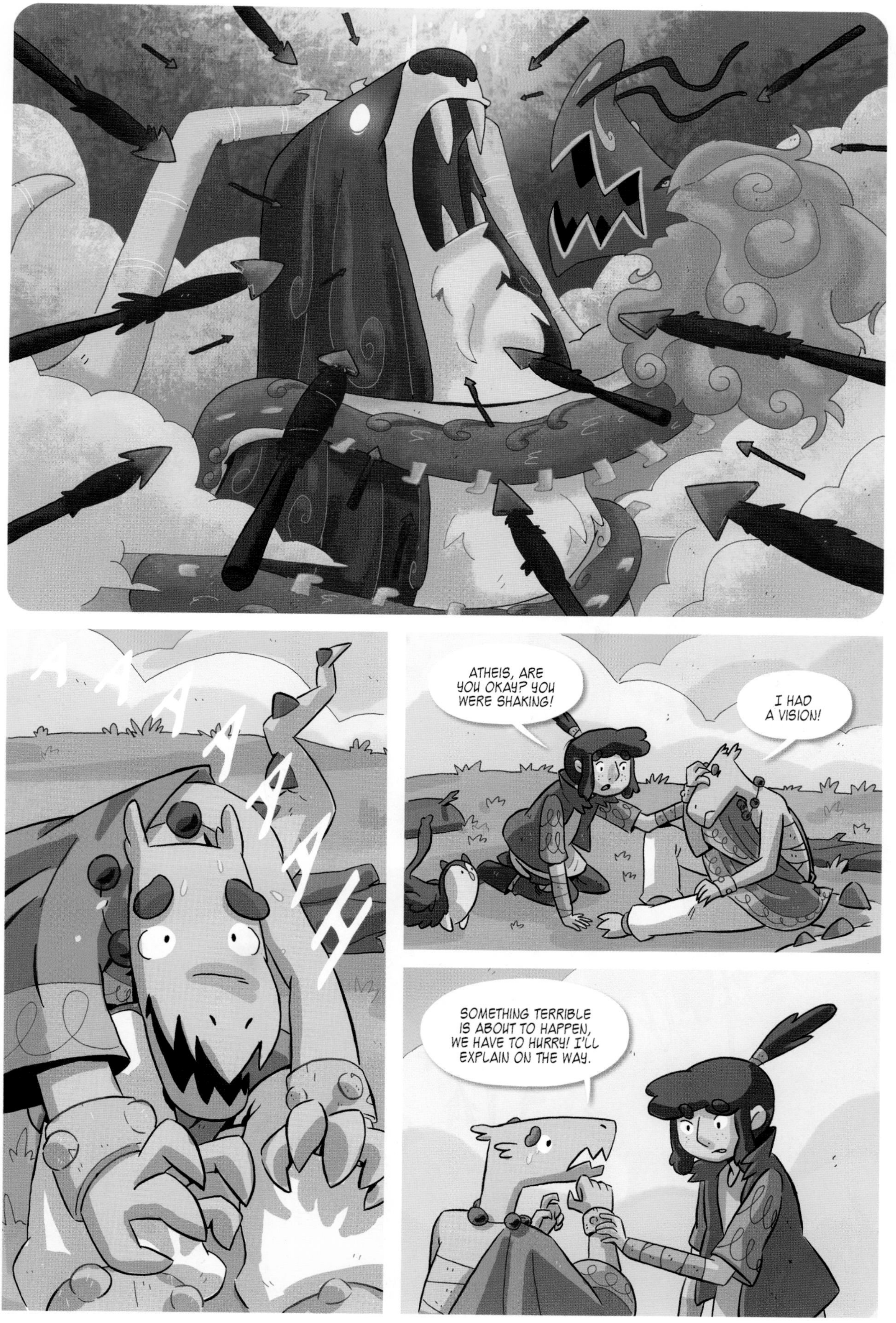
AAAAAAAAAH
ATHEIS, ARE YOU OKAY? YOU WERE SHAKING!
I HAD A VISION!
SOMETHING TERRIBLE IS ABOUT TO HAPPEN, WE HAVE TO HURRY! I'LL EXPLAIN ON THE WAY.

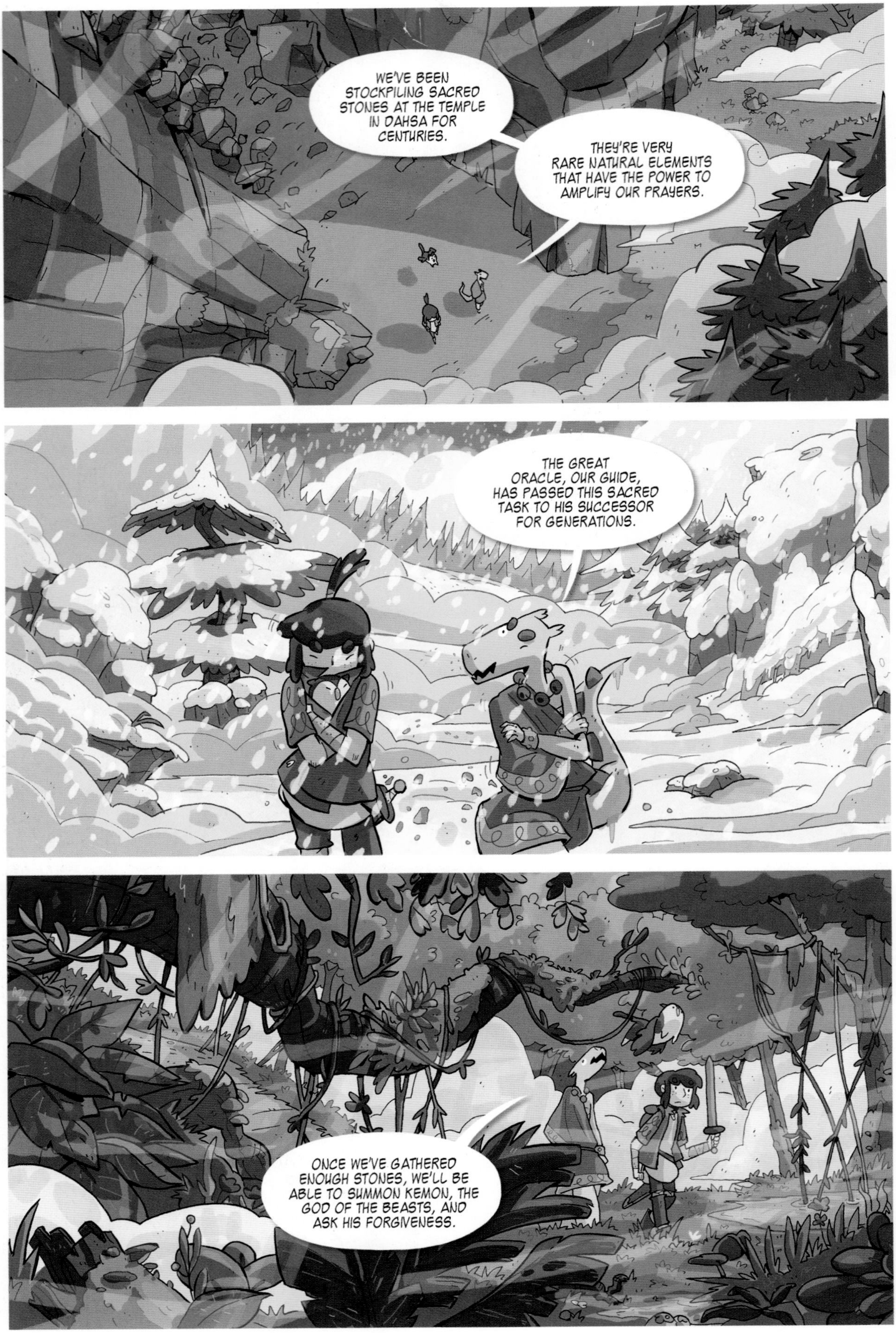
WE'VE BEEN STOCKPILING SACRED STONES AT THE TEMPLE IN DAHSA FOR CENTURIES.
THEY'RE VERY RARE NATURAL ELEMENTS THAT HAVE THE POWER TO AMPLIFY OUR PRAYERS.
THE GREAT ORACLE, OUR GUIDE, HAS PASSED THIS SACRED TASK TO HIS SUCCESSOR FOR GENERATIONS.
ONCE WE'VE GATHERED ENOUGH STONES, WE'LL BE ABLE TO SUMMON KEMON, THE GOD OF THE BEASTS, AND ASK HIS FORGIVENESS.

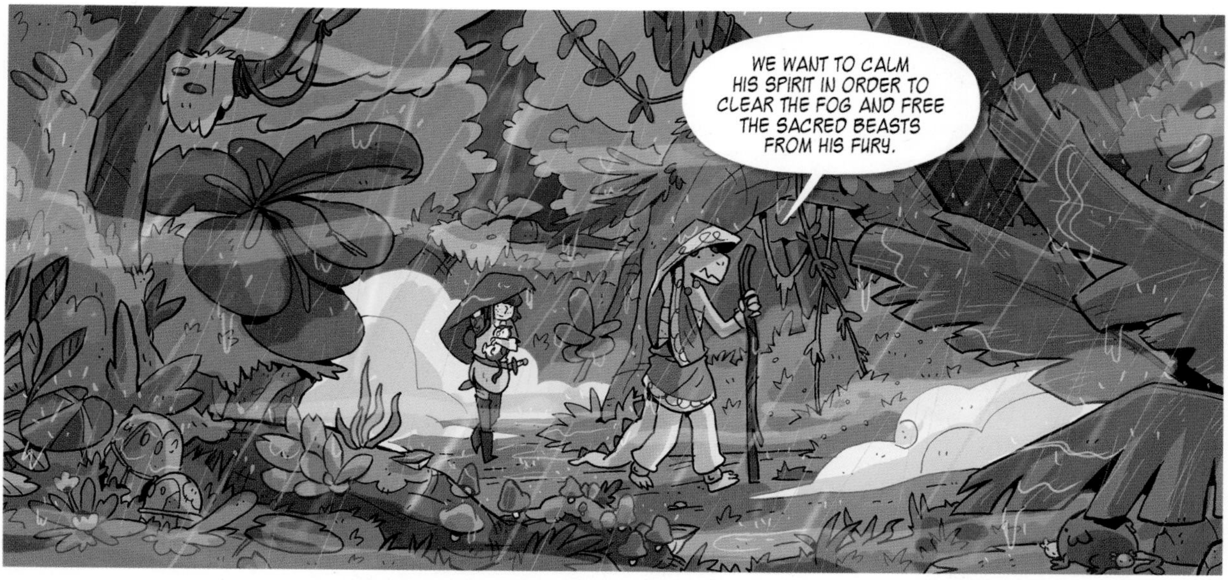
WE WANT TO CALM HIS SPIRIT IN ORDER TO CLEAR THE FOG AND FREE THE SACRED BEASTS FROM HIS FURY.

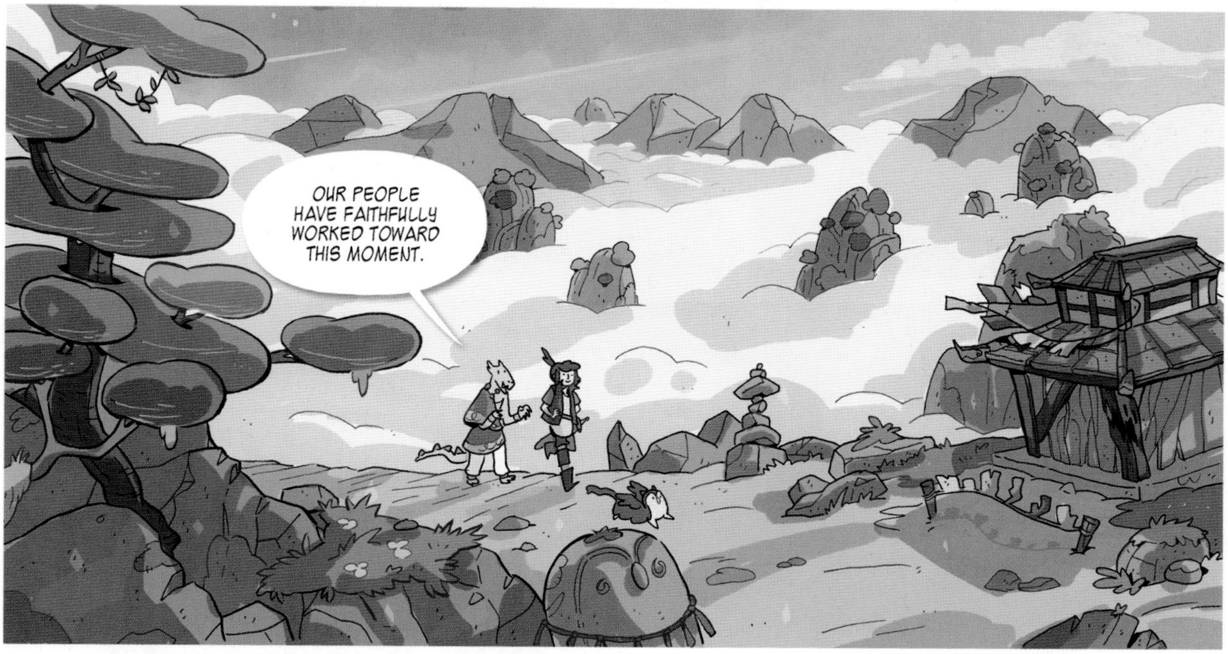
OUR PEOPLE HAVE FAITHFULLY WORKED TOWARD THIS MOMENT.

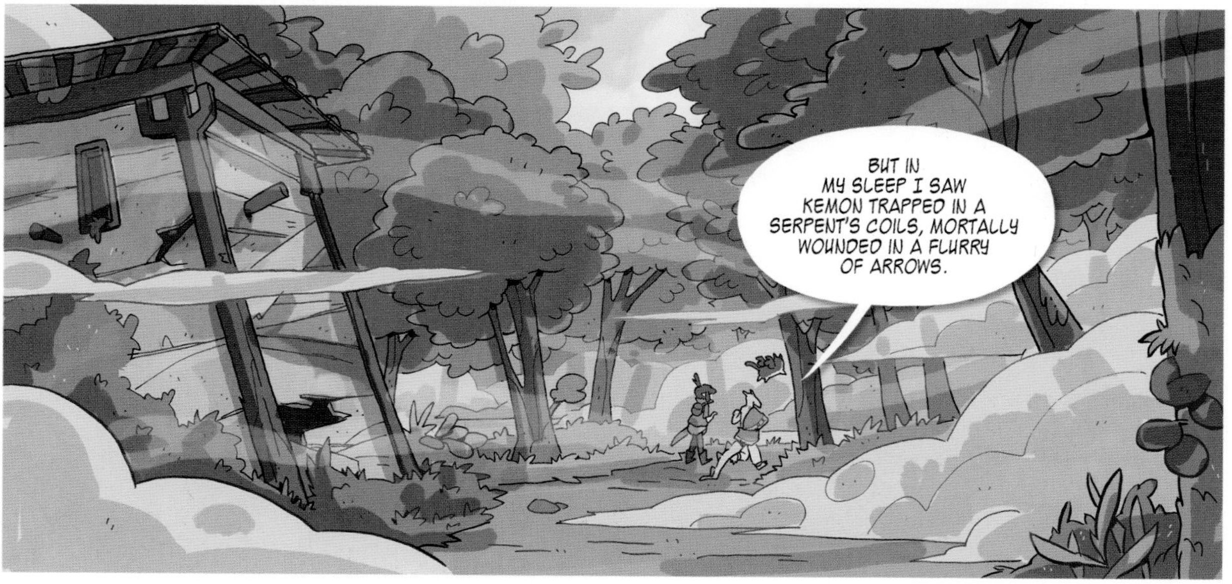
BUT IN MY SLEEP I SAW KEMON TRAPPED IN A SERPENT'S COILS, MORTALLY WOUNDED IN A FLURRY OF ARROWS.

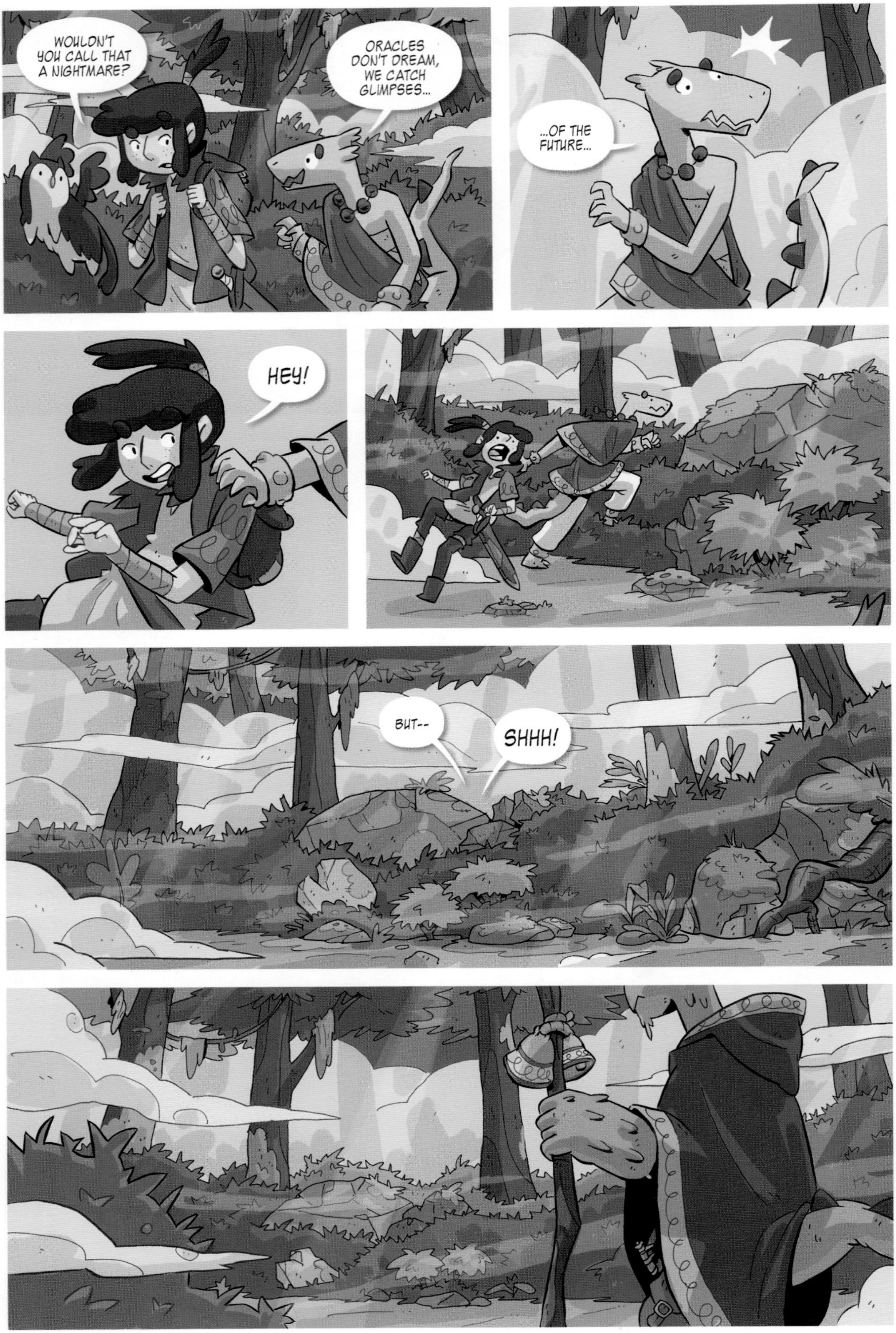
WOULDN'T YOU CALL THAT A NIGHTMARE?
ORACLES DON'T DREAM, WE CATCH GLIMPSES...
...OF THE FUTURE...
HEY!
BUT--
SHHH!

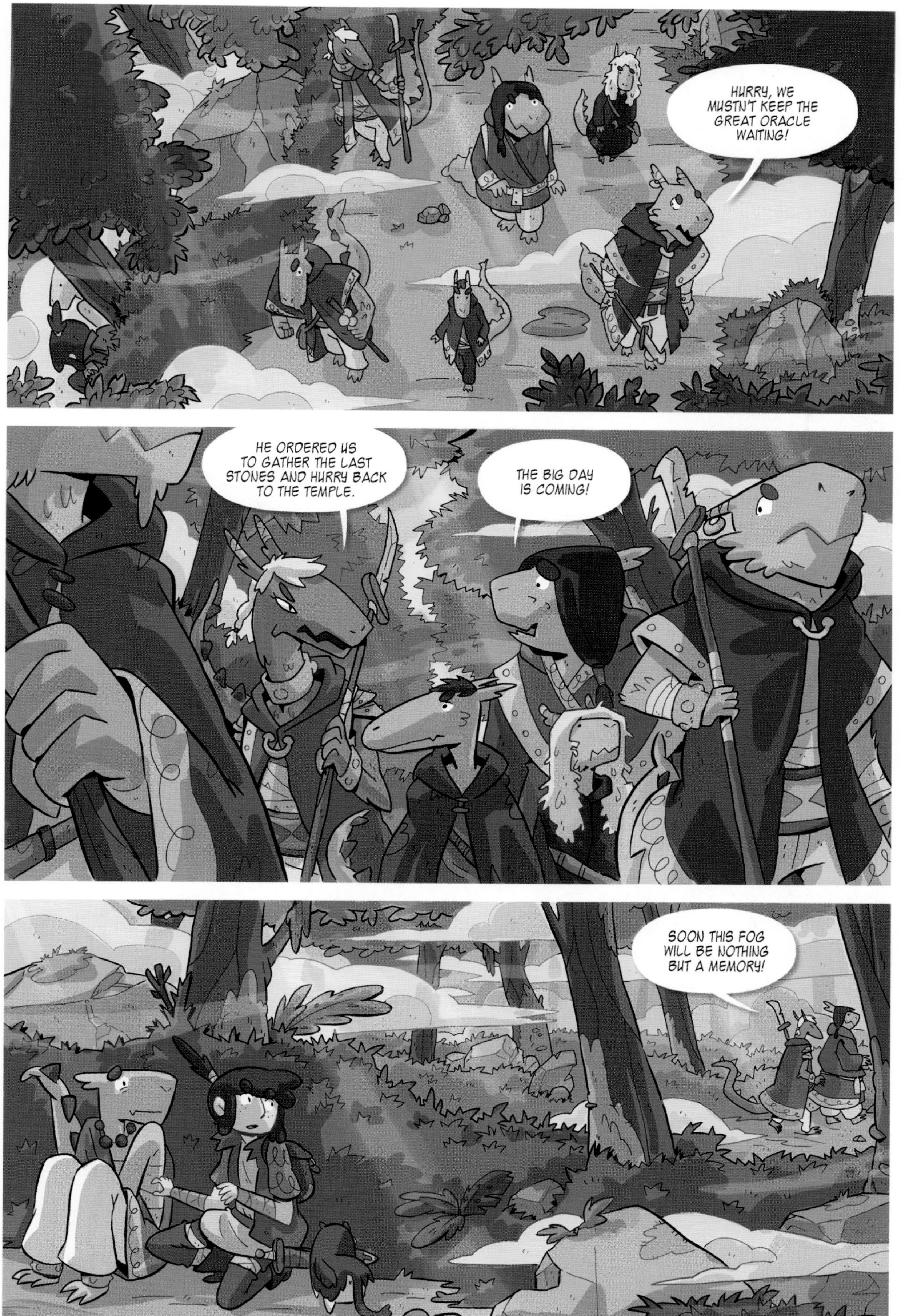
HURRY, WE MUSTN'T KEEP THE GREAT ORACLE WAITING!
HE ORDERED US TO GATHER THE LAST STONES AND HURRY BACK TO THE TEMPLE.
THE BIG DAY IS COMING!
SOON THIS FOG WILL BE NOTHING BUT A MEMORY!

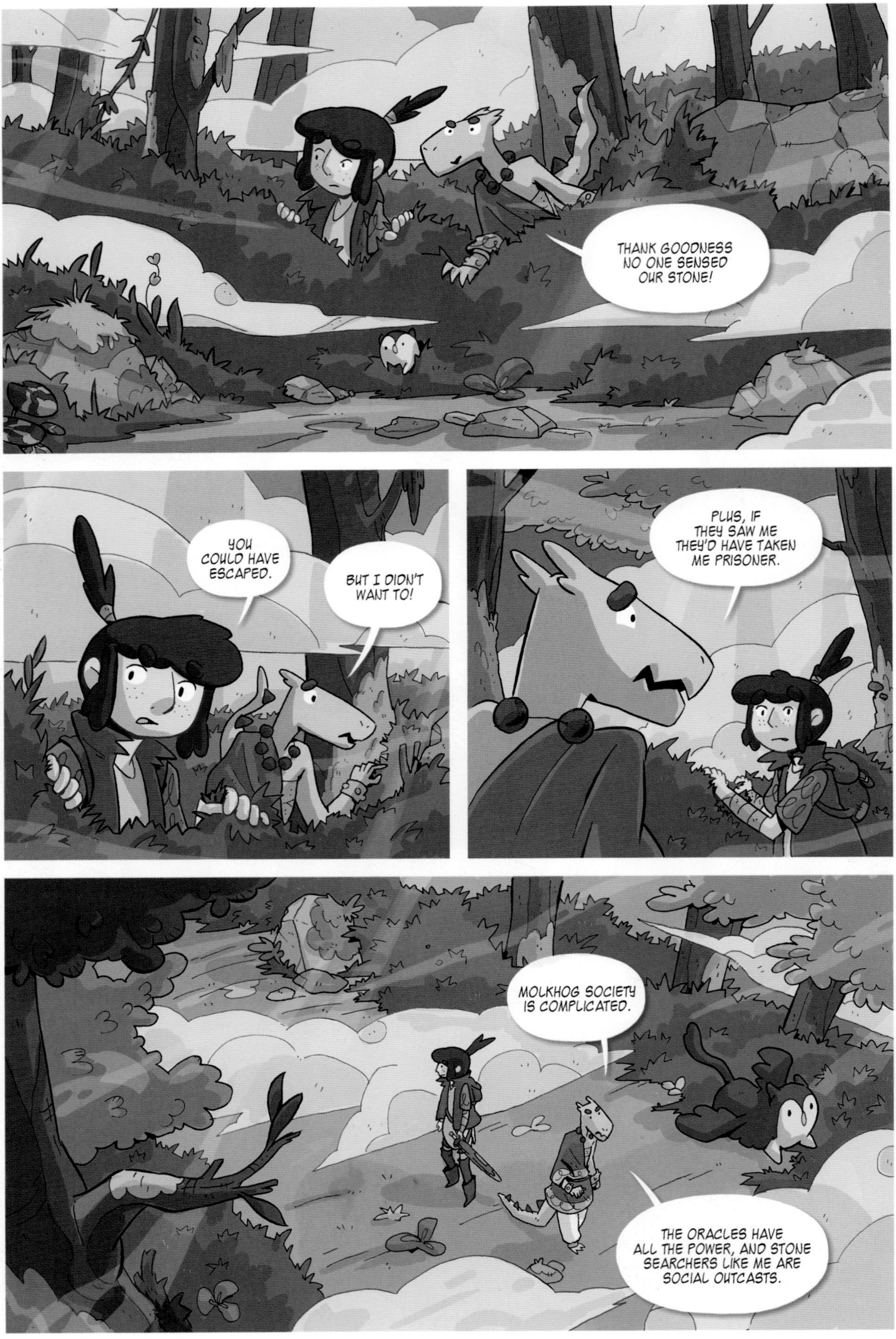
THANK GOODNESS NO ONE SENSED OUR STONE!
YOU COULD HAVE ESCAPED.
BUT I DIDN'T WANT TO!
PLUS, IF THEY SAW ME THEY'D HAVE TAKEN ME PRISONER.
MOLKHOG SOCIETY IS COMPLICATED.
THE ORACLES HAVE ALL THE POWER, AND STONE SEARCHERS LIKE ME ARE SOCIAL OUTCASTS.

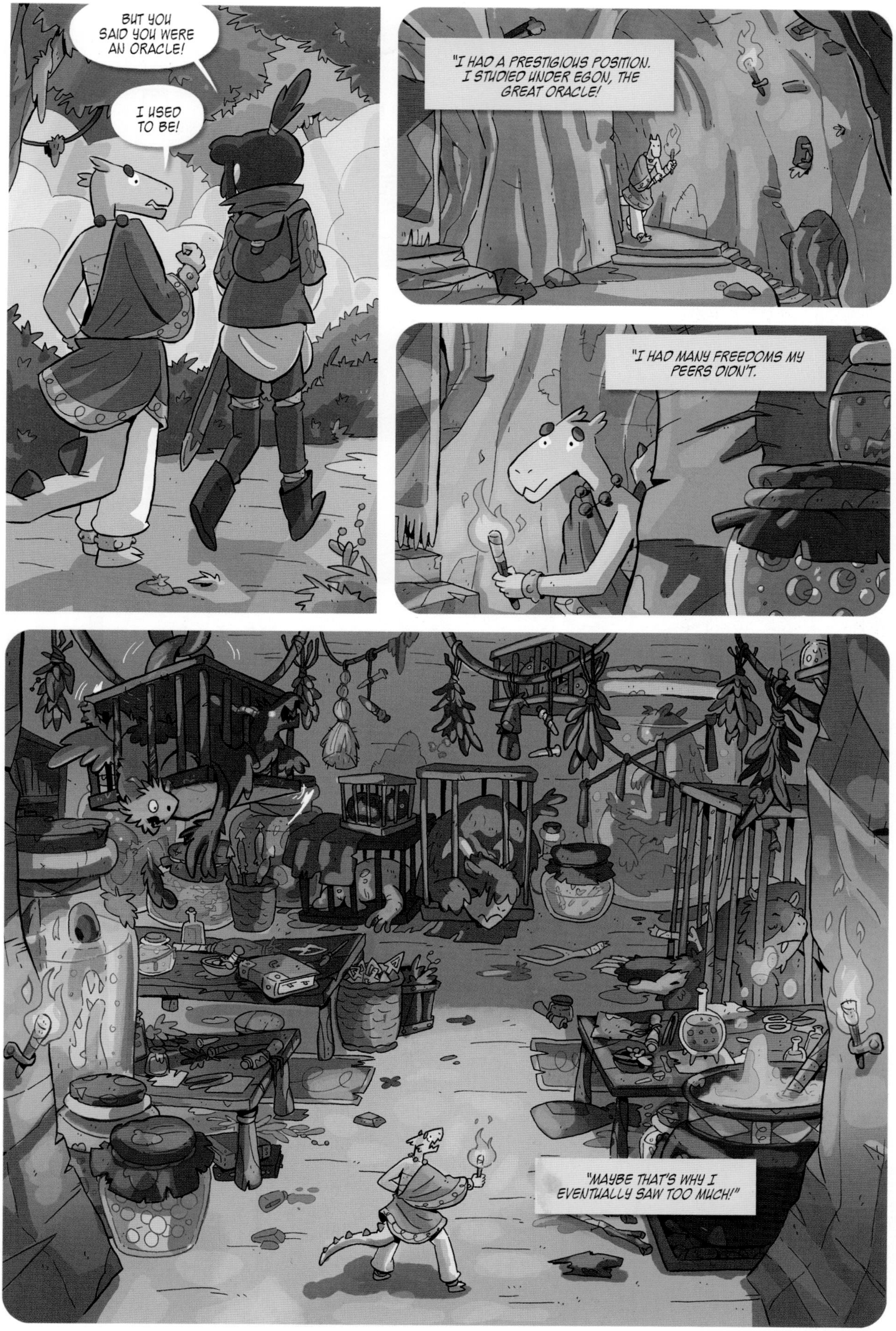
BUT YOU SAID YOU WERE AN ORACLE!
I USED TO BE!
"I HAD A PRESTIGIOUS POSITION. I STUDIED UNDER EGON, THE GREAT ORACLE!
"I HAD MANY FREEDOMS MY PEERS DIDN'T.
"MAYBE THAT'S WHY I EVENTUALLY SAW TOO MUCH!"

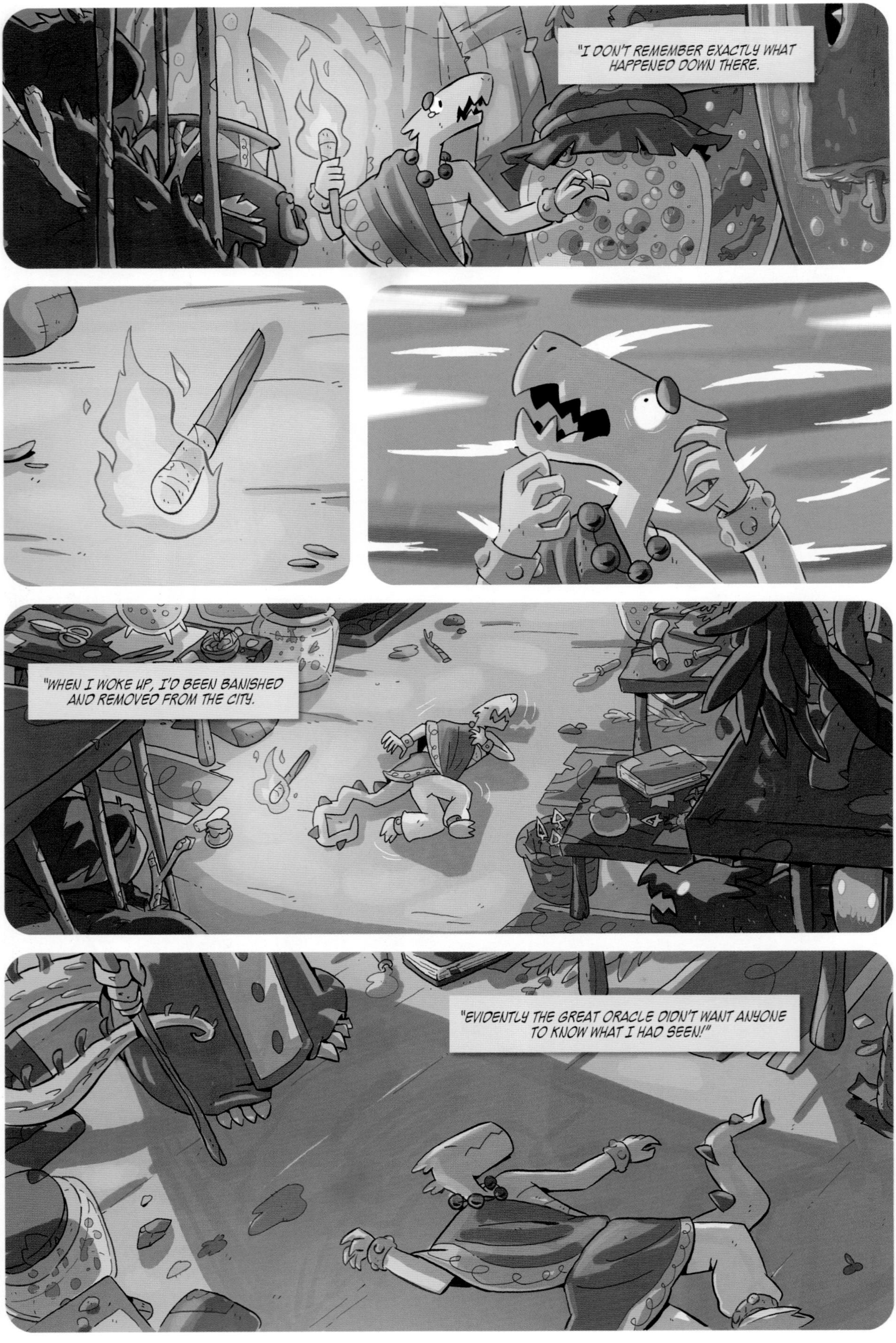
"I DON'T REMEMBER EXACTLY WHAT HAPPENED DOWN THERE.
"WHEN I WOKE UP, I'D BEEN BANISHED AND REMOVED FROM THE CITY.
"EVIDENTLY THE GREAT ORACLE DIDN'T WANT ANYONE TO KNOW WHAT I HAD SEEN!"

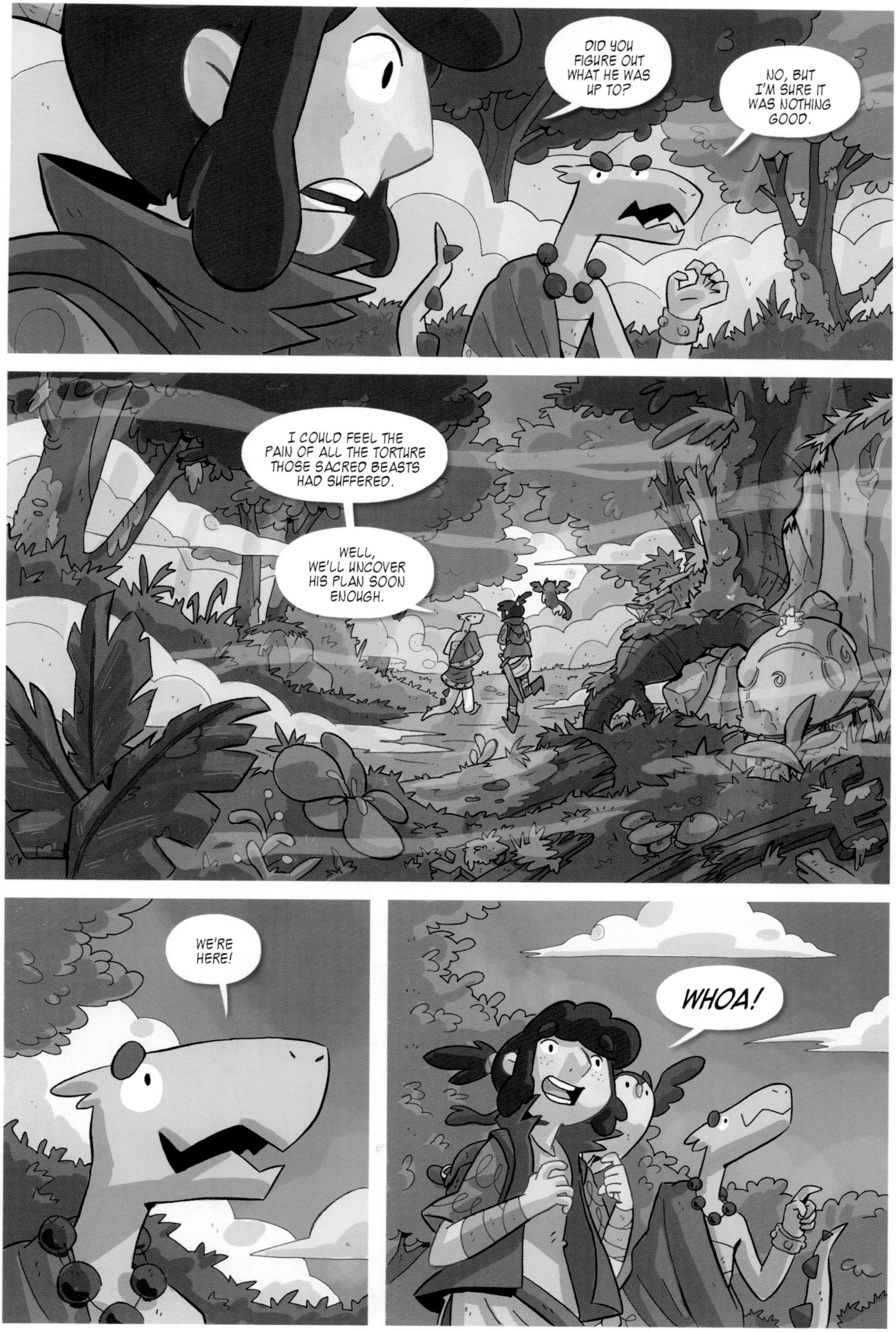
DID YOU FIGURE OUT WHAT HE WAS UP TO?
NO, BUT I'M SURE IT WAS NOTHING GOOD.
I COULD FEEL THE PAIN OF ALL THE TORTURE THOSE SACRED BEASTS HAD SUFFERED.
WELL, WE'LL UNCOVER HIS PLAN SOON ENOUGH.
WE'RE HERE!
WHOA!

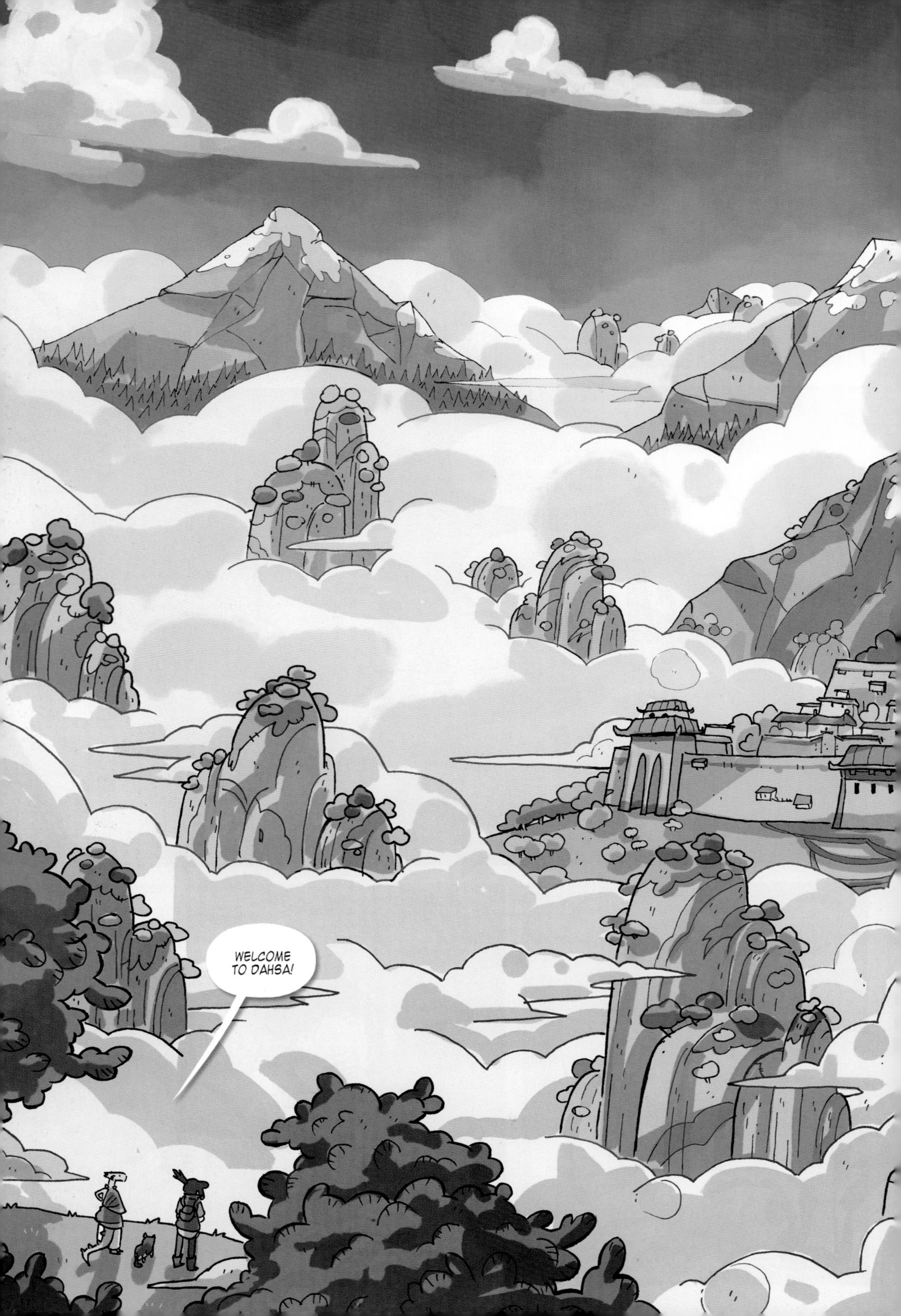
WELCOME TO DAHSA!

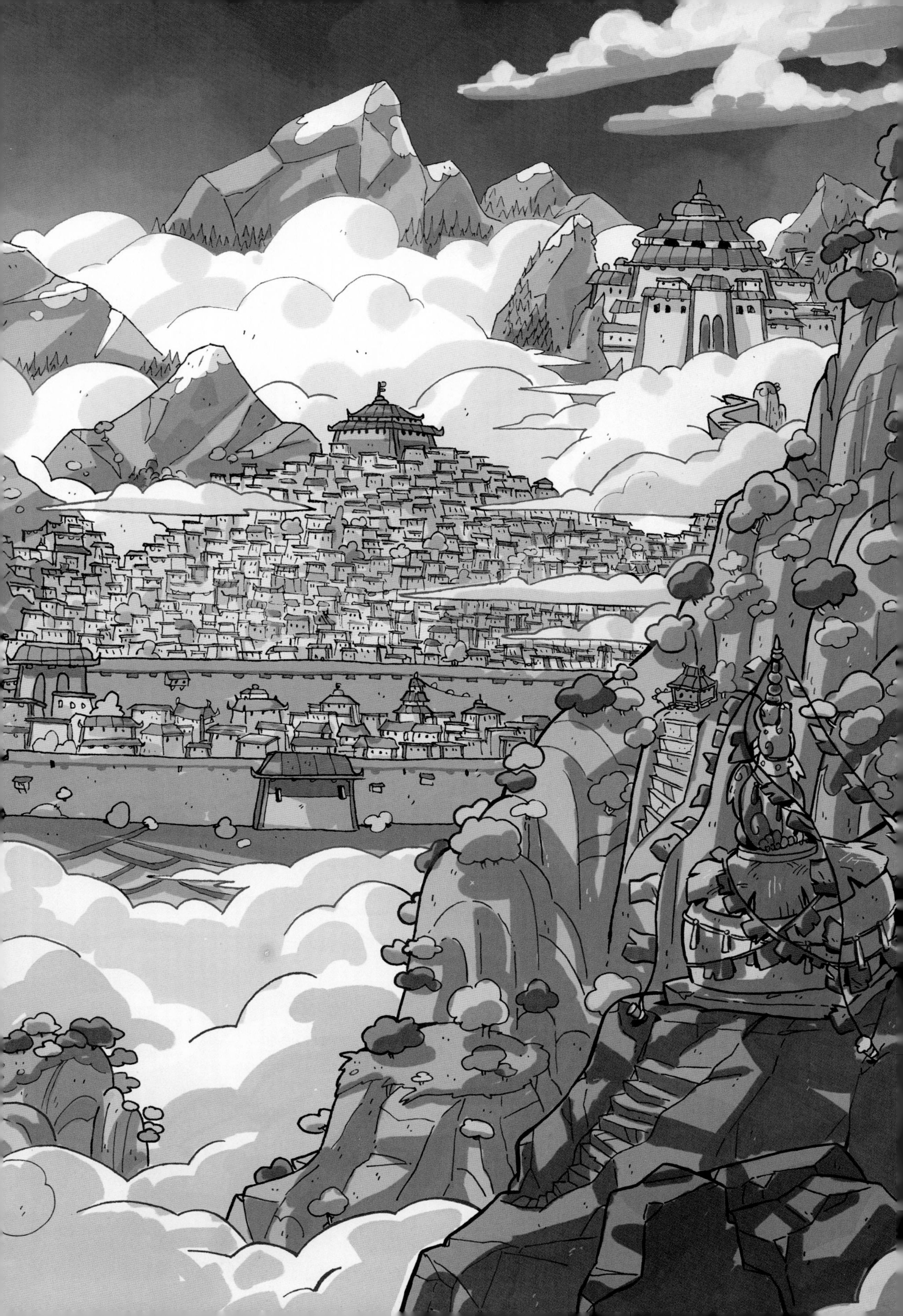

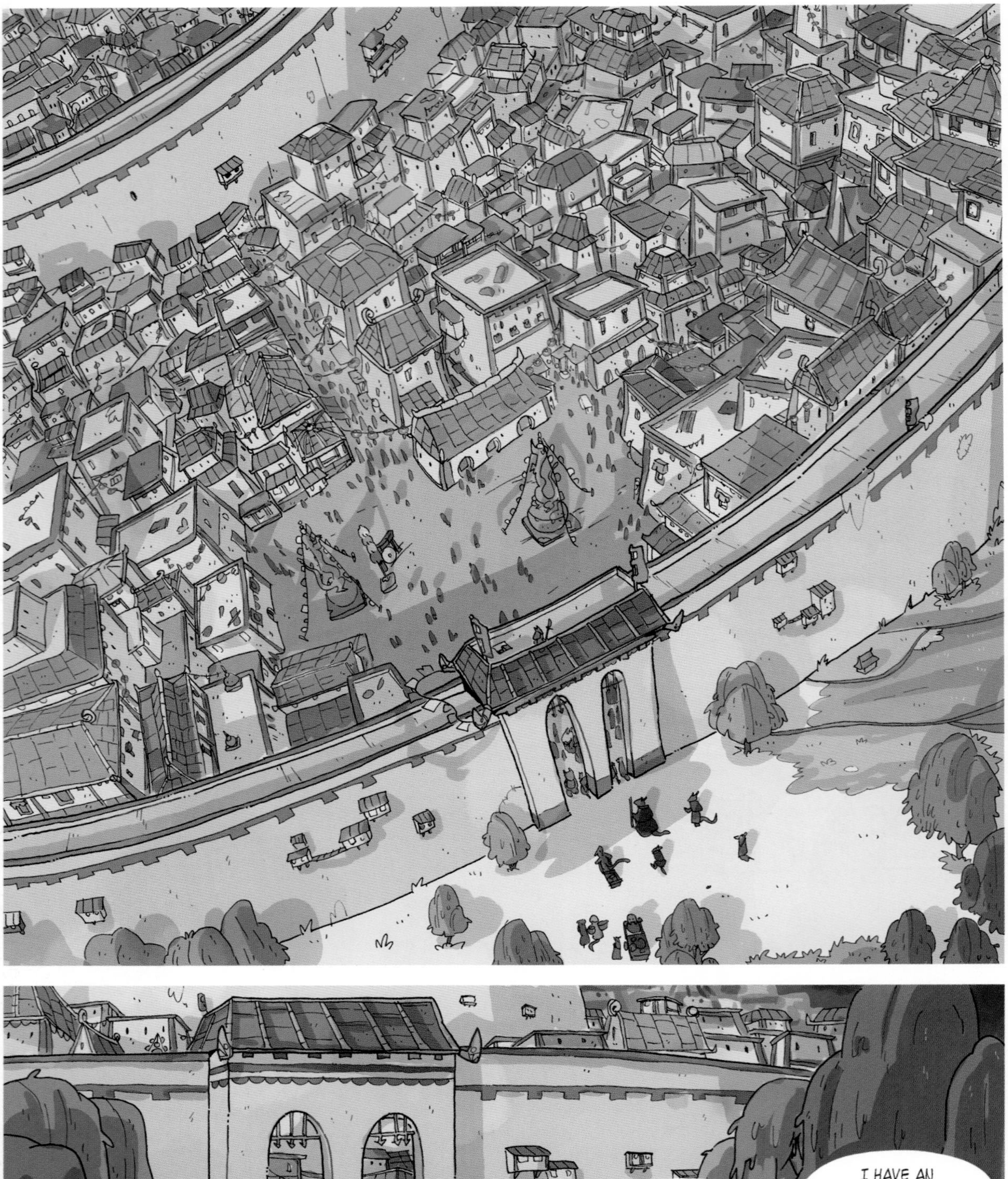

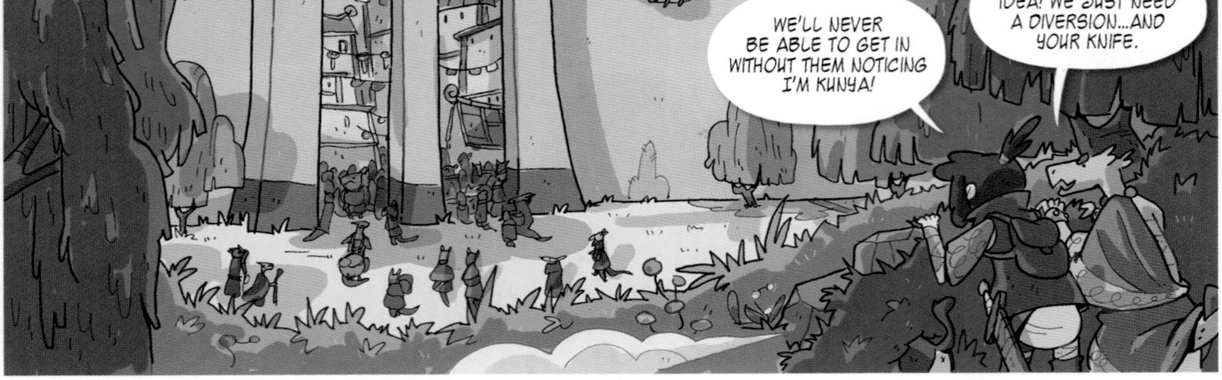
WE'LL NEVER BE ABLE TO GET IN WITHOUT THEM NOTICING I'M KUNYA!
I HAVE AN IDEA! WE JUST NEED A DIVERSION...AND YOUR KNIFE.

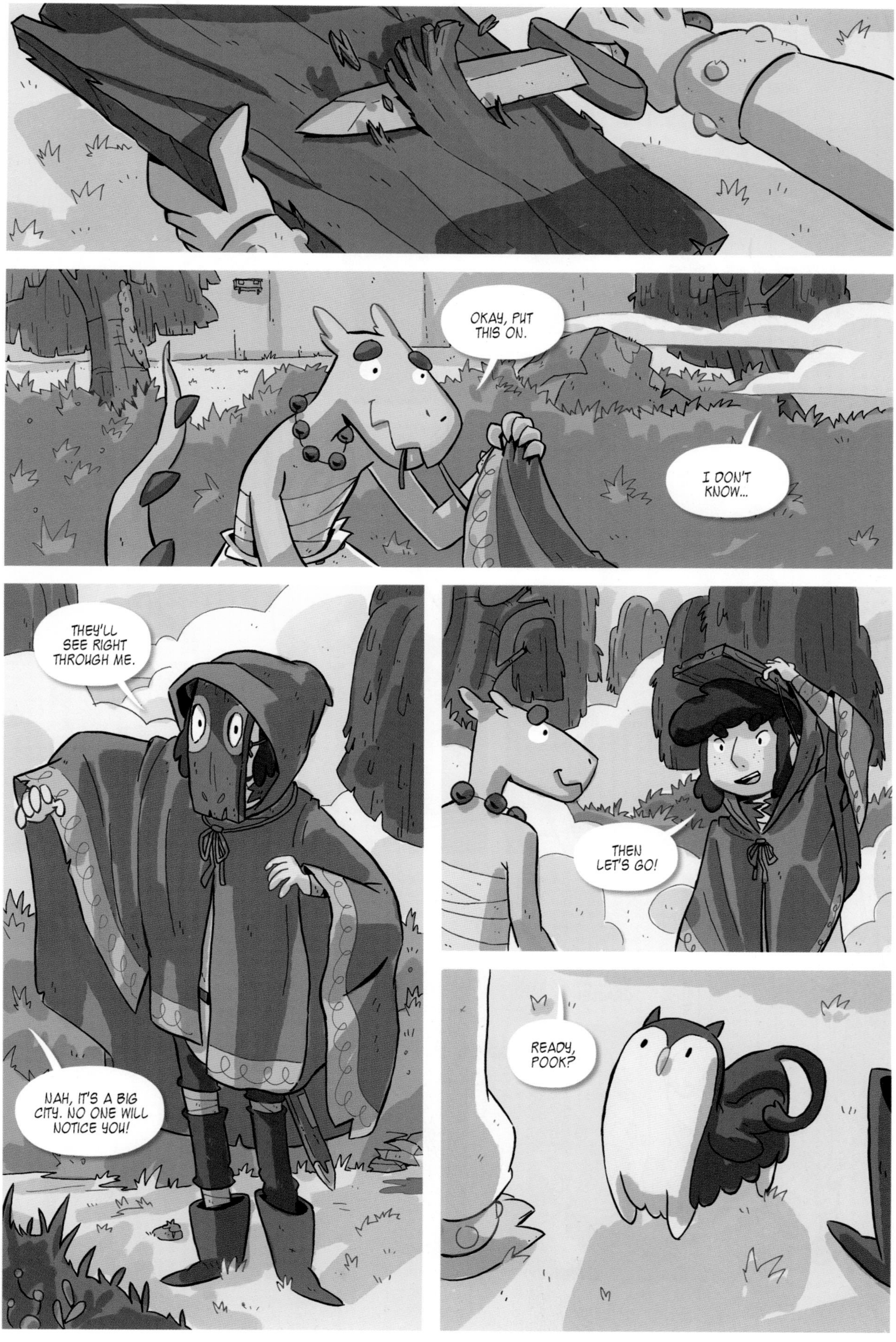
OKAY, PUT THIS ON.
I DON'T KNOW...
THEY'LL SEE RIGHT THROUGH ME.
NAH, IT'S A BIG CITY. NO ONE WILL NOTICE YOU!
THEN LET'S GO!
READY, POOK?

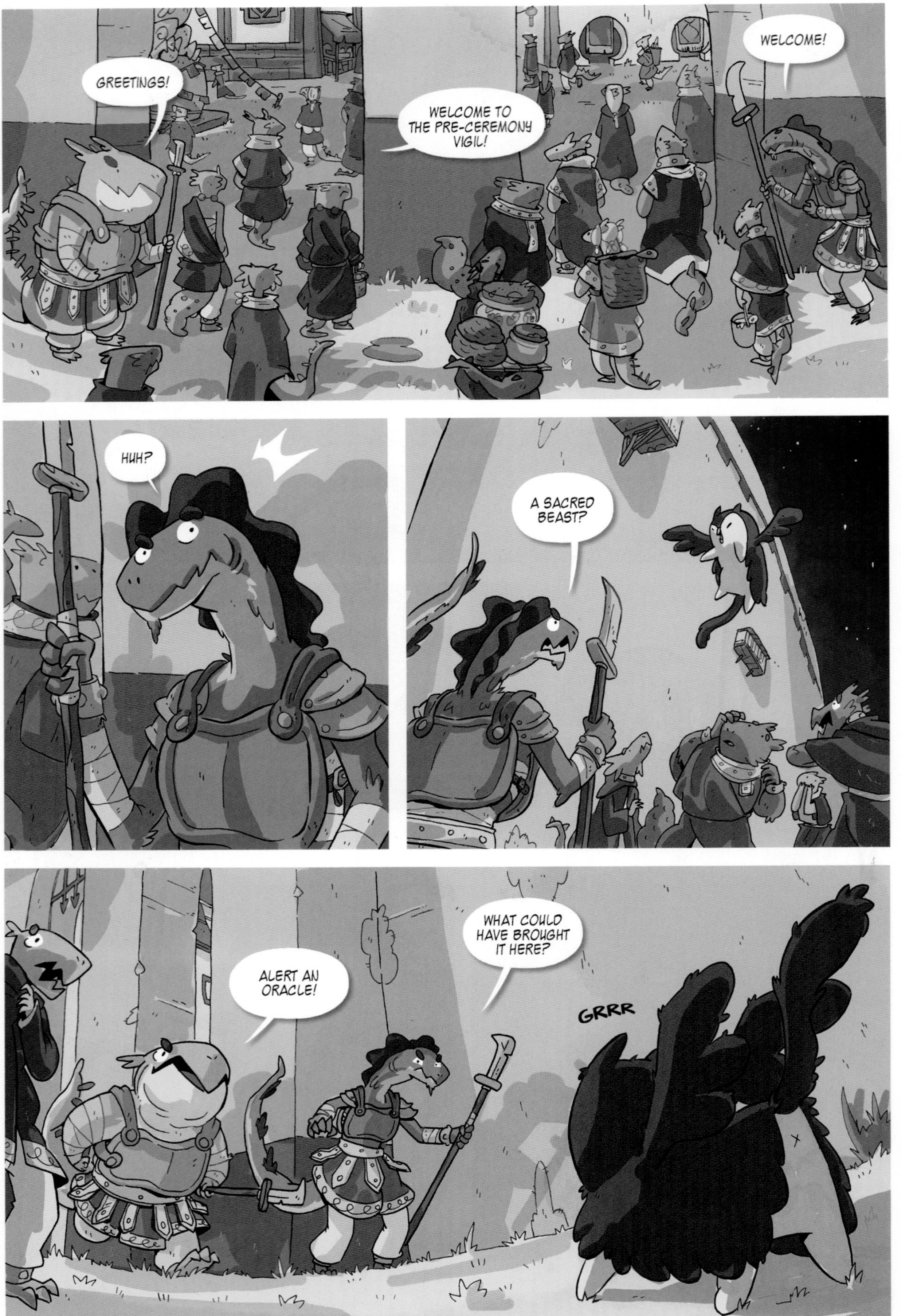
GREETINGS!
WELCOME TO THE PRE-CEREMONY VIGIL!
WELCOME!
HUH?
A SACRED BEAST?
ALERT AN ORACLE!
WHAT COULD HAVE BROUGHT IT HERE?
GRRR

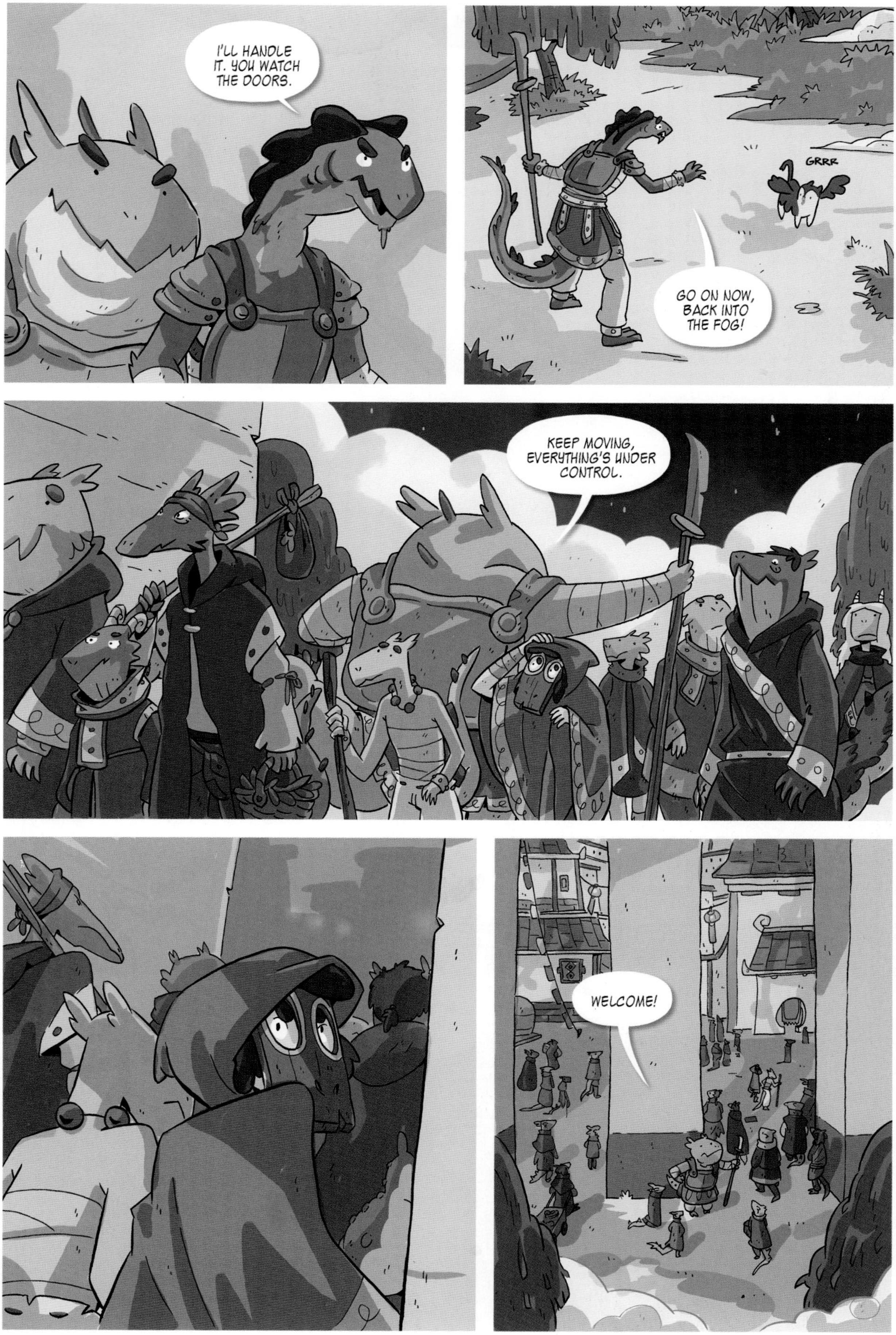
I'LL HANDLE IT. YOU WATCH THE DOORS.
GRRR
GO ON NOW, BACK INTO THE FOG!
KEEP MOVING, EVERYTHING'S UNDER CONTROL.
WELCOME!

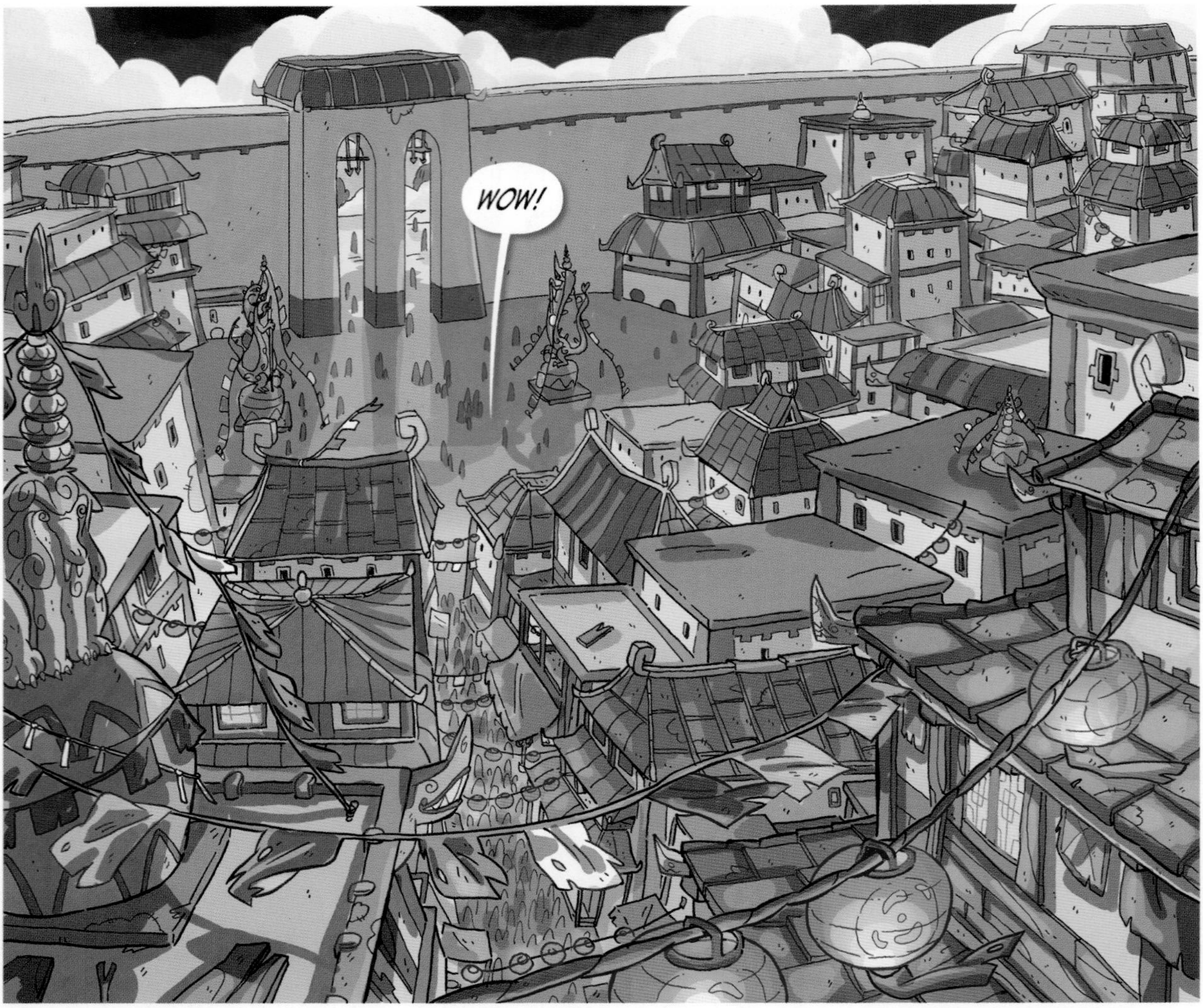
WOW!

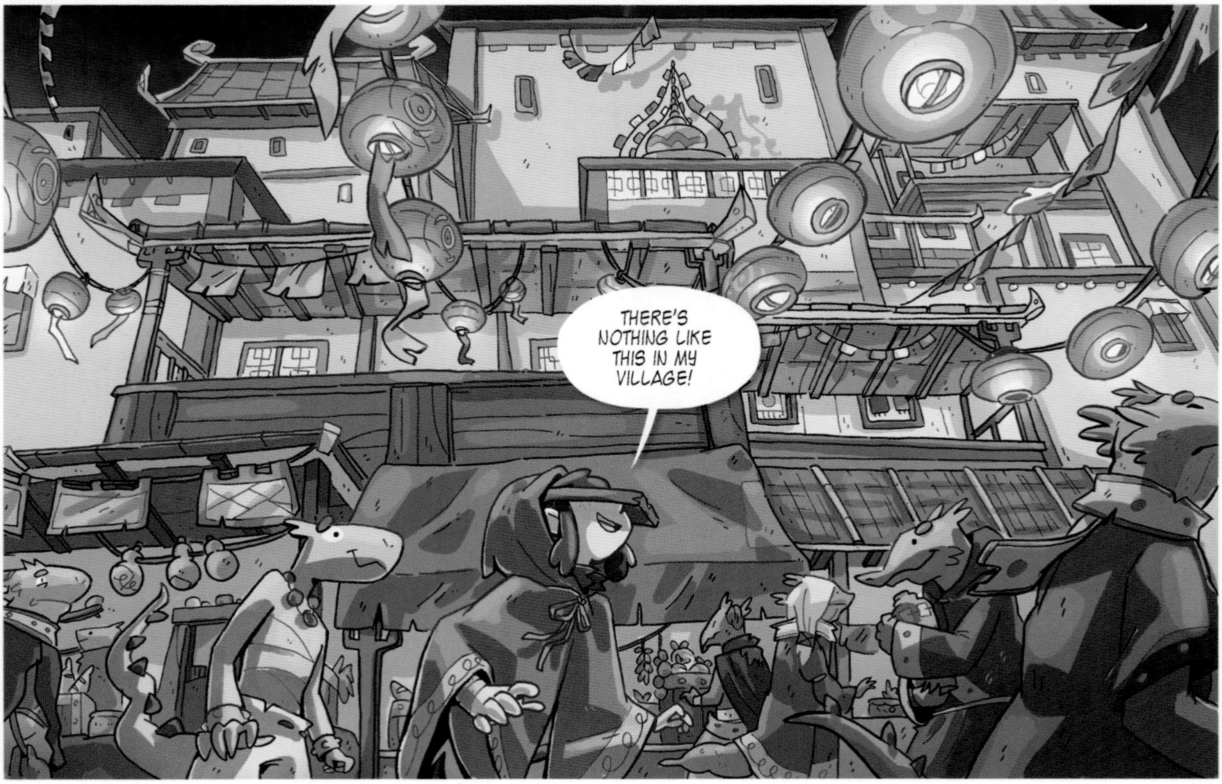
THERE'S NOTHING LIKE THIS IN MY VILLAGE!

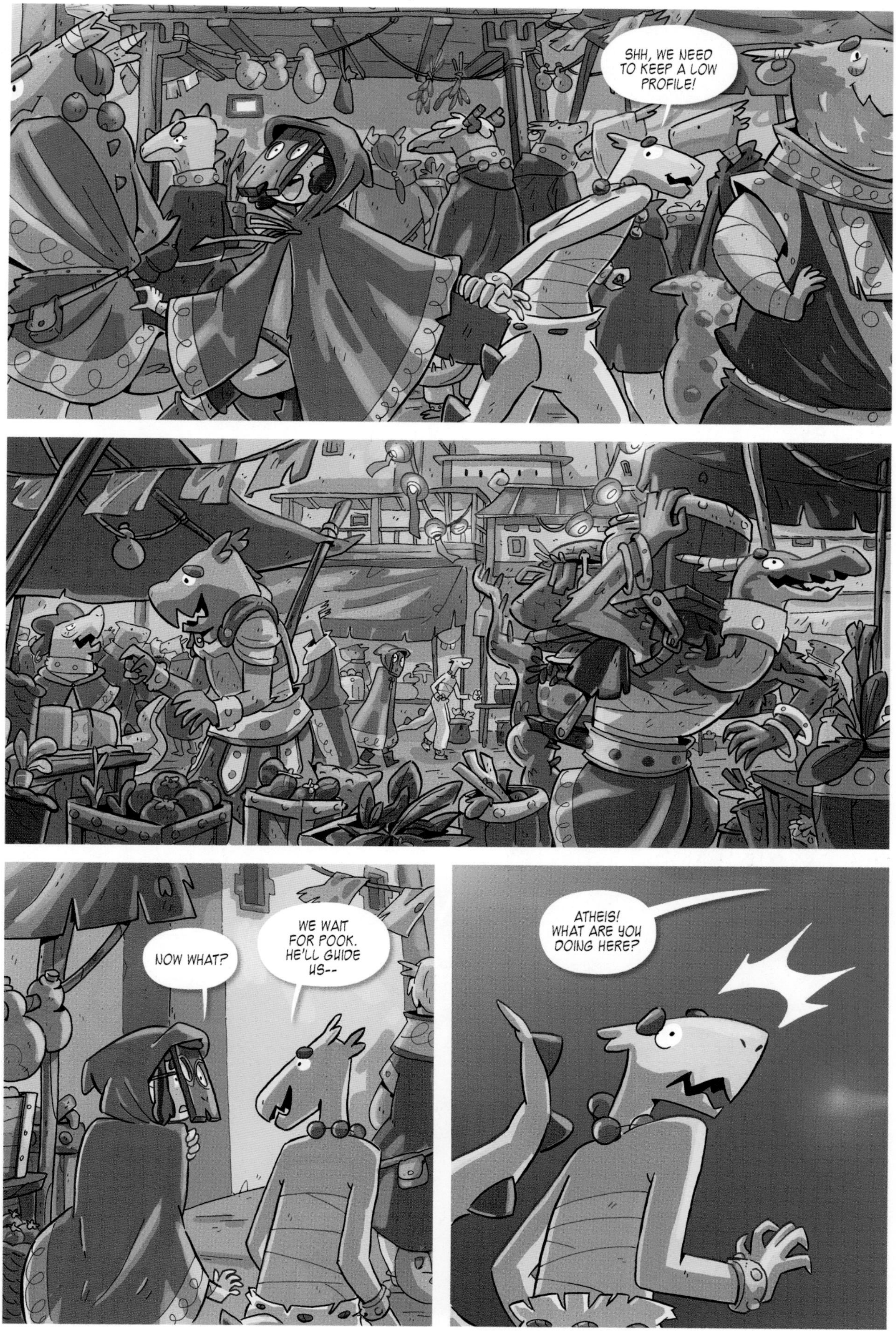
SHH, WE NEED TO KEEP A LOW PROFILE!
NOW WHAT?
WE WAIT FOR POOK. HE'LL GUIDE US--
ATHEIS! WHAT ARE YOU DOING HERE?

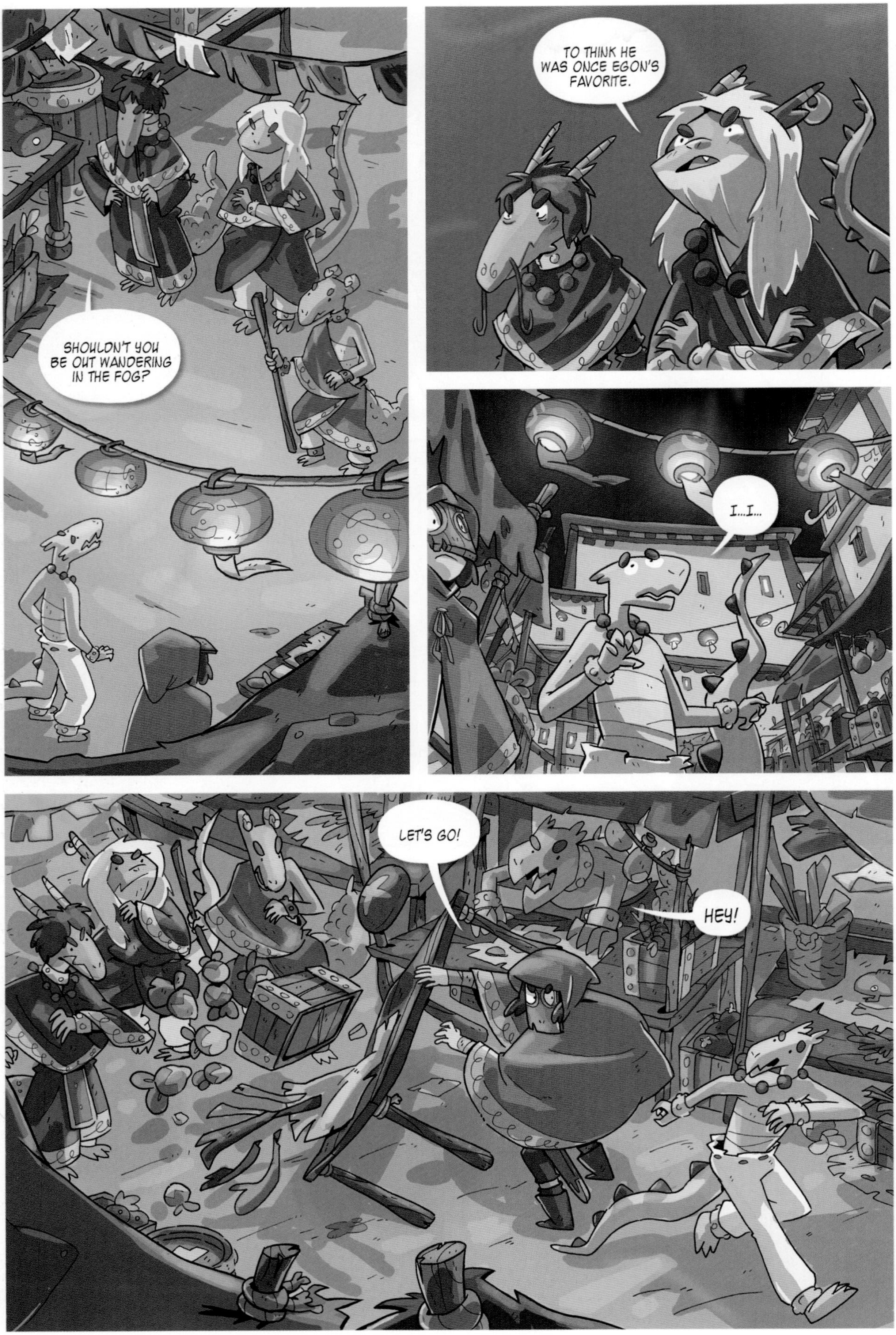
SHOULDN'T YOU BE OUT WANDERING IN THE FOG?
TO THINK HE WAS ONCE EGON'S FAVORITE.
I...I...
LET'S GO!
HEY!

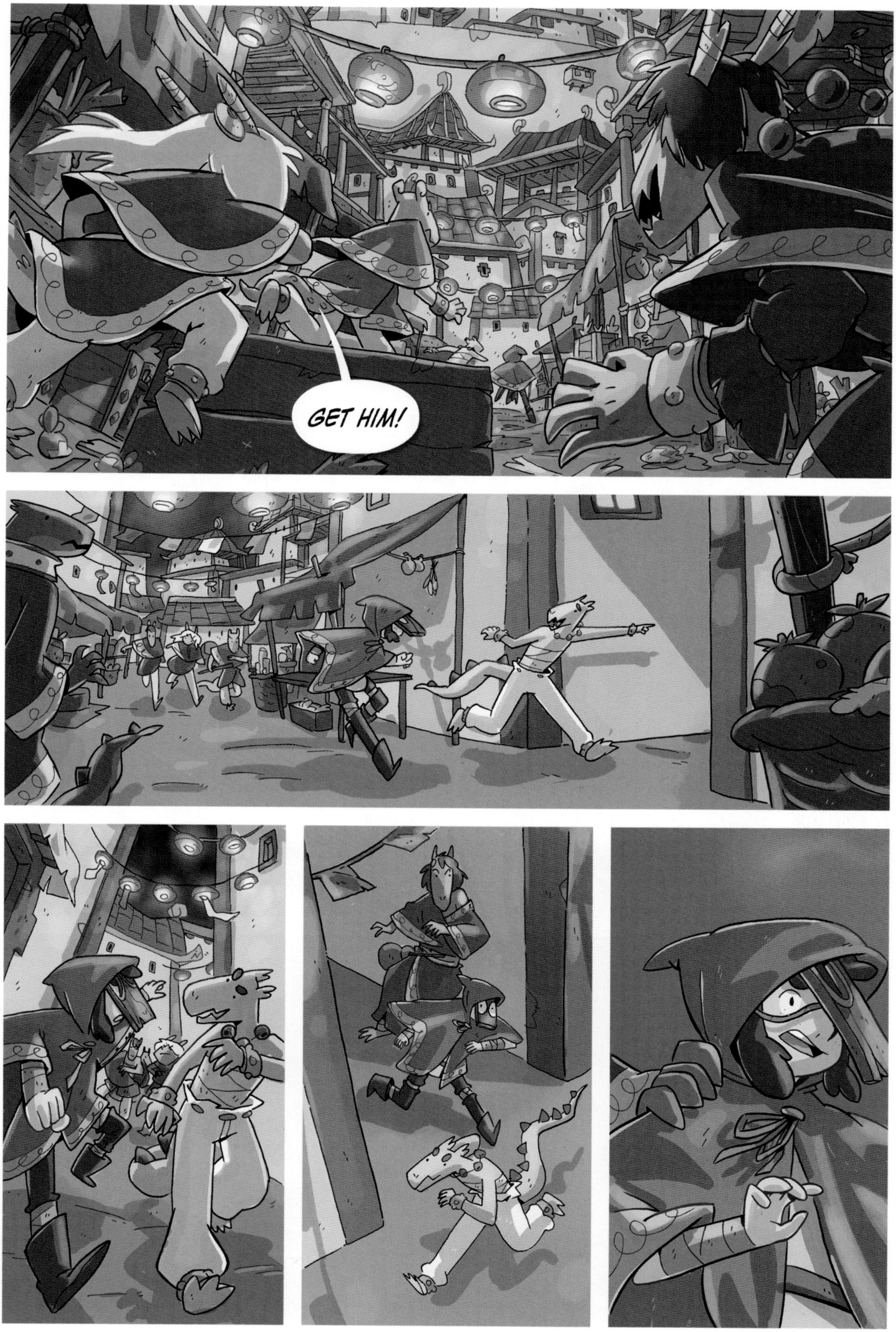
GET HIM!

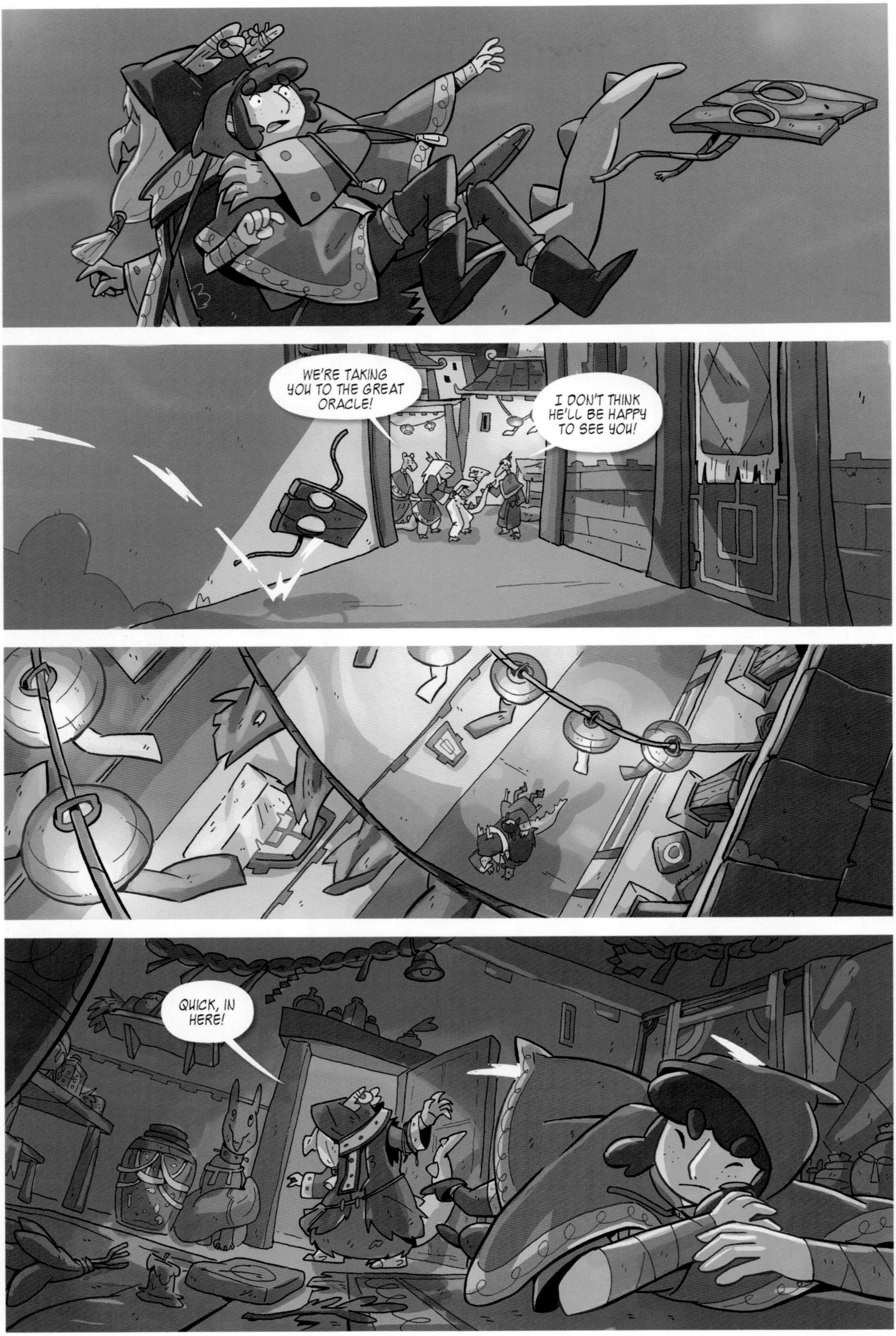
WE'RE TAKING YOU TO THE GREAT ORACLE!
I DON'T THINK HE'LL BE HAPPY TO SEE YOU!
QUICK, IN HERE!

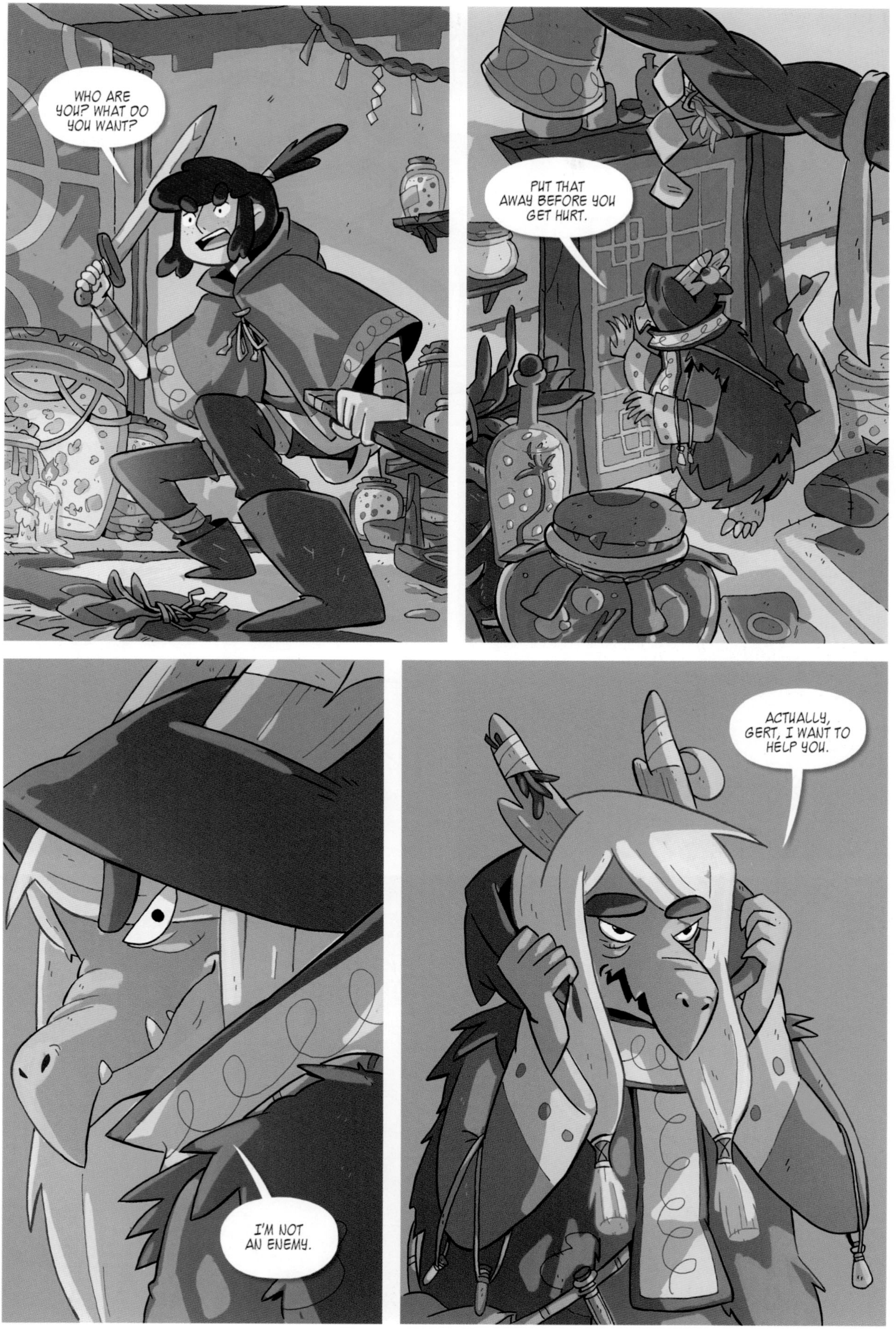
WHO ARE YOU? WHAT DO YOU WANT?
PUT THAT AWAY BEFORE YOU GET HURT.
I'M NOT AN ENEMY.
ACTUALLY, GERT, I WANT TO HELP YOU.

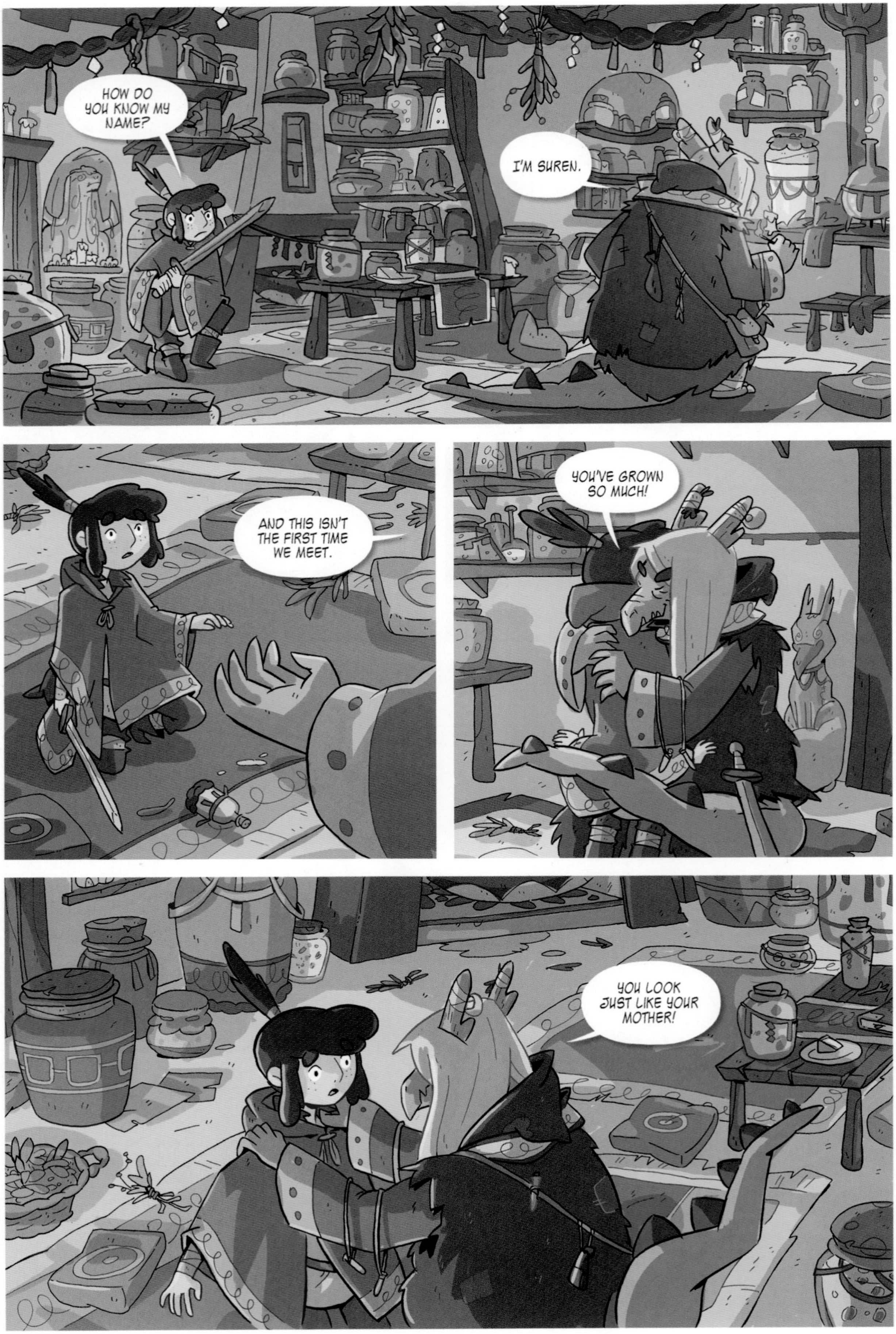
HOW DO YOU KNOW MY NAME?
I'M SUREN.
AND THIS ISN'T THE FIRST TIME WE MEET.
YOU'VE GROWN SO MUCH!
YOU LOOK JUST LIKE YOUR MOTHER!

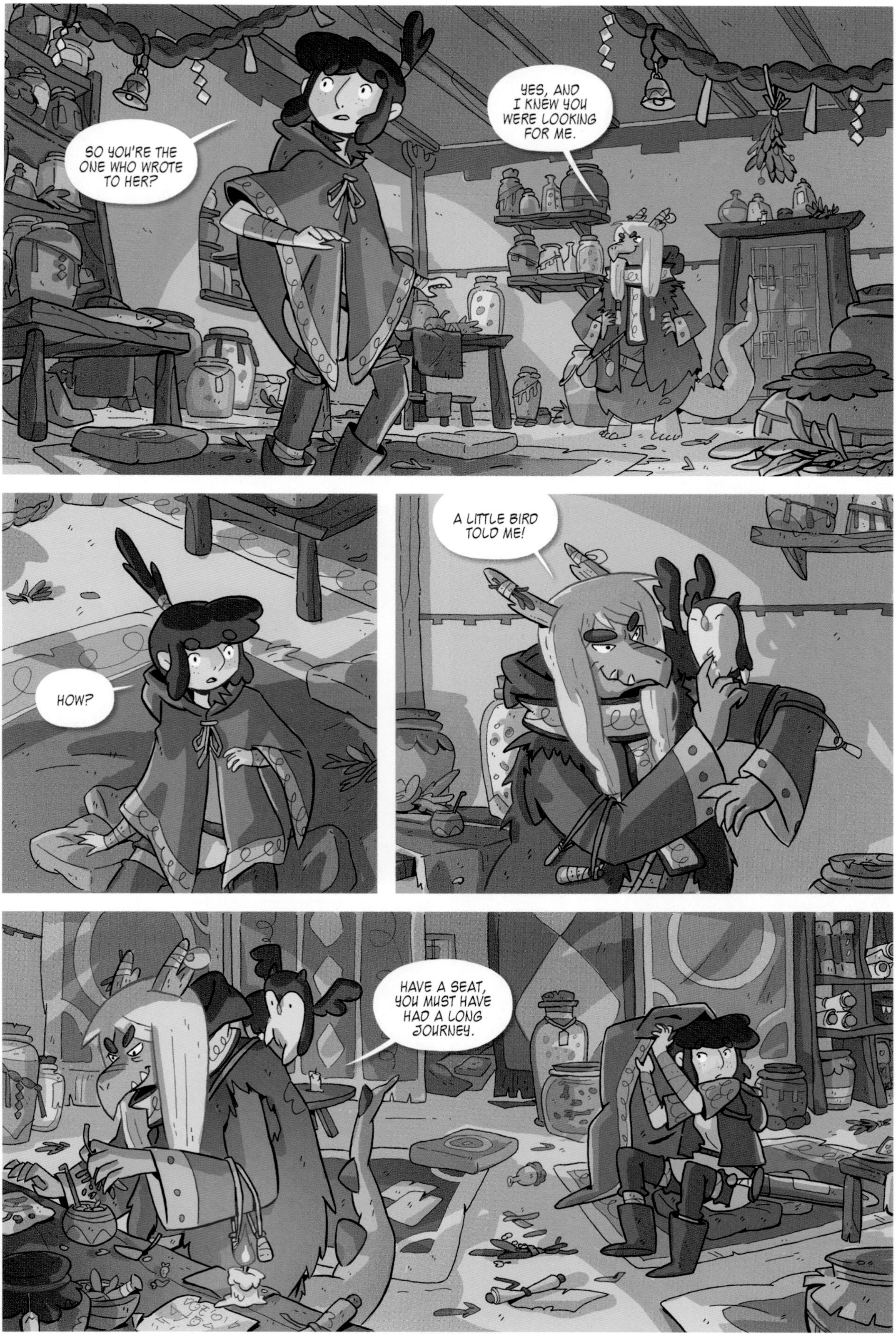
SO YOU'RE THE ONE WHO WROTE TO HER?
YES, AND I KNEW YOU WERE LOOKING FOR ME.
HOW?
A LITTLE BIRD TOLD ME!
HAVE A SEAT, YOU MUST HAVE HAD A LONG JOURNEY.

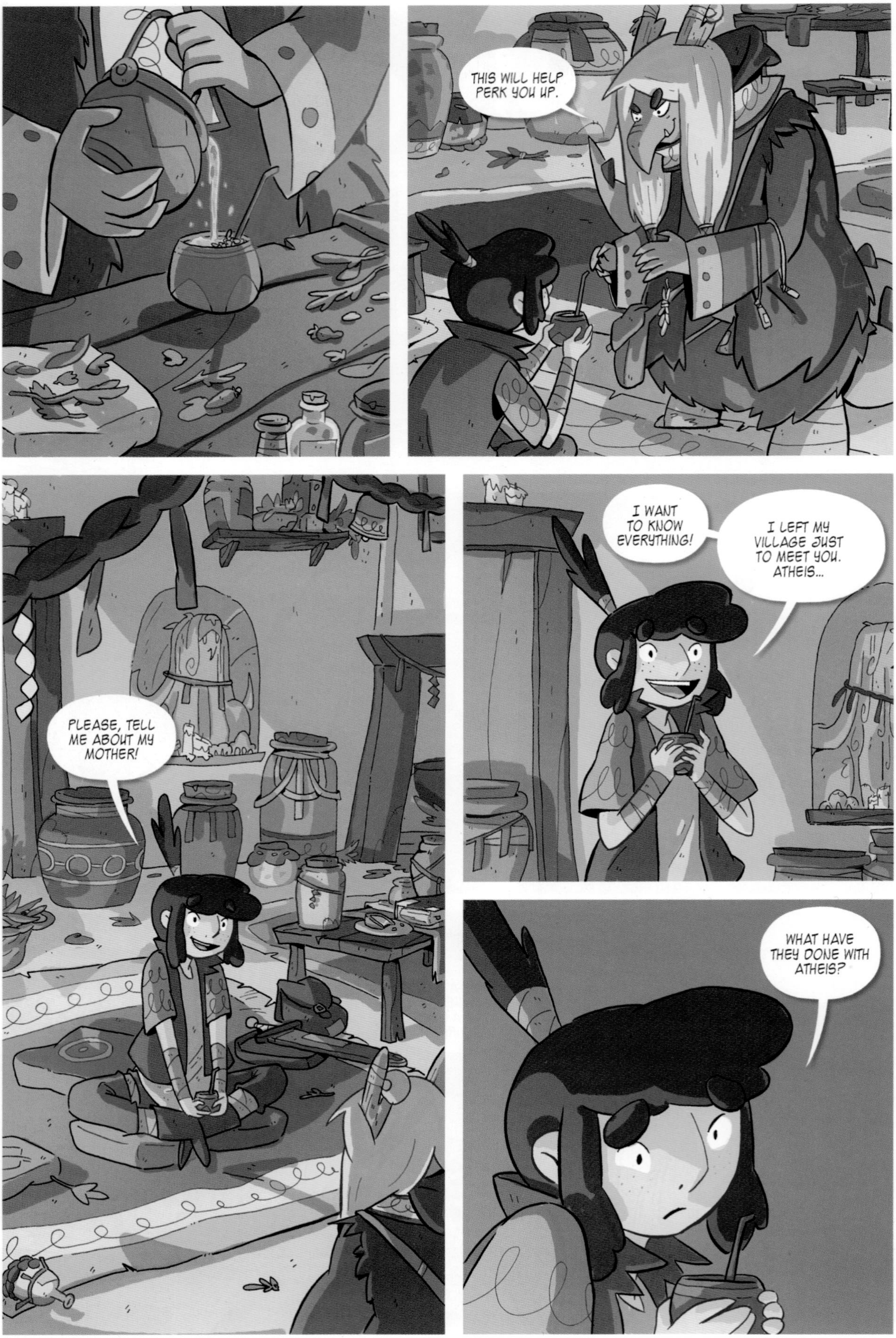
THIS WILL HELP PERK YOU UP.
PLEASE, TELL ME ABOUT MY MOTHER!
I WANT TO KNOW EVERYTHING!
I LEFT MY VILLAGE JUST TO MEET YOU. ATHEIS...
WHAT HAVE THEY DONE WITH ATHEIS?

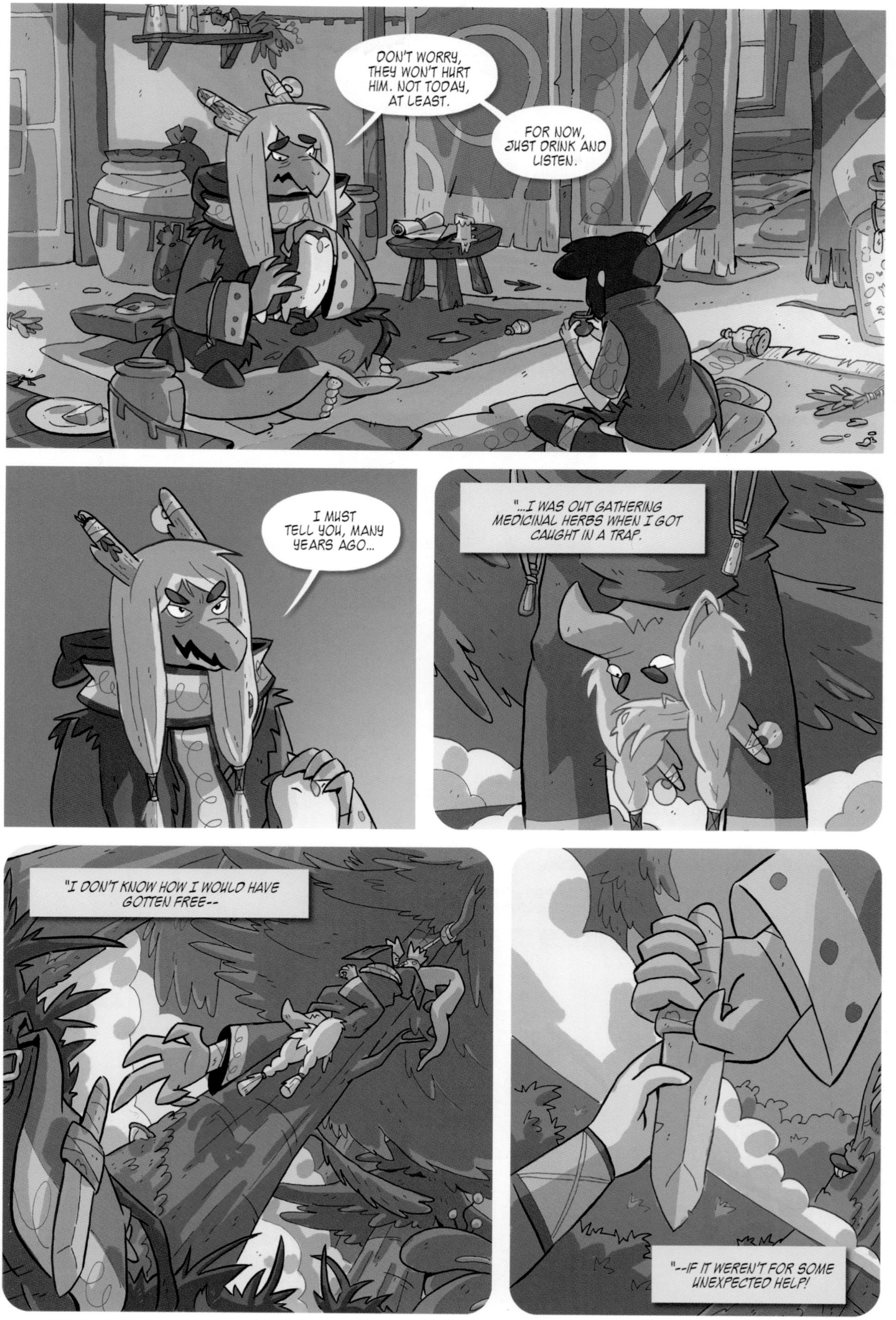
DON'T WORRY, THEY WON'T HURT HIM. NOT TODAY, AT LEAST.
FOR NOW, JUST DRINK AND LISTEN.
I MUST TELL YOU, MANY YEARS AGO...
"...I WAS OUT GATHERING MEDICINAL HERBS WHEN I GOT CAUGHT IN A TRAP.
"I DON'T KNOW HOW I WOULD HAVE GOTTEN FREE--
"--IF IT WEREN'T FOR SOME UNEXPECTED HELP!

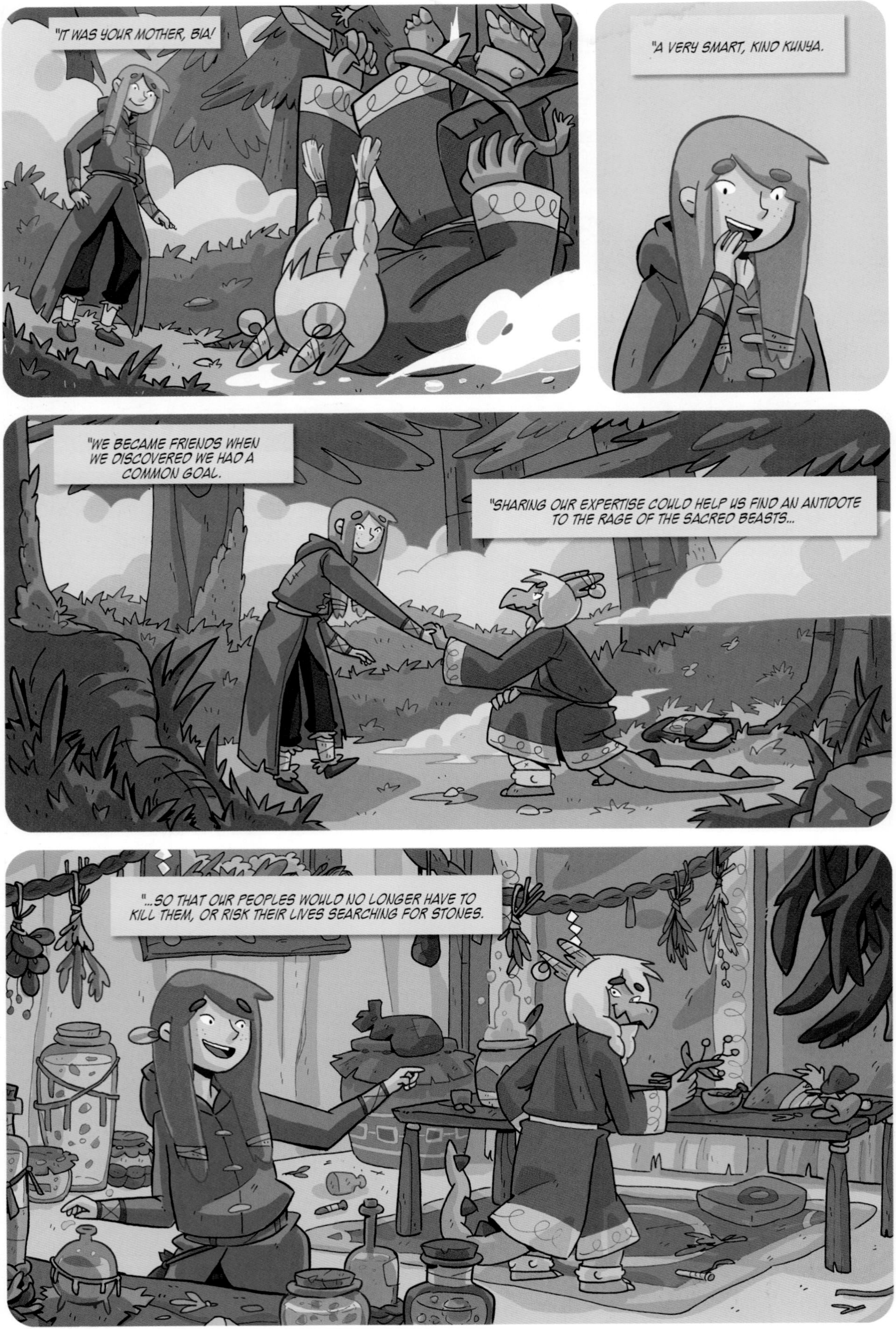
"IT WAS YOUR MOTHER, BIA!
"A VERY SMART, KINO KUNYA.
"WE BECAME FRIENDS WHEN WE DISCOVERED WE HAD A COMMON GOAL.
"SHARING OUR EXPERTISE COULD HELP US FIND AN ANTIDOTE TO THE RAGE OF THE SACRED BEASTS...
"...SO THAT OUR PEOPLES WOULD NO LONGER HAVE TO KILL THEM, OR RISK THEIR LIVES SEARCHING FOR STONES.

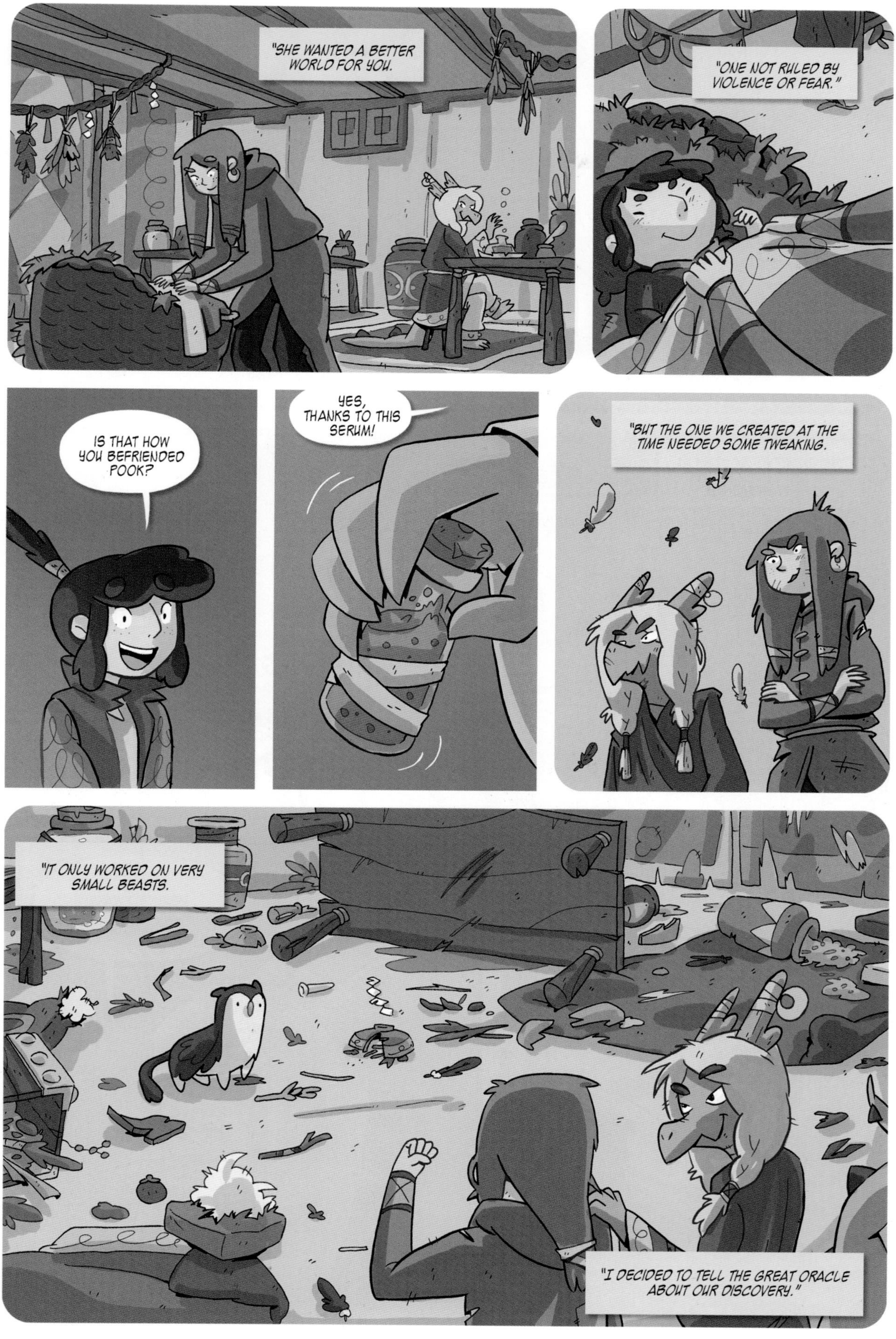
"SHE WANTED A BETTER WORLD FOR YOU.
"ONE NOT RULED BY VIOLENCE OR FEAR."
IS THAT HOW YOU BEFRIENDED POOK?
YES, THANKS TO THIS SERUM!
"BUT THE ONE WE CREATED AT THE TIME NEEDED SOME TWEAKING.
"IT ONLY WORKED ON VERY SMALL BEASTS.
"I DECIDED TO TELL THE GREAT ORACLE ABOUT OUR DISCOVERY."

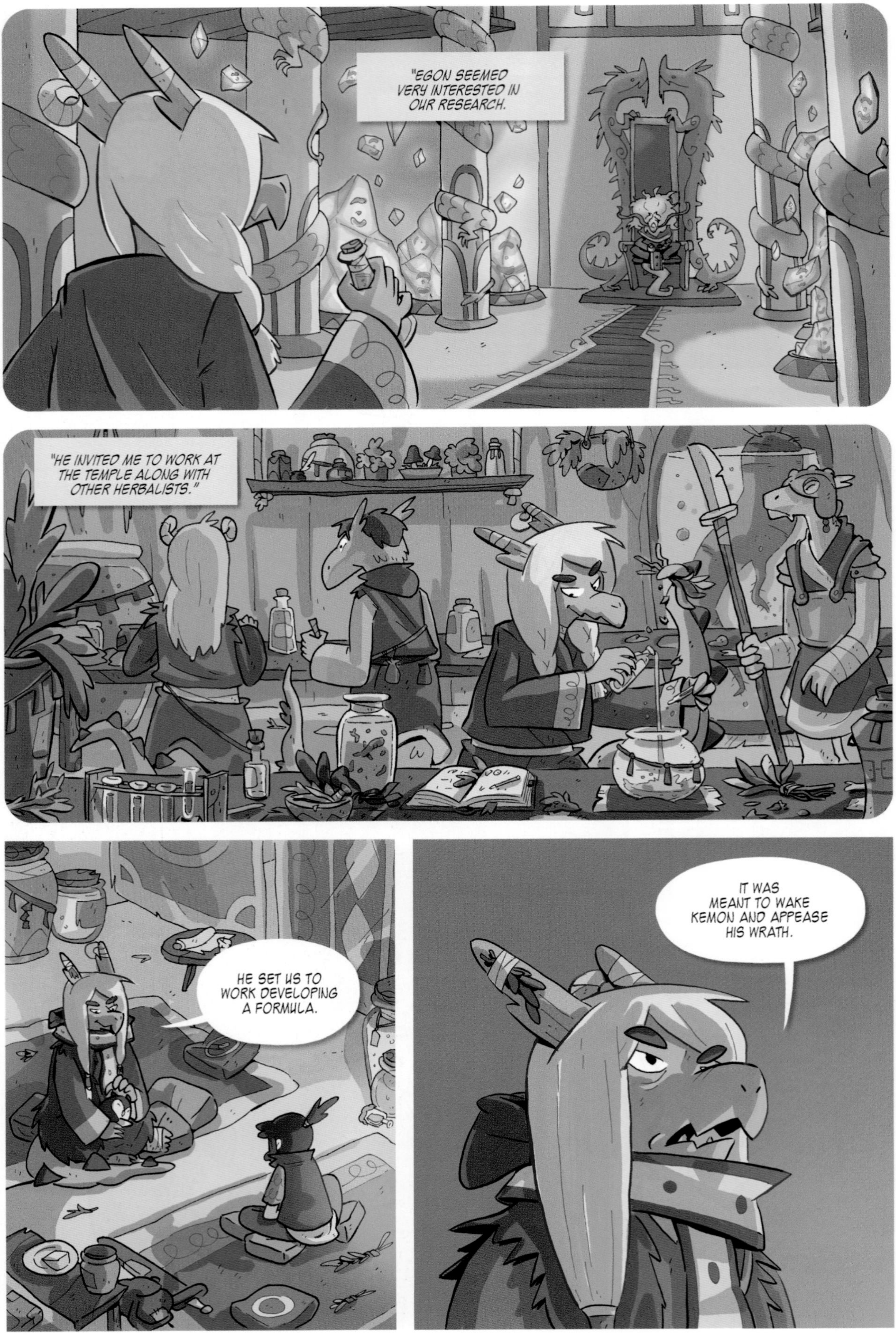
"EGON SEEMED VERY INTERESTED IN OUR RESEARCH.
"HE INVITED ME TO WORK AT THE TEMPLE ALONG WITH OTHER HERBALISTS."
HE SET US TO WORK DEVELOPING A FORMULA.
IT WAS MEANT TO WAKE KEMON AND APPEASE HIS WRATH.

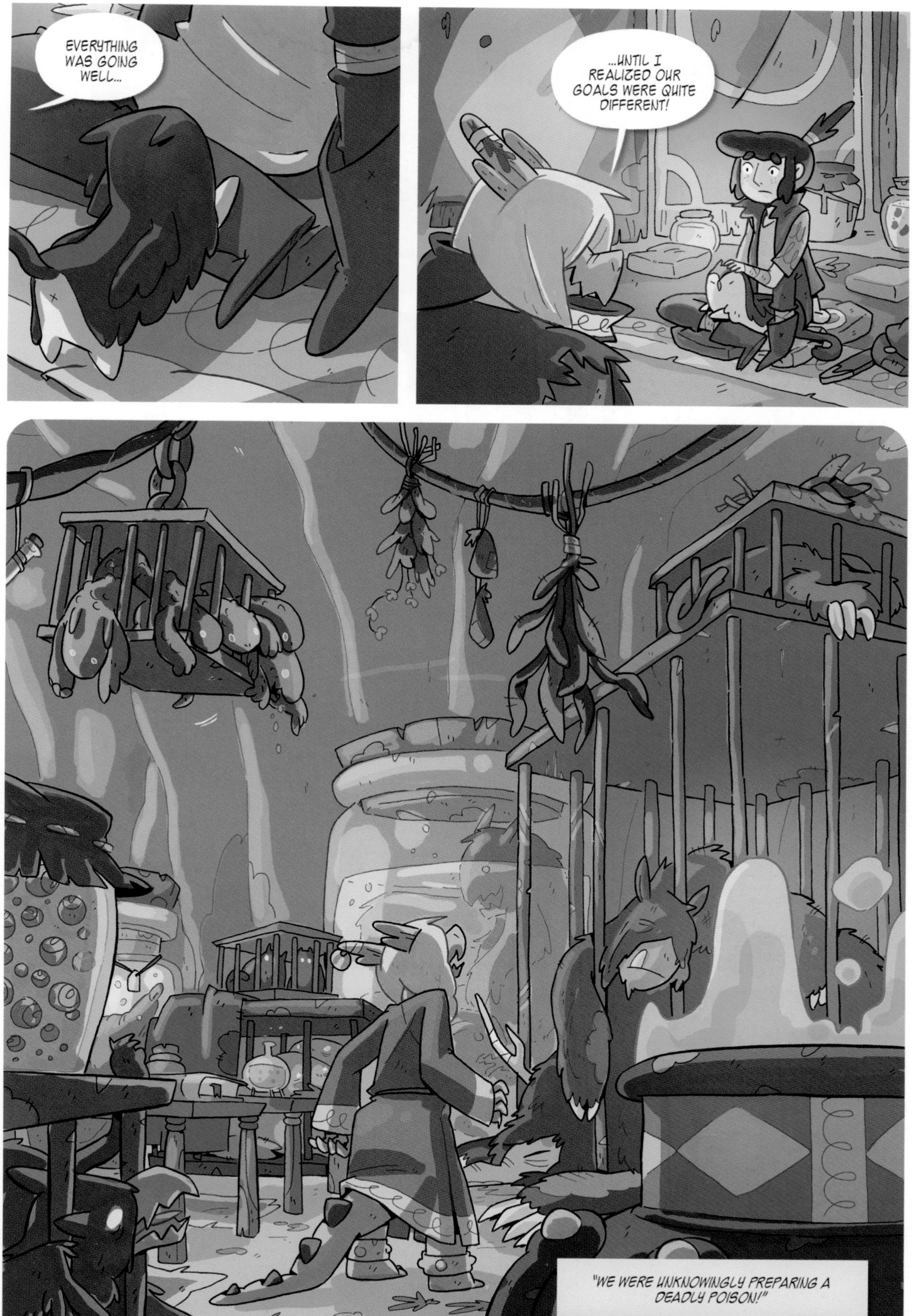
EVERYTHING WAS GOING WELL...
...UNTIL I REALIZED OUR GOALS WERE QUITE DIFFERENT!
"WE WERE UNKNOWINGLY PREPARING A DEADLY POISON!"

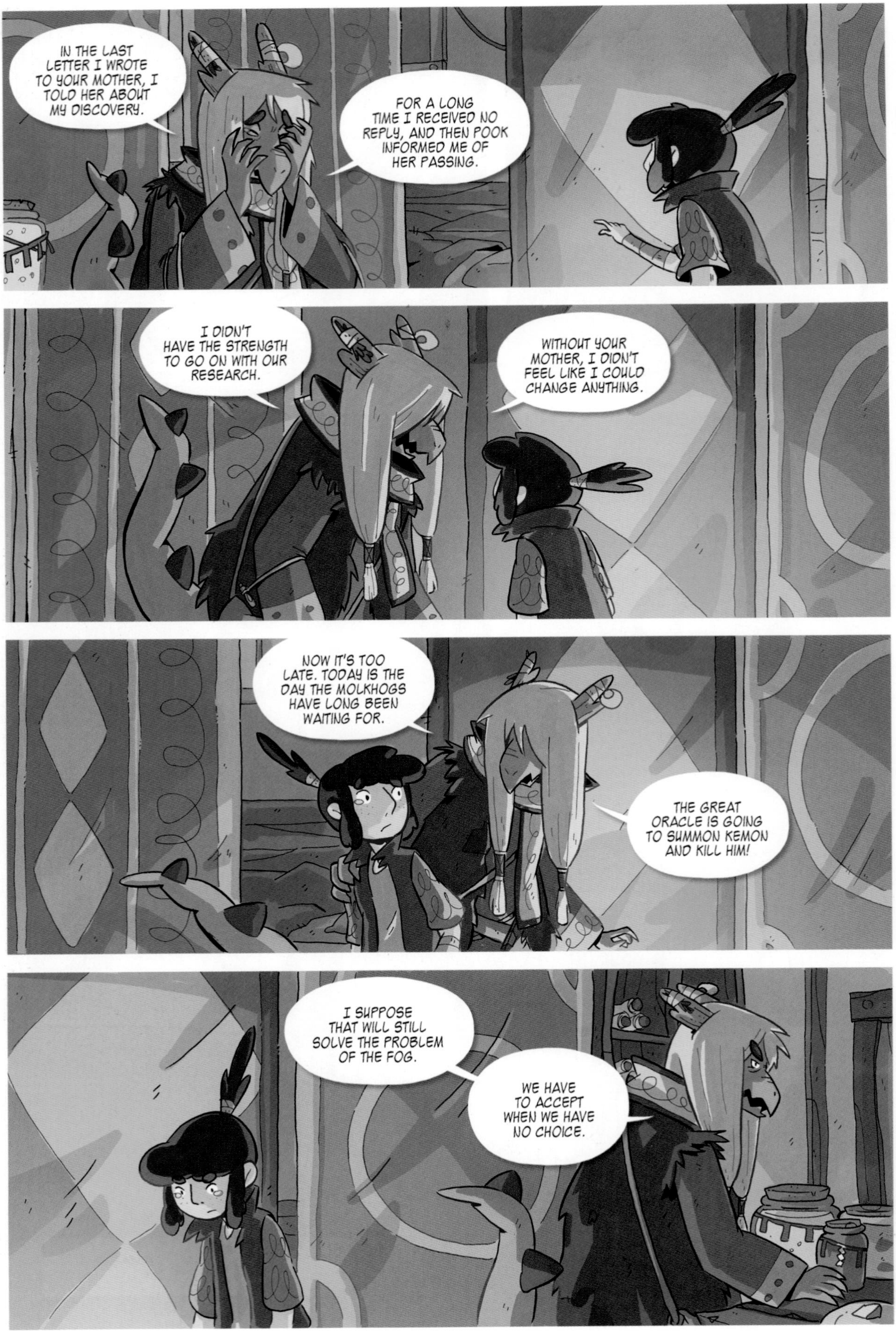
IN THE LAST LETTER I WROTE TO YOUR MOTHER, I TOLD HER ABOUT MY DISCOVERY.
FOR A LONG TIME I RECEIVED NO REPLY, AND THEN POOK INFORMED ME OF HER PASSING.
I DIDN'T HAVE THE STRENGTH TO GO ON WITH OUR RESEARCH.
WITHOUT YOUR MOTHER, I DIDN'T FEEL LIKE I COULD CHANGE ANYTHING.
NOW IT'S TOO LATE. TODAY IS THE DAY THE MOLKHOGS HAVE LONG BEEN WAITING FOR.
THE GREAT ORACLE IS GOING TO SUMMON KEMON AND KILL HIM!
I SUPPOSE THAT WILL STILL SOLVE THE PROBLEM OF THE FOG.
WE HAVE TO ACCEPT WHEN WE HAVE NO CHOICE.

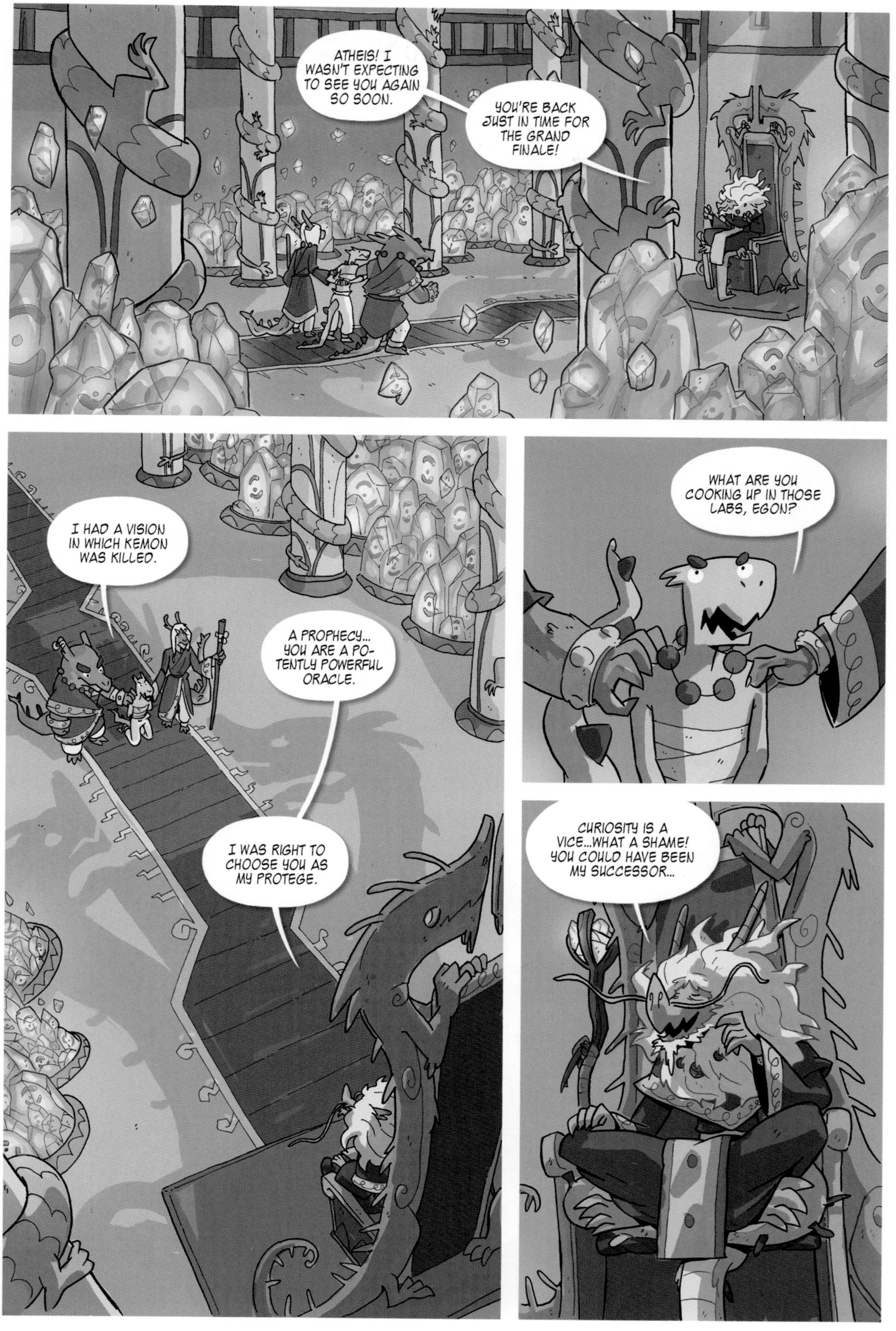
ATHEIS! I WASN'T EXPECTING TO SEE YOU AGAIN SO SOON.
YOU'RE BACK JUST IN TIME FOR THE GRAND FINALE!
I HAD A VISION IN WHICH KEMON WAS KILLED.
A PROPHECY... YOU ARE A POTENTLY POWERFUL ORACLE.
I WAS RIGHT TO CHOOSE YOU AS MY PROTEGE.
WHAT ARE YOU COOKING UP IN THOSE LABS, EGON?
CURIOSITY IS A VICE...WHAT A SHAME! YOU COULD HAVE BEEN MY SUCCESSOR...

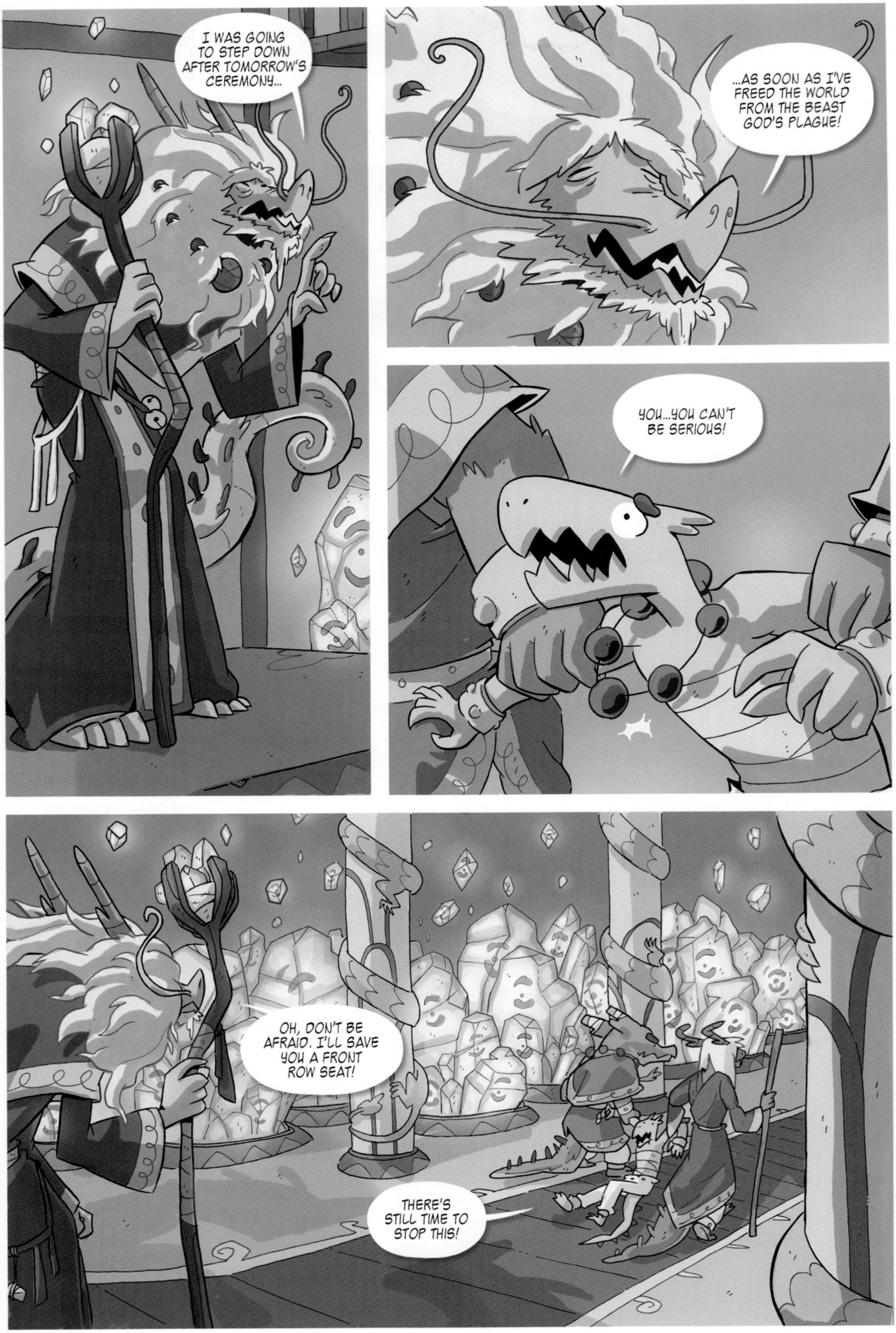

I WAS GOING TO STEP DOWN AFTER TOMORROW'S CEREMONY...
...AS SOON AS I'VE FREED THE WORLD FROM THE BEAST GOD'S PLAGUE!
YOU...YOU CAN'T BE SERIOUS!
OH, DON'T BE AFRAID. I'LL SAVE YOU A FRONT ROW SEAT!
THERE'S STILL TIME TO STOP THIS!

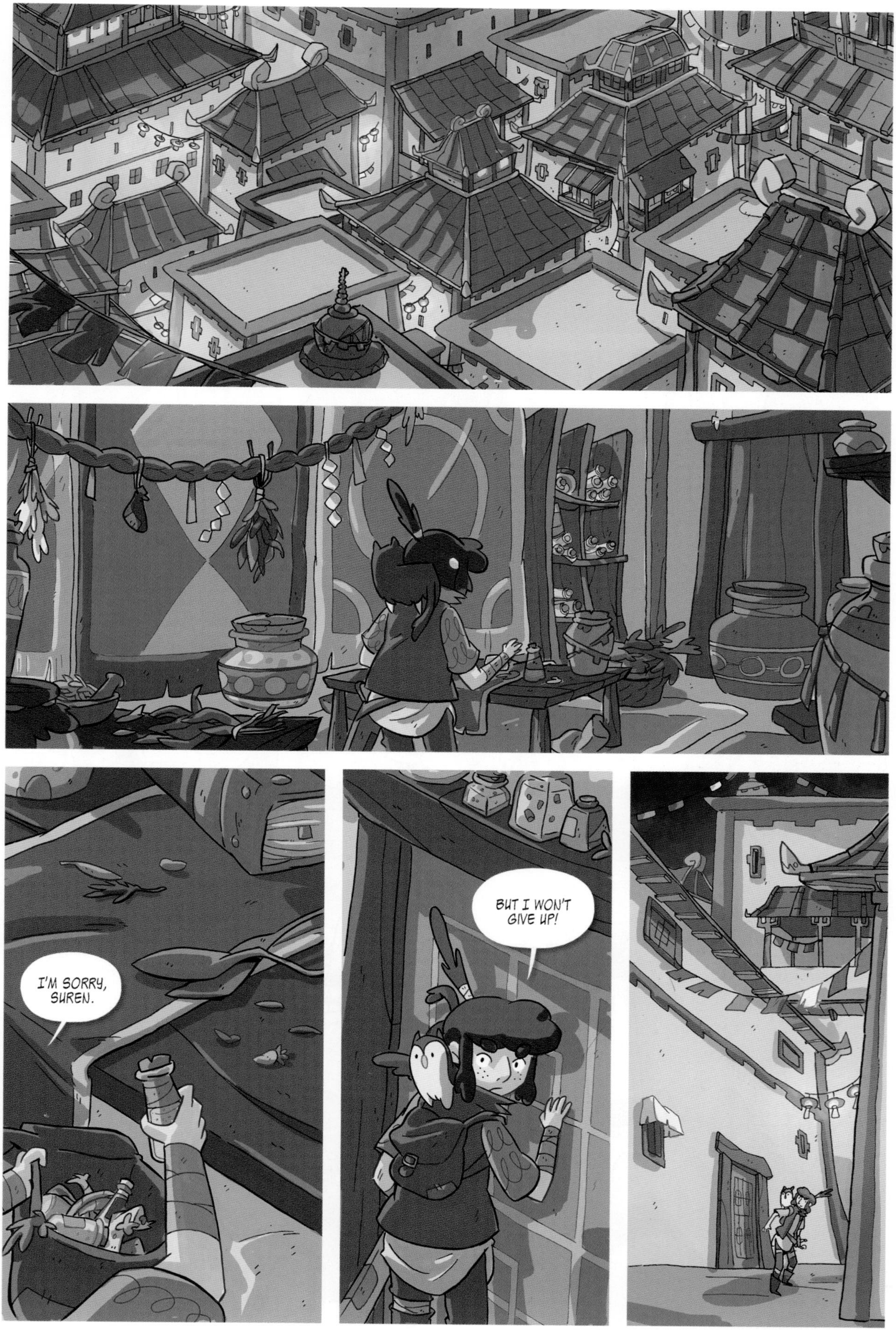
I'M SORRY, SUREN.
BUT I WON'T GIVE UP!

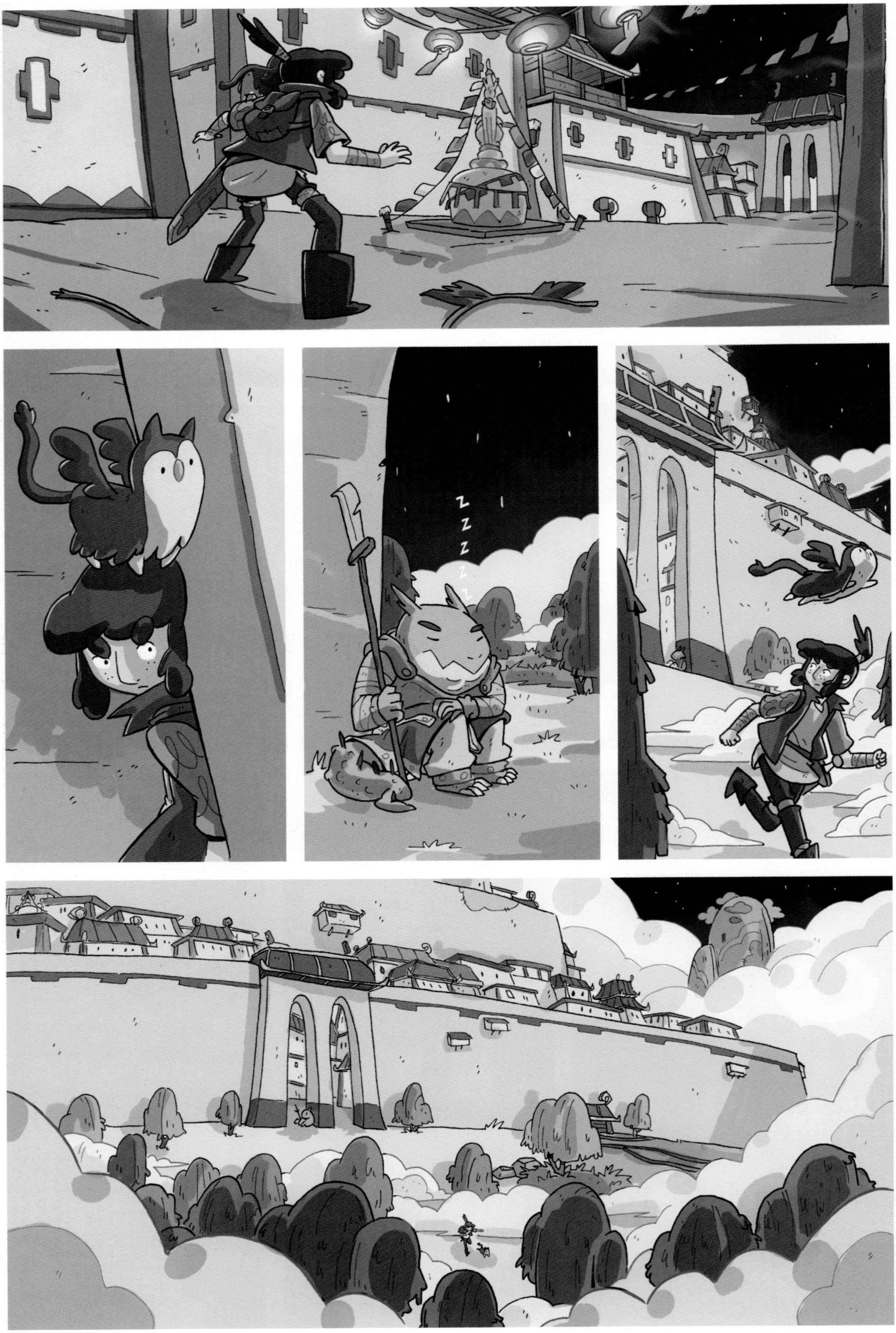
ZZZZ

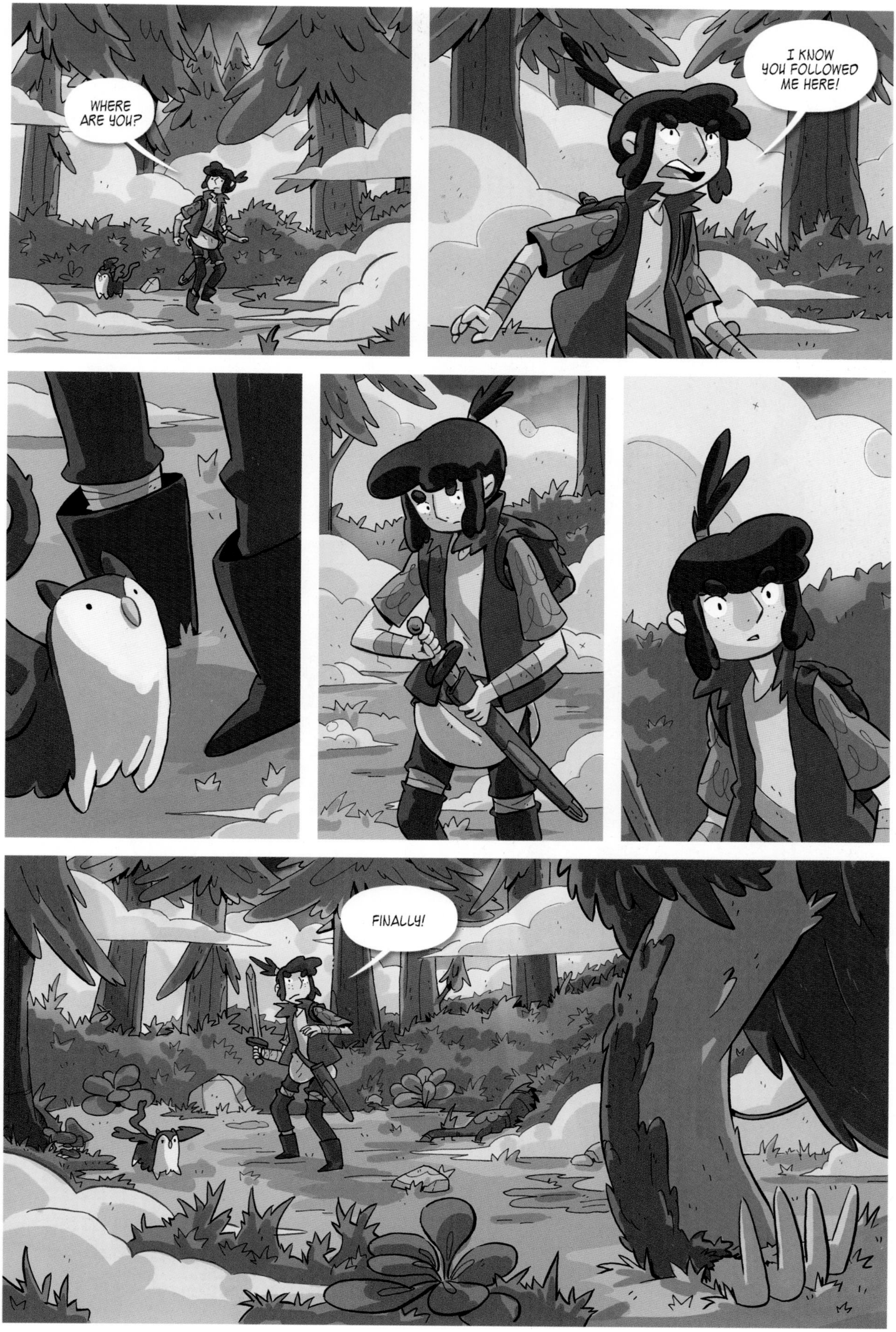
WHERE ARE YOU?
I KNOW YOU FOLLOWED ME HERE!
FINALLY!

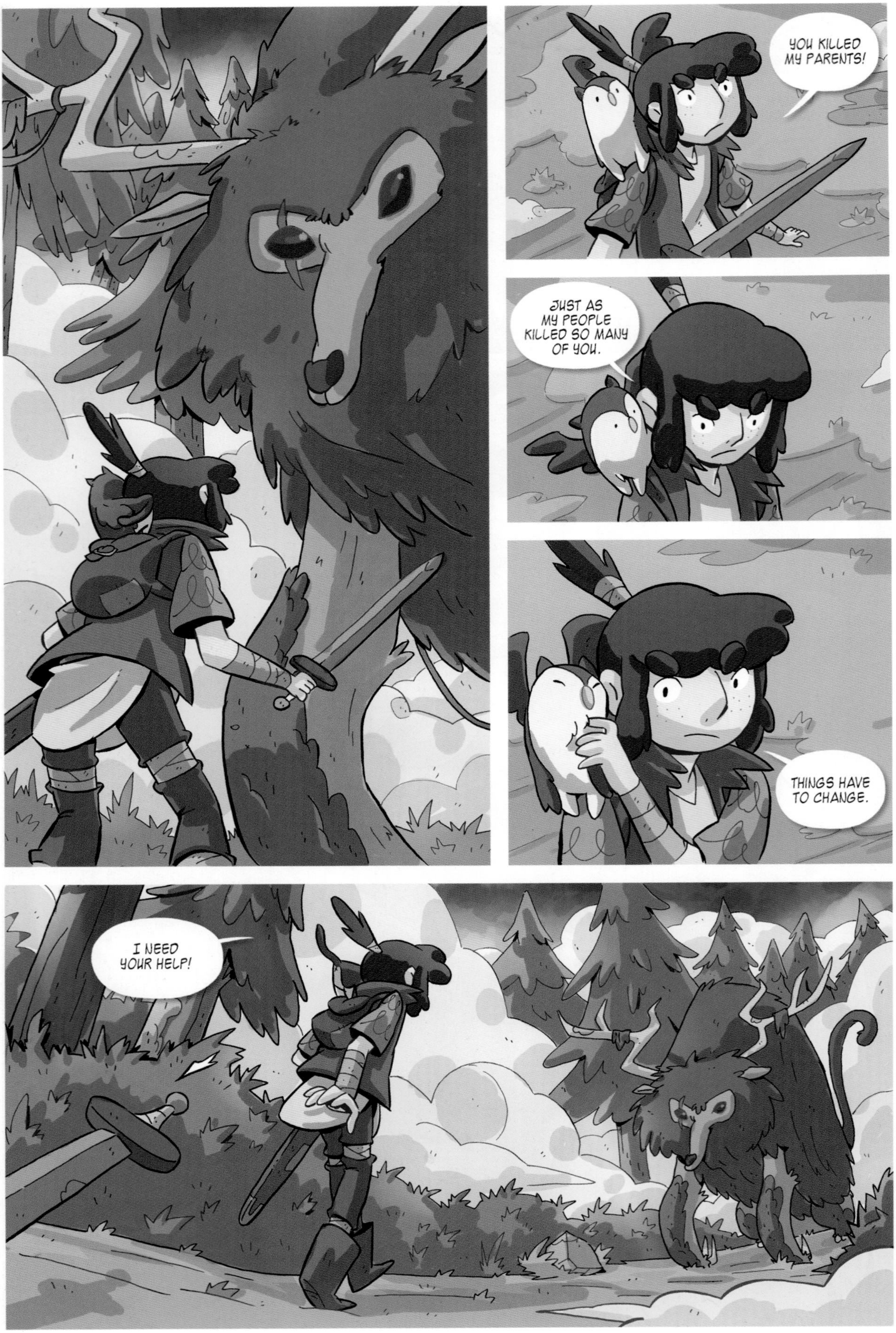
YOU KILLED MY PARENTS!
JUST AS MY PEOPLE KILLED SO MANY OF YOU.
THINGS HAVE TO CHANGE.
I NEED YOUR HELP!

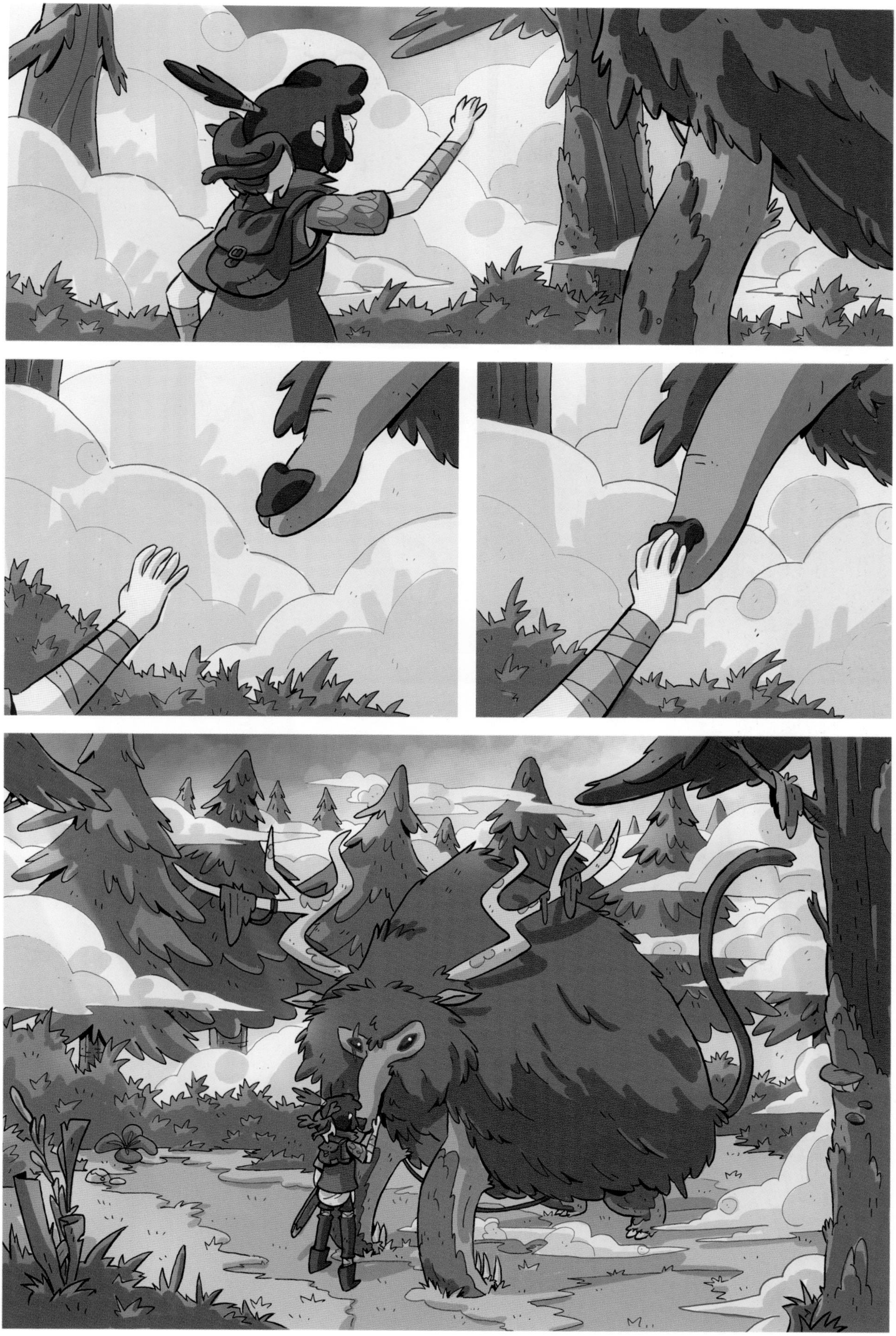

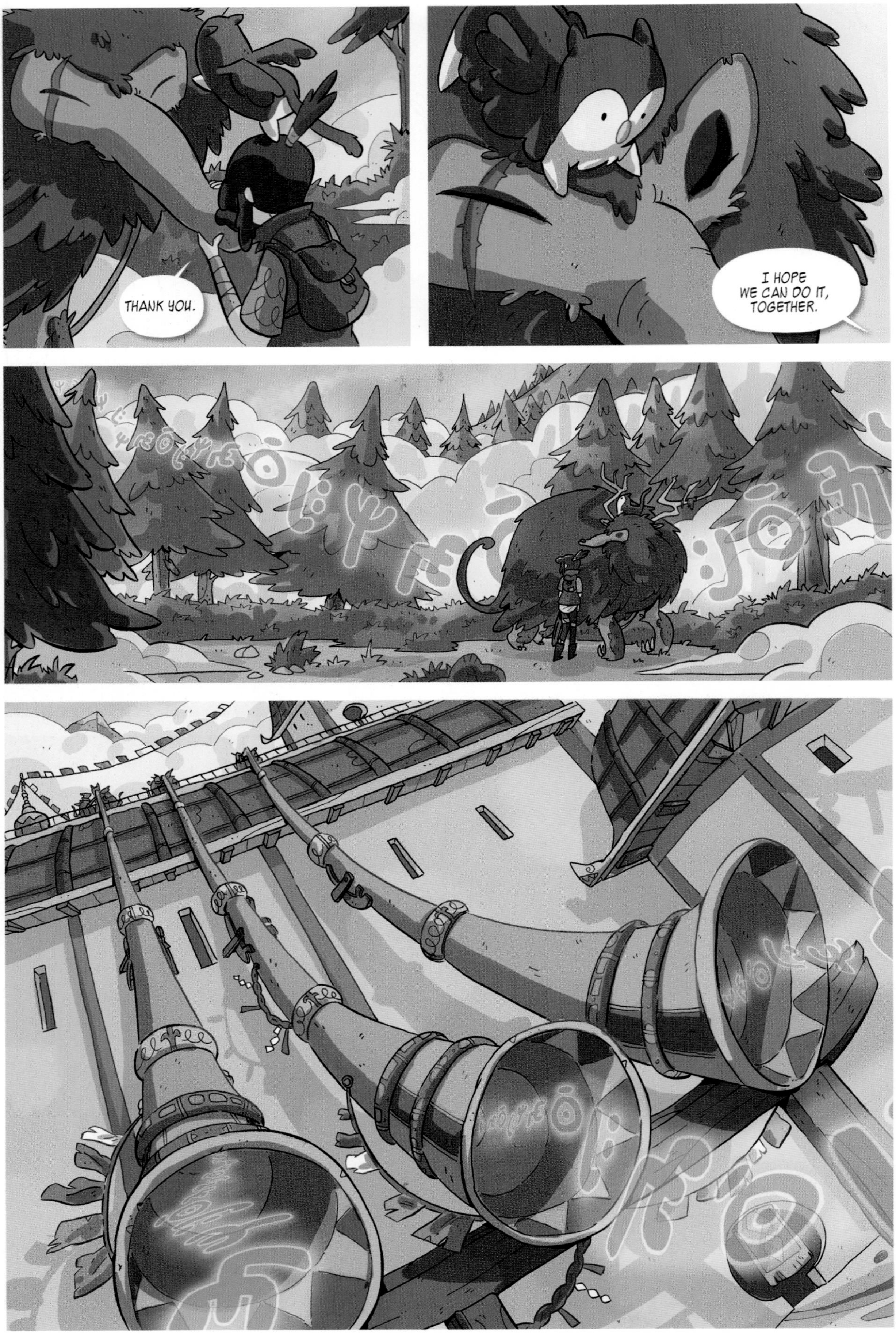
THANK YOU.
I HOPE WE CAN DO IT, TOGETHER.

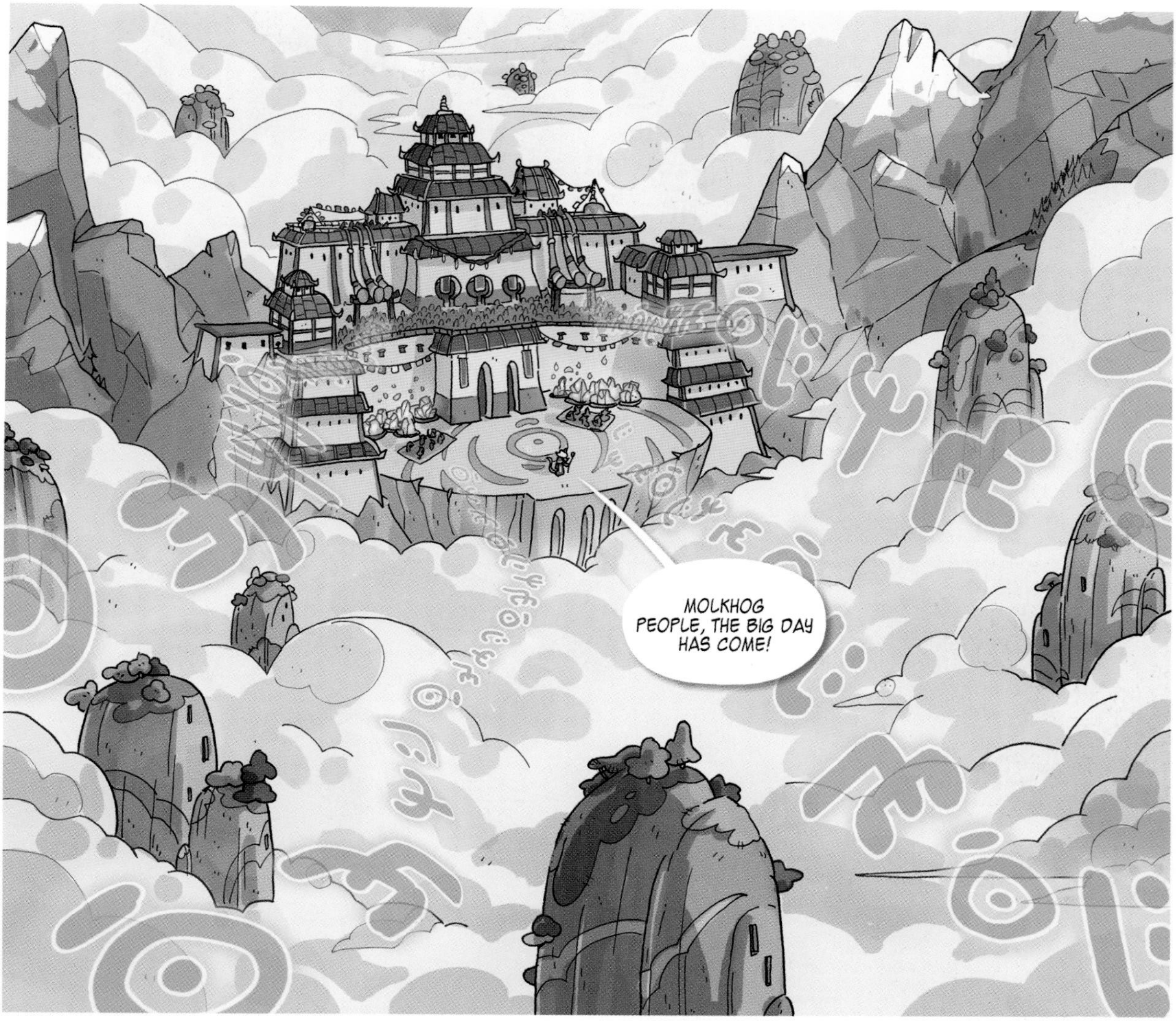
MOLKHOG PEOPLE, THE BIG DAY HAS COME!

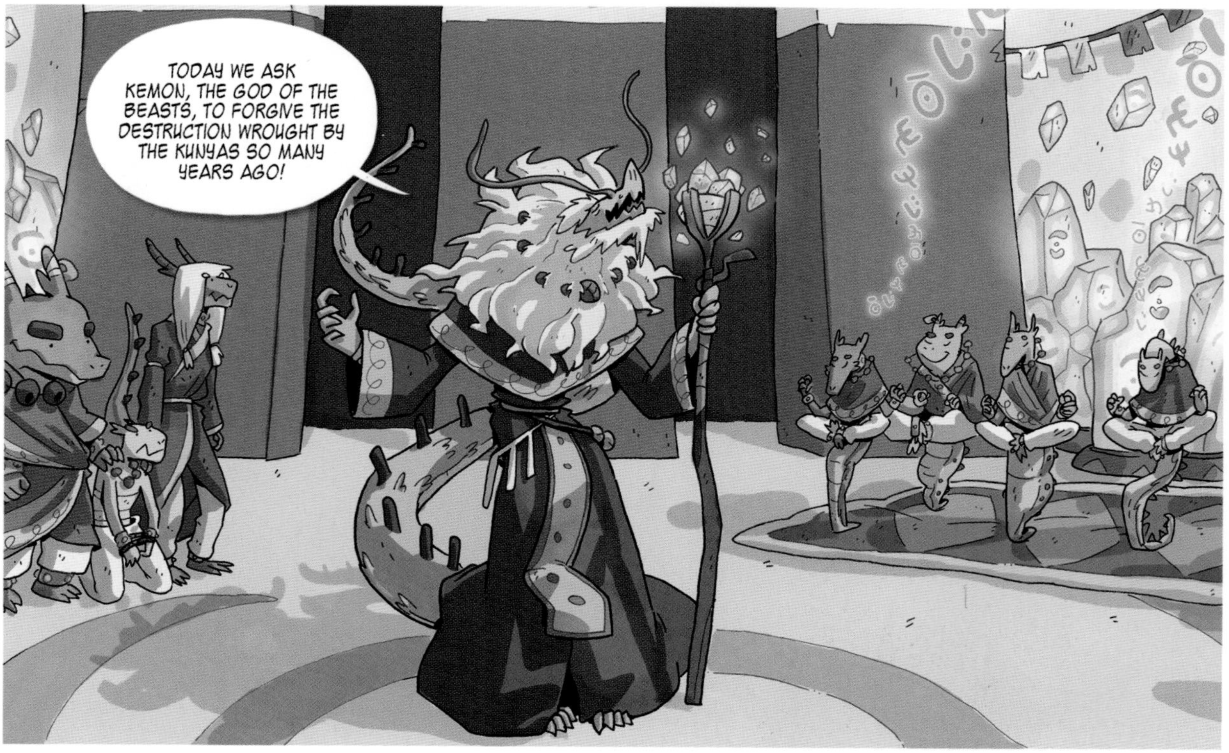
TODAY WE ASK KEMON, THE GOD OF THE BEASTS, TO FORGIVE THE DESTRUCTION WROUGHT BY THE KUNYAS SO MANY YEARS AGO!

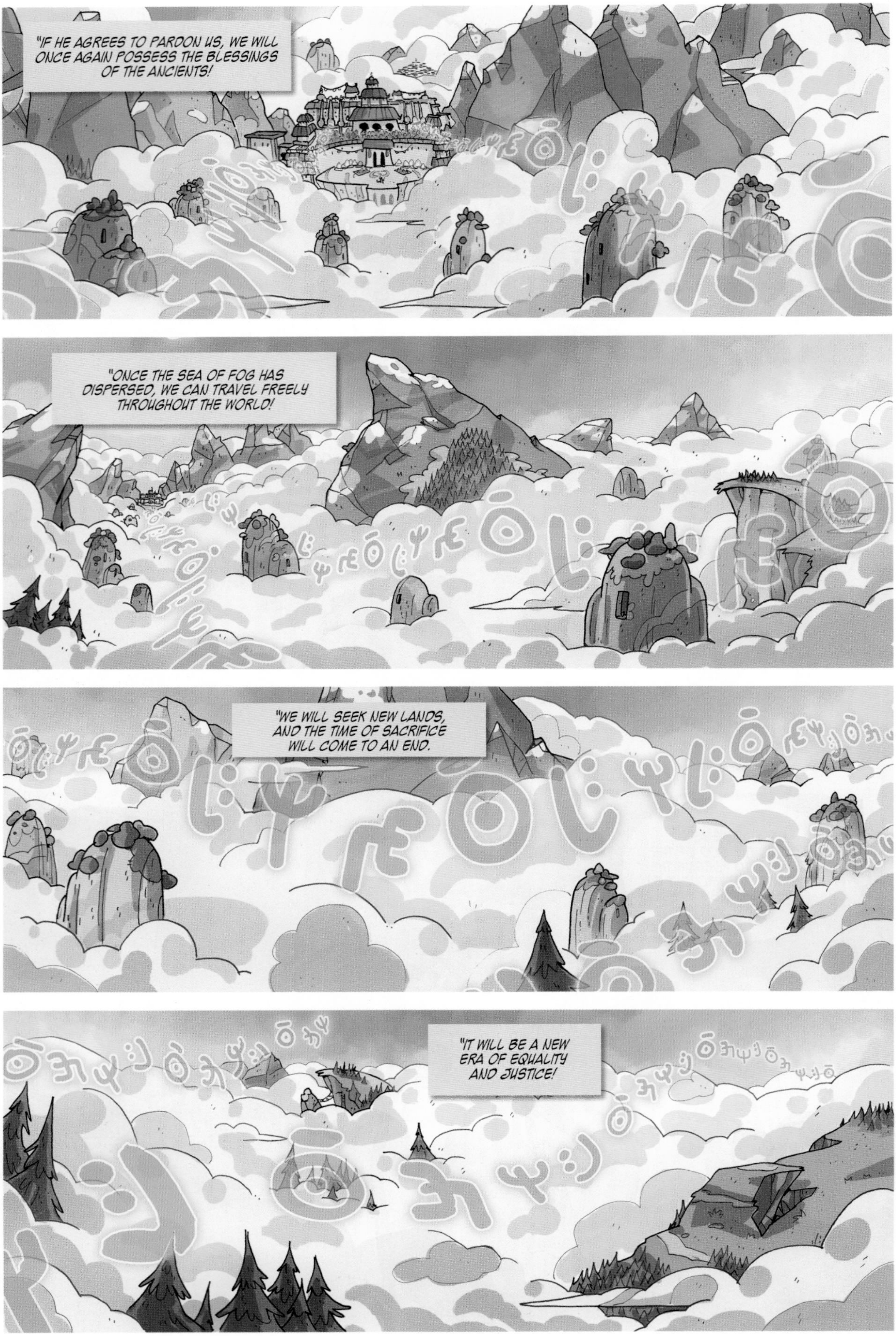
"IF HE AGREES TO PARDON US, WE WILL ONCE AGAIN POSSESS THE BLESSINGS OF THE ANCIENTS!
"ONCE THE SEA OF FOG HAS DISPERSED, WE CAN TRAVEL FREELY THROUGHOUT THE WORLD!
"WE WILL SEEK NEW LANDS, AND THE TIME OF SACRIFICE WILL COME TO AN END.
"IT WILL BE A NEW ERA OF EQUALITY AND JUSTICE!

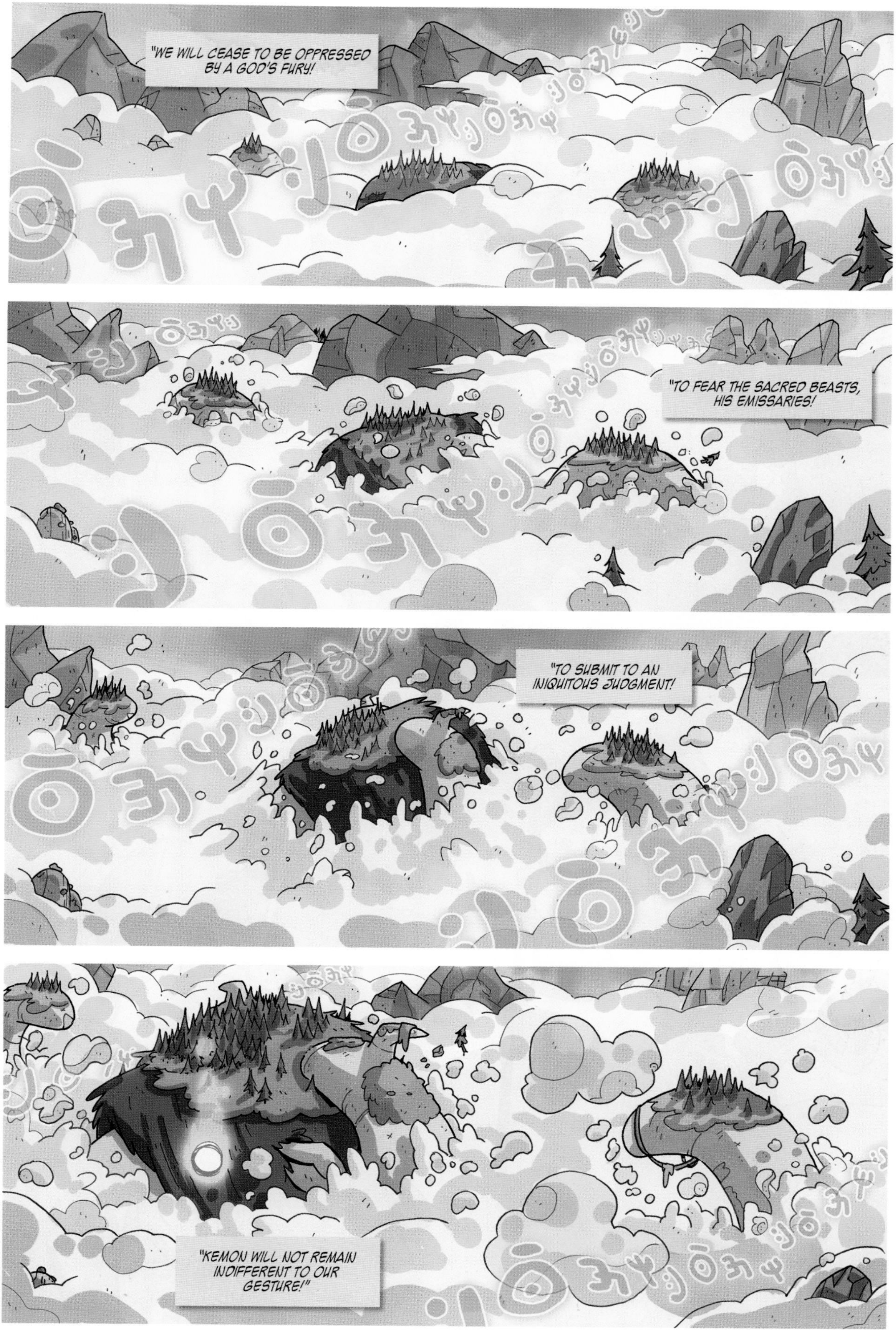
"WE WILL CEASE TO BE OPPRESSED BY A GOD'S FURY!
"TO FEAR THE SACRED BEASTS, HIS EMISSARIES!
"TO SUBMIT TO AN INIQUITOUS JUDGMENT!
"KEMON WILL NOT REMAIN INDIFFERENT TO OUR GESTURE!"

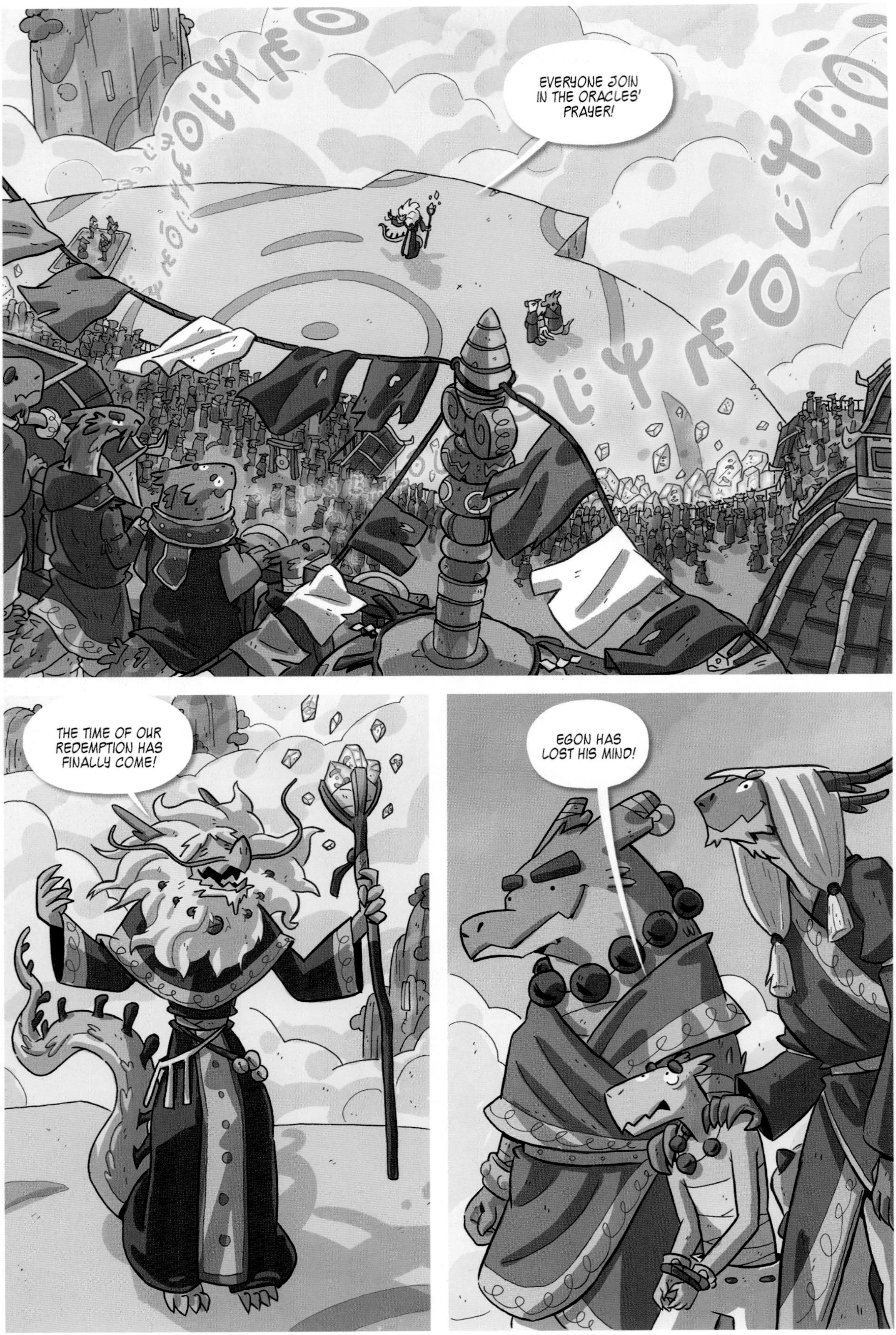
EVERYONE JOIN IN THE ORACLES' PRAYER!
THE TIME OF OUR REDEMPTION HAS FINALLY COME!
EGON HAS LOST HIS MIND!

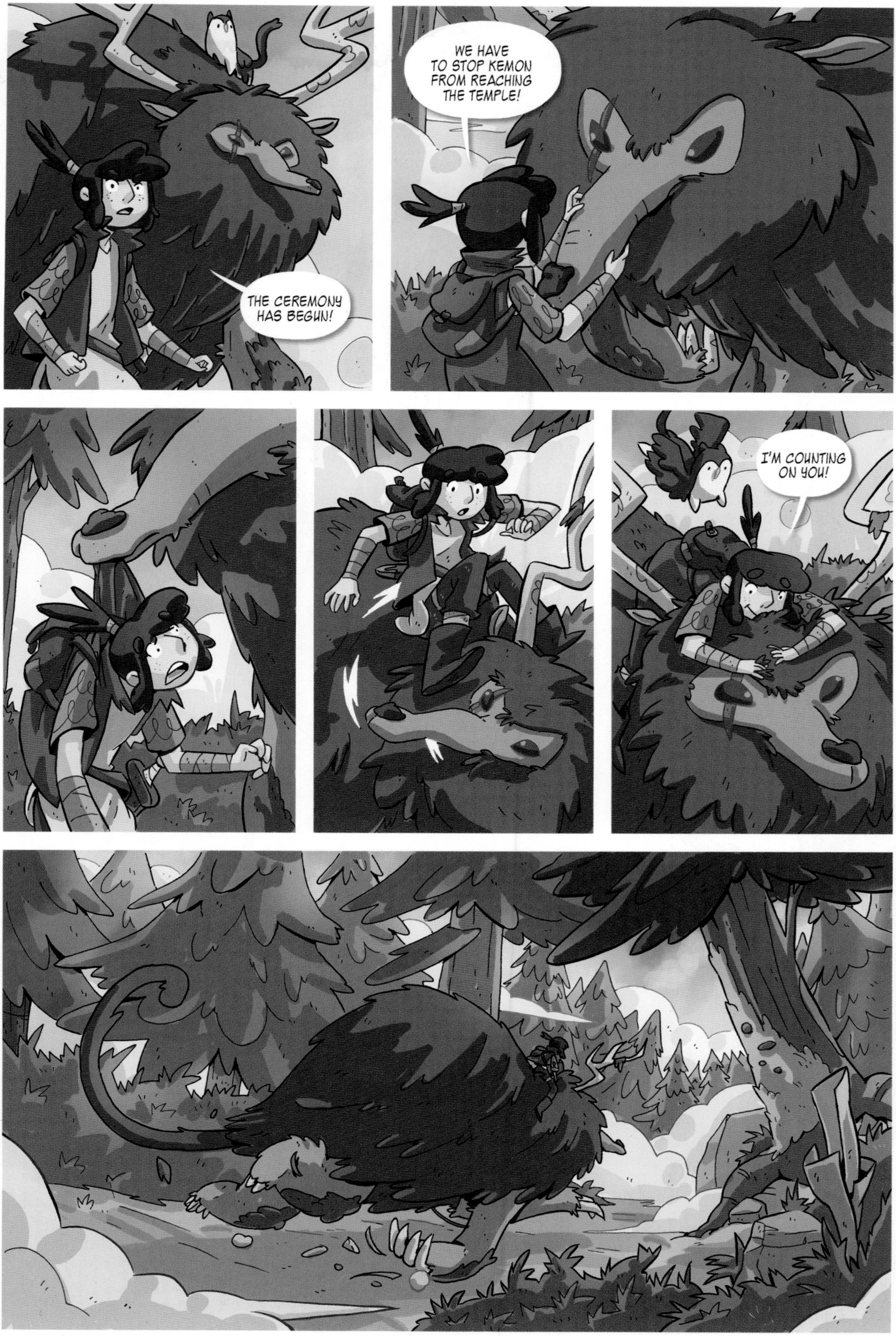
THE CEREMONY HAS BEGUN!
WE HAVE TO STOP KEMON FROM REACHING THE TEMPLE!
I'M COUNTING ON YOU!

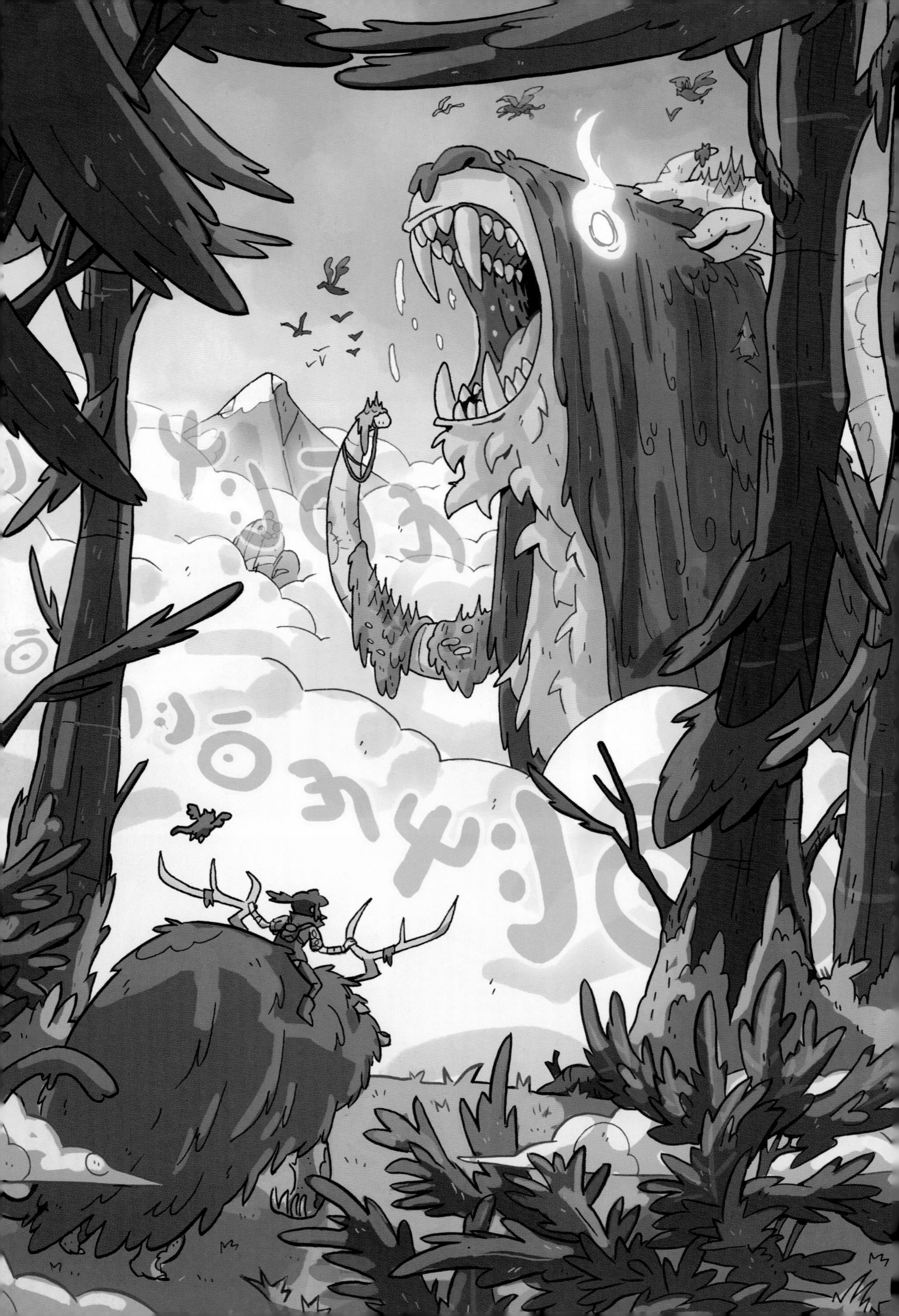

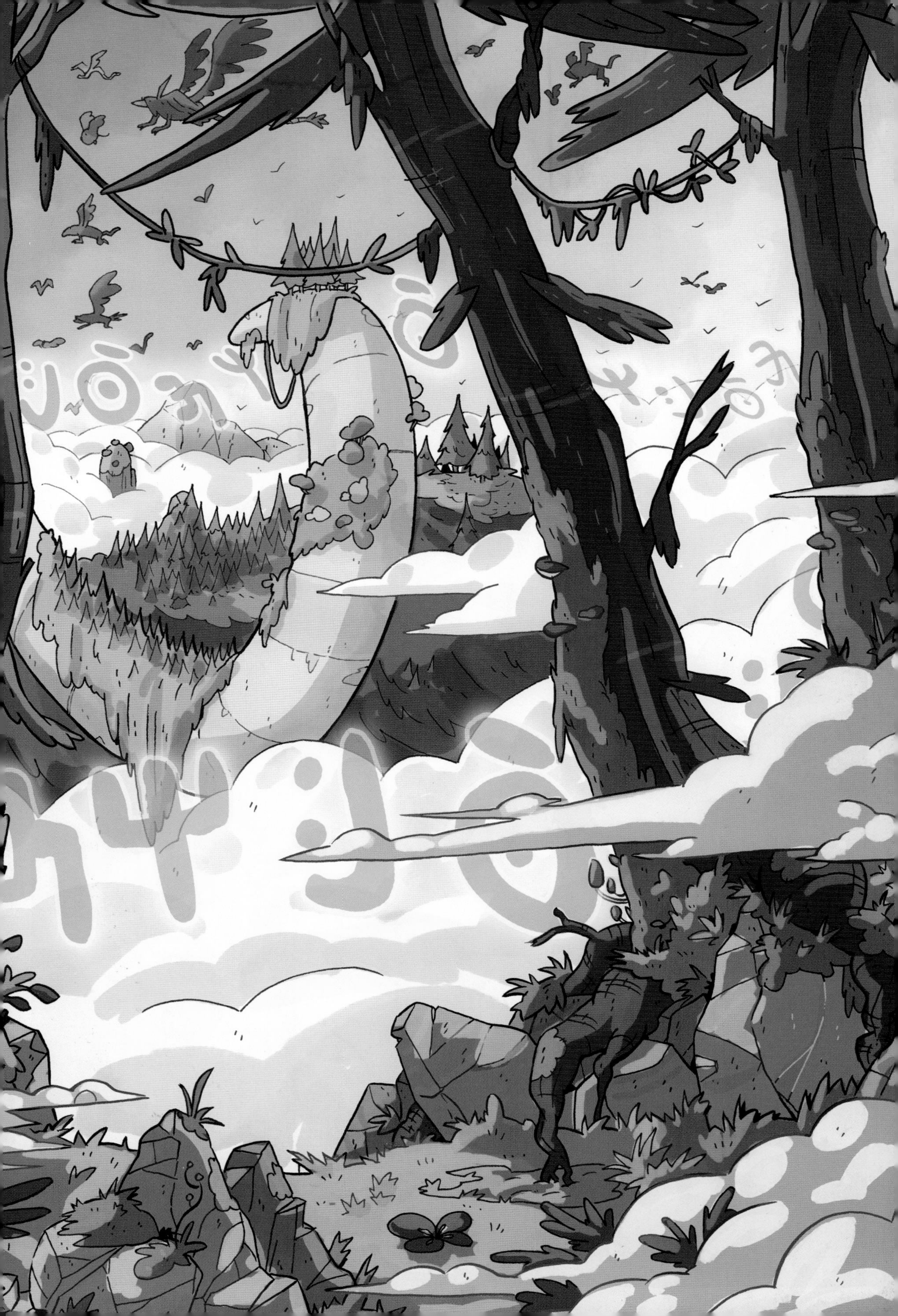

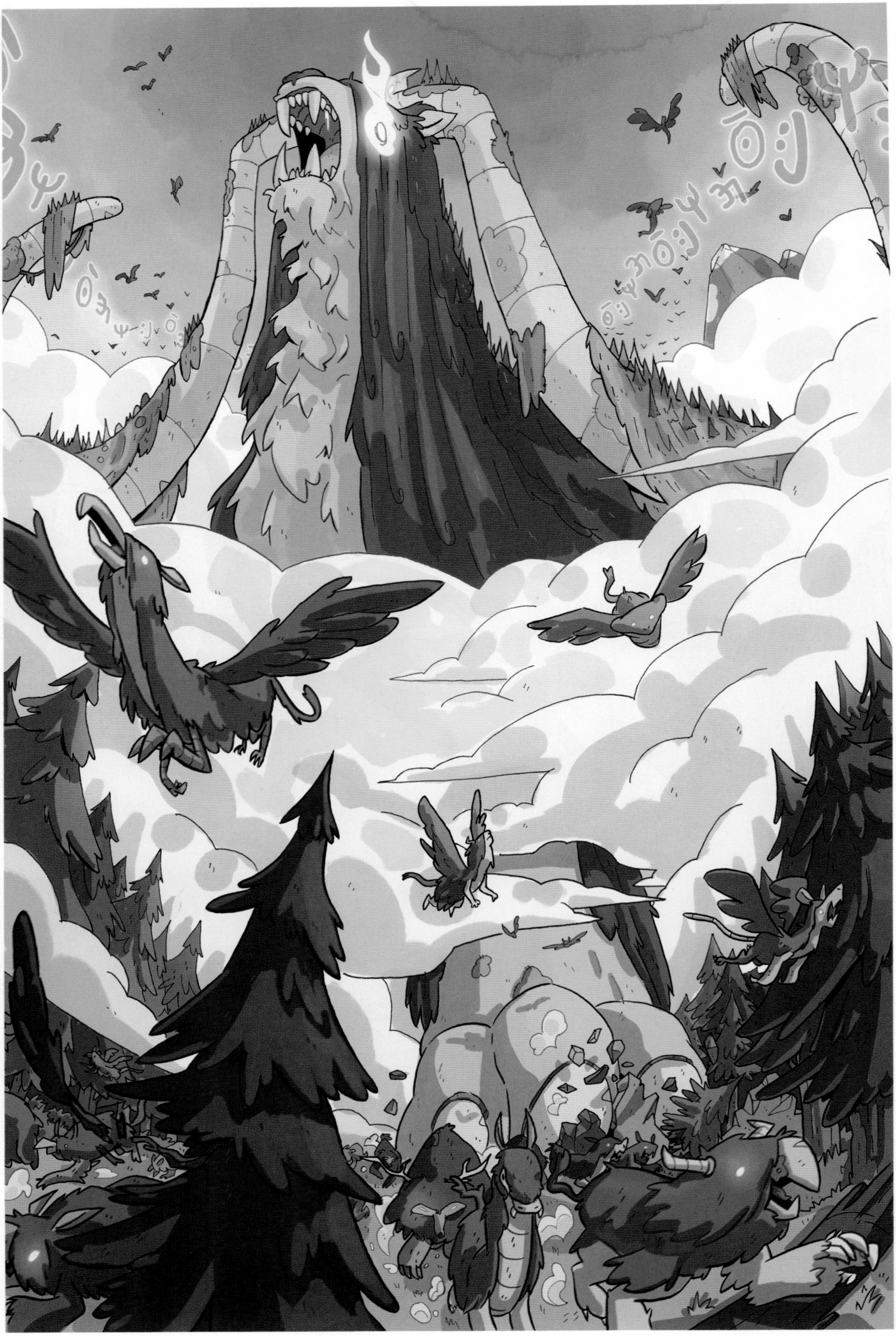

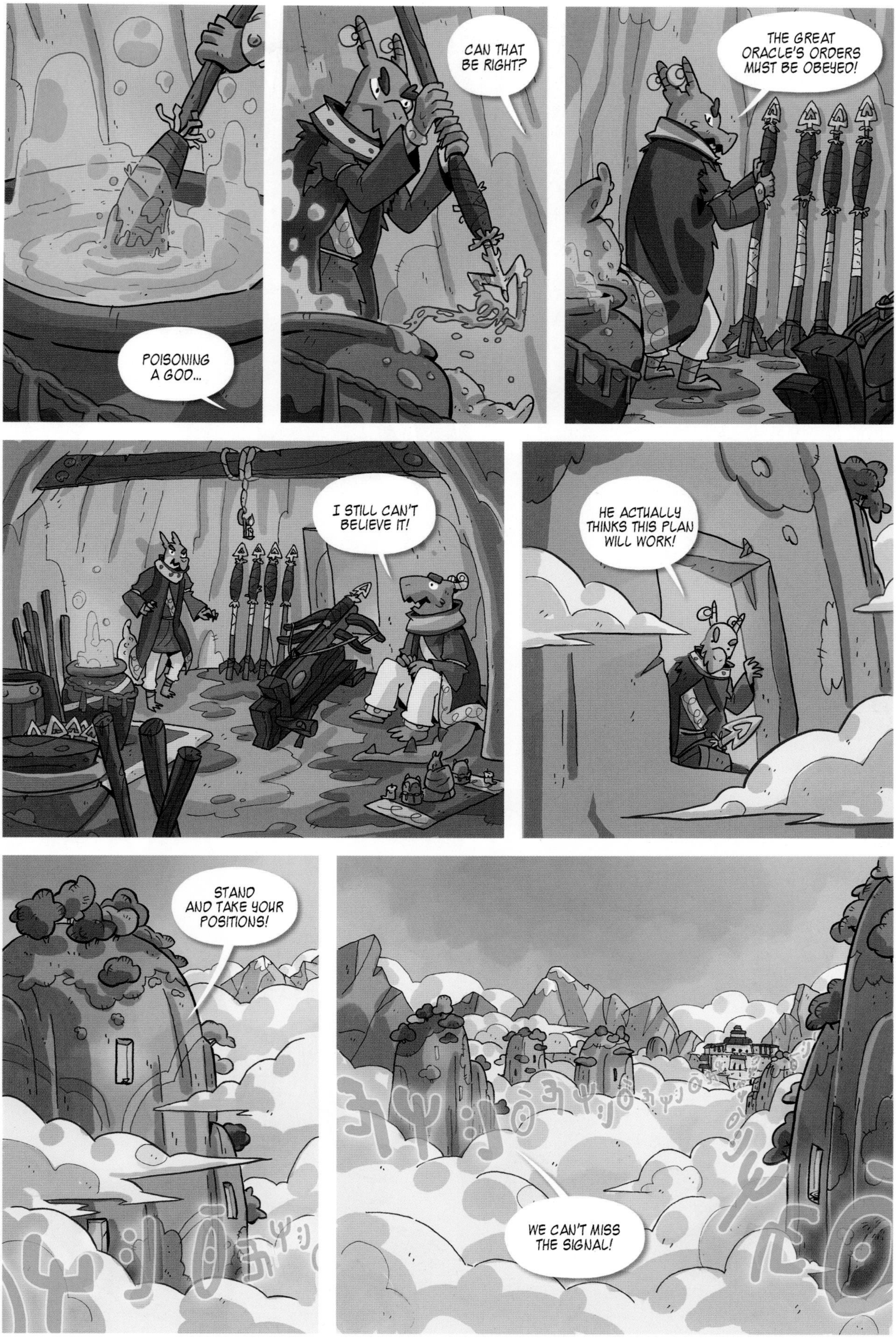
POISONING A GOD...
CAN THAT BE RIGHT?
THE GREAT ORACLE'S ORDERS MUST BE OBEYED!
I STILL CAN'T BELIEVE IT!
HE ACTUALLY THINKS THIS PLAN WILL WORK!
STAND AND TAKE YOUR POSITIONS!
WE CAN'T MISS THE SIGNAL!

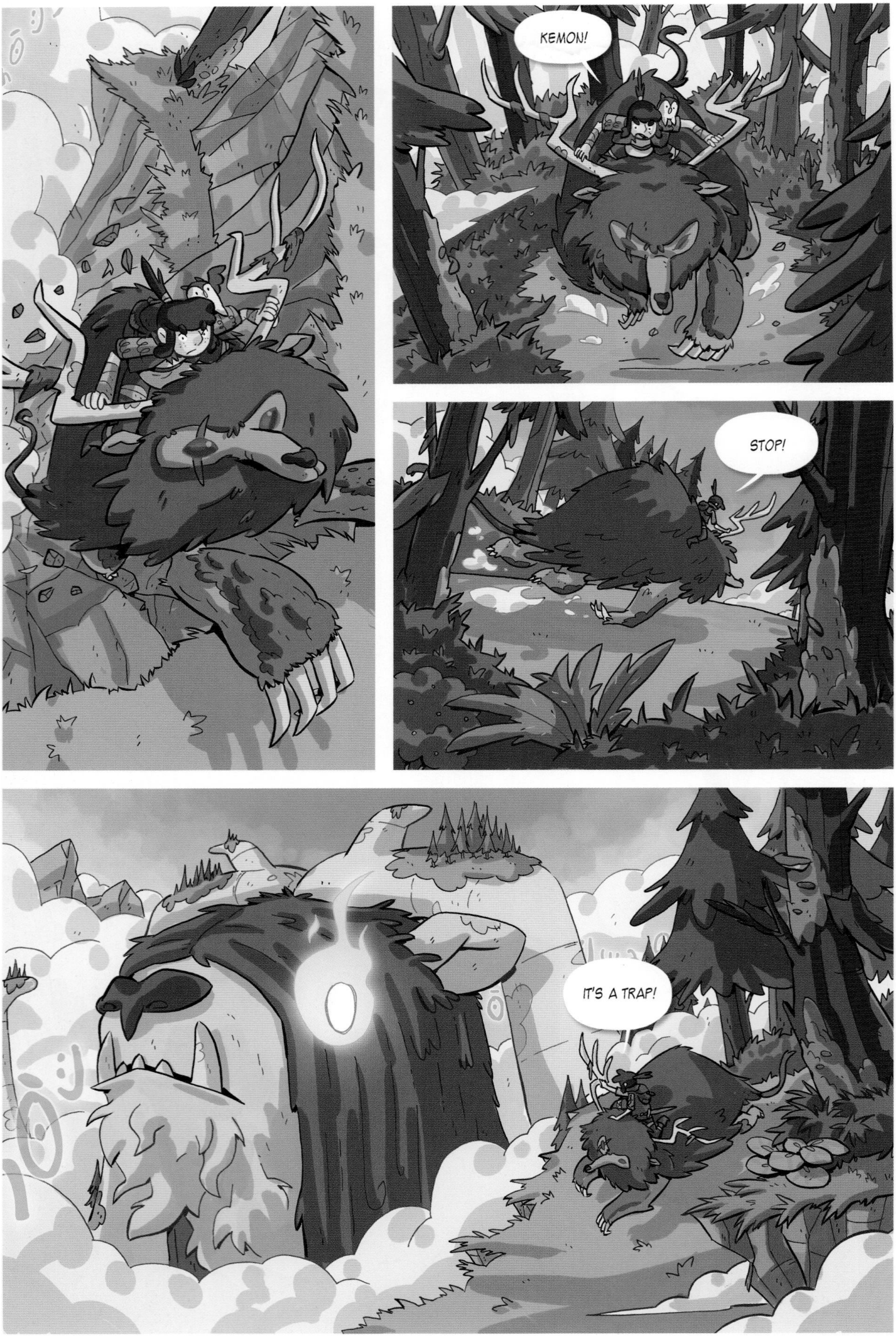
KEMON!
STOP!
IT'S A TRAP!

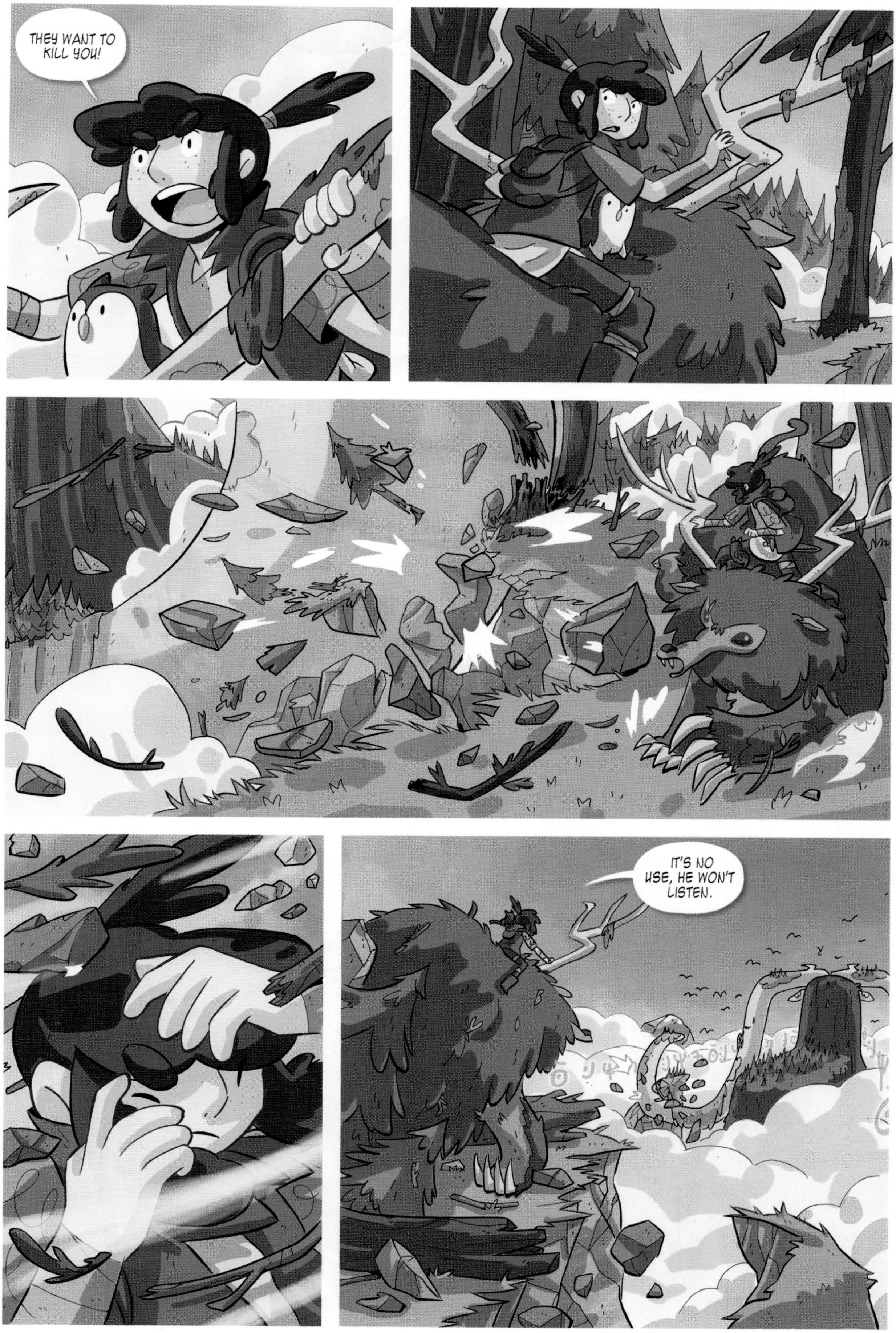
THEY WANT TO KILL YOU!
IT'S NO USE, HE WON'T LISTEN.

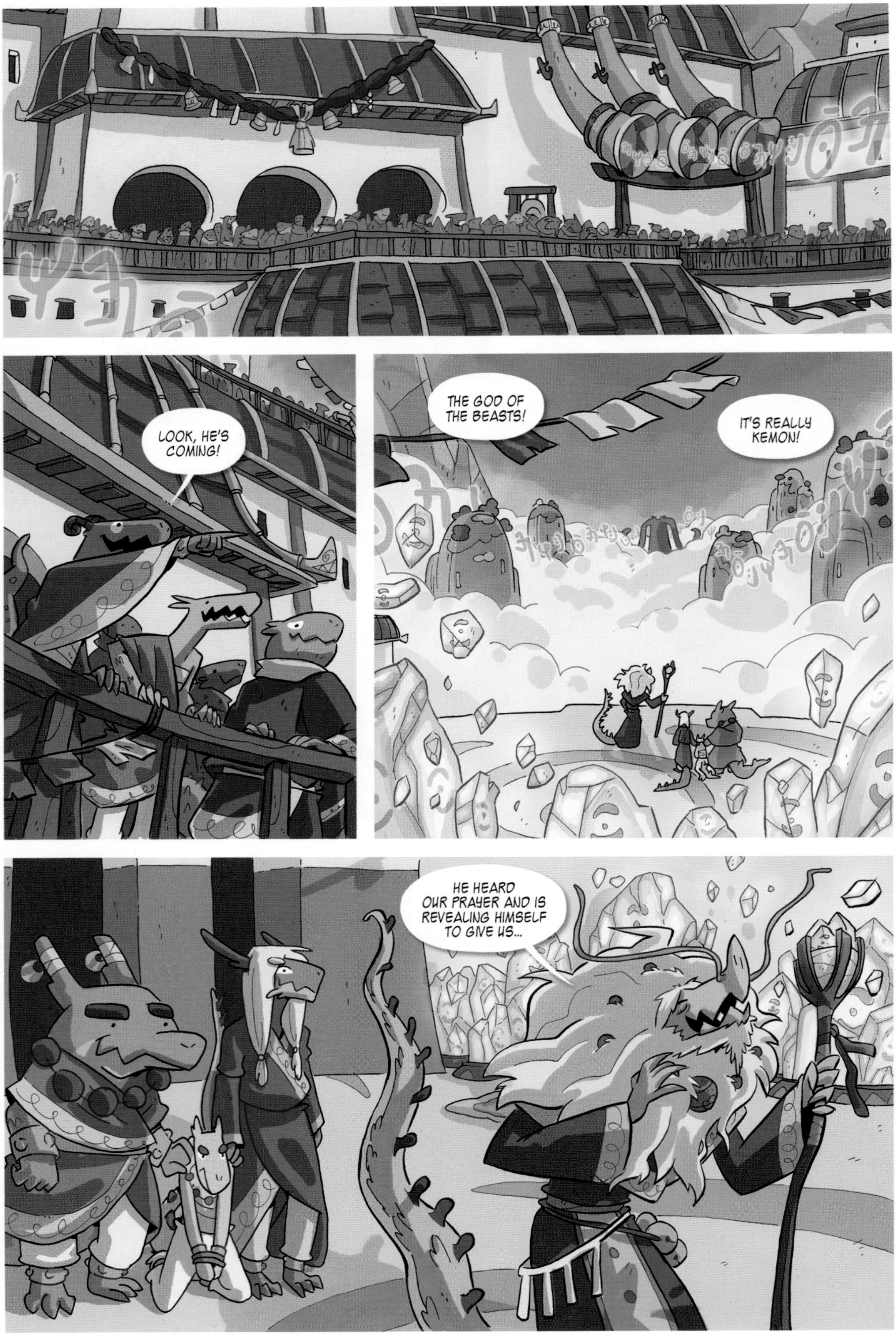
LOOK, HE'S COMING!
THE GOD OF THE BEASTS!
IT'S REALLY KEMON!
HE HEARD OUR PRAYER AND IS REVEALING HIMSELF TO GIVE US...

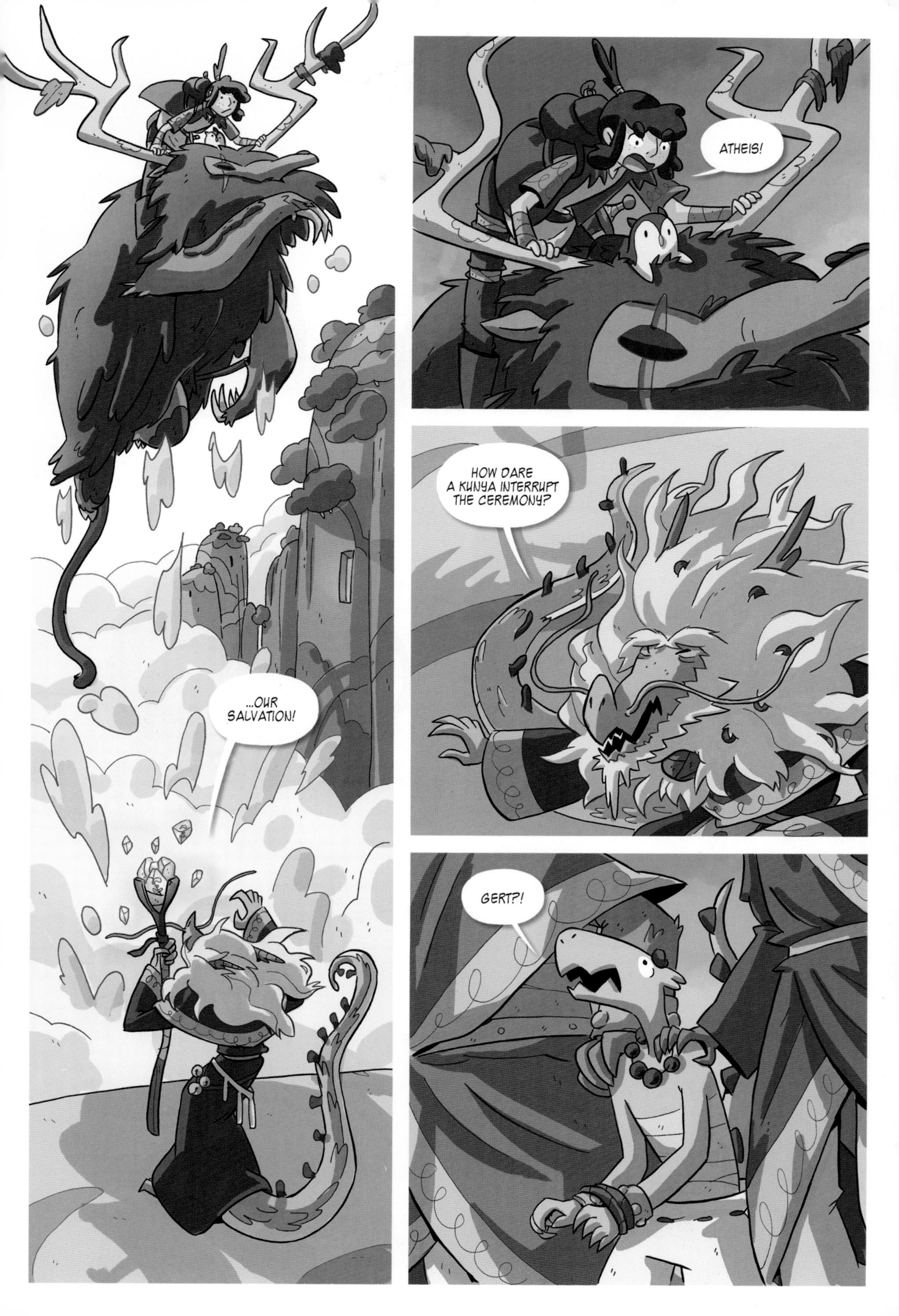
...OUR SALVATION!
ATHEIS!
HOW DARE A KUNYA INTERRUPT THE CEREMONY?
GERT?!

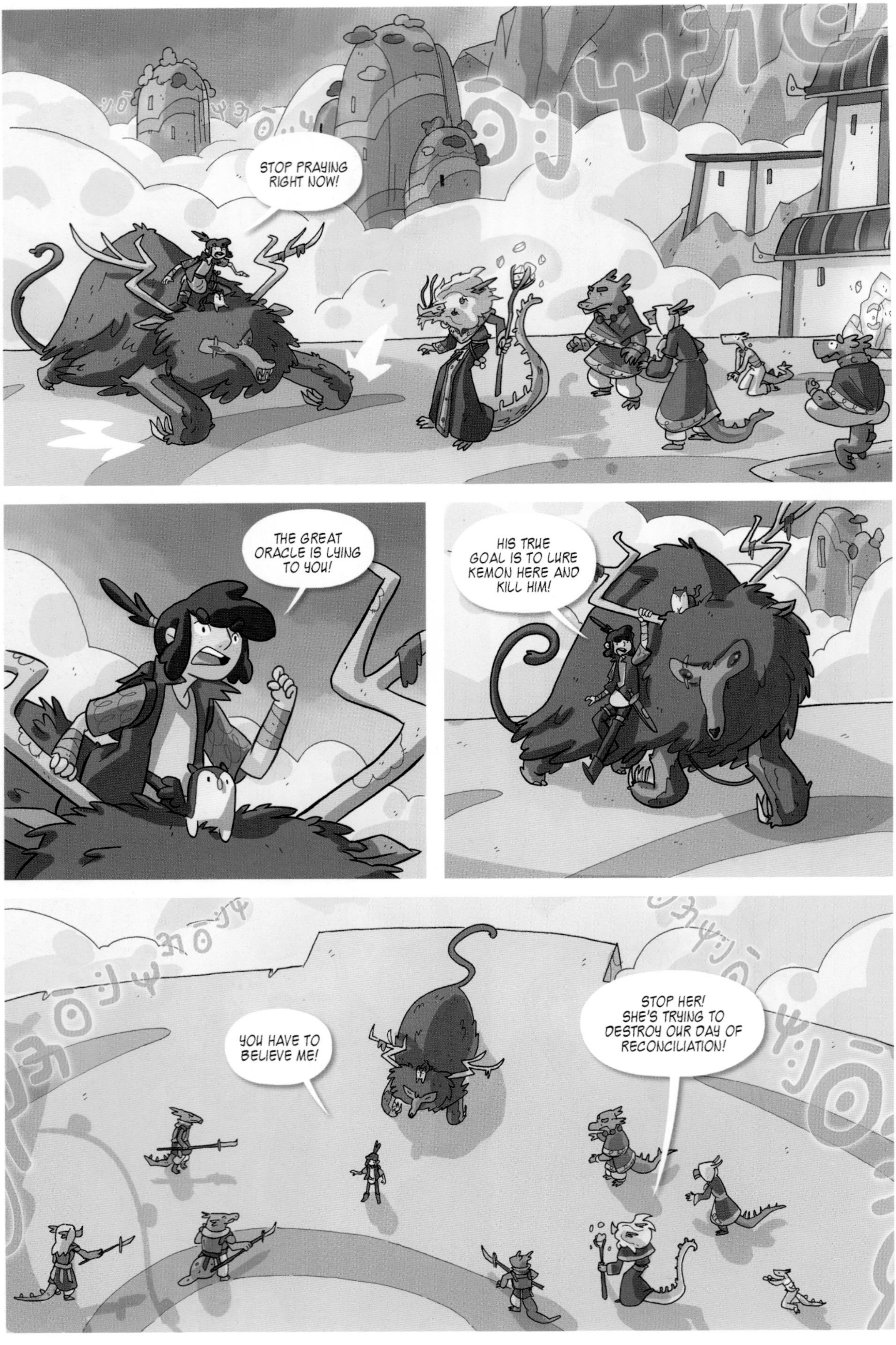
STOP PRAYING RIGHT NOW!
THE GREAT ORACLE IS LYING TO YOU!
HIS TRUE GOAL IS TO LURE KEMON HERE AND KILL HIM!
YOU HAVE TO BELIEVE ME!
STOP HER! SHE'S TRYING TO DESTROY OUR DAY OF RECONCILIATION!

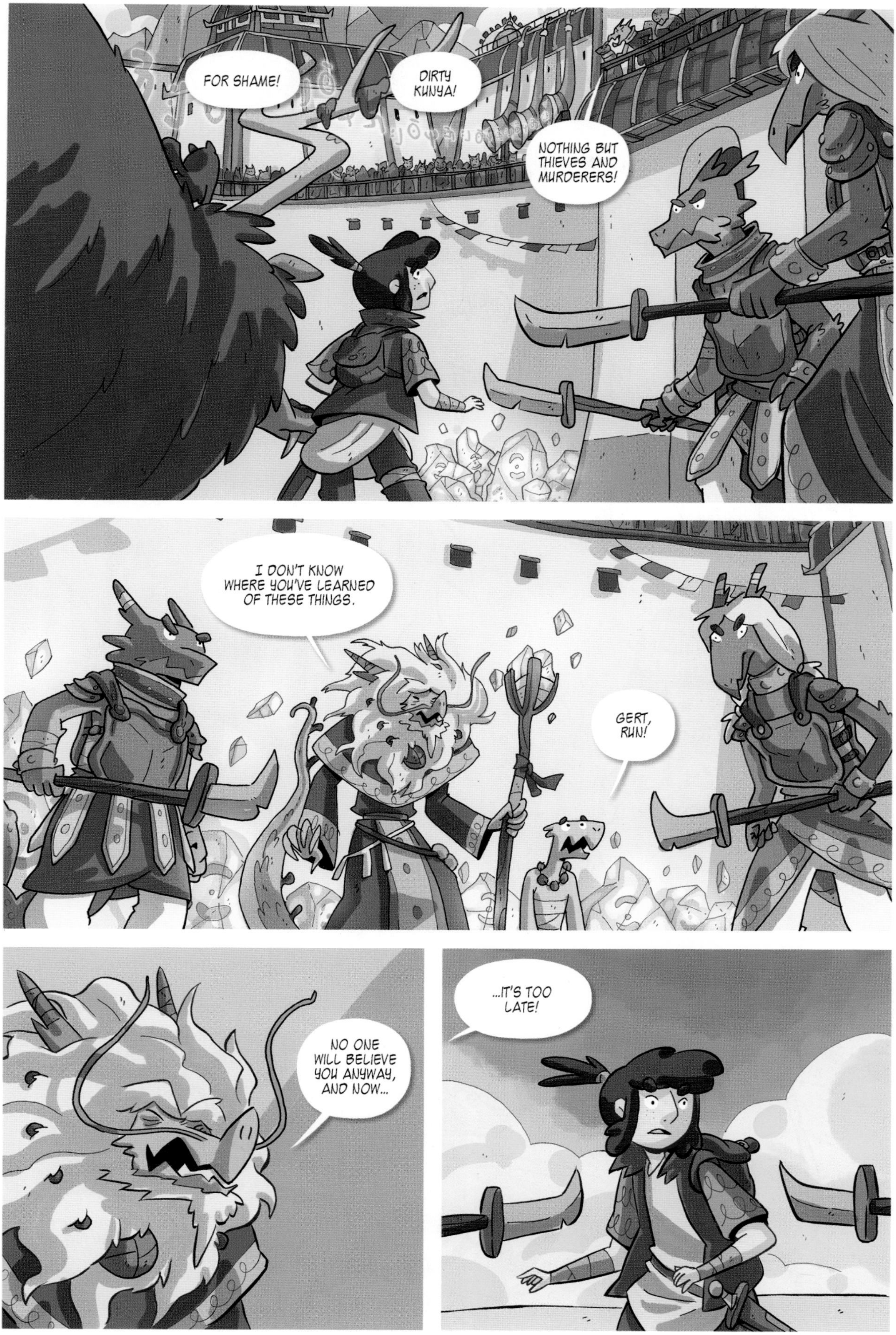
FOR SHAME!
DIRTY KUNYA!
NOTHING BUT THIEVES AND MURDERERS!
I DON'T KNOW WHERE YOU'VE LEARNED OF THESE THINGS.
GERT, RUN!
NO ONE WILL BELIEVE YOU ANYWAY, AND NOW...
...IT'S TOO LATE!

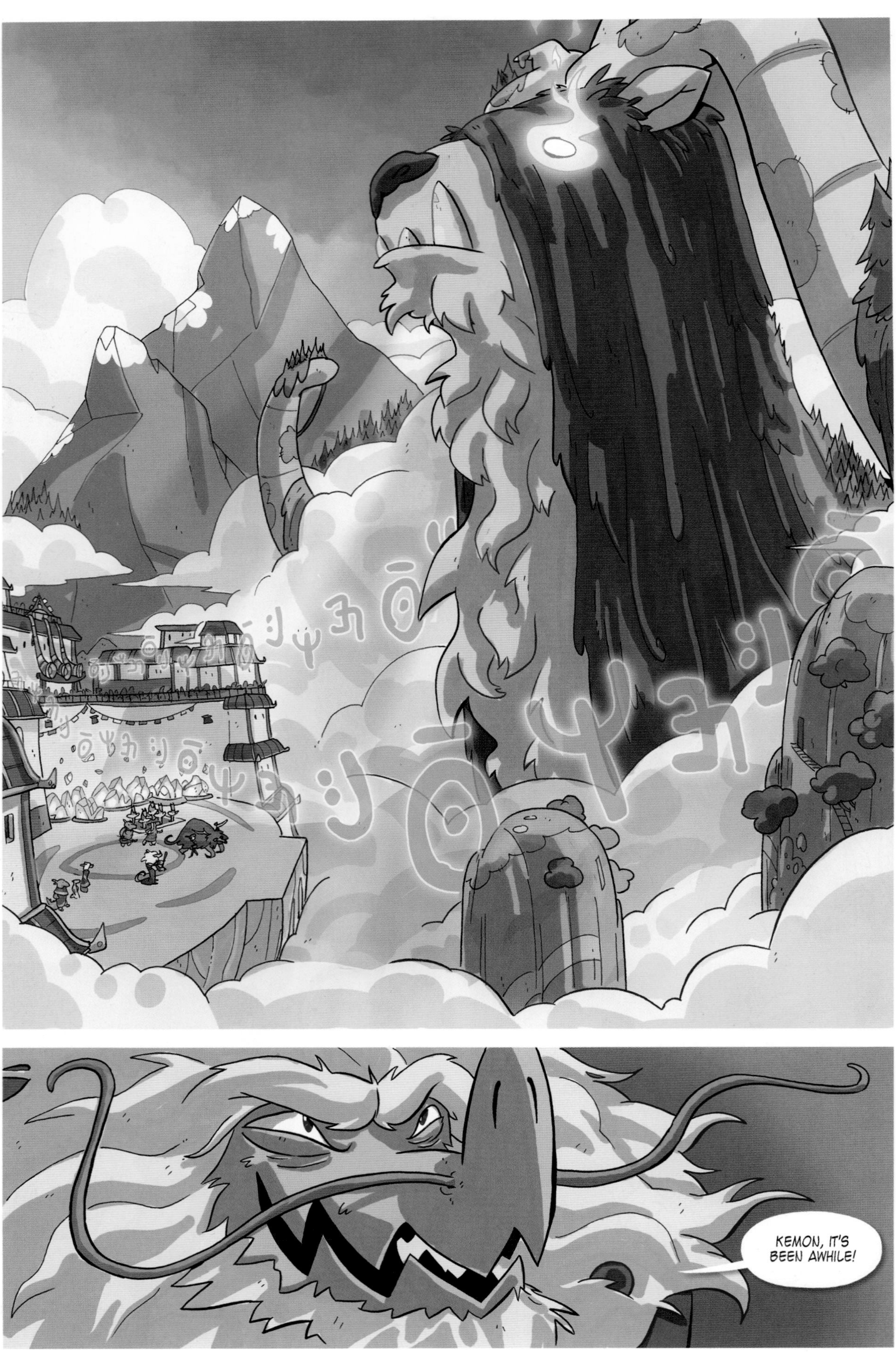
KEMON, IT'S BEEN AWHILE!

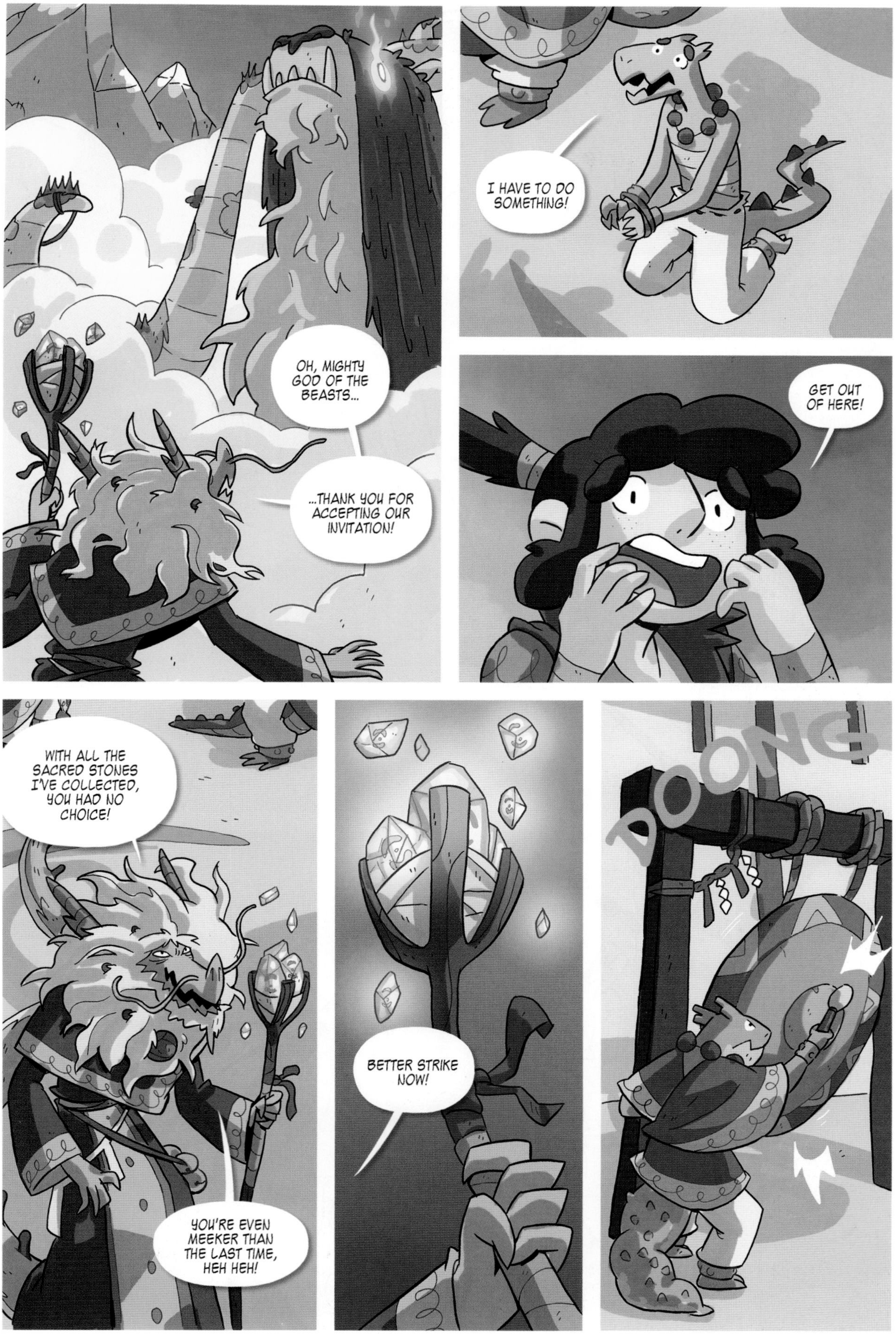
OH, MIGHTY GOD OF THE BEASTS...
...THANK YOU FOR ACCEPTING OUR INVITATION!
I HAVE TO DO SOMETHING!
GET OUT OF HERE!
WITH ALL THE SACRED STONES I'VE COLLECTED, YOU HAD NO CHOICE!
YOU'RE EVEN MEEKER THAN THE LAST TIME, HEH HEH!
BETTER STRIKE NOW!
DOONG

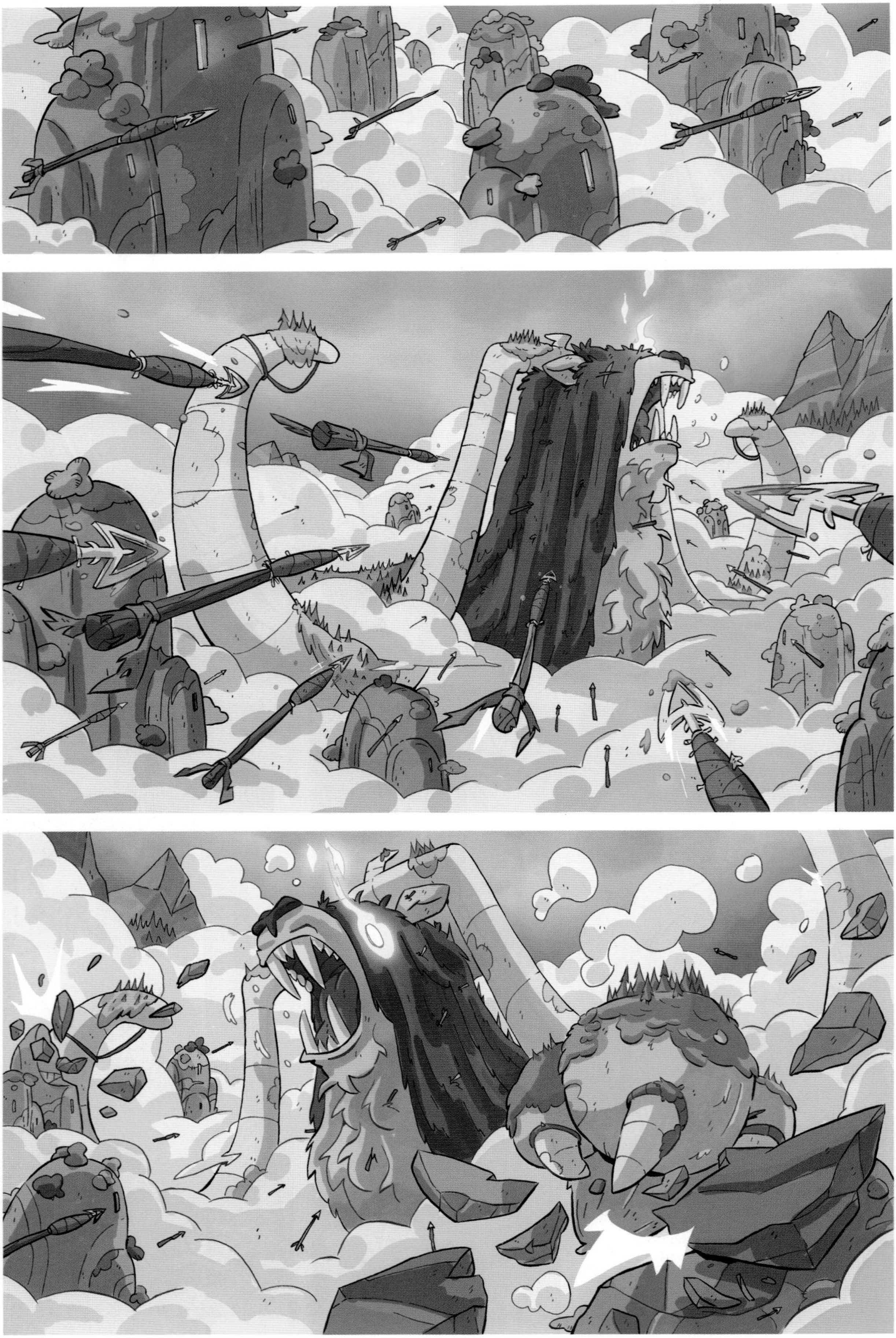

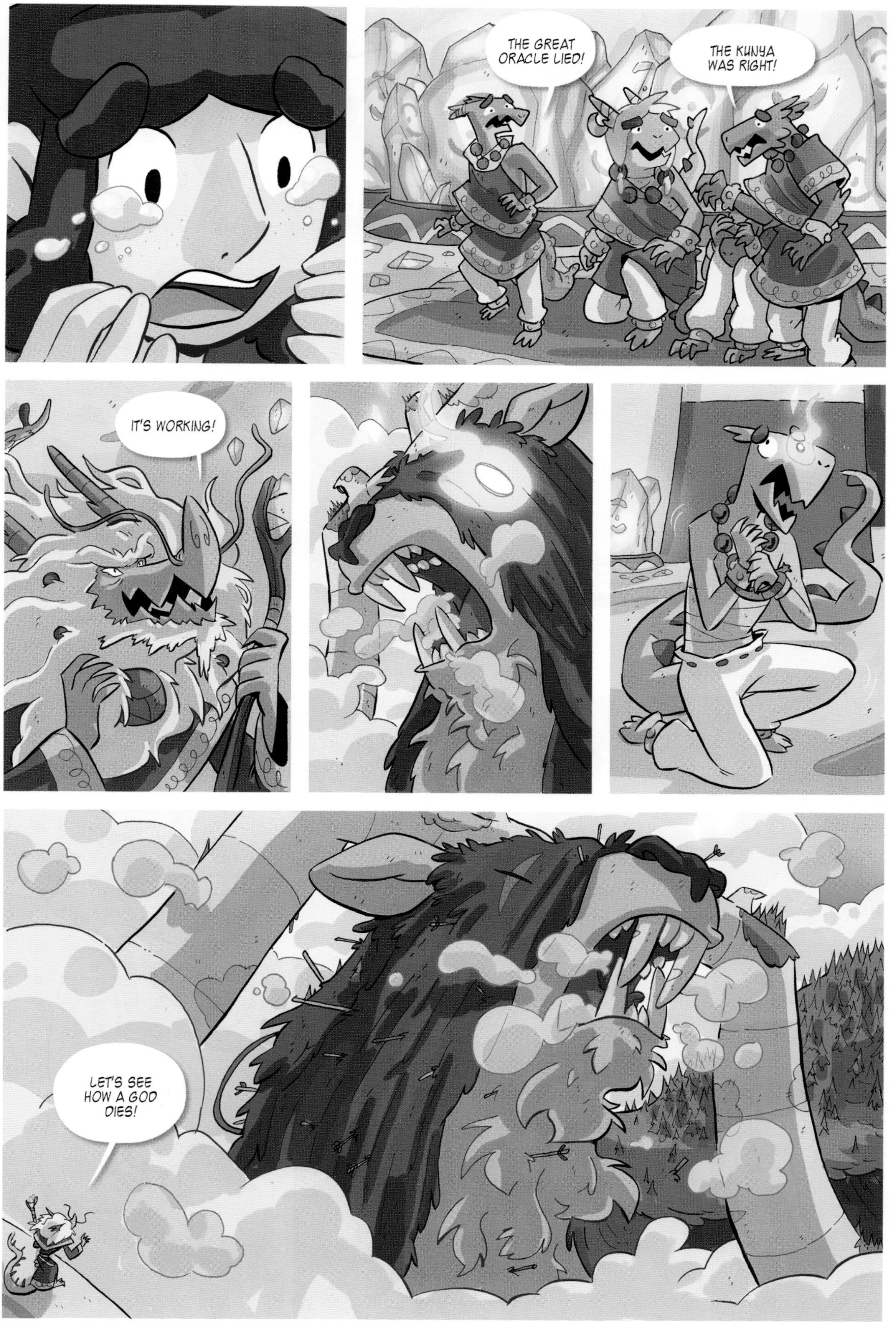
THE GREAT ORACLE LIED!
THE KUNYA WAS RIGHT!
IT'S WORKING!
LET'S SEE HOW A GOD DIES!

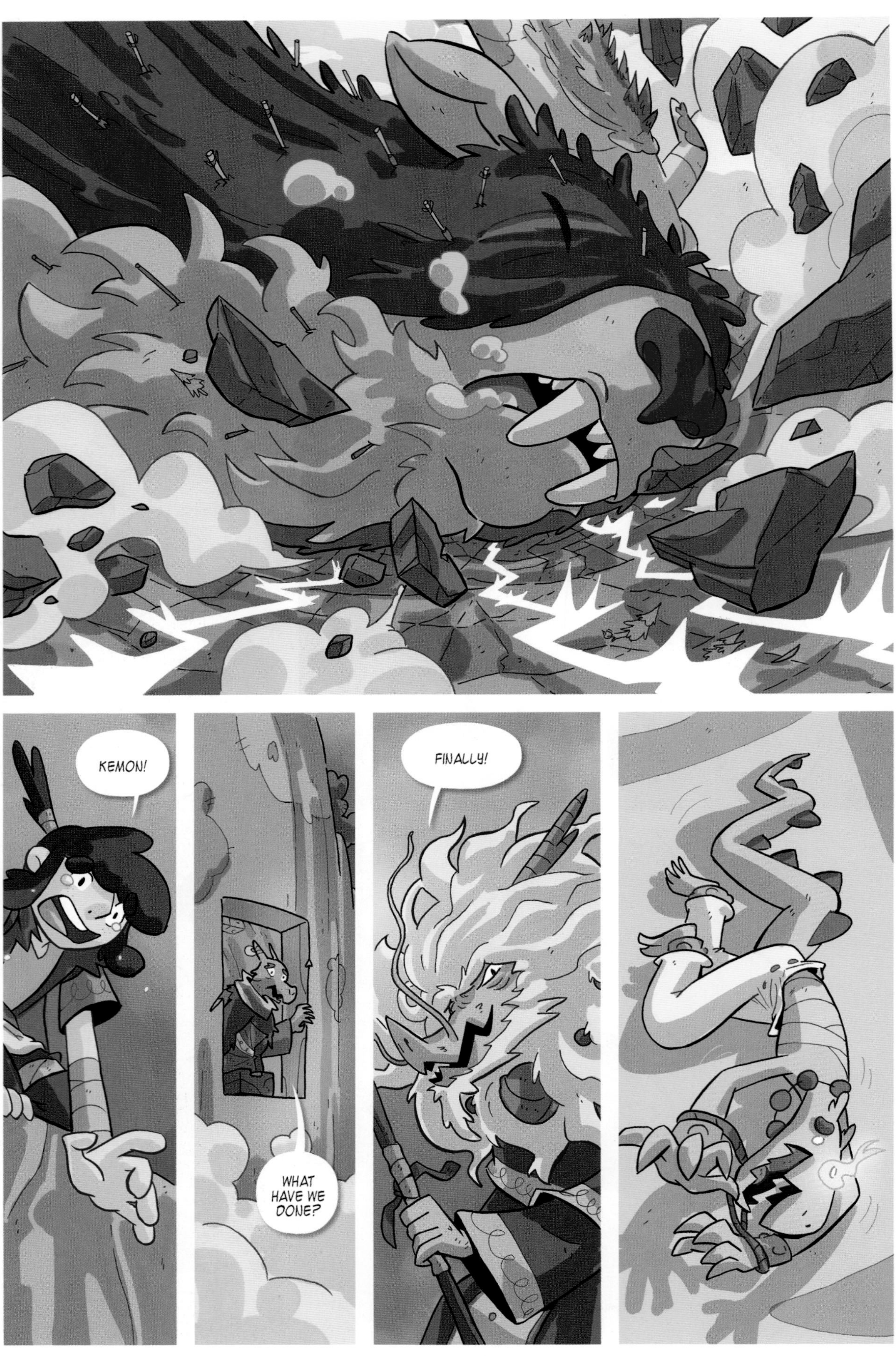
KEMON!
WHAT HAVE WE DONE?
FINALLY!

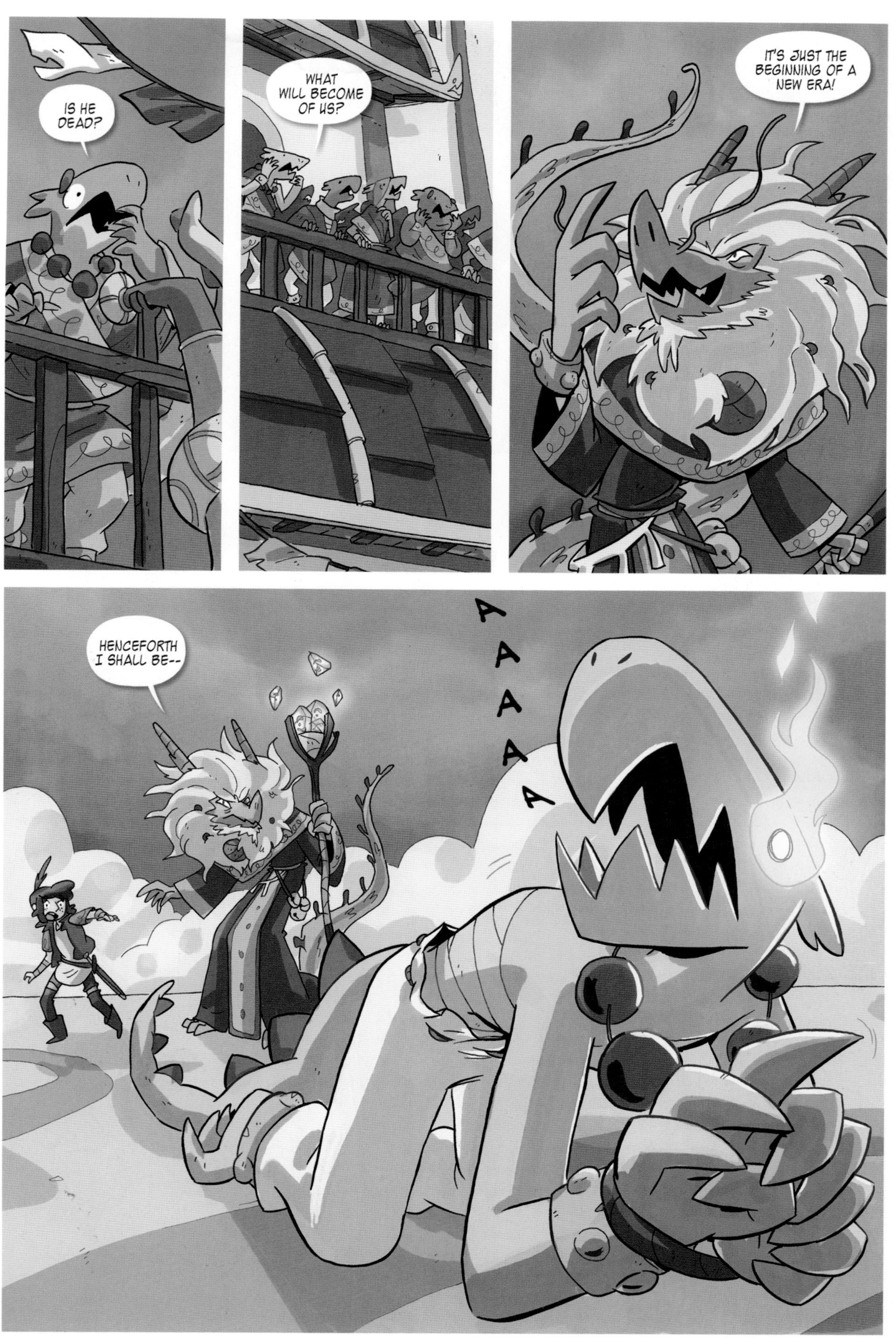
IS HE DEAD?
WHAT WILL BECOME OF US?
IT'S JUST THE BEGINNING OF A NEW ERA!
HENCEFORTH I SHALL BE--
AAAAA

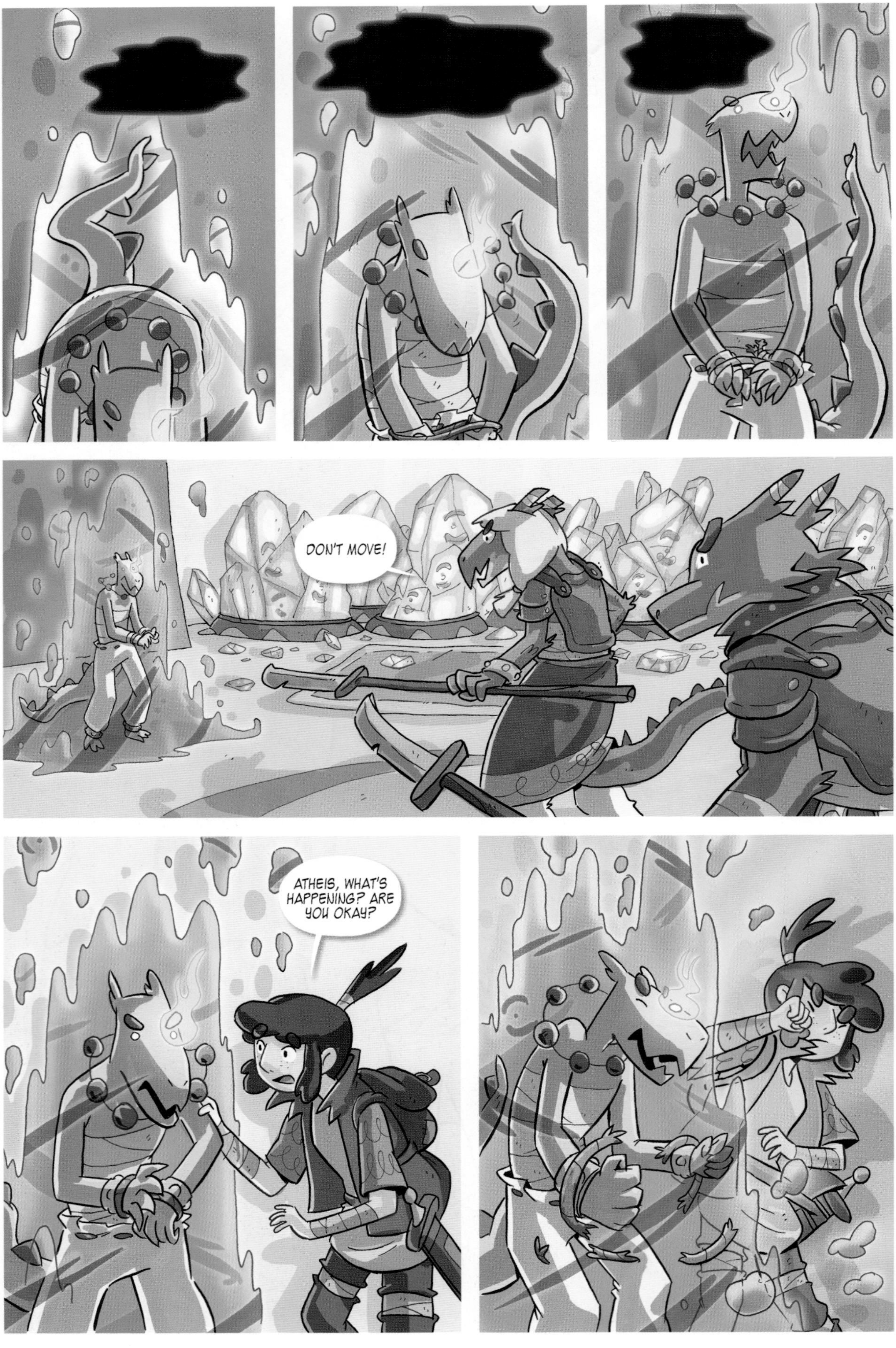

[redacted]
[redacted]
[redacted]
DON'T MOVE!
ATHEIS, WHAT'S HAPPENING? ARE YOU OKAY?

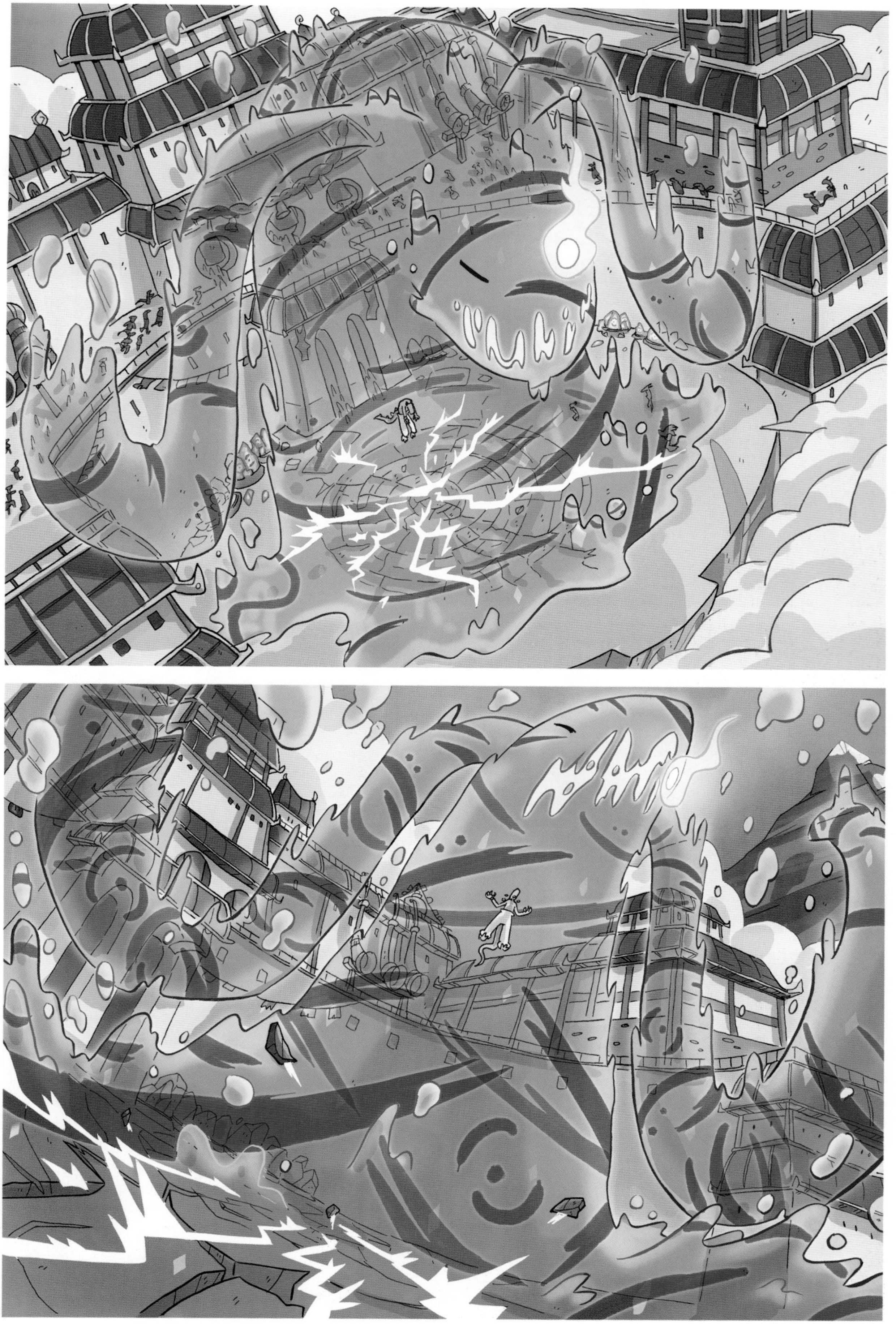

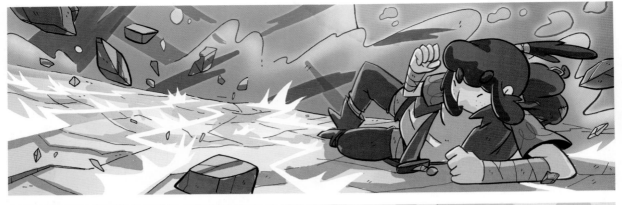

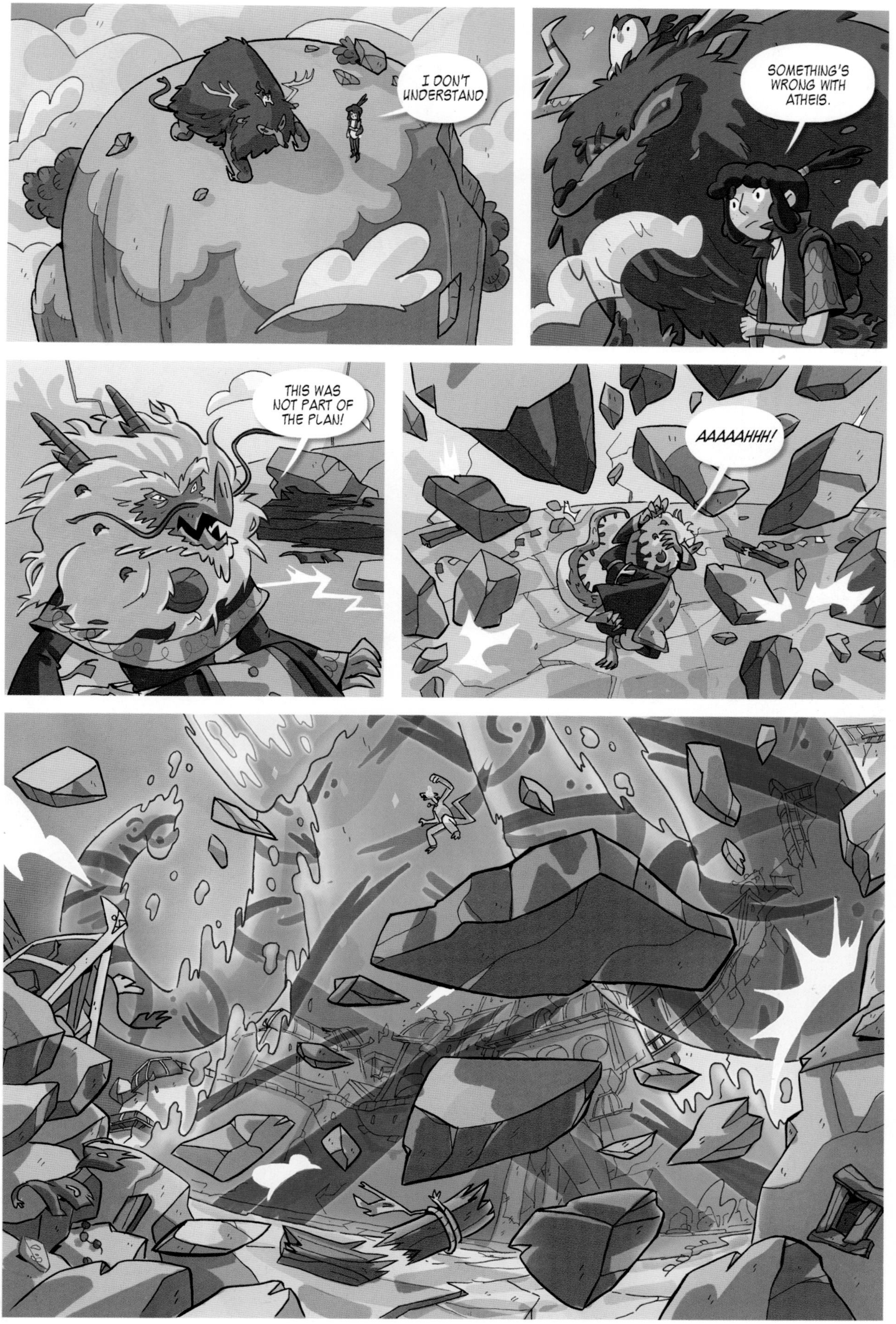
I DON'T UNDERSTAND.
SOMETHING'S WRONG WITH ATHEIS.
THIS WAS NOT PART OF THE PLAN!
AAAAAHHH!

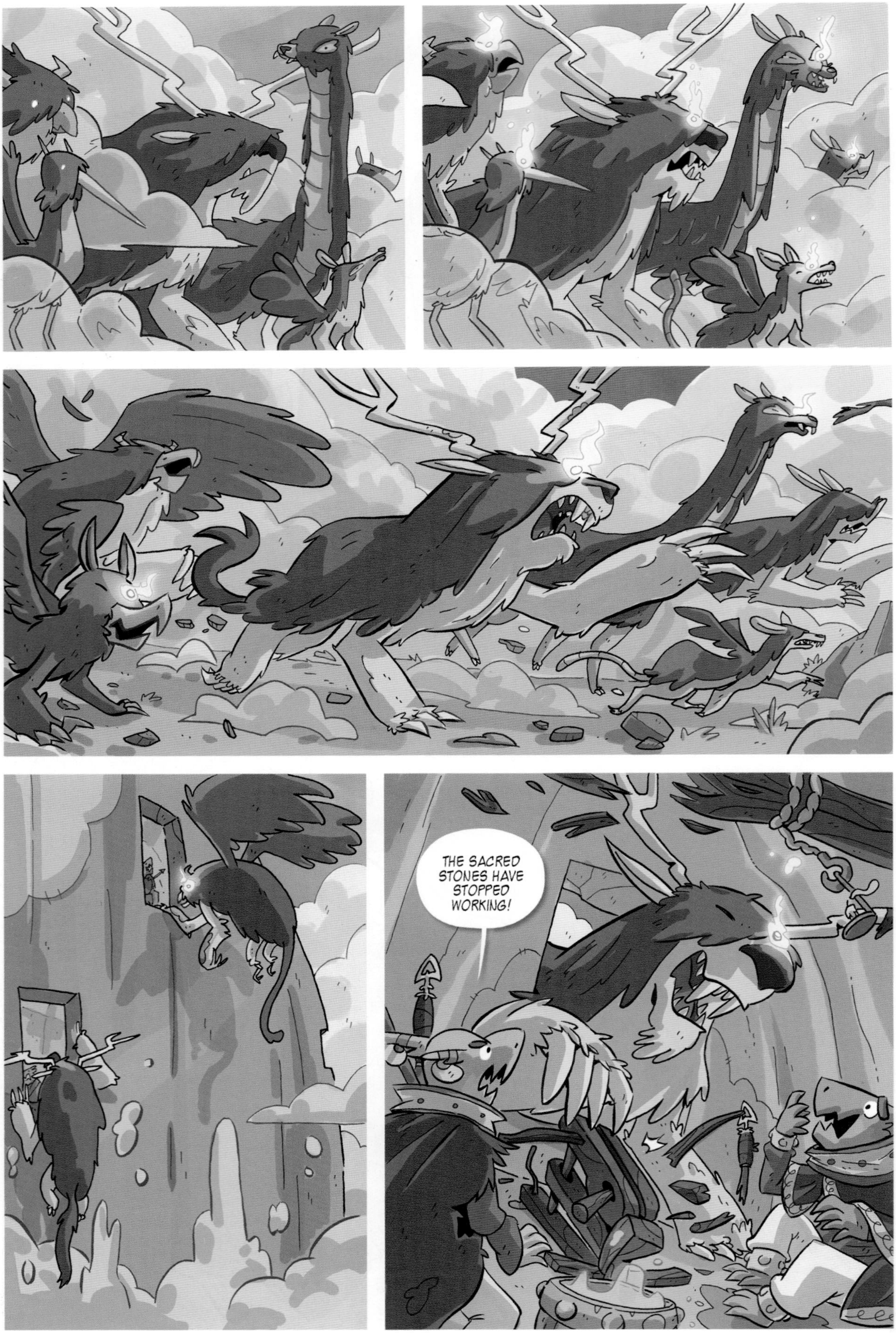
THE SACRED STONES HAVE STOPPED WORKING!

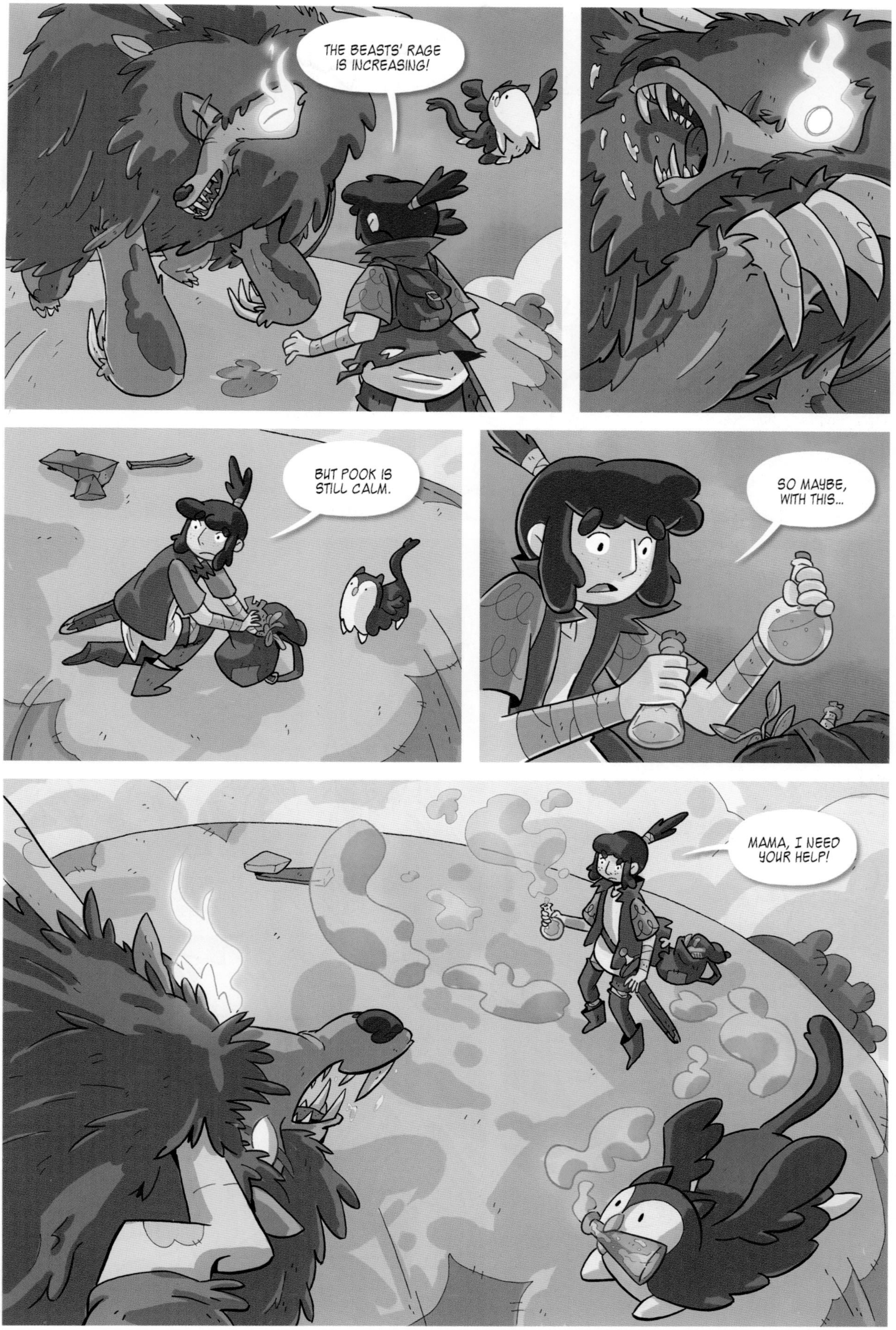
THE BEASTS' RAGE IS INCREASING!
BUT POOK IS STILL CALM.
SO MAYBE, WITH THIS...
MAMA, I NEED YOUR HELP!

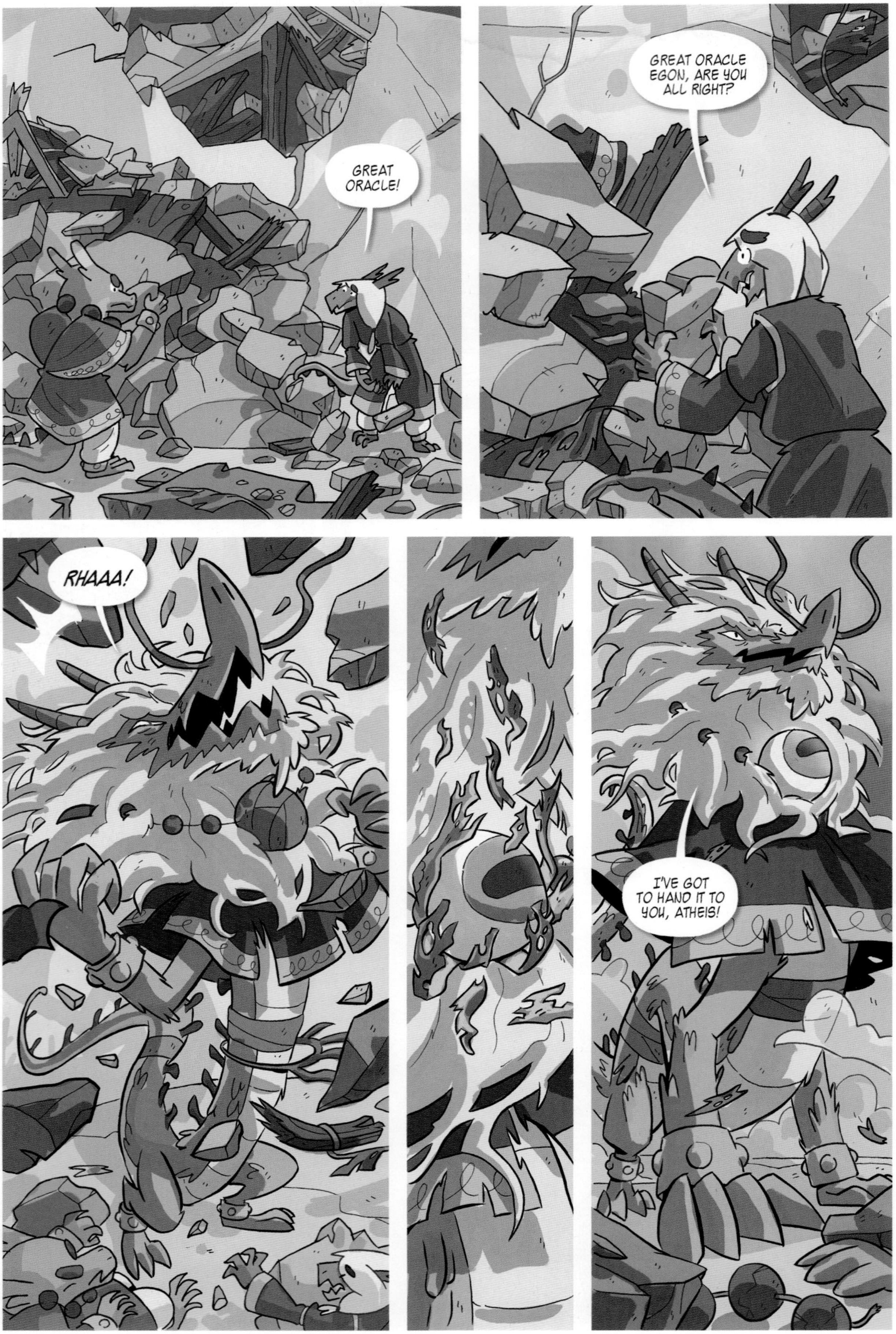
GREAT ORACLE!
GREAT ORACLE EGON, ARE YOU ALL RIGHT?
RHAAA!
I'VE GOT TO HAND IT TO YOU, ATHEIS!

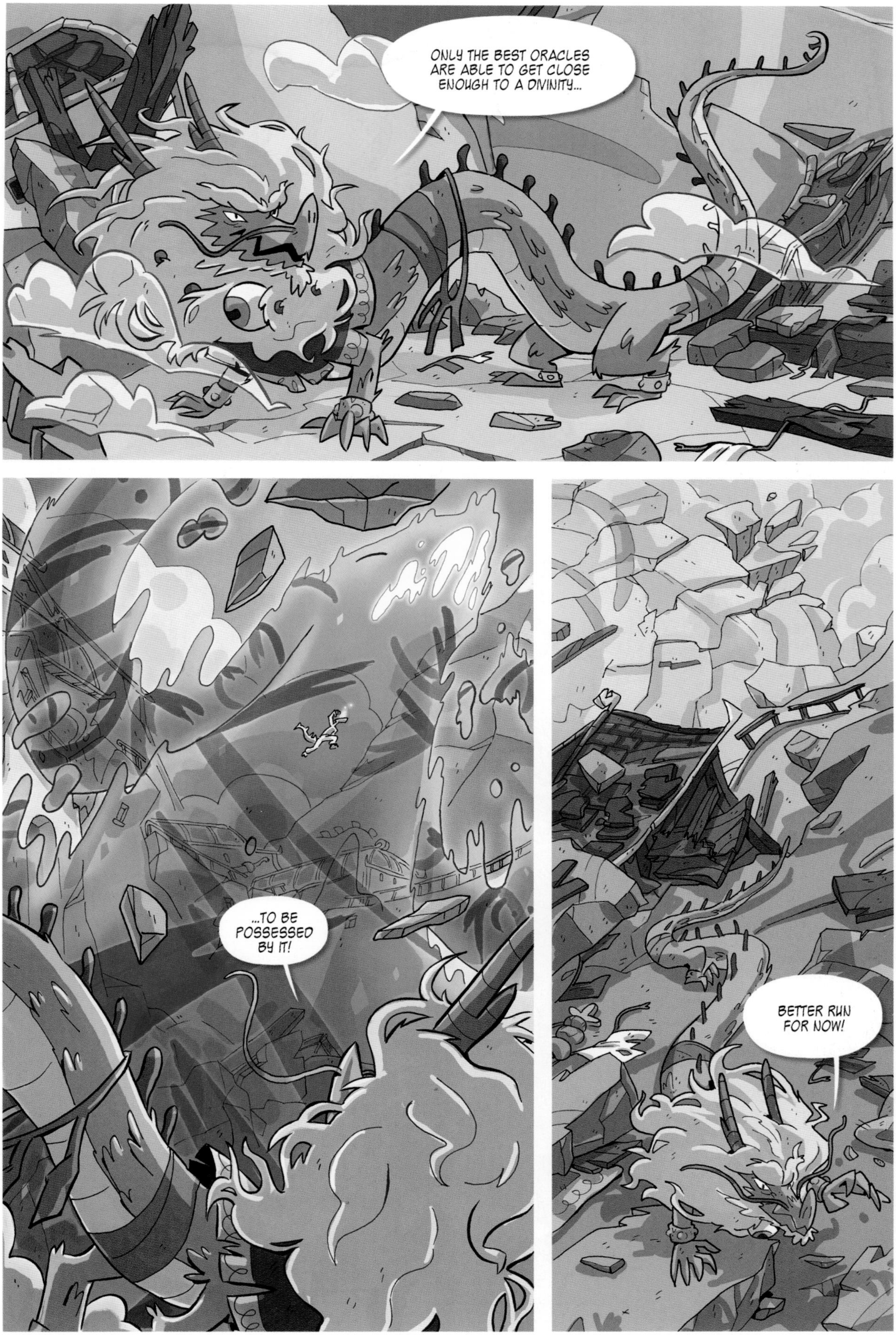
ONLY THE BEST ORACLES ARE ABLE TO GET CLOSE ENOUGH TO A DIVINITY...
...TO BE POSSESSED BY IT!
BETTER RUN FOR NOW!

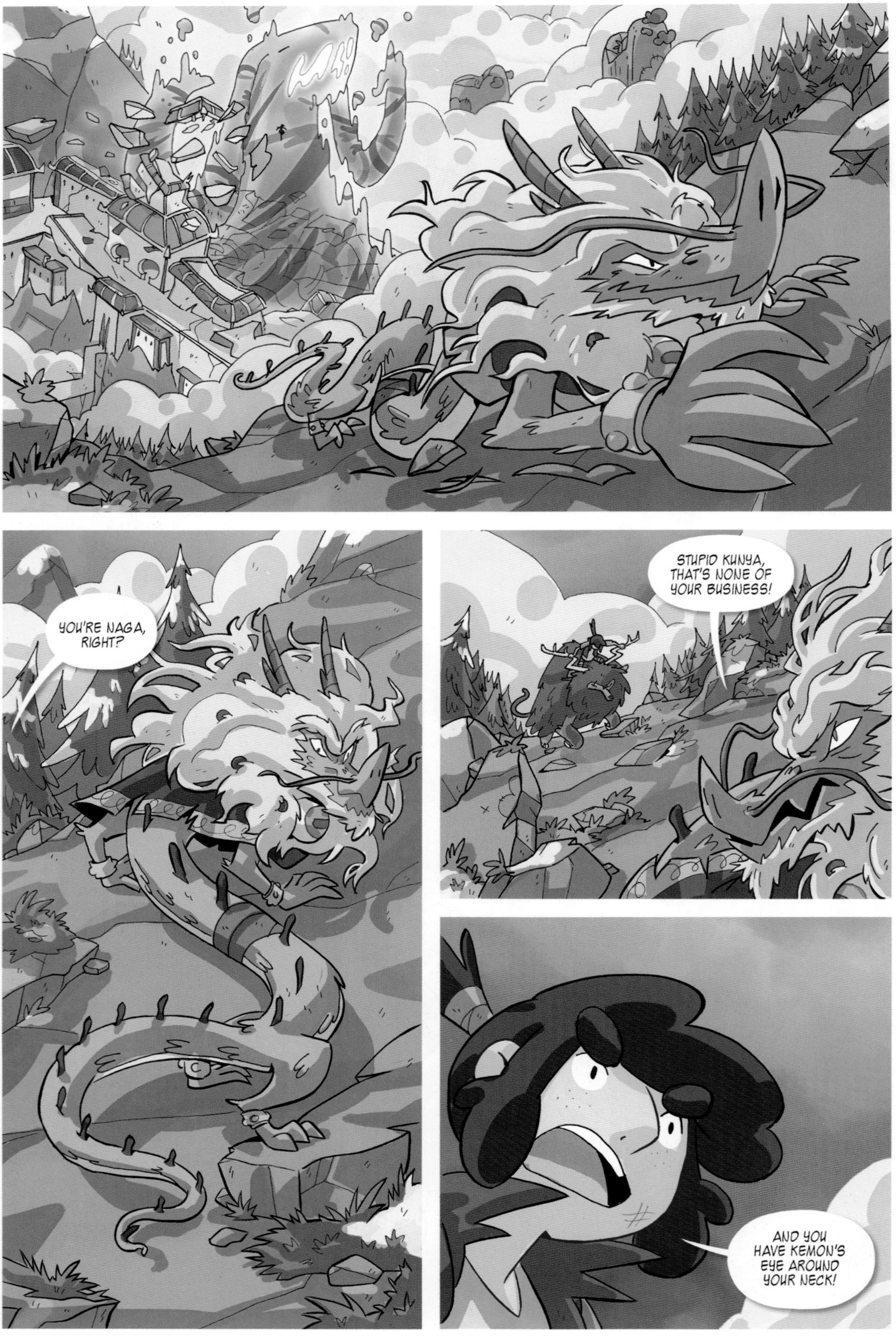
YOU'RE NAGA, RIGHT?
STUPID KUNYA, THAT'S NONE OF YOUR BUSINESS!
AND YOU HAVE KEMON'S EYE AROUND YOUR NECK!

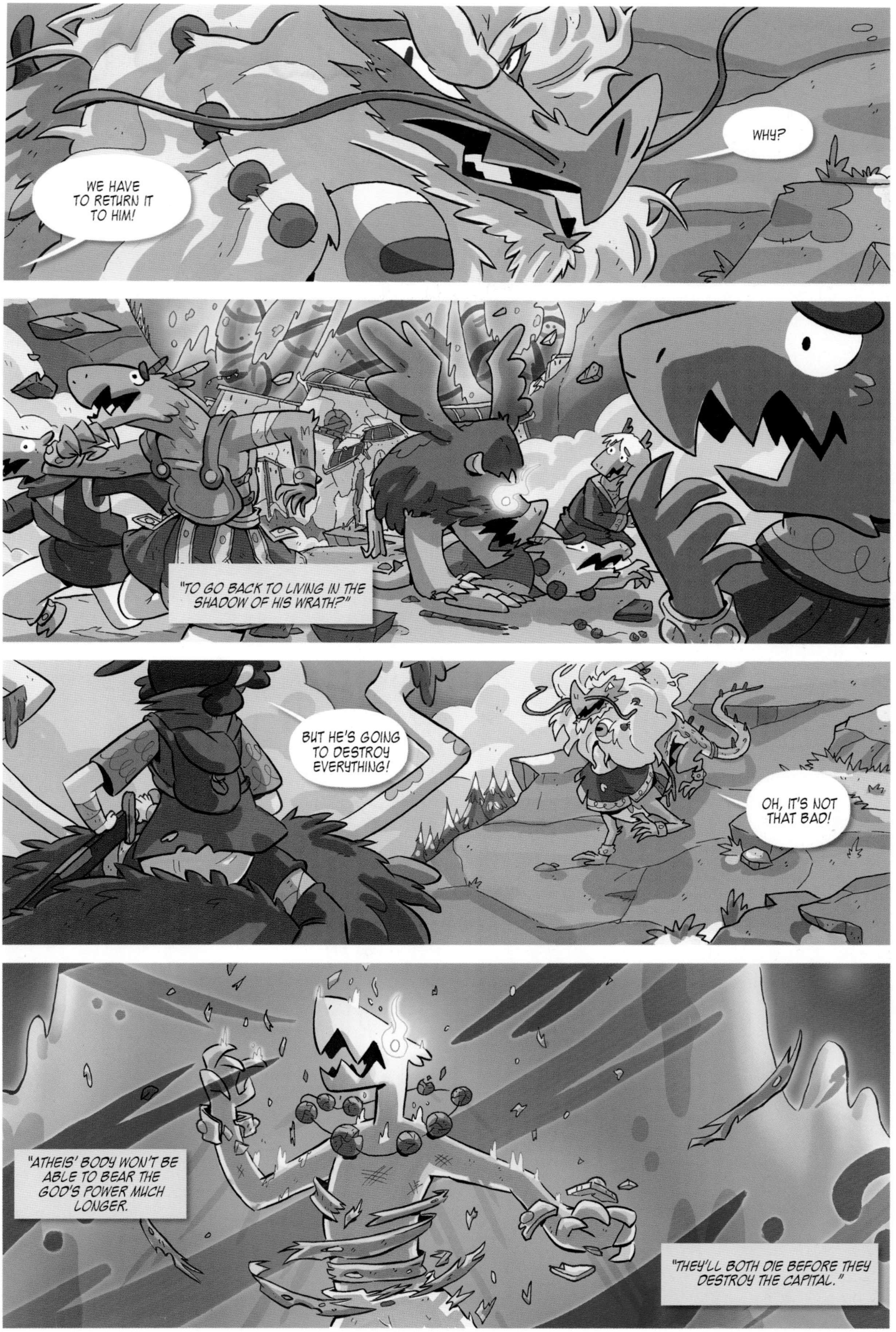
WE HAVE TO RETURN IT TO HIM!
WHY?
"TO GO BACK TO LIVING IN THE SHADOW OF HIS WRATH?"
BUT HE'S GOING TO DESTROY EVERYTHING!
OH, IT'S NOT THAT BAD!
"ATHEIS' BODY WON'T BE ABLE TO BEAR THE GOD'S POWER MUCH LONGER.
"THEY'LL BOTH DIE BEFORE THEY DESTROY THE CAPITAL."

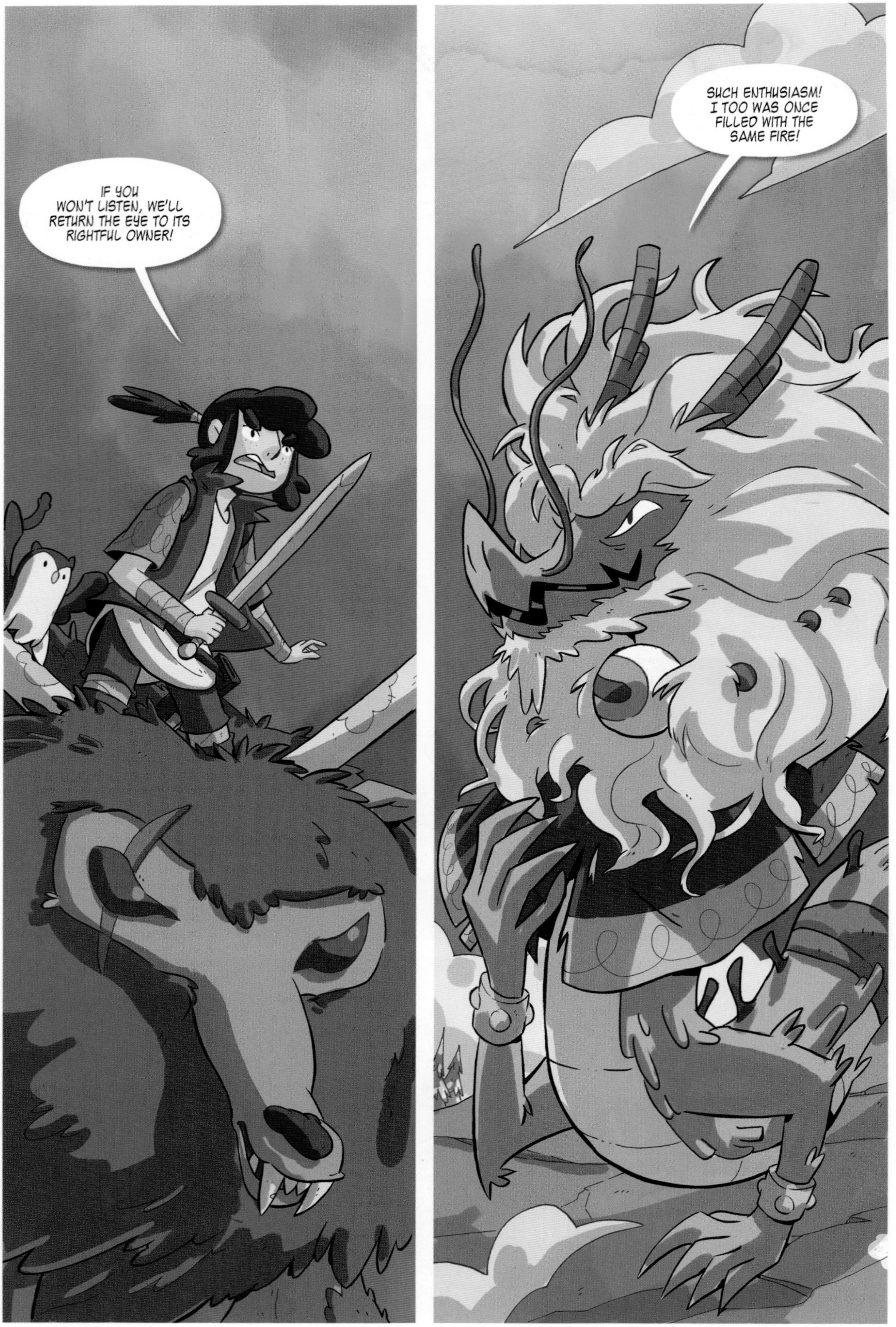
IF YOU WON'T LISTEN, WE'LL RETURN THE EYE TO ITS RIGHTFUL OWNER!
SUCH ENTHUSIASM! I TOO WAS ONCE FILLED WITH THE SAME FIRE!

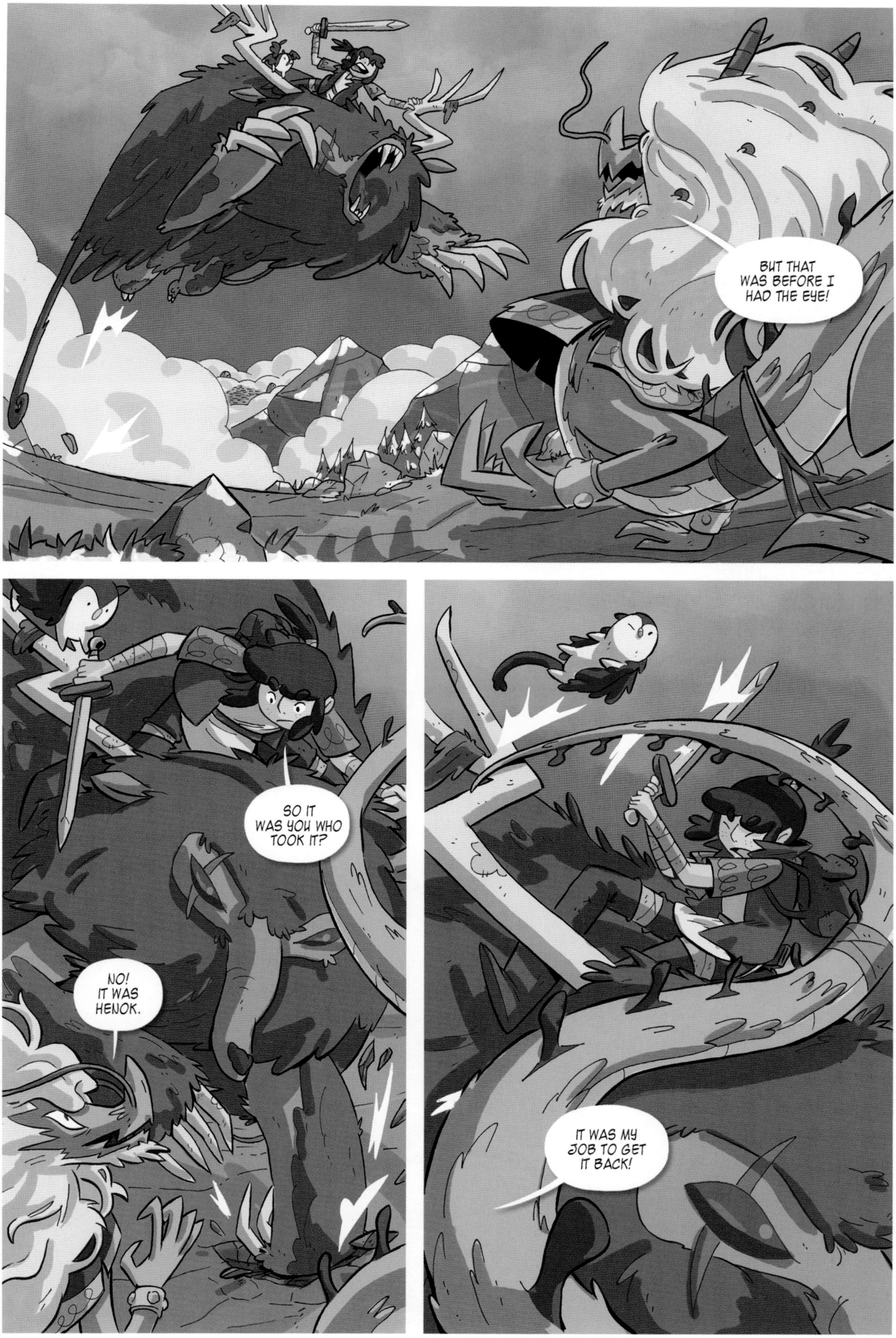
BUT THAT WAS BEFORE I HAD THE EYE!
SO IT WAS YOU WHO TOOK IT?
NO! IT WAS HENOK.
IT WAS MY JOB TO GET IT BACK!

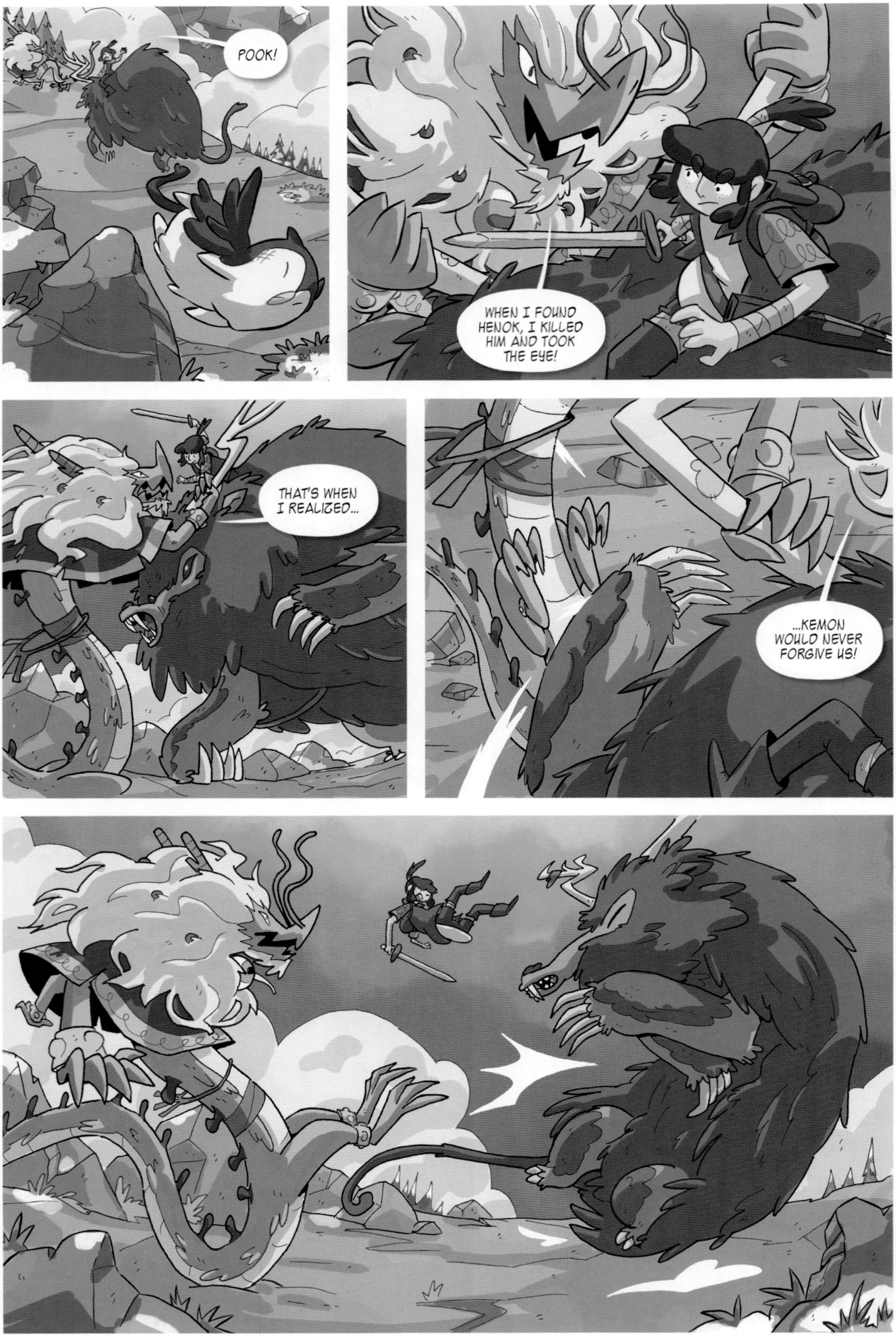
POOK!
WHEN I FOUND HENOK, I KILLED HIM AND TOOK THE EYE!
THAT'S WHEN I REALIZED...
...KEMON WOULD NEVER FORGIVE US!

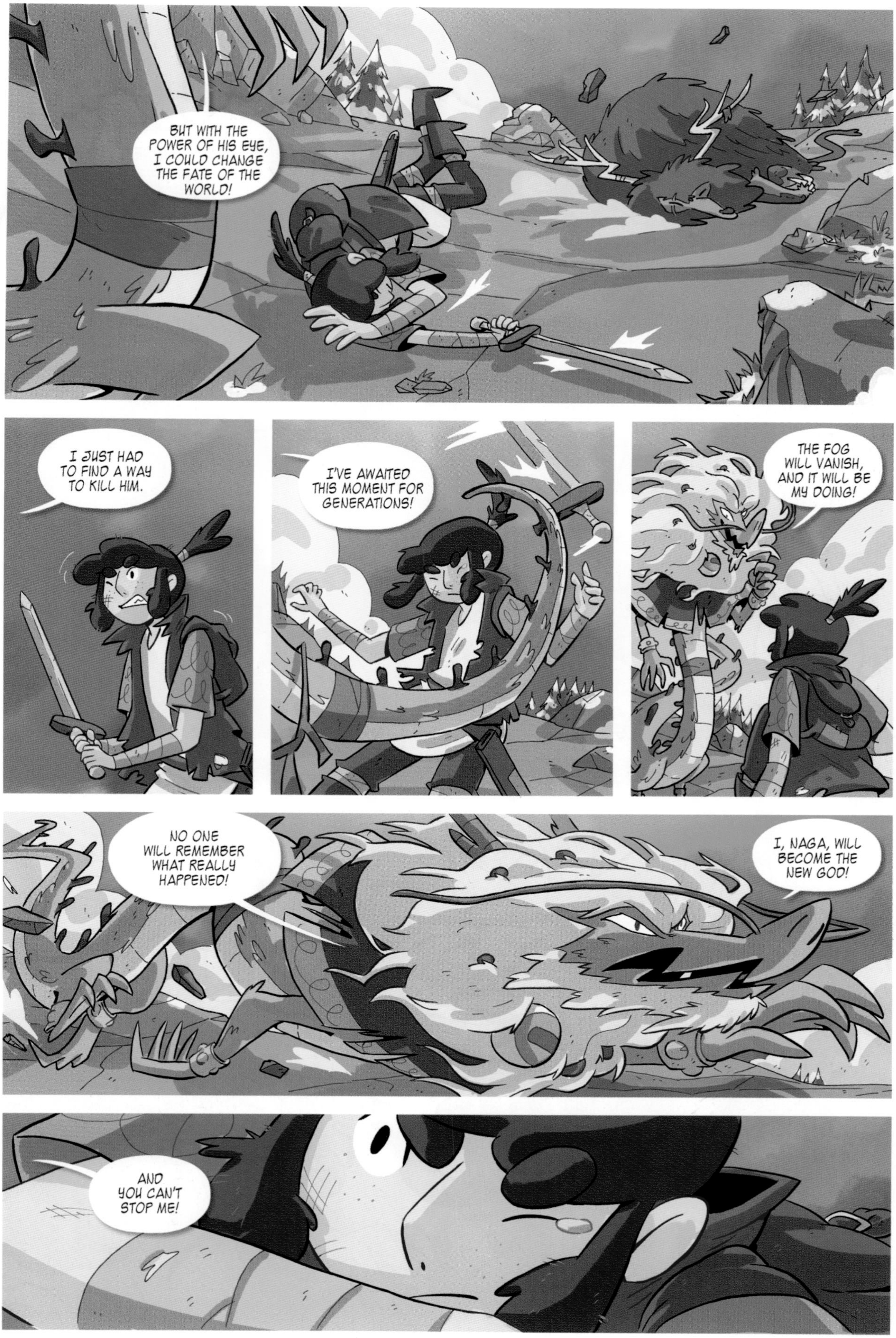
BUT WITH THE POWER OF HIS EYE, I COULD CHANGE THE FATE OF THE WORLD!
I JUST HAD TO FIND A WAY TO KILL HIM.
I'VE AWAITED THIS MOMENT FOR GENERATIONS!
THE FOG WILL VANISH, AND IT WILL BE MY DOING!
NO ONE WILL REMEMBER WHAT REALLY HAPPENED!
I, NAGA, WILL BECOME THE NEW GOD!
AND YOU CAN'T STOP ME!

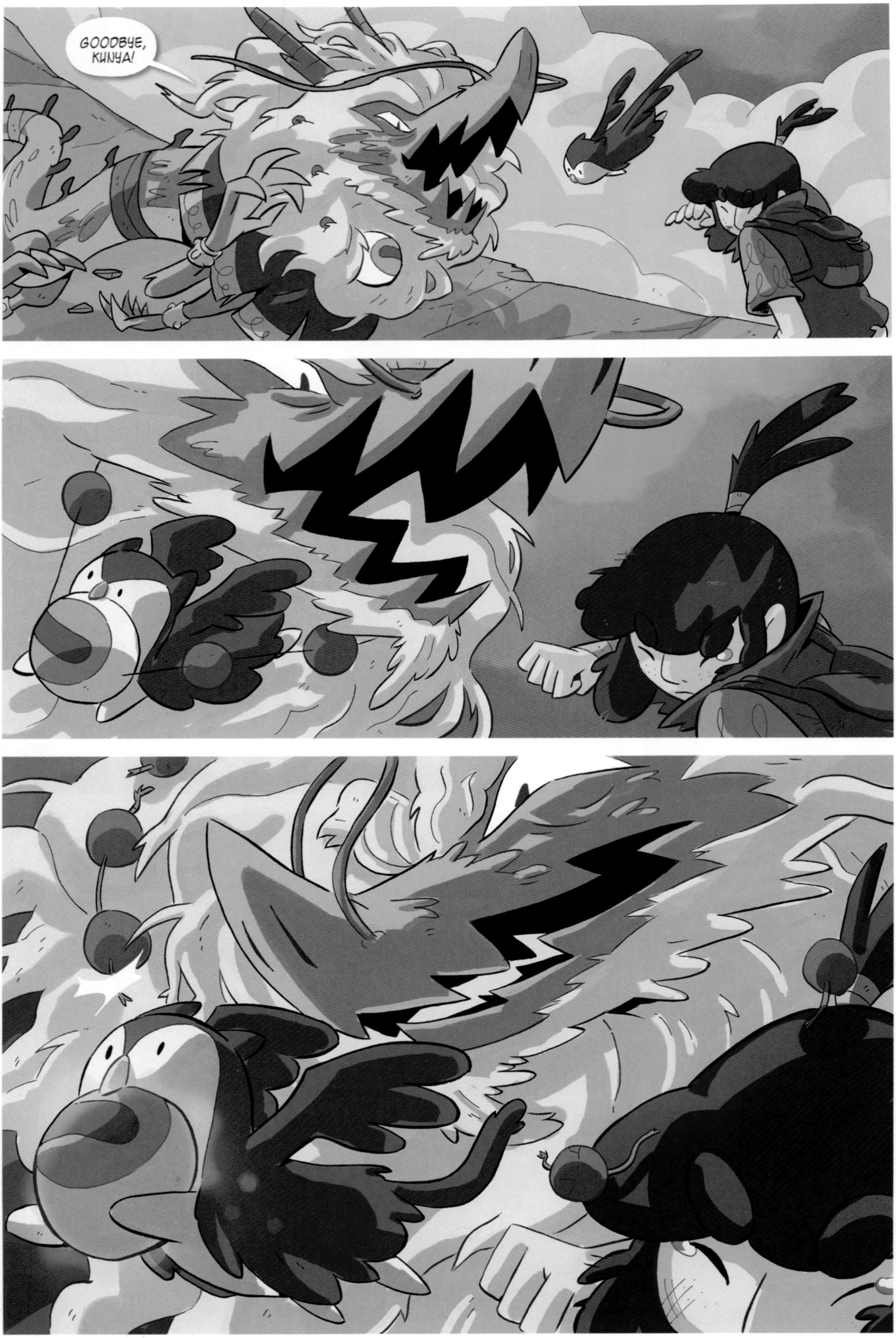
GOODBYE, KUNYA!

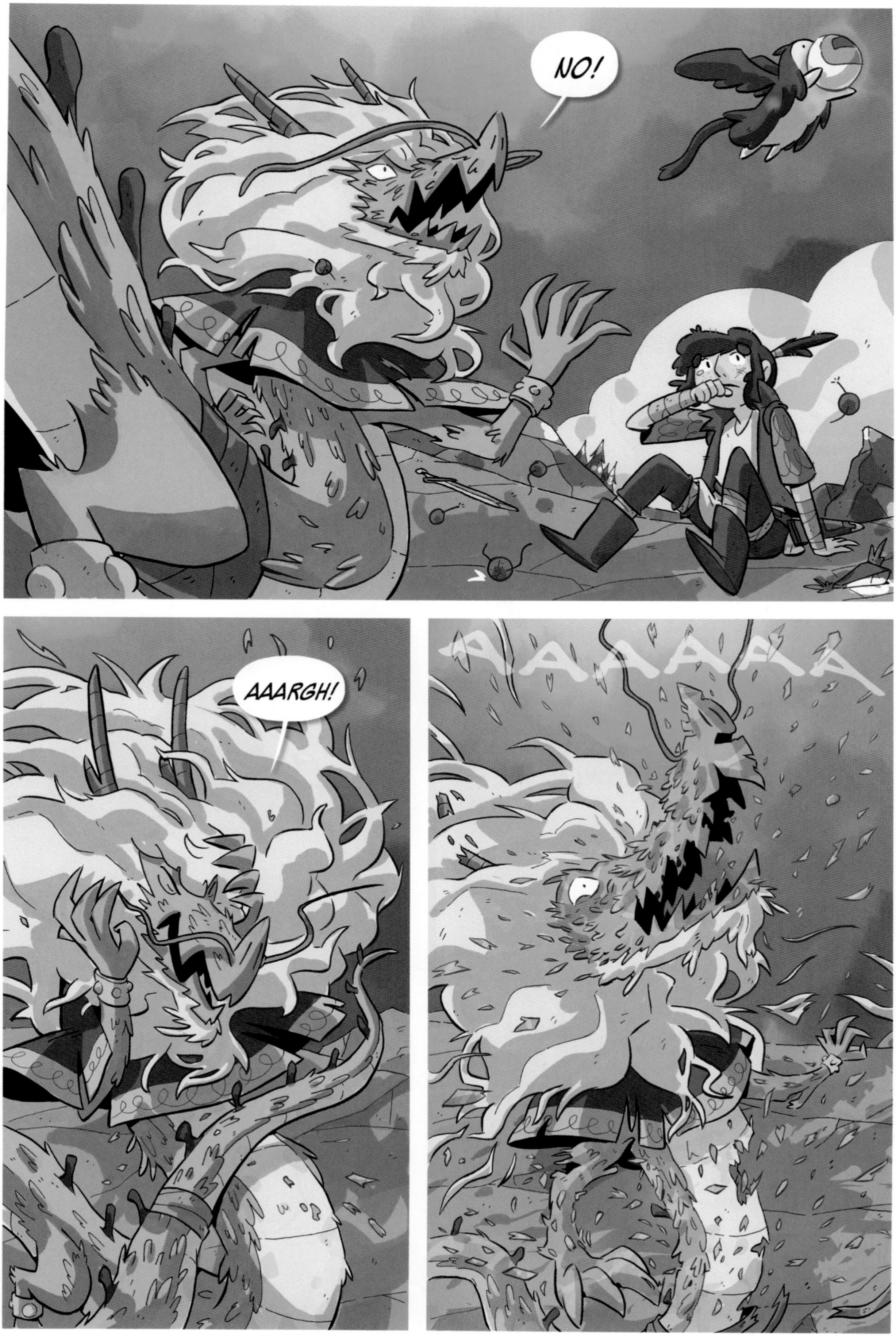
NO!
AAARGH!
AAAAAA

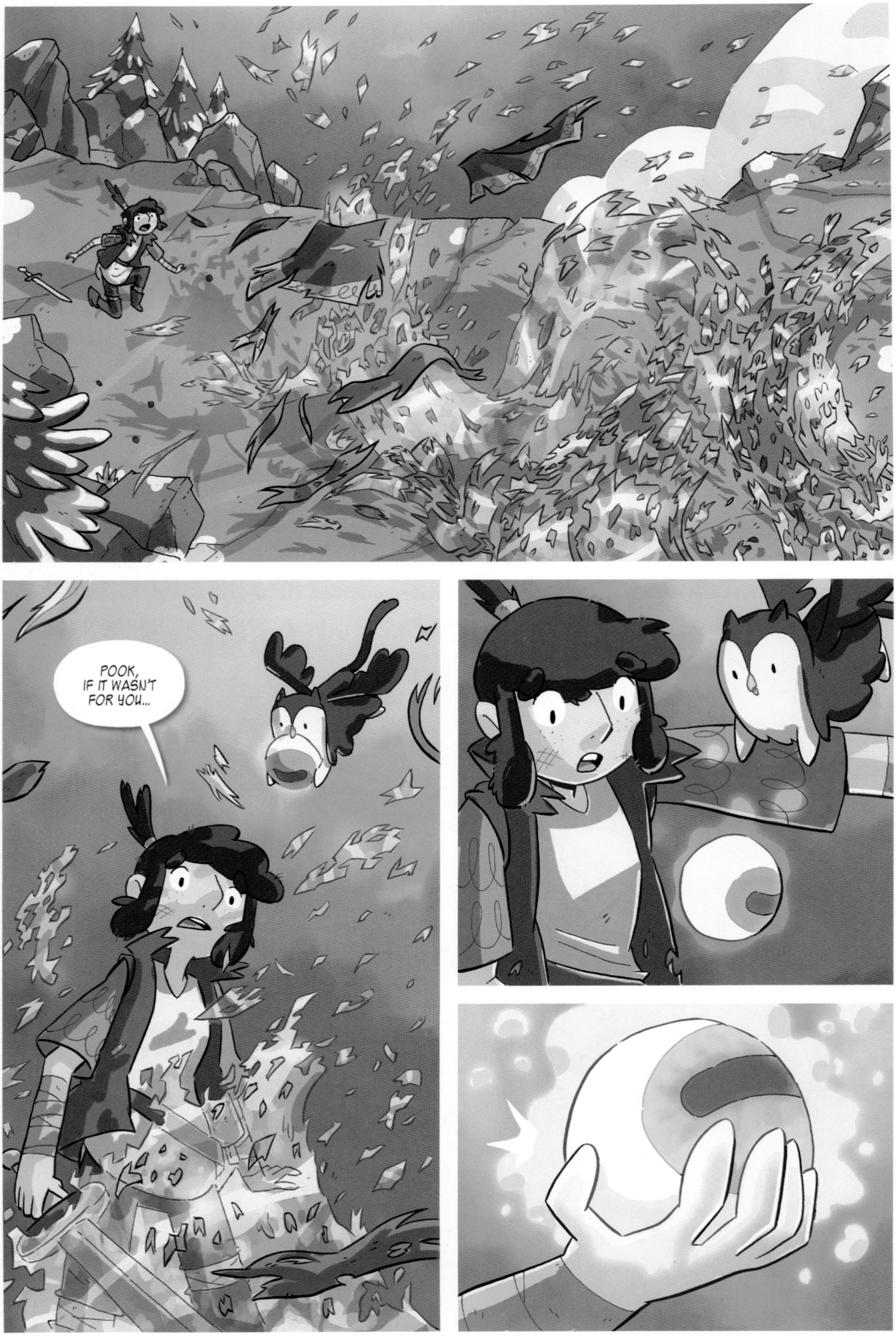
POOK, IF IT WASN'T FOR YOU...

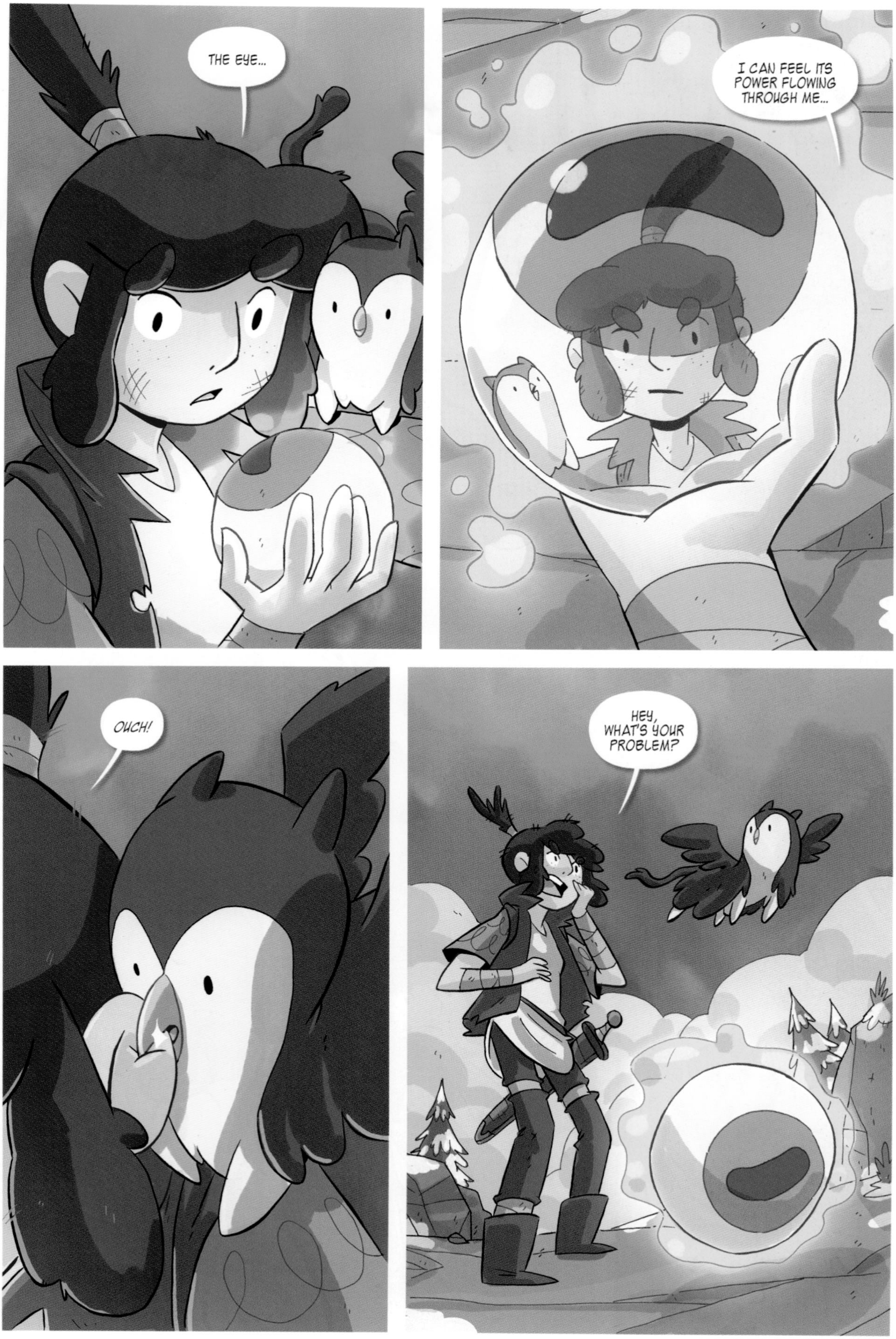
THE EYE...
I CAN FEEL ITS POWER FLOWING THROUGH ME...
OUCH!
HEY, WHAT'S YOUR PROBLEM?

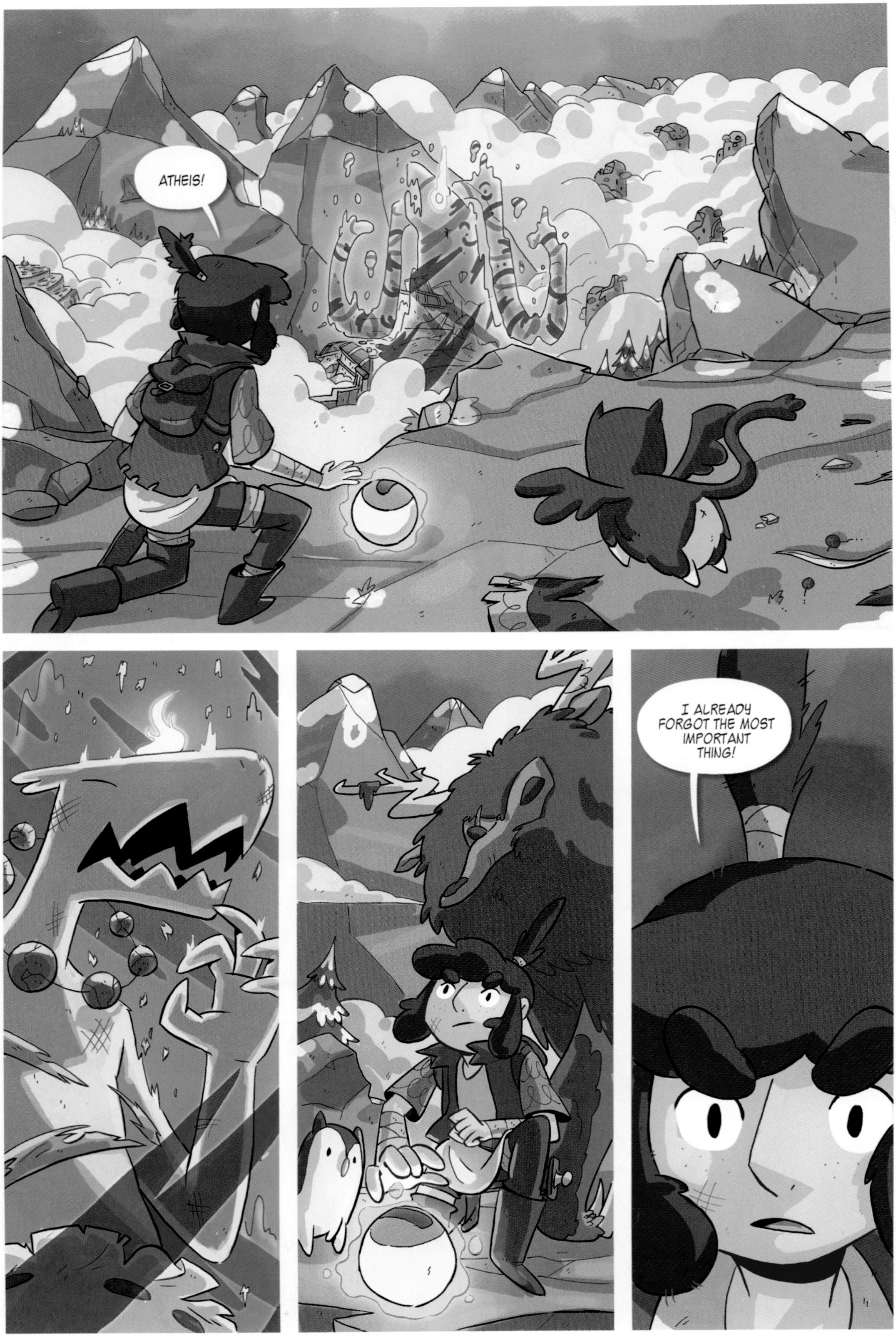
ATHEIS!
I ALREADY FORGOT THE MOST IMPORTANT THING!

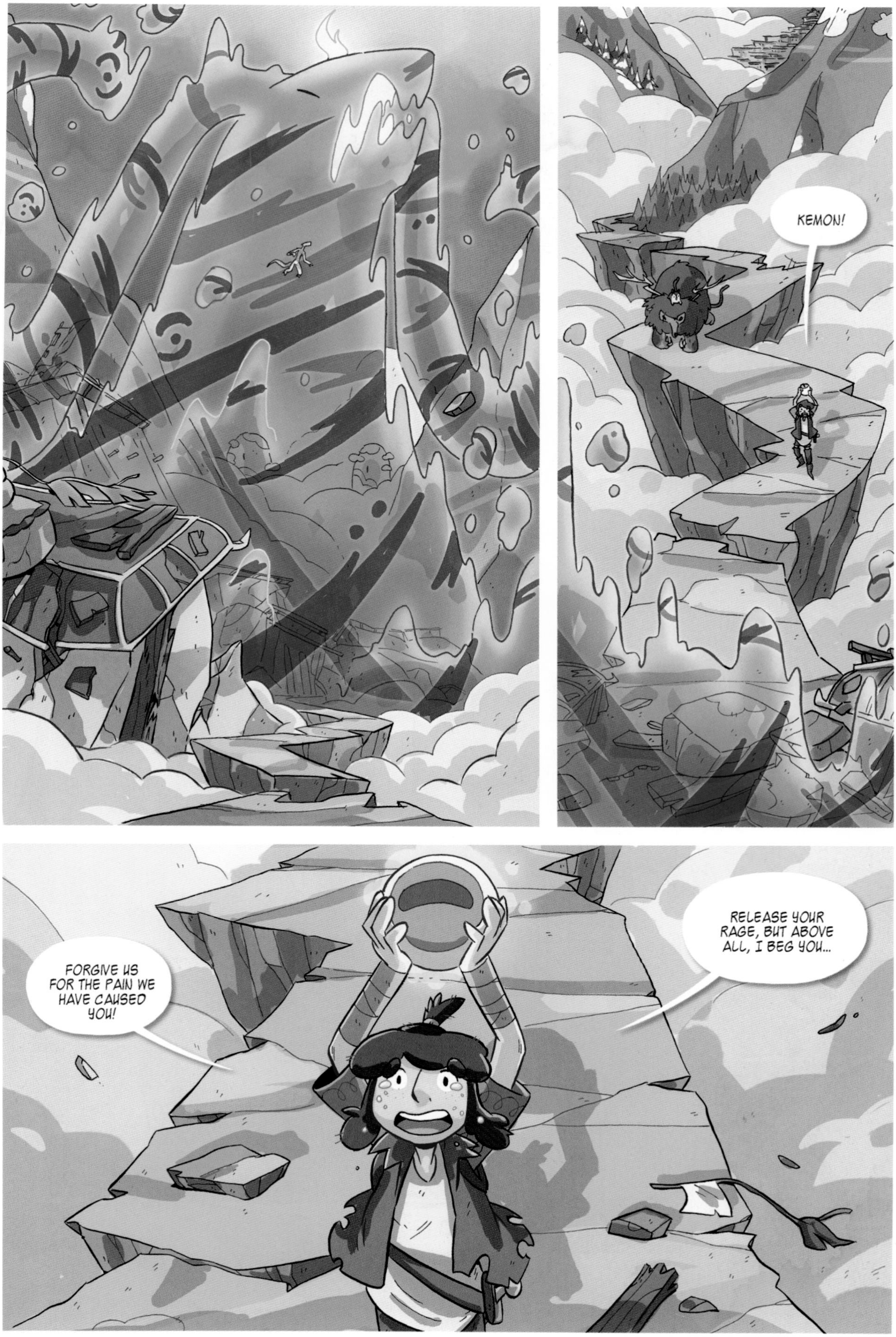
KEMON!
FORGIVE US FOR THE PAIN WE HAVE CAUSED YOU!
RELEASE YOUR RAGE, BUT ABOVE ALL, I BEG YOU...

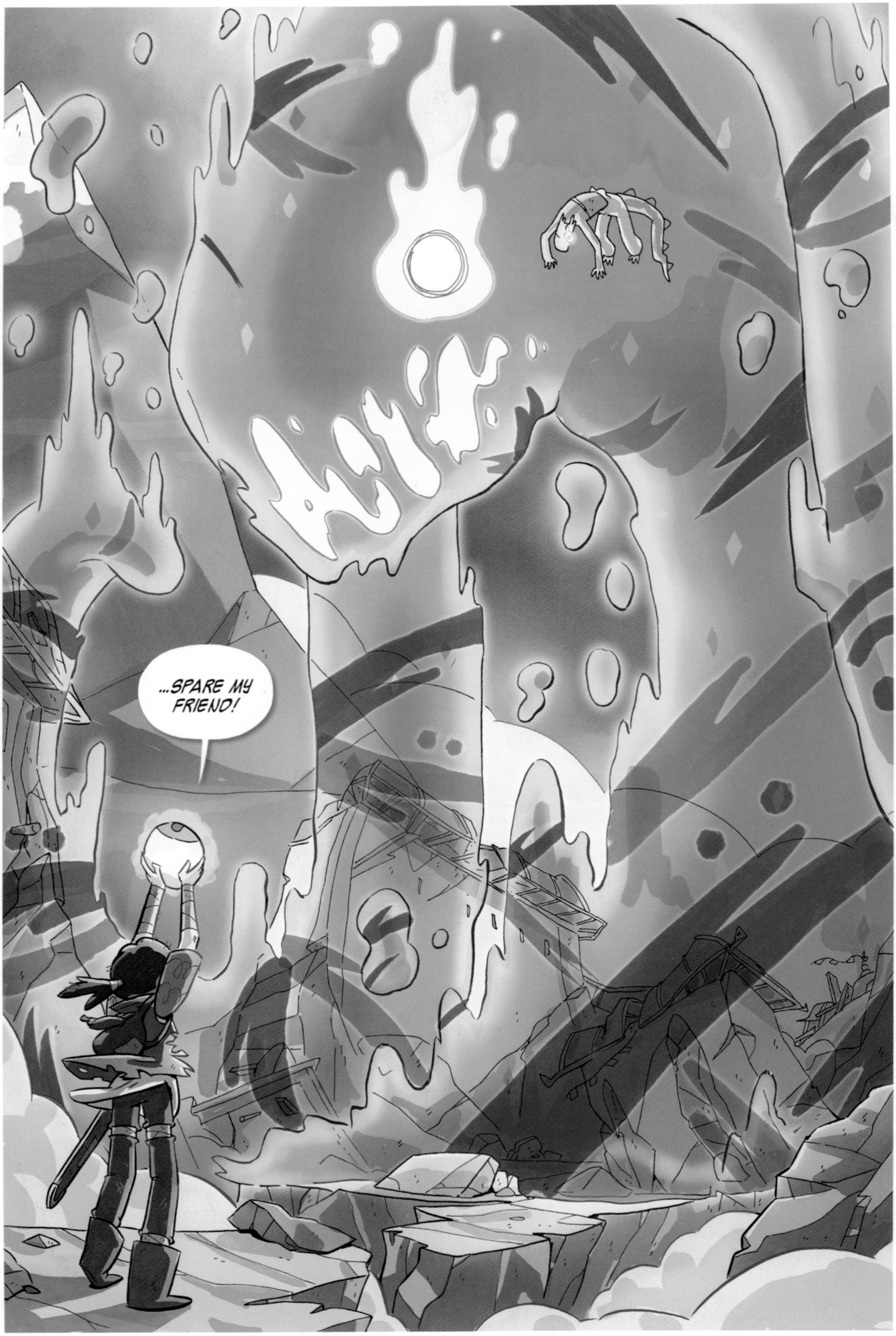
...SPARE MY FRIEND!

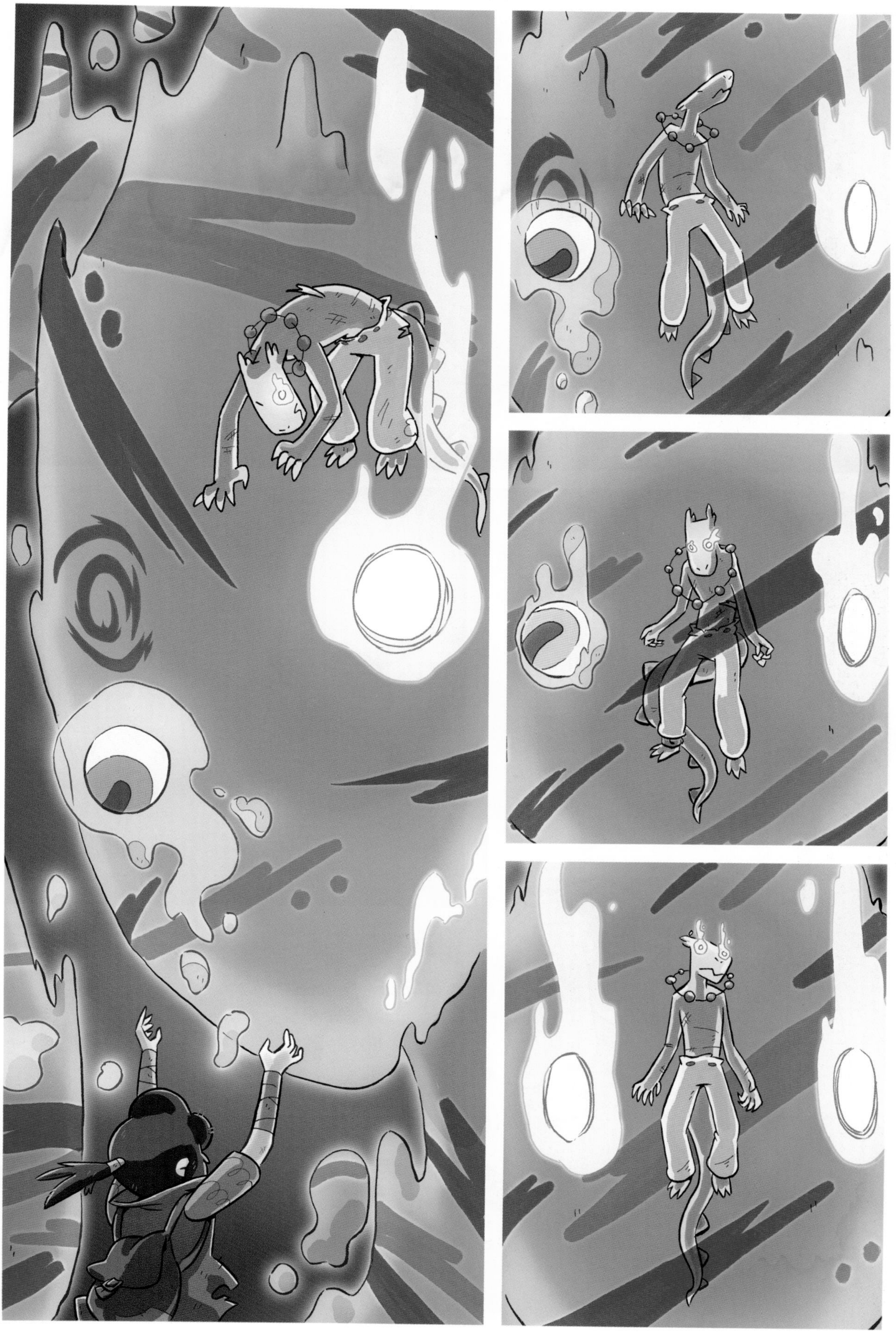

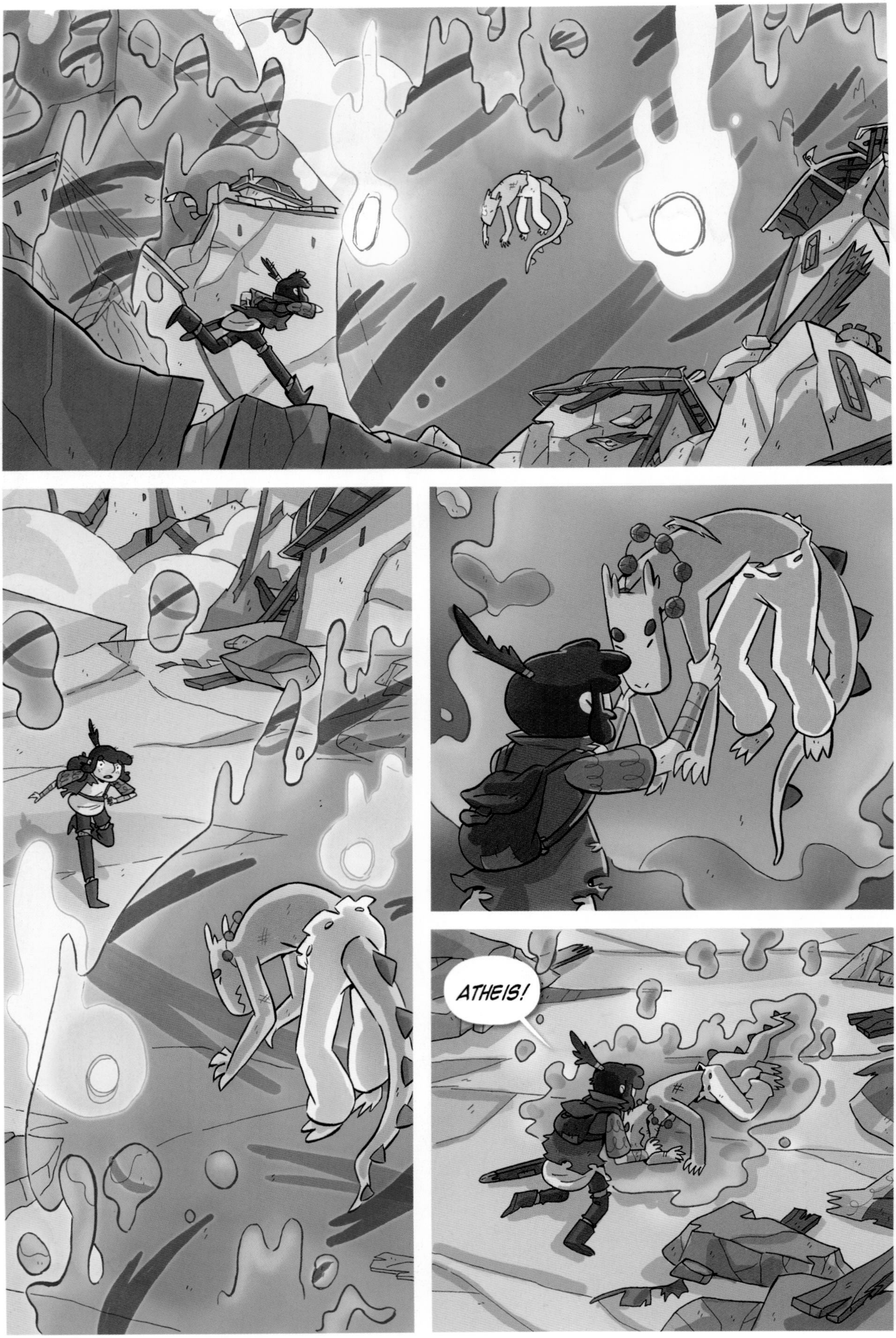
ATHEIS!

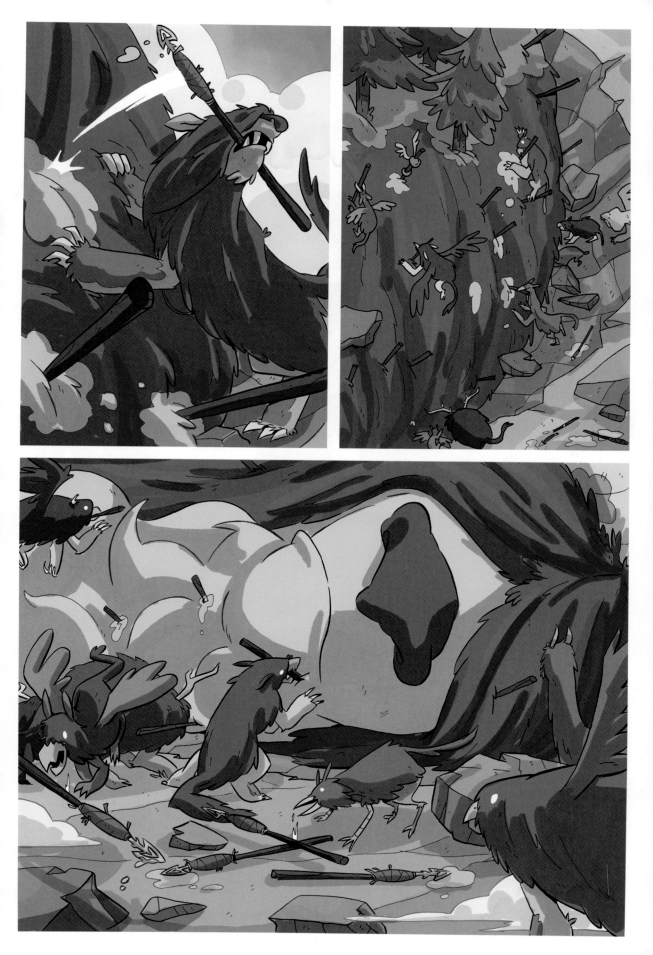

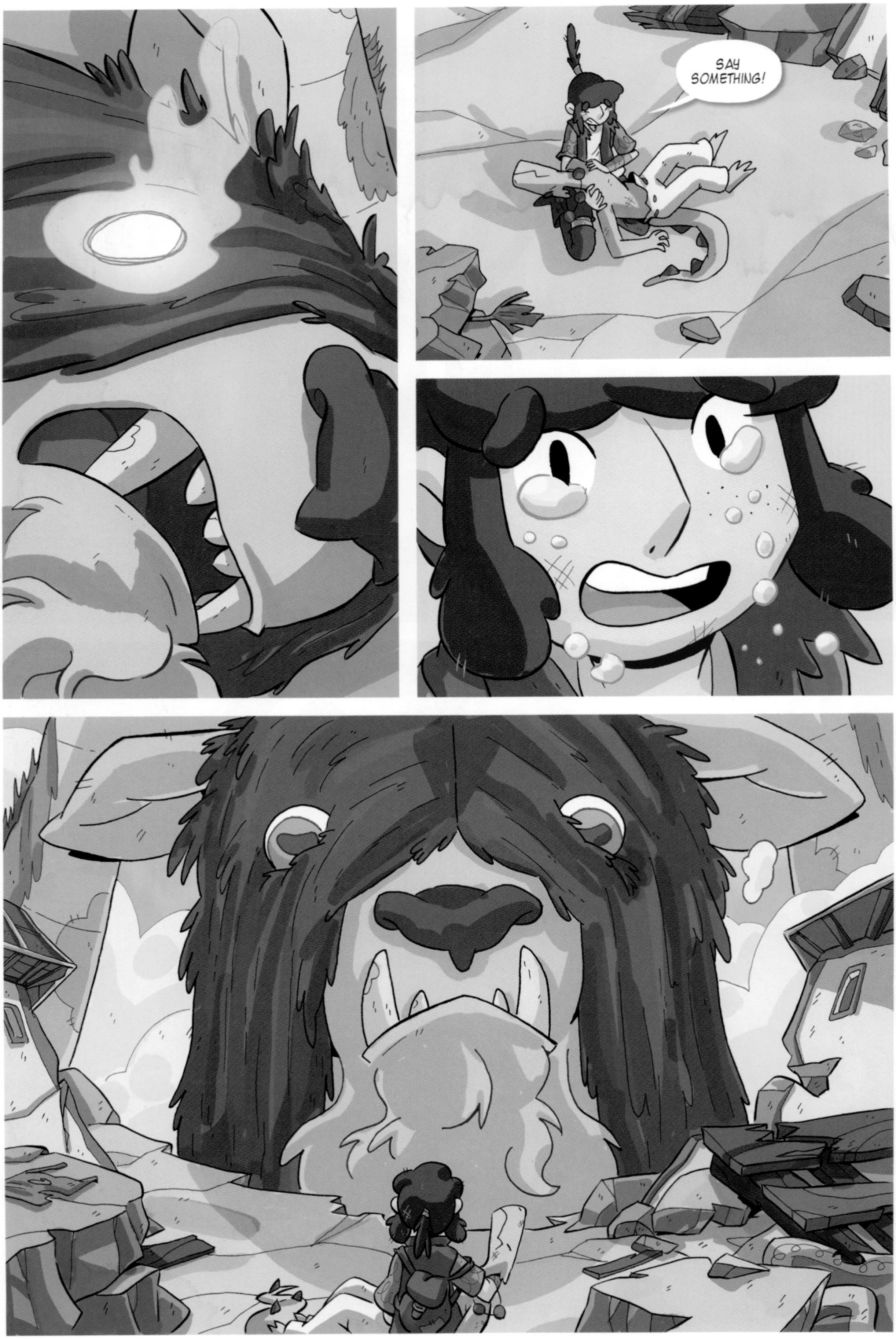
SAY SOMETHING!

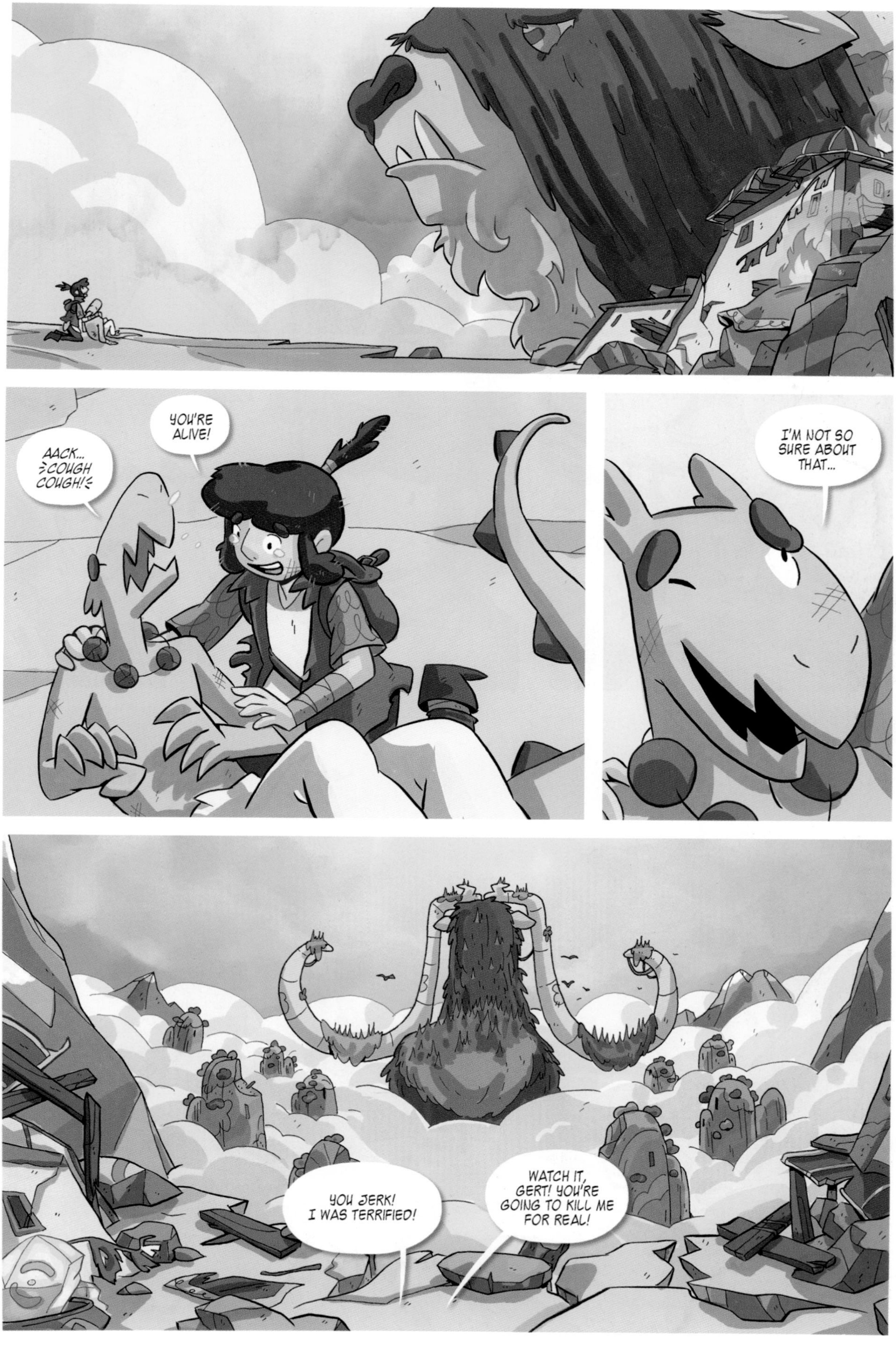

AACK... ⪢COUGH COUGH!⪡
YOU'RE ALIVE!
I'M NOT SO SURE ABOUT THAT...
YOU JERK! I WAS TERRIFIED!
WATCH IT, GERT! YOU'RE GOING TO KILL ME FOR REAL!

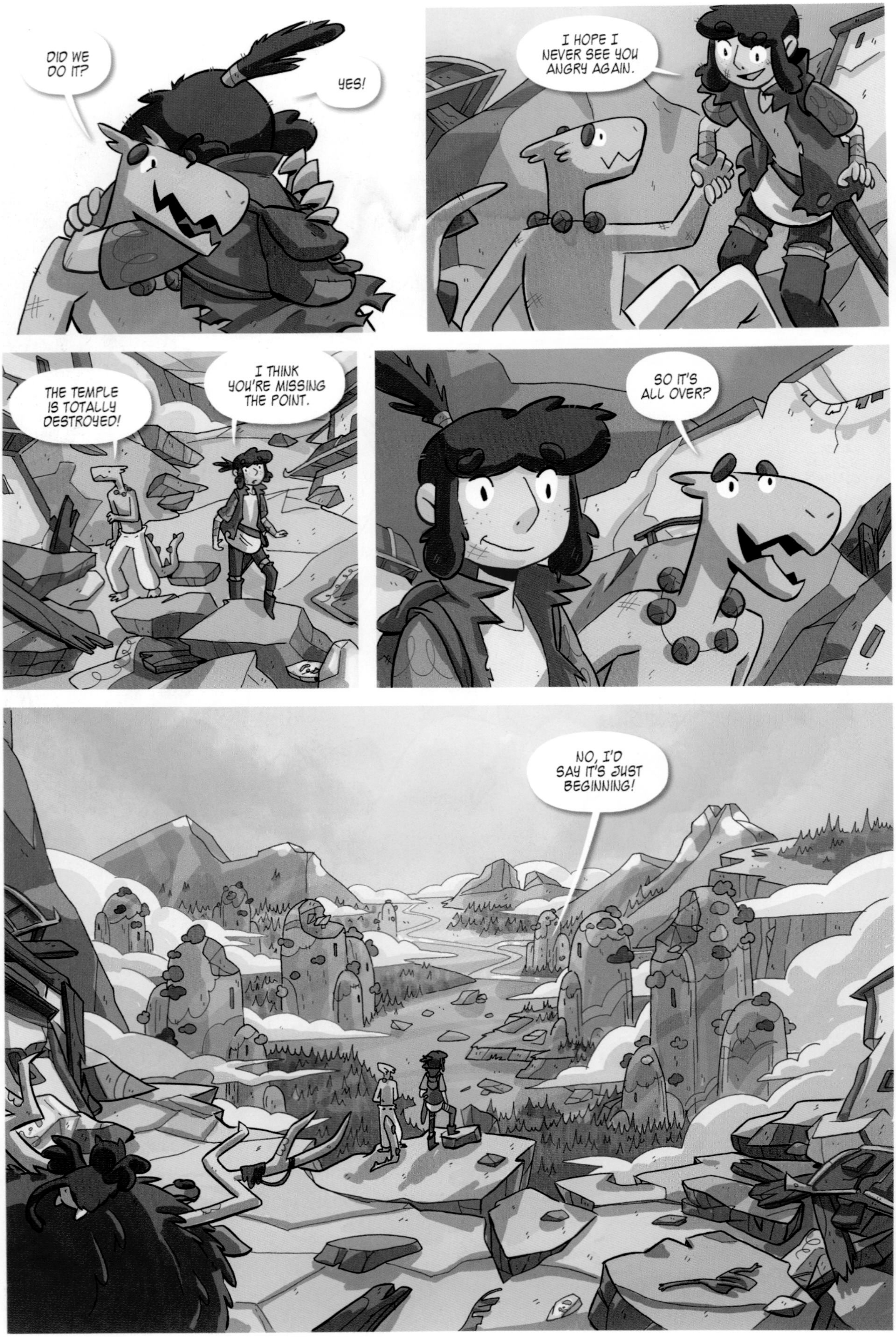
DID WE DO IT?
YES!
I HOPE I NEVER SEE YOU ANGRY AGAIN.
THE TEMPLE IS TOTALLY DESTROYED!
I THINK YOU'RE MISSING THE POINT.
SO IT'S ALL OVER?
NO, I'D SAY IT'S JUST BEGINNING!

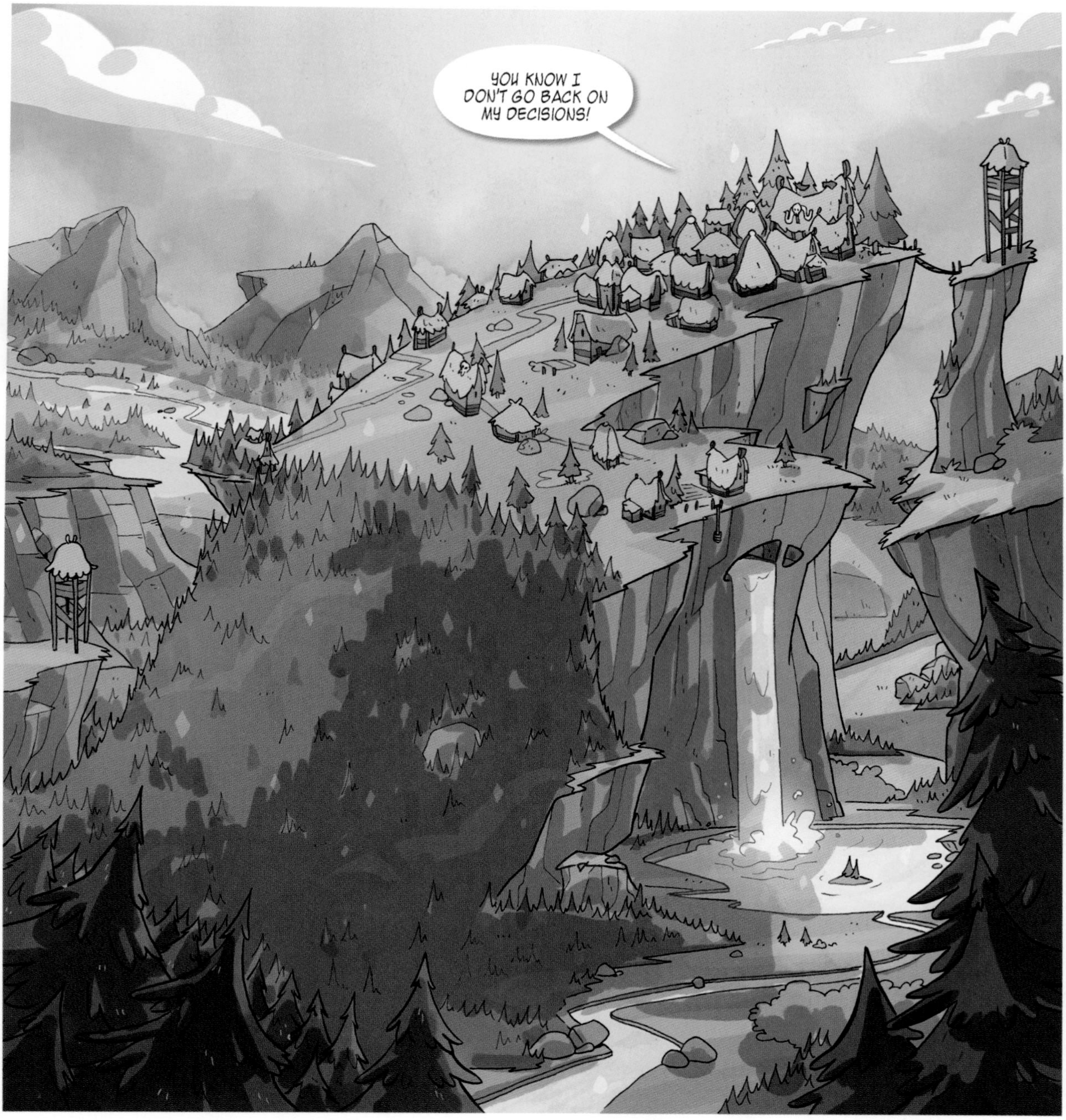
YOU KNOW I DON'T GO BACK ON MY DECISIONS!

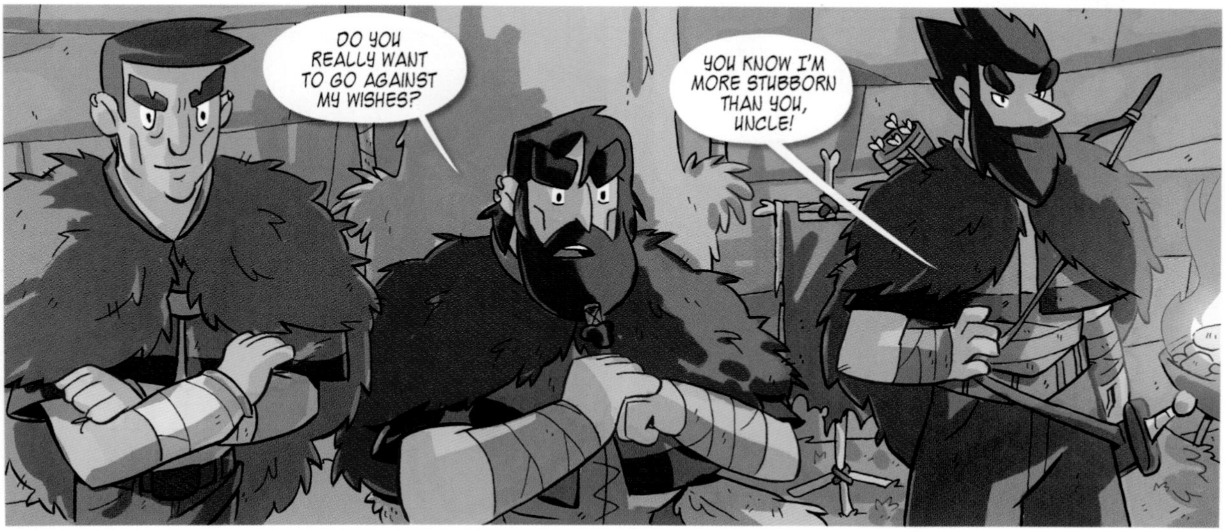
DO YOU REALLY WANT TO GO AGAINST MY WISHES?
YOU KNOW I'M MORE STUBBORN THAN YOU, UNCLE!

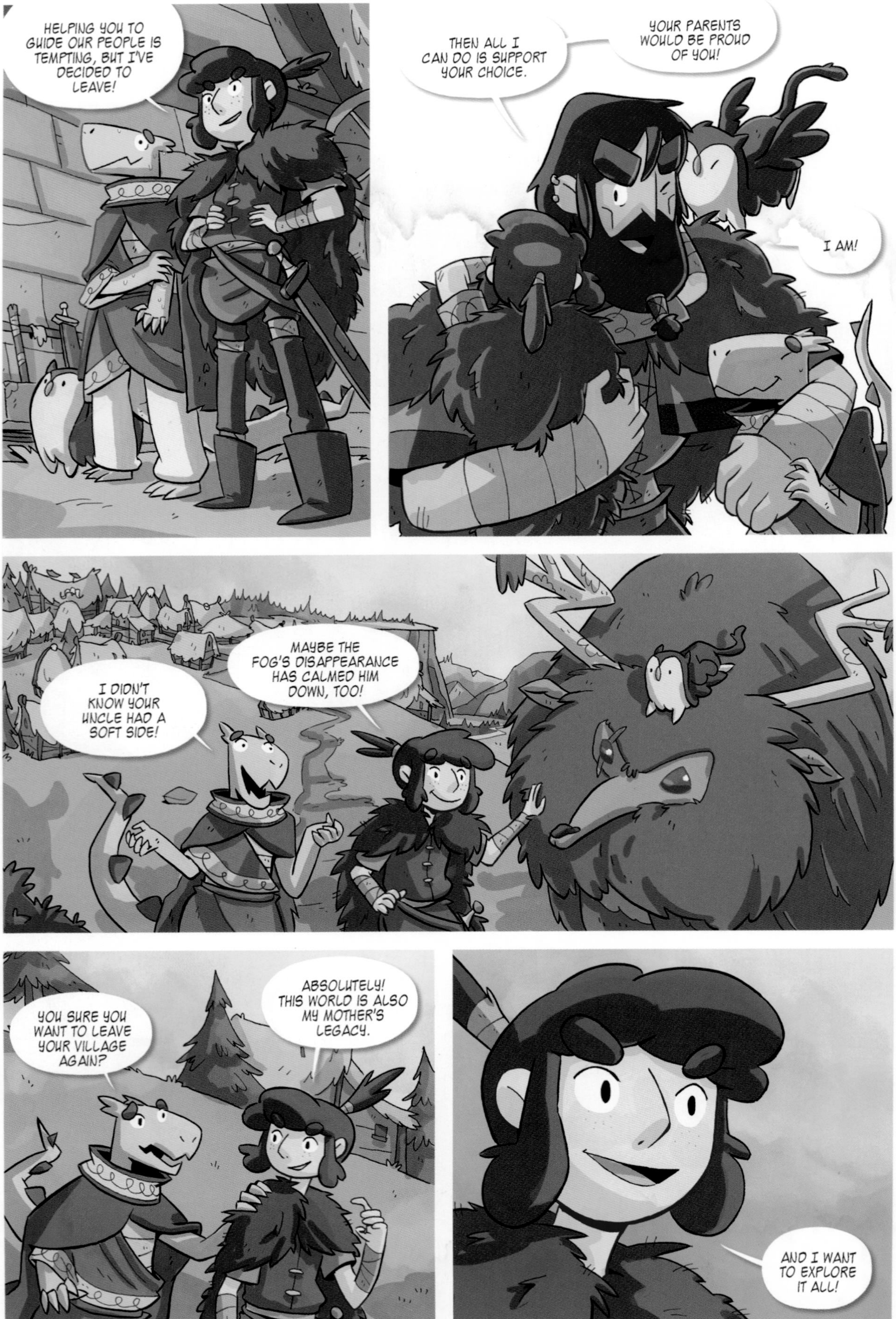

HELPING YOU TO GUIDE OUR PEOPLE IS TEMPTING, BUT I'VE DECIDED TO LEAVE!
THEN ALL I CAN DO IS SUPPORT YOUR CHOICE.
YOUR PARENTS WOULD BE PROUD OF YOU!
I AM!
I DIDN'T KNOW YOUR UNCLE HAD A SOFT SIDE!
MAYBE THE FOG'S DISAPPEARANCE HAS CALMED HIM DOWN, TOO!
YOU SURE YOU WANT TO LEAVE YOUR VILLAGE AGAIN?
ABSOLUTELY! THIS WORLD IS ALSO MY MOTHER'S LEGACY.
AND I WANT TO EXPLORE IT ALL!

This story is about friendships that can change the world, and it would never have existed if I hadn't met Andrea, the best buddy I could have grown up with, and if Bianca hadn't jumped out of the bushes and become my other half.

Whether near or far, you'll both always be a part of me.

I want to thank: Francesca and Sarah for always being there despite distance and duty, you're my Sailor Moons; Francesco, for all the invaluable advice and for giving us an amazing logo; Giorgio for the positivity and suggestions he gave me at every stage of this comic; Roni for spurring me on and believing in me and Pippo for always finding the time to lend me a hand; Antonio, Ester, Naomi and Giovanni, for all the affection and support, you were essential; my mom and dad for raising me with adventures and without prejudice and for believing in all this with me—I'll forever be your wild child; Marco, for loving me and being loved, for making me sublime lunches and dinners to keep me going. Nothing makes me happier than sharing this life and work with you. I am proud of us.

—Francesca

A bow to all of those who have read this far, the attentive or distracted, the ones who read this page even before the beginning, the ones who liked or didn't like our story, readers who are young or no longer so young, but readers nonetheless.

I call Francesca back on to this imaginary stage for a final thank you from both, but especially to her, my joy.

—Marco

To everyone who helped us this year at our time of greatest need, our deepest thanks.

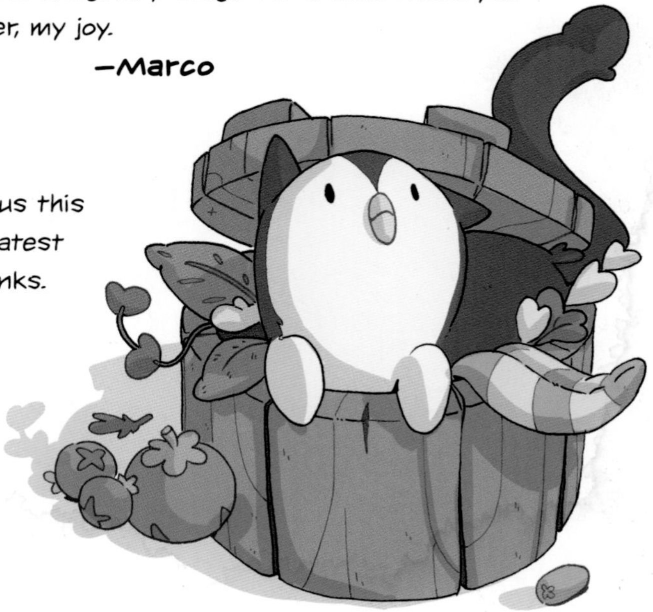

SKETCHBOOK

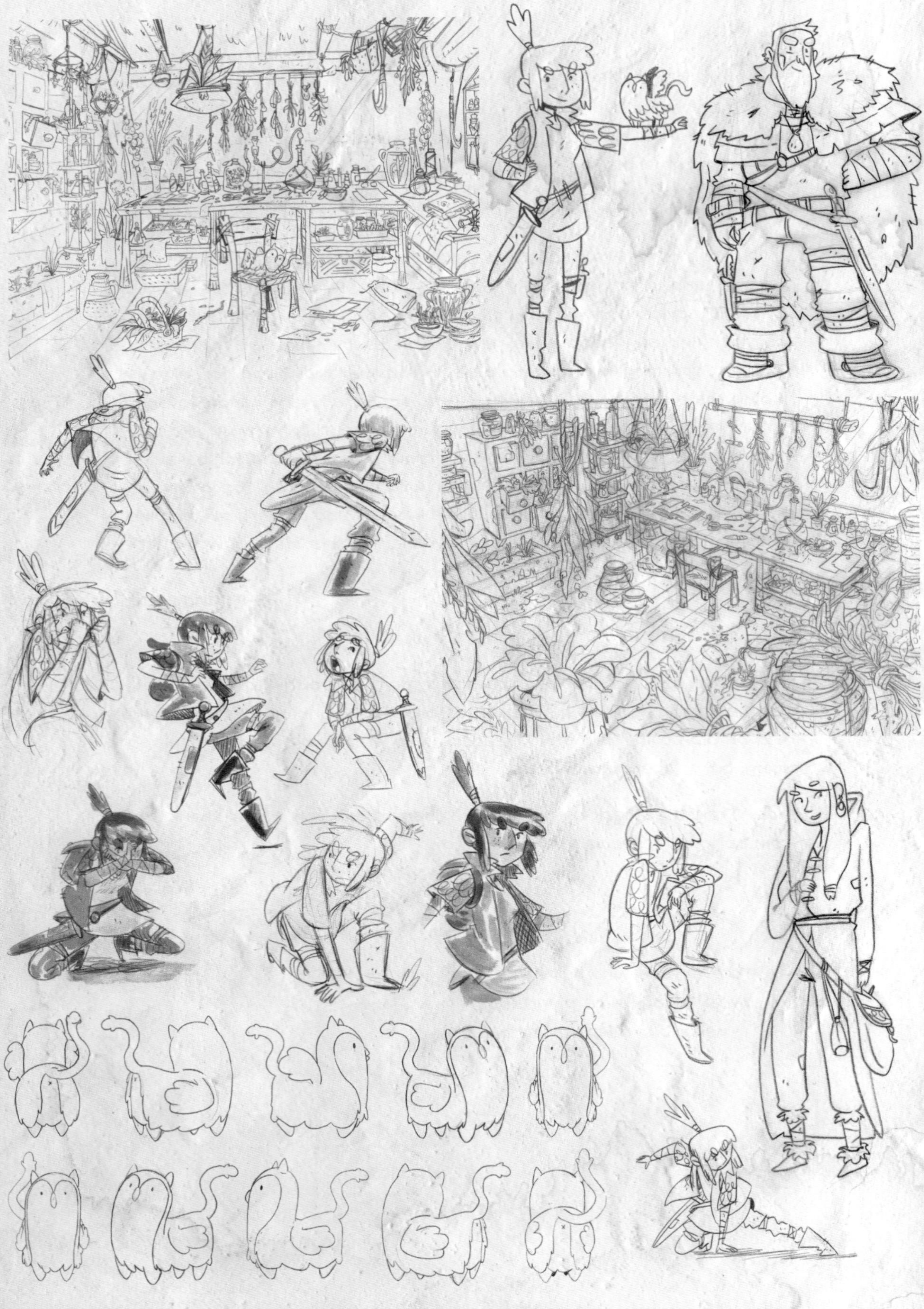

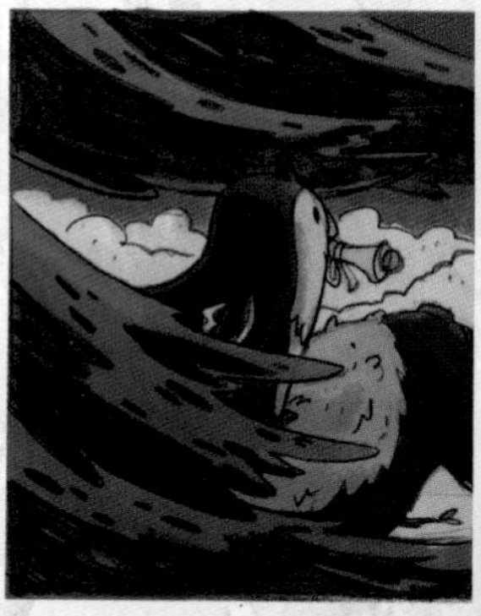
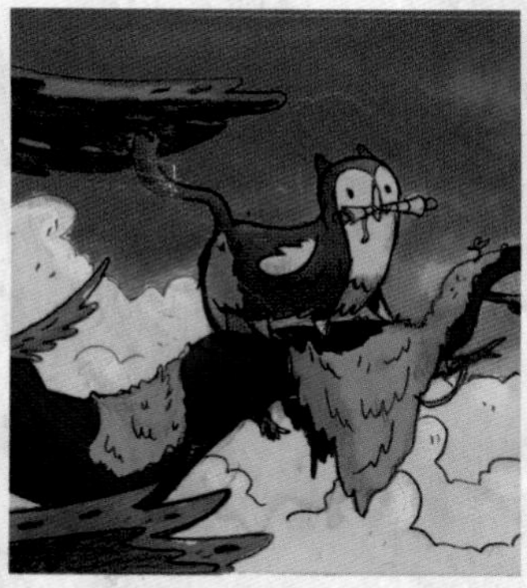
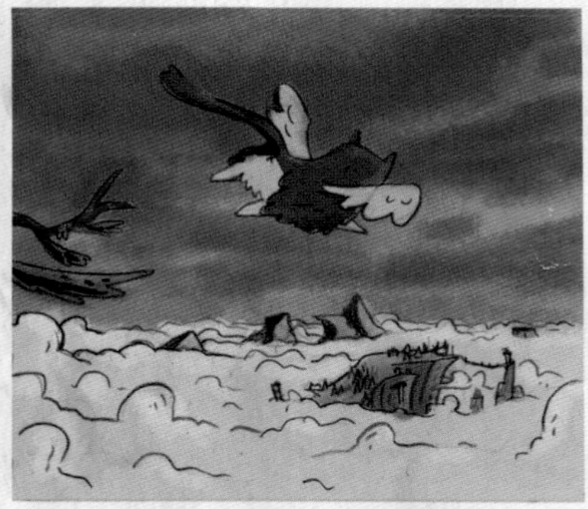
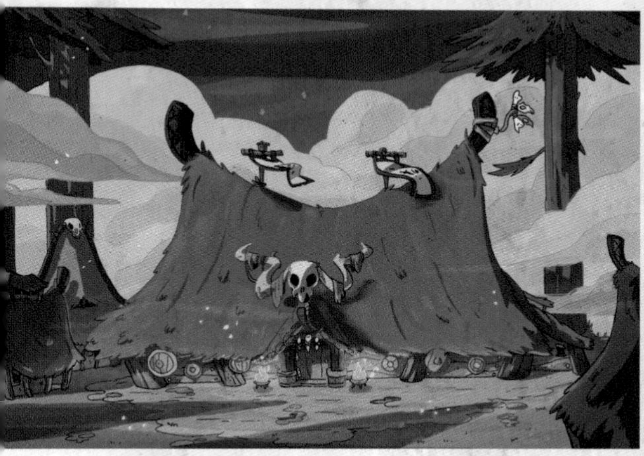
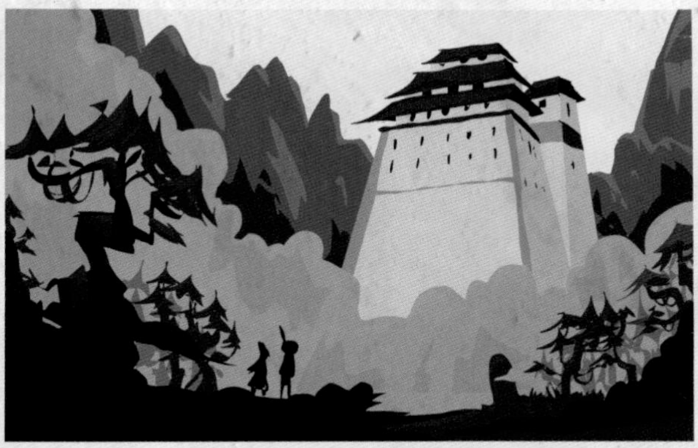
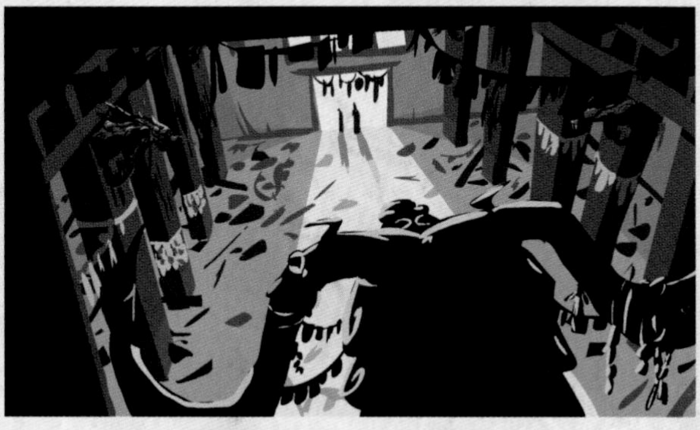
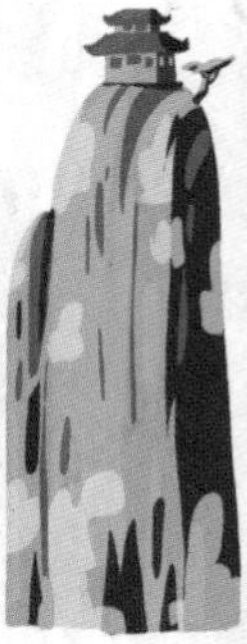
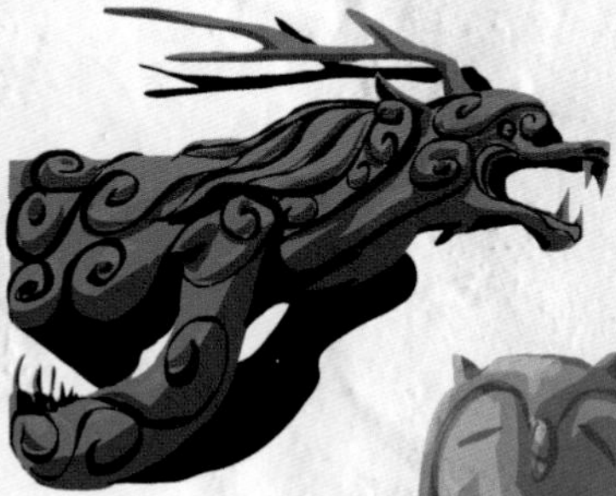
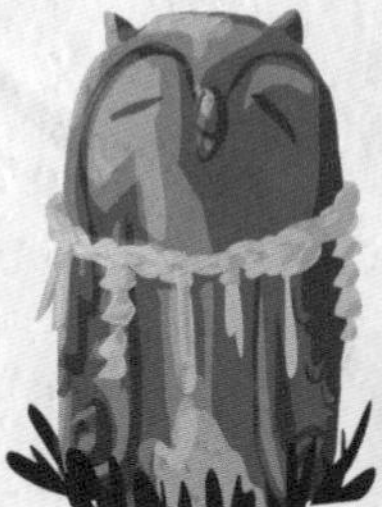
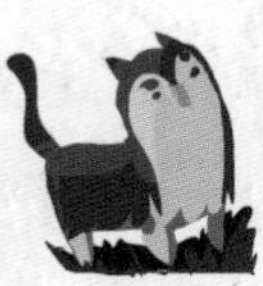
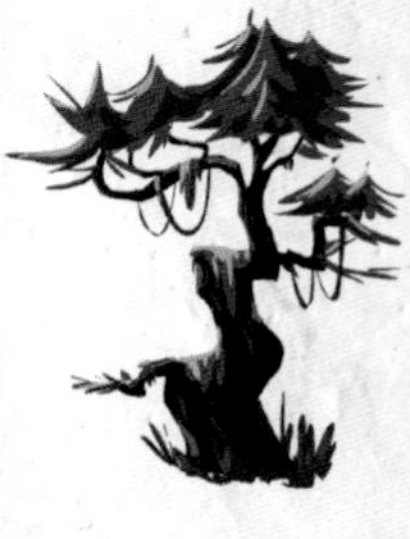
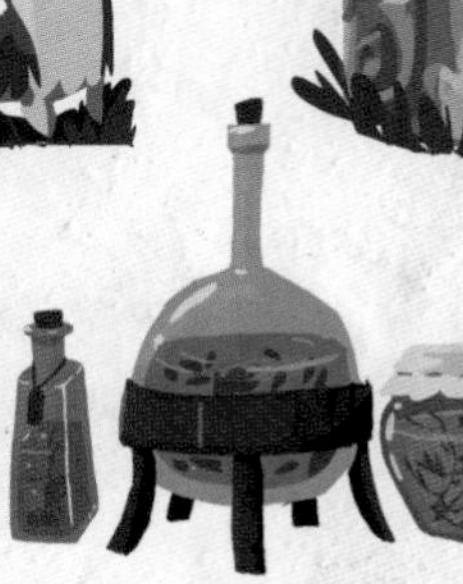
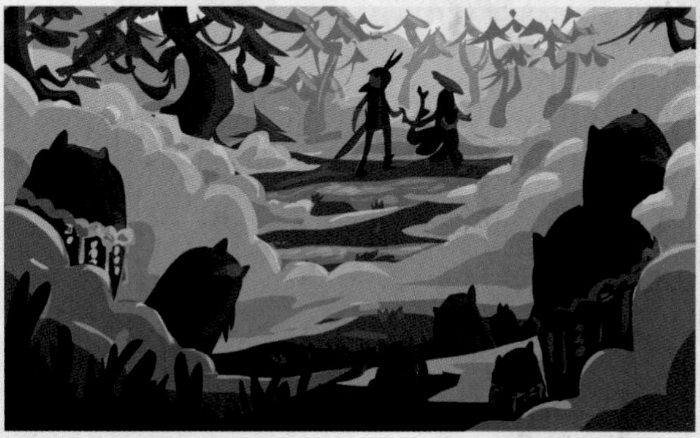
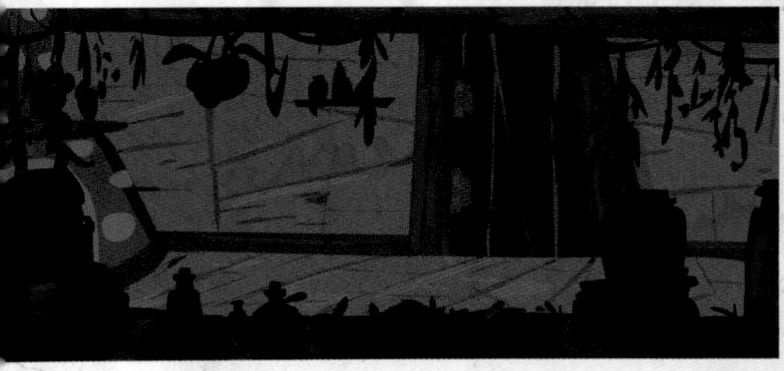
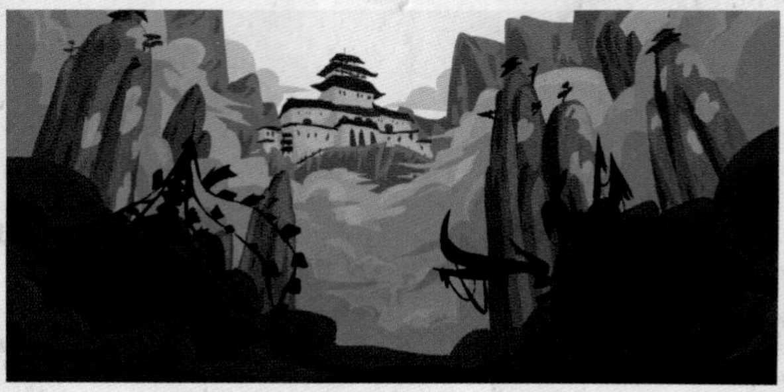

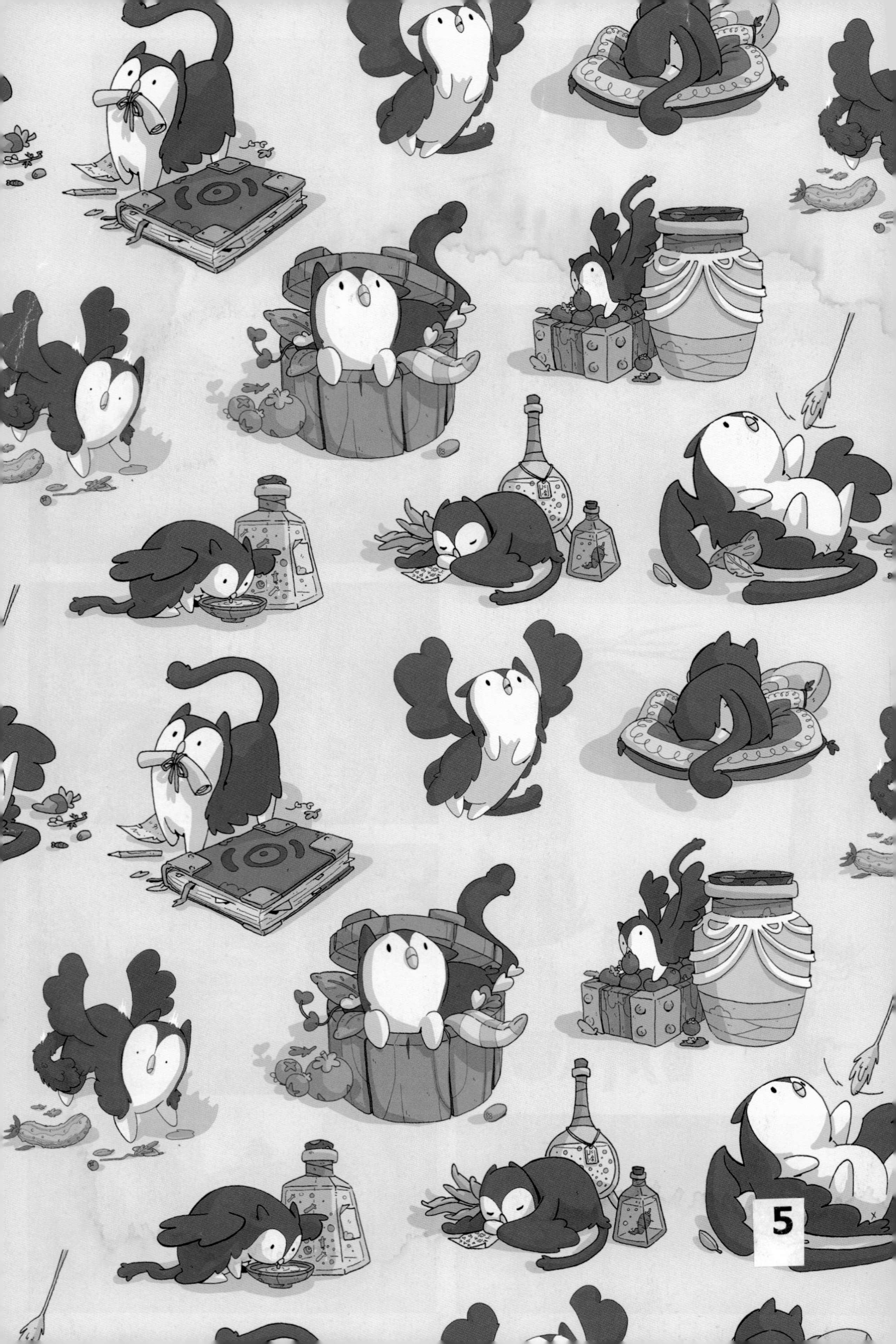